Praise for the Catherine LeVendeur Series

Death Comes As Epiphany

"Breathtakingly exciting and full of mystery and adventure."

—*Los Angeles Times*

"*Death Comes As Epiphany* is a wonderful story, tender and breathtakingly exciting."

—Roberta Gellis, author of *A Silver Moon*

"Fans of Brother Cadfael should rejoice at this new find."

—*Deadly Pleasures*

"Will captivate readers, especially women whose only complaint with Brother Cadfael is his gender."

—*Rue Morgue*

"Gentle humor and a popping plot, the novel offers a most likable heroine."

—*Kirkus Reviews*

"Newman skillfully depicts historical figures and issues in a very different age, one in which piety and great beauty coexist with cruelty."

—*Publishers Weekly*

"This is the sort of novel I love best—an action-filled historical with an exciting, original heroine and a complex mystery at its heart. Newman's twelfth-century French setting comes to brilliant life through her judicious use of detail. Her characters, including the ill-fated Abelard and Heloise, are drawn with exquisite care, and the story moves with the speed of a team of wild horses. I really can't imagine anyone reading the first chapter of this book without wanting to devour it!"

—Molly Cochran, coauthor of *The Forever King*

"The proverbial page-turner . . . as suspenseful as any hard-boiled mystery."

—*Santa Barbara News-Press*

"The author's attention to details makes this book one of the most compelling mysteries I've ever read—it's a passport to a medieval world that might have been."

—Aimee Thurlo, author of *Black Mesa*

The Devil's Door

"History, philosophy, religion, socioculture, murder, and mayhem combined with a sharply defined sense of time and place, original characters, and a magnificently medieval plot—there is little else one can ask for in a book."

—*Ellis Peters Appreciation Society Journal*

"Catherine and company continue to sparkle with intelligence, wit, and compassion."

—*Deadly Pleasure*

"Sharan Newman's fresh, provocative view of women's roles in the medieval milieu offers a background as richly detailed as fine stained glass."

—Carole Nelson Douglas, author of the Irene Adler series

"Strong characters, sparkling dialogue, sound scholarship, and rich historical setting make this series one to read and collect."

—*Poisoned Pen*

"A bubbling brew of nuns, noblemen, not-so-noble-men, conspiracy, and vexing mystery."

—*Mystery Scene*

"I did not think Sharan Newman could surpass *Death Comes As Epiphany*, but *The Devil's Door* is an even better mystery . . . one of the most exciting detectives to come along in many years."

—Andrew Greeley

"Rich in history, romance, and adventure, absolutely impossible to put down. Fans of Ellis Peters will be thrilled to add Sharan Newman's work to their reading list."

—Aimee and David Thurlo, authors of *Second Shadow*

"Newman has an excellent narrative sense and all of her characters are depicted vividly and come to life on the page."

—*Mystery News*

"Sharan Newman is scholarly, clever, earthy, funny, whimsical, warm, tender, and enormously entertaining. This is sure to become a very popular series."

—*Grounds for Murder*

By Sharan Newman from Tom Doherty Associates

Death Comes As Epiphany
The Devil's Door
The Wandering Arm

The Wandering Arm

SHARAN NEWMAN

A TOM DOHERTY ASSOCIATES BOOK
NEW YORK

For Beccy, Meg, Kay and John, who heard
the stories first whether they wanted to or not,
with love.

THE WANDERING ARM

This book is printed on acid-free paper.

Map by Ellisa Mitchell

A Forge Book
Published by Tom Doherty Associates, Inc.
175 Fifth Avenue
New York, N.Y. 10010

Forge® is a registered trademark of Tom Doherty Associates, Inc.

Library of Congress Cataloging-in-Publication Data

Newman, Sharan.
     The wandering arm / Sharan Newman.
         p.   cm.
     "A Tom Doherty Associates book."
     ISBN 0-312-85829-9
     1. France—History—Medieval period, 987-1515—Fiction.
     2. Women detectives—France—Fiction.   3. Nuns—France—Fiction.
     I. Title.
     PS3564.E926W36   1995   95-23237
                                                              CIP

First edition: October 1995

Printed in the United States of America

0 9 8 7 6 5 4 3 2 1

Acknowledgments

Many thanks to the following people for their help in making this book as historically accurate as possible. Without their generosity, I would have made many more mistakes:

Mr. Bob Caplan, for brewing tips.

Dr. Robert Chazan, for advice on Jewish communities in France.

Dr. H.A. Drake, UC Santa Barbara, for Latin obscenities; I didn't think I knew any until he started questioning me at my doctoral exams.

Dr. Richard Hecht, UC Santa Barbara, for advice, reading lists, many Hebrew translations, and for checking the finished manuscript.

Joan Hecht, for reading and commenting on the manuscript.

Rebecca Hill, RN, for looking up medical information.

Dr. Stephen Jaeger, University of Washington, for giving me a copy of his paper on Abelard's silence at Sens.

Dr. Constant Mews, University of Monash, Victoria, Australia, for references concerning twelfth-century scholastics.

Dr. David Rollason, University of Durham, U.K., for helping me find the arm.

Dr. Mary Rouse, UCLA, for finding it first and tracking it further.

Dr. Jeffrey Russell, UC Santa Barbara, for reading and commenting on the manuscript and for putting up with a neurotic writer for a student.

Jennifer Russell, for being a sister in neurosis and telling me where the good parts were.

Dr. Michael Signer, Notre Dame, for information on medieval Judaism.

Dr. Kenneth Stow, University of Haifa, Israel, for advice and references on the Jewish communities of France.

Dr. Judith Tarr, who is not only a brilliant writer but also a fine Latin scholar. Thanks for checking my grammar and for suggestions on streamlining.

Dr. Richard Unger, University of British Columbia, Vancouver, for information on boats and brewing and for giving me a murder weapon.

Dr. Frans VanLiere, Gronigen and Princeton, for information on Andrew of Saint-Victor.

Dr. Bruce Venarde, Harvard, for sending me a copy of his wonderful dissertation, *Women, Monasticism and Social Change: The Foundation of Nunneries in Western Europe, c 890–c 1215* and for being my Harvard library liaison.

Fr. Chrysogonus Waddell, Gethsemani Abbey, for enthusiastic support, editorial comments and liturgical advice.

Dr. M. Theresa Webber, University of Southampton, U.K., for information on Salisbury and its archives.

I would also like to thank all the members of the mediev-l listserv for references, comments and suggestions for further research.

All these people did their best to supply me with information. Any historical errors are due solely to my perversity or lack of comprehension.

For more information on the scholarly work done by many of these people, and other sources used for this book and earlier ones in the series, please send a self-addressed, stamped envelope to me in care of the publisher and I will send the full bibliography for the series.

The
Wandering
Arm

RUE ST. HONORE

RUE DE FOSSES ST. GERMAIN

RUE DU POULE

RUE DE BETHISY

Bourg Germain — St. L'Auxerrois

RUE R. BERTIN POIRE

RUE ST. GERMAIN L'AUXERROIS

SAINT · DENIS

POISSONNIERE

La Seine

King's Palace

TOWER OF LOUIS VI

RUE DE

Priory

RUE DE LA

La Seine

Pré aux Clercs

1 Cimetiere des Innocents (Cemetery of the Innocents)
2 St· Merry
3 Cimetiere St Jean (Cemetery of St. Jean)
4 St· Jacques
5 St· Germain – L'Auxerrois
6 Chatelet
7 Le Pet du Diable (Devil's Fart)
8 St· Gervais
9 St· Jean
10 St· Barthelemy
11 St· Eloi
12 St· Denis de la Chartre
13 Synagogue

St Germain des Pres

14 Port St Landry
15 Port Notre-Dame
16 St· Etienne
17 St· Jean-Le-Rond
18 Notre-Dame (Ste· Marie)
19 Rue de la Draperies
20 Les Hules
21 St· Marine
22 St· Pierre aux Boeufs
23 St· Christophe
x Hubert's House

RUE DE LA HARPE

Jewish Cemetery

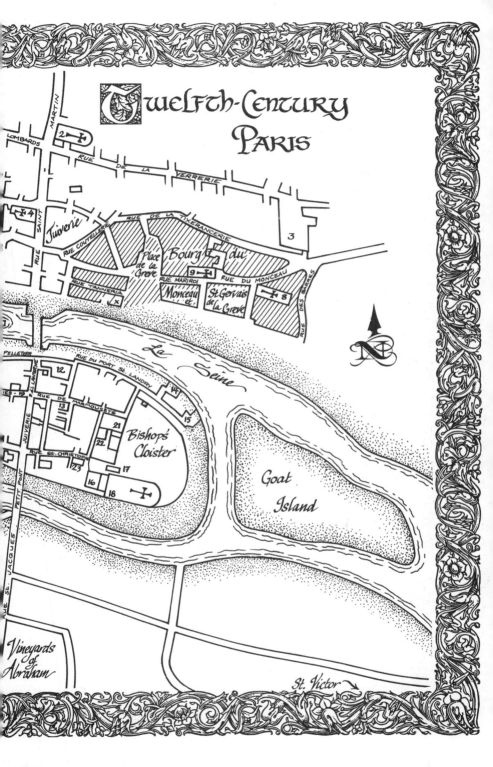

Prologue

The bishop's palace at Old Sarum,
Salisbury, Christmas 1139

Rogero deffuncto, Rex annisus est Philippum quemdam sufficere
cancellarium suum, sed tam legato quam clero Sarisburiensi
retinentibus destitit ab incepto.

When [Bishop] Roger died, the king strove to elect as
successor a certain Philippe, his chancellor, but he was
robbed of it from the start by the resolute stubbornness of
both the legate [Henry of Winchester] and the clerics of
Salisbury.
—De praesulibus Angliae commentarius

$\mathcal{P}$hilippe d'Harcourt, dean of Beaumont and Lincoln, archdeacon of Evreaux, chancellor of England and, in his own mind at least, bishop-elect of Salisbury, was tired of the greasy manners of the Norman nobility at dinner. He leaned back onto the cushion of his personal folding chair and viewed the assorted revelers with annoyance.

His patron, Stephen, King of England, had clearly come to terms with the arrogant canons who had refused to accept Philippe as their new bishop. The king had given them places of honor at the table and they were all dining together in the utmost amicability. Philippe was saddened but not surprised. In return for the unobstructed pillaging of all the secular and some of the ecclesiastical treasure of the see of Salisbury, Stephen had restored property to the canons and donated handsomely to the monastery of Malmesbury. The king had also made a tentative peace with his brother, Bishop Henry of Winchester, who had had his own candidate for the see. But, watching him from across the hall, Philippe noticed that Henry seemed nearly as irritated as he was, either by the behavior of the gathering or by some secret insult. The realization comforted him.

All the combatants of the recent struggle were at this moment gorging themselves hugely at Stephen's expense. It was a necessary investment. Stephen needed to win all the support he could to keep his throne from the eager seat of his cousin, Matilda, who never let anyone forget she was the last surviving legitimate child of King Henry I, not to mention widow of the Holy Roman Emperor and, lately and reluctantly, countess of Anjou.

King Stephen ordered another cask of wine to be opened. The hall echoed with cheering.

Everyone was content at this joyous season. Even Bishop Henry allowed a page to pour him another cup of wine.

Philippe d'Harcourt was the lone exception. Politics and family connections aside, he *deserved* to be bishop of Salisbury. And he knew how he could prove it in such a fashion that no one would dare challenge him.

He looked down at his plate and felt his stomach turn. Despite his certainty that his cause was just, the enormity of the possible consequences of what he planned destroyed his appetite.

Just as well, he thought. One should fast before encroaching upon sacred space even for the purest of motives.

Eventually the dinner descended to the level of such dissolution that the haughty Norman nobles were challenging each other to Saxon drinking games. By the time the shouts of *"Waes Heal! Drinc Heal!"* began to be interspersed with the sounds of retching, Philippe felt the moment was right to withdraw. He signaled his wish to King Stephen, who waved him out. Philippe was known to be a serious cleric who preferred his books to an evening of carousal. No one thought it odd that he would leave early. Few noticed his departure at all.

It was well past midnight. Those who weren't still drinking were surely asleep or at least otherwise occupied in bed. Philippe met no one as he made his way from the palace to the church. As he entered, he noticed two men kneeling before the high altar. He called to them softly. They blessed themselves, then rose and came to him.

"Did you get the keys?" Philippe asked.

"Yes, my lord."

The younger man held them out and Philippe took them.

"Do you have the other box?" he asked.

The elder opened the sack he carried to show Philippe the contents.

"Good," he told them. "You are both worthy servants. I'll not forget you."

"Thank you, my lord," the elder said. "But we seek only to be remembered in your prayers."

"Of course," Philippe answered. "But I shall remember you in other ways as well, never fear. It would be better if one of you stayed up here to watch, but I need you both as witnesses. Therefore, we must rely, as always, on divine protection. Are you prepared?"

"Yes, my lord," the younger man said. "We have spent the entire evening here praying that we might be judged worthy of this task."

"We have eaten nothing since the host passed our lips at Mass this morning," the elder said. "Both Father Geronce and I are resolved to accompany you and support you to the end."

"I thank you both," Philippe said. "Our Lord must know that we do this not for vainglory or profit, but only to allow His will to be made manifest to those men of clay who care only for worldly power."

The three men knelt again for one final prayer. Then Philippe turned the key in the iron gate. It swung open with a grating creak. Father Geronce shuddered and the other priest winced, but Philippe entered without hesitation.

His steps slowed as he reached the reliquary. Motioning to the others to stay back, he tried to swallow. His mouth was suddenly dry with terror. What if he were mistaken?

No. It wasn't Stephen who had intended Salisbury for him. The king was only the instrument. Philippe was sure that it was God's will that he become bishop.

And God had little patience with the faint of heart.

Philippe knelt before the wooden box. He fumbled with the keys until he found a smaller one that fit the lock. He took a deep breath and crossed himself again, his lips moving in prayers of supplication. Behind him, he could hear the murmured support of the priests.

He opened the box.

The jewels glittered in the lantern light: ruby, topaz, beryl, sapphire, all set into brightly polished silver. Looking over Philippe's shoulder, Father Geronce reflected that one of the Salisbury canons must have dedicated his life to seeing that no tarnish ever appeared on the reliquary. Of course, he considered, something in daily contact with the divine might well assume aspects of incorruptibility. The young priest swayed slightly. Hunger was making him lightheaded.

Philippe took a pair of linen gloves from his sleeve and put them on. He wanted to prove to the saint that he meant no disrespect.

"Blessed Aldhelm," he addressed the relic. "You who were bishop here before all others, you who brought the heathen Saxon to the Light with your wisdom, show me your mercy. Help me prove that you find me worthy to be your successor. Accompany me to France until such time as we may return here together. I ask you this with a humble heart.''

Even though he was convinced of the righteousness of his plea, Philippe trembled as he reached out and opened the reliquary.

Inside the bejeweled silver casket lay the arm and hand bones of a man. Brown with age and brittle, they lay quietly in their place, the earthly remains of a soul now in heaven.

Philippe licked his lips. Would Aldhelm allow this or would he strike at the one who would desecrate his body? The saint had once caused a band of would-be looters to be thrown paralyzed to the ground where they lay helpless until found by the canons. Everyone knew the holy ones needed no guards.

"Oh, blessed Aldhelm," Philippe begged. "Believe my heart is pure.''

His gloved hand touched the bones.

The lanterns flickered. Somewhere there was a draft.

Nothing else happened.

Philippe's knees went wobbly and he leaned against the case in relief.

"Quickly! Bring the box!" he ordered.

Father Geronce brought the box and opened it. Inside was another reliquary, made of wood, carved in the shape of an arm and covered in gold leaf.

"Hurry!" the other priest whispered. "I hear someone coming.''

The bones were quickly snatched from the silver reliquary and placed in the wooden one. Philippe shut the original box and locked it. The men doused the lanterns and felt their way slowly back into the nave.

"I must stay with my master, the king," Philippe told the priests. "Go under the protection of the good saint who travels with you. Also take with you the box of vessels for the Mass that is in my chamber. I will meet you in Evreaux before Ash Wednesday. Above all, guard the relic closely. You are responsible for it to heaven and to me.''

Both priests bowed and swore they would die rather than allow the relic to be harmed. Philippe smiled as they departed, satisfied that the will of the saint agreed with his own. When the canons of Salisbury learned that he had the support of Saint Aldhelm, their opposition to his election would evaporate.

He slept that night with a clear conscience in the sure and certain belief that, with the support of their first bishop, the canons would soon welcome him as their leader.

Saint Aldhelm had other plans.

One

The keep at Vielleteneuse, north of Paris, Feast of Saint Julian: martyr;
and Saint Basilisa, his wife: virgin,
Thursday, January 9, 1141

Ele va par ses chanbres, se le duet molt li ciés,
Ses dens estraint ensanle, ses mal et enforciés.
Les dames qui soufroient des enfans les mesciés
Savant bien le malage, . . .

She goes to her rooms, and she suffers greatly there,
Her teeth clenched together, her pain increases.
Women who suffer the pains of childbirth
They know the agony well, . . .
—La Naissance du Chevalier au Cygne
lines 1241–1244

*C*atherine screamed.

In the room just below, Edgar leaped to his feet in an effort to reach her. Two strong pairs of arms restrained him.

"Let go of me!" he shouted. "They're hurting her!"

His father-in-law, Hubert, pushed him firmly back in his chair. Warily, Guillaume, Catherine's brother, and Solomon, her cousin, released their hold on him.

"I promise you, Edgar," Guillaume said. "She doesn't want to see you now."

"Of course she does," Edgar insisted. "She's calling my name."

Catherine screamed again. "Edgar!"

The hands descended on his shoulders once more.

"Damn you, Edgar!" Catherine's voice echoed down the staircase. "Damn you for an English bastard. Damn you and your family and the boat that brought you here! *Edgarde! Maledicite! Edgarde, viescat verpa tua!*"

Edgar gasped.

Upstairs Catherine took another breath and screamed with the contraction. *"Verrucosaque fiat verpa tua!"* Then lower, as the pain subsided momentarily. *"In tres partes confracta canibus devoretur verpa tua!!* And the same to every man from Adam on. And damn Eve, too. . . ."

Edgar sank back, his face even paler than usual. Hubert chuckled.

"Don't worry, boy," he said. "If she can still make a noise like that, she's fine."

"But did you hear what she said?" Edgar asked.

"I didn't catch all of it," Hubert admitted. "Catherine has a marvelous vocabulary. I suppose it's from all those years in the convent."

Edgar shook his head in awe. "She never learned those words at the Paraclete. Are you sure she's all right?"

Guillaume nodded. "When our first child was born, I sat in the

next room and listened until I thought I deserved gelding for putting
Marie through all that. For the second, I went hunting. It's better
not to know what your wife thinks of you at these times. She won't
remember it afterward, or that's what she'll tell you."

"But it's been hours," Edgar said.

"Only since dawn," Hubert assured him. "Here, have some more
wine."

Involuntarily the four men glanced out the window, where the
short winter afternoon was ending. Solomon, who wasn't married,
relaxed. Hubert and Guillaume didn't. Catherine was nineteen and
strong. But it had been all day and, by the midwife's reckoning, it
was a month too soon. Guillaume poured more wine and wished
he'd taken Edgar hunting, despite his protests.

Upstairs in the birthing room, Catherine's imprecations were
greeted with cheers.

"That's right, dear," the midwife said. "Sons of whores, the lot of
'em. Yell all you like. But don't blame poor Eve; she was beguiled by
a serpent, just like we all were. Samonie, warm a little more oil to
rub her stomach with and drip some onto my hands. She needs a bit
of help. Then you'd best bring that bowl of holy water Father Anselm left. Put it on the floor here."

Catherine's servant did as she was told. Over Catherine's bowed
head she exchanged a worried glance with Guillaume's wife, Marie.
The pains were close enough. More should be happening. As Samonie put the oil on the midwife's hands, the old woman whispered to
her.

"Give the girl a few sips of the hot ale and dittany." She shook her
head in worry. "Then be ready to hold her. I've got to turn it."

Samonie bit her tongue to keep from crying. Catherine sat on the
birthing stool, dark curls plastered to her face, too exhausted to
blink as the sweat rolled into her eyes. Samonie signaled to Marie
what must be done. Marie closed her eyes a moment and began reciting a prayer to the Virgin, begging her to summon the child forth
safely. But she knew from her own experience of three stillbirths
that the Virgin and the saints didn't always heed such supplications.

Catherine had said nothing for several minutes. She ached all over
from trying to rid herself of this baby. The rim of the birthing stool
was digging into her buttocks. Her hands and feet were freezing de-

spite frequent rubbings with vinegar and salt. Even her eyes hurt. The room blurred and shimmered every time she opened them.

Someone forced a warm liquid down her throat. She gagged on it, then swallowed. Arms went around her shoulders and Marie's cheek pressed against hers.

"Mother of God, care for your daughter," she chanted. Catherine weakly nodded agreement.

"Ready?" the midwife said.

"We have her," Samonie answered.

The midwife put her hand in to push up the tiny foot that had just appeared.

Catherine screamed again. Then there was silence.

In the room below the men looked up, hardly daring to breathe, hoping for the feeble wail of new life. They only heard the rustle of feet in the rushes on the floor above. Edgar buried his face in his hands.

"I should have left her in the convent," he muttered. "She was happy there, safe. Now I've killed her."

"Don't say that!" Hubert snapped.

Edgar looked up, startled.

"We don't know what's happened," Hubert continued. "She may only be resting between the pains. My daughter is not going to die!"

He turned his back to the others, groping for the wine pitcher. Like Guillaume, he had generally managed to be somewhere else during his wife's confinements. At the moment, he hated Edgar passionately for causing Catherine to be in such danger. Even more, Hubert feared that this was simply a continuation of God's punishment on him. But was the divine retribution for letting himself be baptized rather than slaughtered with his mother and sisters? Or was it for returning to the Jewish faith of his ancestors? If he knew which, he could repent, but no sign had been sent to tell him, so he simply muddled on. And upstairs, Catherine's suffering continued.

The door opened. The men all stood. Solomon put a hand on Edgar's arm.

Marie stood in the doorway. The look in her eyes made Edgar's heart jolt.

"We tried," she said. "The child was turned wrong. We got it out, but it was too late. It had strangled on the cord."

Edgar tried to speak but couldn't get his mouth to move.

"And Catherine?" Guillaume said it for him.

"She's alive," Marie said. She swallowed the lump in her throat. "The bleeding isn't too bad. If we can stop it, if she doesn't get the fever, if she doesn't die of grief, she'll survive to go through this again. I did."

She leaned against the door, worn with the hours of fruitless work, and glared at all of them for being male. Guillaume ignored the look and went to her. She buried her face in his shoulder, crying.

Edgar fell back into his chair, too numb to cry. Catherine was alive; that was all that mattered.

"Can I see her?" he asked.

"We've given her a sleeping potion," Marie told him. "They're cleaning her now and putting her to bed. You may look in on her when they've finished, if you don't wake her."

"And the baby?" Hubert added.

"We can bury her with the ones I lost, in the corner of the garden, by the chapel wall," Marie answered.

They all knew the child couldn't be buried in consecrated ground since it hadn't lived to be baptized.

Edgar lifted his head. "It was a girl?"

"It would have been," Marie said. She wiped her eyes and nose on her husband's sleeve, turned and went back up the stairs.

"Edgar . . ." Solomon began. He searched for some words of comfort, thought of none and then realized that Edgar wouldn't have heard them anyway. Instead he sat on the floor next to his friend, hoping that his presence would be comfort enough.

Hubert sighed and left the room, followed by Guillaume. Catherine was alive; that was all that mattered. She was the one child who loved him despite knowing his darkest secret. The one who had his mother's face. Losing her would have been more than he could bear.

But there was nothing more he could do. It was time to return to his own business.

At the final turn in the stairway before the Great Hall, Guillaume caught Hubert's arm.

"Father," he said, "how could you have let that man stay with us at such a time?"

"But Edgar is her husband," Hubert answered, bewildered.

Guillaume glared at him. "Not Edgar, that associate of yours," he said. "That Jew. Did it ever occur to you that he might have done something to make Catherine's pregnancy go wrong?"

"Guillaume!" Hubert was frightened by the vehemence of his son's accusation. He wished he had the courage to tell him that Solomon wasn't some chance trading partner but his own nephew, the son of his lost brother, Jacob, and blood cousin to Catherine and Guillaume himself. Catherine knew and accepted the fact. But his other daughter, Agnes, had found out by accident the summer before and hadn't spoken to him since. This was not the time to enlighten Guillaume about family connections.

"You're speaking nonsense," Hubert said at last. "Solomon is devoted to Catherine. He has been since they were children and played together at the fairs. I could always trust him to look out for her while I was doing business. And he and Edgar are good friends. Solomon would never hurt them."

"But it is known that those people are adept at potions and evil magic," Guillaume responded.

"I don't know it," Hubert answered him sharply. "And neither do you. If that were so, there'd be no children born dead among the Jews. You've only to see their cemetery at Saint-Denis to know that's not true."

Guillaume shook himself as if to rid his head of a nightmare. Reluctantly, he nodded. "Yes, I suppose you're right," he said. "But it seems strange that Solomon showed up the evening before Catherine's pains started."

"He brought a message for me, from the silversmith Baruch at Saint-Denis," Hubert explained. "The abbey has more work for us."

He knew that was a good way to end any conversation with Guillaume. His son was not proud that Hubert's wealth came from trade. Never mind that it had bought Guillaume military training, a wife from the lower nobility and a position as castellan for Abbot Suger. It was embarrassing. Hubert sighed. That was the penalty for raising one's son to better things.

They entered the Great Hall. A little boy broke away from his nurse and ran to them. He was about three years old. He had the

golden curls of his mother but dark eyes that made him irresistible
to the ladies already, as well as a curve to his nostrils and a tint to his
skin that might have betrayed his Jewish ancestry, if anyone had
thought to look for it.

"Papa!" he shouted as he threw himself into Guillaume's arms.
"Do I have a new cousin?"

Guillaume held him close, remembering once again the joyous relief he had felt when they had told him that this child would live.

"No, Gerard," Hubert answered for him. "The baby didn't survive, but Aunt Catherine will be all right."

Clumsily, the boy blessed himself. Guillaume nodded approval.
The nurse was doing her job.

"Is it in heaven, then?" Gerard asked.

Guillaume opened his mouth to lie. But he couldn't. "Only Our
Lord knows that," he equivocated.

The child seemed satisfied. At this point in his life, God was just a
force, like the king or abbot or his father, to be feared or ignored as
need dictated.

Hubert smiled on him. He doted on his grandson as well as Guillaume and Marie's second child, a daughter, born the previous summer. It would have been nice for them to have a cousin.

"I have to go meet with the silversmith," Hubert repeated. "I'll be
back at first light to see Catherine. Ask Solomon to stay with Edgar
for the night. He'll need a friend."

It was past dark when Hubert arrived at the house of Baruch,
which was in the town of Saint-Denis, which surrounded the great
abbey. He was admitted at once.

"*Shalom*," Baruch greeted him. "You look terrible. Is anything
wrong?"

Hubert told him.

"Thank the Almighty One your daughter survived," Baruch con-
soled.

"I do," Hubert said. "Now, what is this Solomon was telling me
about a parcel of pearls and gold chain?"

"Prior Hervé summoned me to the abbey today," Baruch explained. "It seems that Natan ben Judah has been to see him, offering this parcel at a suspiciously low price."

"What was his story?" Hubert asked.

"Natan told the prior that he had taken the gems as pledge from a nobleman in England who has since lost his lands in the war there and can't redeem them."

"What does Prior Hervé say to that?" Hubert grinned.

"The prior is no fool," Baruch said. "He says the pearls have the look of having been pried loose from something. There are scratches on them, bits of glue. And he suspects the chain may have been part of a censer."

Hubert nodded. "The anarchy in England has allowed many people to acquire church property, some from looting in the course of battle. But I can't imagine Natan entering a church for any reason, even theft. His story could be true. How the nobleman came by the parcel is not his concern."

"I agree," Baruch said. "But if Natan knew the property was stolen from a church, would he have refused to take it, as you and I would? This dealing in their holy objects is bad for all of us. Oh, forgive me, do you want some ale?"

"Yes." Hubert answered the second question first. He took a long draught and set the cup down with a clink. "I don't trust Natan," he said. "He's been known to buy horses and sheep from men who clearly couldn't have been the true owners. But up to now, he's only been an animal trader. This is the first I've heard of his dealing in gems. I wouldn't have thought he knew anything about them. What price did he ask of the prior?"

"Two marks," Baruch answered. "That's what roused Hervé's suspicions."

Hubert smiled. "It's a good thing he went to Hervé and not to Abbot Suger. The prior may not be a scholar, but he's a sharp trader. He knows the tricks. Suger would simply have thought it was another example of good fortune attending his building program."

"Good or bad, who knows?" Baruch said. "I don't like it when the Edomites can point a finger at us, even at one like Natan."

"It's true, he could cause trouble for us all," Hubert said. "Perhaps if the matter is taken up with the entire community of Paris we can exert enough pressure to convince Natan to change his ways. I'll ask my brother."

"Perhaps." Baruch sounded doubtful. "He doesn't seem to care much for the opinion of the community. But for now, what am I to tell Prior Hervé?"

"Don't worry, my friend," Hubert sighed. "I'll speak with him. He has so many other concerns that he should be happy to leave this one to us."

Baruch smiled sadly at his old friend. "You have enough worries of your own, Hubert. This life is too hard on you. Why don't you simply give up the pretense and rejoin us? You can go to my cousin in Arles and start again."

Hubert shook his head as he rose. "It's a kind offer," he said. "But it's too late. I'm not truly a Jew anymore, even if I only move through the rituals of being a Christian. I have responsibilities and people I love. I can't abandon them now. Catherine says that her Master Abelard teaches that it is our intentions that are judged, more than our acts. My only hope is that the Almighty One knows that I'm doing the best I can with what He has given me."

"How could He not?" Baruch asked. "Now, where are you going? Not to bed so soon? Don't you want to sit up a while, have some cheese, play a friendly game of tric-trac?"

"Thank you, no," Hubert said, as he continued on his way to the stairs. "It's been too long a day. I can't bear hearing my child crying out like that and not be able to ease her pain."

"I know," Baruch said. "There's nothing worse. Here, take another cup with you. You may wake up in the night and need it. Sleep well. May your dreams be empty of omens."

The little oil lamp by the bed sent flickers and shadows across Catherine's face as though the spirits of light and dark were fighting over her still. She lay motionless, her skin so pale that Edgar had to put his mouth to hers and feel her breath before he was reassured that she was alive.

Gingerly, he laid his hand on her stomach. It felt spongy, like a sack of new cheese. He swallowed and tried not to imagine further.

"Edgar?"

Her eyes were still closed and her voice so soft that he thought he must have imagined it. Then her lashes moved and there was the glint of tears in the lamplight.

"I'm sorry, Edgar," she said. "I failed. It never even cried."

None of the thousand things that raced through his mind seemed adequate to tell her what he was feeling. He bent over and, very carefully, kissed her.

At first, she didn't respond at all; then she put her arms around him. He knelt by the bed, afraid to jostle it and hurt her more. After a moment, she lowered her arms, too exhausted even for comfort.

"Stillborn, they said," she sighed. "Its soul is lost now. Poor baby, wandering alone . . . all alone."

"Catherine," Edgar said quickly. "Don't think about it now. You have to rest."

"I'm cold," she answered. "Hold me."

He could tell that she was still hazy from the sleeping potion. She spoke as if from another world. If frightened him to think how close she had come to leaving this one. It wasn't the first time she had been in danger of death, but it was the first time he had been the one responsible for putting her in danger. Her request was no problem. He wanted nothing more than to hold her, to reassure himself from one instant to the next that her heart was still beating. He took off his shoes and lifted the covers to slip in beside her.

"Saint Margaret's sacred milk! What do you think you're doing here!"

Edgar lost his balance and landed on the floor with a thump. The midwife was standing over him with a pitcher in one hand and a clay cup in the other.

"You foul *mesel!*" she shrieked. "Thinking of your own lusts after what she's been through. You don't touch her until she's been churched, young man. And if you have trouble with that, I'll be happy to give you a kick that will put the idea out of your mind even longer."

"Edgar?" Catherine's hand appeared over the edge of the bed, groping for him. "Are you all right?"

Edgar scrambled to his feet. He patted Catherine's hand on his way up. Then, straightening himself to his full six feet, he glared down at the midwife.

"No one, not even you," he said clearly, "has the right to tell me how to care for my wife. I will stay here as long as she needs me. You will not speak to me in that tone again."

The woman glared back at him, her jaw clenched. Then she

turned and stomped from the room. She turned at the doorway.

"I will return only when this foreigner, this *English*, is gone," she announced. "Or, my lady Catherine, when you decide which of us you need more."

Edgar maintained his glare until the woman had flounced out. Then he looked ruefully at Catherine. "I'm sorry, *leoffedest*," he said. "I don't like being treated like some serf of the family. It's been harder these past few months. I'm used to having a place in the world."

Catherine tried to smile. "I know. Are you sorry now you married me?"

"Absolutely not," he said, and he meant it.

He bent over and kissed her again, to assure her. As he released her, her hand dropped to her stomach. She pushed at it and gave a cry.

"Edgar, my stomach! It squishes like a bag of new cheese! That's disgusting! Oh, sweet Saint Melania, what's happened to me?"

Samonie, the maid, came in just then to find Catherine in tears with Edgar hovering over her like an ill-fed egret repeating that everything would be fine, and that cheese had never even occurred to him. Samonie had no idea what was happening, but she took pity on him and guided him out of the room.

"Catherine will be better soon," she told him. "Give her time to rest and accept what has happened. Come back tomorrow. Bring her a rose."

"A rose?" Edgar stopped. "It's midwinter."

"That's right," Samonie answered. "So you should be kept well occupied in finding one."

At the bottom of the staircase he found Catherine's cousin, Solomon, in the process of pulling on his warm hose. His cloak and boots lay on the bench next to him.

"What are you doing?" Edgar asked. "You can't be leaving now; it's pitch dark out."

"I believe my claim to hospitality here has worn thin," Solomon told him. "Your brother-in-law has said clearly that tonight they plan to have pork sausage. He looked straight at me in a very pointed manner as he spoke. I got the feeling he would be happy to excuse me."

"Guillaume does have a certain lordly way about him," Edgar admitted. "I don't think he's accepted me into the family yet. I wonder what he would do if he found out you were already a member."

"I don't want to wonder." Solomon shuddered.

"Well, I find it an interesting intellectual problem," Edgar continued, seating himself next to him on the bench. "You know, I feel more comfortable with you than with anyone I've met in France, except Catherine, of course. Certainly more than any other of her family. Why should that be? Let's see, if I'm Guillaume's brother-in-law and you're his cousin—"

"Not-in-law," Solomon interrupted.

"What does that make us?" Edgar finished.

Solomon fluttered his lashes. "Too closely connected ever to marry?" He smiled sweetly.

Edgar cuffed him hard enough to knock him off the bench. "You are no scholar," he said.

"And you are no knight," Solomon replied. "I barely felt that. But," he continued, "my unscholarly opinion is that we're friends because we're both foreigners here."

"You're not a foreigner," Edgar argued. "You were born in Paris!"

"I was born a Jew," Solomon said quietly. "I'm a foreigner everywhere. Is there any more wine in the pitcher, do you think? I wouldn't mind a cup for the journey."

"Take what you like," Edgar replied absently. He circled the room, scuffing at the rushes, peering into the corners.

"What are you looking for?" Solomon asked as he poured.

"A bit of wood."

"What for?"

"I have to make a rose for Catherine."

Solomon left the keep soon after and set off into the black night. He cursed his own pride as he slid on the ice in the wagon ruts of the road. He could have supped on bread and wine and left for Saint-Denis in the morning. But he would rather freeze to death than stay in a place where he was considered less respectable than the dogs under the tables.

He slipped again and landed on his knees, the frozen mud jarring his bones. From the church at Saint-Denis, three miles distant, he heard the bells calling the monks to prayer.

Even out here, he thought. *It's all around me. I am trapped in a land that will never accept me, amid people I can never trust.*

He shouldn't have had that last cup of wine. Red wine always made him maudlin.

He reached the river Croult and turned east for Saint-Denis, keeping an eye peeled for a likely spot to cross. The river split into two branches, north and south of the village, and then rejoined to make a dignified entrance to the Seine, barely a mile away. There was a glaze of ice on the river, but Solomon didn't trust it and, while the water was no more than a foot or so deep, he had no desire to walk the last mile in boots that squelched and with feet cold as the welcome given him by his cousin, Guillaume.

He was so busy watching his step in the road and looking for a ford that he nearly caught his neck on the thin rope stretched across the way, tied to trees on either side of the river. Someone must have left it earlier in the day, while there was still light to find solid footing. Holding on to it with one hand, Solomon tested the bank with his feet. Yes, there were stones across the stream in a line straight enough to cross on.

He gave the rope a quick pull. Although it was no thicker than his finger, it didn't give. It would be enough to keep his balance with as he eased from one slippery rock to the next. Cautiously, he started across.

The man must have been watching all along. He waited until Solomon was in the middle, one foot braced on a rock point, the other reaching for the next.

"*Hé! Malfé!*" he taunted. "A cold night for a journey. Afraid to baptize your toes in the river?"

"Cold, indeed, friend," Solomon answered, planting his left foot firmly on the next rock. "One doesn't have to be the devil to mislike wading on a night cold as this."

He swung his right arm over so that he was holding on with both hands and both feet were on the rock. He looked over his right shoulder. The man hadn't moved. He was too far back in the shadows for Solomon to make out his features. He could be just another traveler, caught by winter darkness, trying to get home, but Solomon was not about to assume anything so harmless.

"What will you pay for dry feet?" the man asked as he gently shook the rope.

"Abbot Suger has given you the tolls for this elegant bridge?" Solomon responded as he gauged the distance to solid ground. "Or have you set up to compete with the Trecines Bridge?"

There was one more rock. Could he make it to the other side before the man made his move? He slid his hands along the rope and prepared to leap.

He let go just in time as the man jerked hard on the rope in an effort to throw him into the river.

Solomon scrambled up the bank as the man tried to push him back. Despite having the upper ground, the assailant wasn't strong enough to stop him. He realized his misjudgment quickly and backed away as Solomon approached.

"I have a knife!" he yelled in panic.

"Do you?" Solomon answered. "Let's see it, then!"

As he spoke he drew his own knife, not the stubby one he kept for the table but the long one he kept sheathed and tied to his left arm by a leather strap. Even in the dim starlight, it glinted menacingly. The man moved back another step, into a tree.

"Don't kill me," he begged. "I'm only a poor farmer, but I'll give you whatever I have."

Solomon considered. "What's that you're carrying?" he asked. "A weapon?"

"Only food, grain and beans for my family," the man answered. "It's alms from the monks at the abbey. Our crop was bad this year and we've nothing left. You wouldn't have my children starve, would you?"

"Show me," Solomon ordered.

He was puzzled by the sudden change in the man, from bluster to whine. Did this peasant really believe Solomon was an outlaw about to slit his throat? Was the man really no more than some villein bringing back food for his family? His lack of a knife would suggest it. Still, there was something wrong about the whole business. Solomon felt a frisson at the back of his neck.

The man was waiting for someone. Maybe several someones, armed and accustomed to casual murder. He was stalling until they arrived to save him.

The man dropped the bag and began to open it slowly, apparently struggling with the knots. Solomon kicked him away from it and picked it up.

"If this truly came from the monks," he said, "I'll see that your family gets it tomorrow. If not . . . then I suggest you cross the river now and follow your nose north before your friends discover your cowardice. Now!"

The man felt the prick of the knife in his back as he hesitated. Quickly, he splashed across, his boots slipping on the rocks. As soon as he had reached the other side, Solomon slashed at the icy rope until the knife frayed it and it snapped. The rope fell into the water and the peasant grabbed it and pulled it to his side of the river, winding it around his arm.

"This won't stop them, you know," he shouted to Solomon. "They have horses. Big horses . . . and dogs. They have swords and crossbows and . . ."

He realized he had gone too far. A force like that would be heard for miles in the still evening. But Solomon wasn't about to wait to find out how much the man had exaggerated. He threw the sack over his shoulder and ran for the town.

Luckily, the guard at the Pontoise Gate knew him and merely waved him through. "More goods for the abbot?" he asked without much interest as he closed the door behind them. "I hope he pays you more than me for freezing your *nache* off on a night like this."

"Not likely," Solomon grunted. "I'm just the messenger boy."

"Well, a good night to you, anyway," the guard answered. "On a night like this, I look forward to Hell, just to warm my toes again."

"Save me a place when you get there," Solomon agreed. "If the bishops haven't taken all the best seats."

The guard laughed and returned to the gatehouse. Solomon continued through the quiet streets until he reached the wall of Baruch's house. Baruch had long ago given him the key to the door by the stables. He took care to lock it again behind him.

There was an oil lamp hanging on a hook near the still-glowing hearth. Solomon took a spill from the kindling box and ignited it on the coals. He lit the lamp from that. He pulled off his gloves, holding his hands over the coals until he could feel his fingers again. Then he turned his attention to the bag.

The knots were pulled tight. Doubt again hit him. Had the man been telling the truth? He cut the cords and opened the bag. Grain fell out onto the stone floor. Baruch's wife would be furious with him for making such a mess. He reached gingerly inside the bag. There was something cold and hard stashed in the center. Slowly he took it out and held it up to the light. It sparkled, silver, gold, red and green. The monks had certainly been very generous with their alms. He shook the grain off the thing and then gasped in horror as he realized what it was. He dropped it with a loud clank.

Quickly, he stepped away from it, rubbing his hands against his *braies* to wipe away the very feel of the thing.

He had thought it was a cup, stolen from some lord's table. But there was no mistaking what the peasant had been carrying.

It was a chalice.

Two

The home of Baruch, silversmith of Saint-Denis, Friday, January 10, 1141 / 1, Shebat, Rosh Hodesh 4901

Concessimus etiam ut Judei, qui ad presens sunt vel habendi sunt in burgo seu in castello sancti Dionysii, usque ad quinque, cum familiis suis liberi sint ab omni justicia nostra, et ab omni exactione nostra, tantum sub jure vel justicia sint abbatis.

We have granted that the Jews who are at present living in the village or the citadel of Saint-Denis, up to five householders with their families, are to be free of all our judgments and our taxes, and that they be placed under the jurisdiction of the abbot.
—Privilege of Louis VI granted in 1111 and renewed by his son, Louis VII, in 1143

*G*et rid of it!" Baruch stood across the room from the chalice. "I don't want it in my house. How could you have brought such a thing here?"

"I didn't know it was in the bag," Solomon said. "The man said it was food from the abbey."

"I won't be dragged into the wickedness of the Christians," Baruch insisted. "Let them traffic in their own idolatrous wares. Throw it in the midden, or even better, the river. I won't have it near me."

"There are plenty of brethren who will," Solomon retorted. "Are you telling me you never took their holy vessels as pledges?"

"Never!" Baruch lifted his chin proudly. "I don't care what Rabbi Solomon said. It's trafficking in sacrificial wares. And I pity those who are driven by necessity or greed to do so. Such a thing can only bring a curse upon our house."

"Calm yourself, Baruch. You can give it to me," Hubert interrupted. He had been awakened by Baruch's cry of horror at seeing Solomon's find and, hurrying downstairs, had been greeted by the sight of the two men standing across the room from the golden cup, glaring at it as if it were a griffin poised to strike at them.

"I'll take it to the prior," Hubert continued, "and tell him that it was found near my son's keep. I doubt it was stolen from the abbey. They guard their treasure too closely now for theft, but Hervé may know where it came from. He can deal with the problem of returning it. Is that acceptable to you, Solomon?"

"Of course," Solomon answered. "I don't want it any more than Baruch."

Hubert rubbed his eyes. He wasn't completely awake yet. His sleep had been heavy and full of dreams that he couldn't remember but which upset him all the same. Something was amiss.

"Solomon, what are you doing here?" he asked. "I thought you were staying with Edgar last night."

"Your son convinced me I'd prefer staying with my own people,"

Solomon answered. "Don't worry. When I left, Catherine was already resting more comfortably. Edgar had spoken with her. He said she showed no signs of fever."

"That is a comfort," Hubert answered. "I could not have borne to lose her." He sighed and returned to the problem at hand. "It's too early to go bothering the monks; they'll all still be at their prayers. Give me some bread and cheese and a cup of ale to fortify me for the ordeal and then I'll take this jeweled monstrosity off your hands."

He took it from the table and examined it carefully. Hubert had started out as a dealer in wine and spices, but during the years he had been supplying the abbot of Saint-Denis with these provisions he had also become more and more involved with Abbot Suger's quest for precious jewels to glorify his abbey church or to sell to finance its rebuilding. Hubert had of necessity developed some knowledge of craftsmanship and quality.

"However much you may abhor its use," he commented to Solomon and Baruch as they brought in the bread and cheese, "one can't help but admire the beauty of the work. See how each pearl and garnet in the foot is set into the filigree. The silver wire is almost as thin as a strand of hair."

Baruch kept his eyes on the cheese he was cutting. "Lovely, no doubt," he grunted. "Although either of my apprentices could do better. But a pig in silk is still a pig. And no less forbidden for all its fine wrapping."

Hubert nodded. In his heart, he agreed. He chewed thoughtfully awhile; then something occurred to him.

"Solomon," he asked, "did anyone see you with this thing? Could the man you took it from recognize you again?"

"The only one who saw me was the guard at the west gate, Maro, I think he's called. He asked me no questions about the bag. As for the thief I stole this from, I never got a good look at his face and I doubt he saw mine. I'd know his voice again, though."

"Are you quite sure he was a thief?" Hubert prodded.

Solomon squirmed on his bench. "Nearly certain," he said. "He didn't have the air of a man protecting his own property, but of one who feared being caught in a crime."

Hubert shook his head. "All the same, I wish you'd left it on the road for the first traveler of the day to pick up."

"Perhaps I should have let the *mescrûus caiel* throw me into the

Croult, bash my head in and add my purse to his collection," Solomon suggested angrily. "Or I could have taken it to Natan, instead. He would have pried out the jewels and melted the gold into bars before dawn and asked no questions."

"And slit your throat to be sure you gave no answers!" Hubert answered. "Don't be a fool, Solomon."

"*Dayenu!*" Baruch raised his hands, palms out. "Enough of this arguing. Forgive my bad temper, Solomon. You acted just as anyone might, meeting a stranger alone in the dark. I was wrong to chastise you. Hubert will take the chalice away with him and we will never speak of it again."

Hubert wrapped the golden cup in an old sack and shoved it to the bottom of his pack. He wished he had any confidence that the matter could be disposed of so easily. It was tempting to consider taking the chalice apart and creating something else from it, something secular. Thieves did it all the time. He was probably a fool for taking it to the prior. A chalice this elaborate didn't come from some village parish church. Somewhere there were powerful people who wanted it back—influential churchmen or robber barons or both, working together. Hubert sighed and thought fleetingly of a little house in Arles where he could sit all day and study the Law. Then he forced his attention back to reality, hefted the bag to his shoulder and set off for the abbey.

The morning was icy. It was so cold that even the light seemed to creak as it forced its way through the slits in the windows of the women's room.

Catherine lay beneath a mound of coverlets and furs, but she was still freezing. And there was a numb frost that lay in her heart and seeped through her body, worse than the harshness of winter.

Both of them could have been warmed by having Edgar lying beside her.

That stupid woman! Did she think there was only one reason for her husband to want to share her bed? She remembered all the nights they had lain together, holding each other and whispering nonsense, laughing sometimes so loudly that a boot would bounce against the bed curtains, reminding them that others in the hall wanted to sleep.

And now, when she needed him most, they had shut her up in a place almost as restricted as the convent, only allowing him to visit for a few minutes. They didn't want him to worry her, they said. Idiots, every one of them! What about his worry, his grief? Didn't they have the right to mourn together?

Catherine?

She opened her eyes. She didn't look around for the person who had spoken. All the other women and children were asleep. Catherine sighed. She had never been sure if the voices in her mind were angels or demons, conscience or madness, or just the memory of all the admonitions of Sister Bertrada, who had supervised her morals and behavior during her days at the Paraclete. All she knew was that they surfaced at the most annoying times.

Catherine, they repeated. *You are not alone. Have faith.*

Catherine clenched her teeth. She was not in a mood to be told that God had not forsaken her. She wasn't ready yet to forgive God for letting her child die without even the promise of heaven. And if those voices were reminding her that they were always with her, she wanted none of it. They were welcome to go harass some other poor *fatua.*

"Catherine?"

"Leave . . . me . . . alone!" she begged, putting her hands over her ears.

Wait. That voice was real.

"It's all right, dear. I know how you feel."

Her sister-in-law, Marie, was standing beside the bed. "I was up early and had the cook steep some herbs and honey for you. I think I strained most of the leaves out."

She uncovered the thick clay bowl. Steam rose from it.

Catherine smiled an apology and pushed herself to a sitting position. She took the bowl in both hands and drank the posset down in one long draught. Much of the heat had already escaped but there was enough to warm her a bit.

"Thank you." She handed the bowl back. Marie patted her cheek and smiled in sympathy. Catherine felt the tears gather at the edges of her eyes. "How can we bear it?" she asked.

Marie shook her head. "I don't know how," she answered. "We just do. Most of us. I'm not a theologian, Catherine. I don't really understand why, if we are in this life only to prepare for the next, we should want so deeply to live here and now. I don't know why, when we try our best to obey God's law, we should still be given such pain. I asked Father Anselm once, and he said the desire for pleasure was a snare of the devil and we should accept the pain as our lot. But I don't think he was any more satisfied with his answer than I was."

In earlier days, Catherine would have been happy to explain various theories of temptation and salvation, but now she only nodded. Life was certainly much easier when she had set it out in *sententiae*, with all the positions of the Fathers of the Church in neat rows. She wondered if Saint Augustine had been able to remain philosophical when his son had died. She would have to look it up when she was better.

"Marie," she said, "if they won't let Edgar stay with me up here, can't I be moved back down to one of the alcoves off the Hall?"

Marie shook her head firmly. "You mustn't be jostled yet, not until we're sure the bleeding has stopped. Furthermore, you need to rest. You've had a hard time. It always takes a while to get your strength back, even when everything goes well."

Catherine gave the fur coverlet a feeble, frustrated thump. Dust rose from it, making her sneeze.

"Aiee!" she cried. Her eyes crossed. "Now I know why Saint Perpetua didn't fear the gladiator's sword. It couldn't have hurt more than childbirth."

Marie nodded calmly, checking under the covers to make sure Catherine hadn't caused any damage with the sneeze.

"I suspect," she said, "that's why most of the stories of the female martyrs make such a fuss about their being virgins. Now you see why you shouldn't be moved."

"But I will go mad just lying here," Catherine answered. "Where's Edgar? Will you let him come in when the other women have wakened and dressed?"

"He was sitting by the hearth when I passed through the Hall on my way up here," Marie told her. "I don't think he slept last night. Of course he may visit you when the others have gone."

There was a moment of silence. Catherine sighed again. "Guillaume must have told you how many stillborn children our mother had," she said. "At least two between his birth and mine, then sev-

eral after Agnes and little Roger. I remember once, after she had mis-
carried, sitting on the staircase listening to the men telling my father
it was no great tragedy. He could make another child all that much
sooner. They laughed at his grief. Such 'comfort' would only hurt
Edgar. We need each other now."

"I'll do what I can, if you'll be quiet for now and try to go back to
sleep."

Marie started to smooth the covers, then, remembering the dust,
let them be.

She found Edgar sitting on a stool by the fire, just as he had been
all night. There were wood shavings all around him and he was rubbing at something with a cloth. As she approached, he held it out to
her.

"Catherine's rose," he said. "It's the best I can do for now. You
may look at it but I will give it to her myself."

Marie took the flat piece of wood. Edgar had made the rose in
relief, so that it appeared to be floating just above the surface. The
oak was not of good quality; the work had been done quickly; but all
the same, there was something about it that was more than merely a
crude representation of a flower. The petals were just opening and
Marie felt that if she touched one, it would move, revealing the heart
of the rose. Carefully she handed it back to Edgar.

"Did you make this with magic?" she asked.

"No." He smiled. "I made it with love."

Hervé, prior of Saint-Denis, looked gravely at the chalice Hubert
had placed on the table before him.

"It is exquisite," he sighed. "But not from the abbey. I have never
seen it before, I'm sure. If it was stolen, there will certainly be a
clamor put out against the thieves. We may hear of it."

"You think it may not have been stolen?" Hubert asked.

Hervé sighed again. "Perhaps, perhaps not. You know as well as I
do, Hubert, that such things are sold or pawned often enough. Some
priests are venal, others care more for feeding the poor than having
splendid vessels for the altar. If they must find a way to save their
flock in time of famine, they might prefer to trade the fine church
treasures for food. If that is what happened, then we may never discover where it came from. I'm only relieved that this hasn't been

dismantled, like the pieces the man, Natan, tried to sell me. You should warn Baruch that traders such as he can only bring trouble on his people."

"Baruch knows that well, Prior Hervé," Hubert assured him.

Hervé lifted the chalice and examined the stem. "Was there anything else found with it?" he asked.

"It was in a sack of grain," Hubert told him. "Nothing but that. What else were you thinking of, the paten?"

At first the prior seemed not to be disposed to answer him. Then he leaned closer and whispered, "There have been rumors that the altar vessels of the churches are not all that is being traded recently." His voice tightened in horror. "I have heard that the blessed saints themselves are being kidnapped from their homes and their reliquaries, even their holy bodies, violated and broken into pieces by soulless demons in the form of men."

"How can that be?" Hubert asked. "The saints protect their relics, don't they, as they do the churches where they are venerated? Would not any man who committed such an act be struck down at once?"

Hervé nodded. "I would have thought so. Perhaps the saints have allowed it as a punishment on their congregations for not caring for them properly. They may be using these thieves in their search for a more worthy resting place. But I feel it is sacrilege all the same."

"So do I," Hubert agreed. "And I want no part in such matters. If the saints wish to find new homes, I hope they never ask my aid in transporting them."

The prior was quiet a moment, his lips pursed in heavy consideration. "And yet," he said slowly, "if they did ask, we could hardly dare to refuse them."

He stared at Hubert as if sizing him up for the Last Judgment.

Hubert felt a sense of disquiet in the pit of his stomach that had nothing to do with the bread and cheese resting there. He knew well that Abbot Suger believed that any treasure that came to Saint-Denis was intended to be there by the grace of God and Saint Denis himself, who naturally desired the further glory of his abbey and of France. If a valuable relic were brought to his door, no argument would convince Suger that it was as a result of the larceny of men rather than the will of the saint in question.

"My Lord Prior." Hubert held his hands up to ward off any request. "I am only a simple merchant. I buy wine and spices and occasionally agree to carry a few small trinkets out of respect for the good abbot. I'm sure none of the saints would consider me worthy of their notice. I would not so presume."

"Your humility honors you, Hubert." Prior Hervé folded his hands across his robe and smiled. "But, as we know, God often chooses the most humble of his children to serve him."

There was a rumble from Hubert's bowels. "I beg your pardon, Prior Hervé," he said quickly. However, he fully agreed with his inner opinion. Still, there was nothing left but to face the inevitable. "I am, of course, always at the service of Our Lord. I seek only to serve him through serving you and Abbot Suger, his good servants."

"Nicely put," the prior said. "There is something more you should be aware of. We have had word from Archbishop Hugh of Rouen that one of the priests of his diocese was found murdered recently, his throat cut by brigands on the road."

Hubert crossed himself. It was the fear of every merchant. "The poor man!" he said. "But what has that to do with us?"

"The archbishop has given me to understand that this priest, a Father Geronce, was carrying something of great value with him at the time, something that had been taken by stealth from the church of Salisbury and that he had vowed to deliver safely to Archbishop Hugh."

Hubert's eyes flickered toward the chalice.

"Yes." Hervé nodded. "I believe that may come from the same hoard. It has the look of English work. Archbishop Hugh believes those who attacked the priest knew what he carried. Father Geronce was traveling with another man, a canon of Paris, as I understand."

"Was it he who reported the theft?" Hubert asked.

"No, the man has vanished," Hervé replied. "Whether he has also been killed or is instead in league with the brigands, I have no guess. Warn your friend Baruch of this."

"I'm sure Baruch would have no dealings with murderers or thieves," Hubert insisted.

"Perhaps not," Hervé said. "But his people do not respect our holy things and many of them have a great resentment toward all Christians. He should be reminded of the tolerance we of Saint-

Denis have shown the Jews, allowing them to flourish in our midst."

Hubert forced his teeth to unclench. "I will do so," he said and bowed.

"Thank you." Hervé smiled. "And we shall be sure to remember you in our prayers. Now I sense that you are eager to be about your business. Thank you for your honesty in bringing this to me. I will let you know if I find the true owner. If it is from Salisbury, the archbishop may decide to reward you for your help."

Hubert rose and made his way from the prior's house, through the gate and out into the courtyard between the row of smaller churches and the looming grandeur of the half-finished abbey church. The narthex of Saint-Denis had been dedicated with great ceremony last summer and the work on the choir begun soon after. Now construction had been halted for the winter, but even incomplete, the church seemed too powerful for him. Hubert hunched his shoulders and quickened his pace toward the gateway. He pulled his cloak more tightly and bent his head into the wind. They would find him out one day; he knew they would.

He cringed inside his cloak. The air crying through the towers reminded him of the screams of his sisters and his mother as the crusaders dragged them away to be slain. The people of Rouen had done nothing to save his family from the soldiers of God. Only he had been spared, hidden by a neighbor to whom he had run for help. The family had adopted him, baptized him, changed his name and raised him to be a good Christian merchant.

What would his mother say to him, if she knew he had remained with the people who murdered her? Her martyred soul must cry out every time he denied his faith.

"Lord, forgive me," he whispered.

The feeling of impending doom lay on him until he was back within the walls of Baruch's home.

"What's wrong?" Baruch's wife asked, as she took his cloak and handed it to a maid. "Did the prior accuse you of stealing from the church?"

"No, no, everything is fine," Hubert answered. "I'm just tormented by the weather and my stomach."

"Ah, if that's all, I can help you," she said. "There's a fine pot of fish soup hanging above the fire at this very moment. I'll have some sent to you. Baruch is waiting upstairs to speak with you. Solomon is still with him."

"Thank you." He made an effort to smile. It was not as difficult as he had feared.

"May the Almighty One bless you," Baruch said perfunctorily as Hubert entered. "Well, what did the prior say?"

"He's worried about holy objects being stolen and traded," Hubert answered. "He said you should concern yourself with Natan's activities."

"Does he think the community here would engage in the kind of business *that* one does!" Baruch rose angrily.

"Sit down," Hubert said calmly. "No, he gave no indication that he had anything but respect for you. He only implied that anything Natan did would reflect on all of us . . . you, I mean."

"As if I didn't know that already." Baruch shook his head.

The maid came in with a tray. On it was the soup for Hubert and cups of cider for all three men. They waited until she had left. Hubert drained his mug before he spoke again.

"What rumors have you heard, Baruch?" he asked. "Why is Natan, who is corrupt but neither brave nor very lucky, suddenly appearing with pearls and golden chains? This is a man who buys cows and horses from raiders who live in the forests and have no more need for churches than we do. Who has hired him and why?"

"If I knew that, Hubert," Baruch answered, "I could start sleeping at night instead of lying awake worrying and listening to my hair falling out onto the pillow." He rubbed the top of his head, where the hair had long ago completed its exodus. "But I have heard that Natan has been seen coming and going with great regularity"—he paused, took a deep breath, and continued—"from your brother's house."

Now Hubert stood in anger, splashing the soup over his legs as he rose. "How dare you say that my brother would have anything to do with that *mamzer!*" he shouted. "Eliazar is a pious man. He gives more than his allotment to the community. He reads the Law three hours every day. Even the *parnas* of Paris comes to consult with him. Of all the men I know, he is the most righteous. Didn't he take in and raise Solomon when his father was lost to us? He even sheltered my daughter and her English husband at the risk of his own life. He was under no commandment to help them. I will hear nothing against Eliazar!"

He sat down again, arms folded, and looked away from the others.

Baruch started to defend himself, but Solomon motioned to him to wait.

They waited.

After a moment, Hubert uncrossed his arms. "So," he said. "What should we do about it?"

"Well." Baruch leaned forward, lowering his voice. "Solomon and I do have a plan. Solomon says this English boy is uncommonly good with his hands for a nobleman. Is that true?"

"He carves bits of wood," Hubert admitted. "I never really noticed."

"You should," Solomon said. "He once managed to convince the sculptors of Saint-Denis that he could carve stone."

"Did he?" Hubert asked. "I had forgotten that. That's right. It was here that he met my Catherine."

The memory did not seem to enchant him.

"Nevertheless," Baruch continued, "if he could fool the craftsman here, he must be very good. What I want to know is, how grateful is he to Eliazar for saving his life?"

Catherine was delighted with her rose.

"Is there something inside it?" she asked.

Like Marie, she had the sense that within the wooden petals there was a genuine flower.

"There will be, someday," Edgar said. "I promise."

He bent to kiss her. "Oh, Catherine, don't start crying again."

"I'm sorry," she sniffed. "I don't mean to. It's lying here all day with nothing to do but think. If you could get me a book, maybe a good commentary on the Epistle to the Romans, I would stop this brooding."

"In this place, *carissima*, it would be easier to find you a real rose."

"Then tell me a story," she said. "One of those from your land. You know, the ones with battles and dragons and such."

"They never sound the same in your language," Edgar complained.

"Then tell me a bit in yours," she said.

He thought a moment. "I know." He sat down cross-legged beside the bed, leaned his head against her and began reciting:

> "*Ongin mere secan, maewas ethel,*
> *onsite saenacan, thaet thu suth heonan*
> *ofer merelade, monnan findest.*"

"I like that," Catherine said. "It has a lot of those odd blowing sounds. What does it mean?"

"It's part of a story—well, a letter, really, from a man who's been exiled, asking his wife to come to him. 'Follow me, across the ocean, the home of the gulls, over the seaway. South from here, you will find your husband,'" he translated. "But that's not exactly it. You don't have enough words for water in French."

"There does seem to be a lot of it in all your stories," Catherine said. "Did she go to him?"

"The story doesn't say. What do you think?"

"I think she did," Catherine answered.

She let her fingers slip though his long, pale hair. Would their daughter have had hair like his and eyes the color of storm clouds? Would she have learned to pronounce those funny "eth" sounds?

"Edgar, I think I could bear it if only she had lived to be baptized," she blurted. "I keep imagining her like that man in your other story, who wandered all alone over the seas with no kin and no one to care for him. It's not right."

Edgar took her hand. "I know. I feel that way, too. But we must try to accept it, even if we don't understand."

There was a thumping on the stairs and a wheezing. Edgar got up quickly as the midwife came in to see how Catherine was doing.

"I'm leaving," he said before she could start.

"I should hope so," the woman grunted. "I hear you're some sort of scholar, like they have in Paris. Is that why you've nothing better to do than come up here and worry your wife?"

She looked at him in disgust. Edgar could guess what she'd heard about the scholars of Paris. She seemed about to say more, but turned instead to Catherine.

"Better today, dear?" she asked. "Your color is back some. You haven't been crying again?"

She glared at Edgar.

"What have you been saying to the poor thing?" she demanded.

"He said nothing," Catherine told her. "It hurts us both very much that the child didn't live long enough to be baptized."

"Not baptized?" the midwife asked. "Who told you that?"

"She was stillborn," Edgar said. "Marie told me she was dead when she appeared. How could she . . . .?"

"What do you learn in Paris, then?" the midwife asked. "The child was wiggling when I turned it. As soon as that little foot appeared, I dipped my hand in the holy water Father Anselm gave me and said as I pushed it around, 'Child of God, I baptize thee in the name of the Father, Son and Holy Spirit. May Satan never claim thee.' Just as I was taught."

"You did?" Edgar and Catherine spoke together, so pleadingly that the midwife softened to them.

"You poor children," she said. "I will take an oath on it, if you like. Here you've been harrowing your souls and all you had to do was ask me. That's a penance for pride, that is."

"It is, indeed!" Edgar said and, to her great astonishment, he grabbed the old woman and kissed her. "I am well and truly penitent. Thank you."

Catherine was trying without success not to start crying again. She felt as if there had been a thick pillow pressing down on her, smothering her, and then all at once it had been released. She took a deep breath.

You see? the voices were smug. *We told you to have faith.*

She was so relieved, she let them gloat.

Three

Paris, the home of Eliazar, scholar and merchant, Feast of Saint
Timothy, follower of Saint Paul, Friday afternoon, January 24,
1141 / 13, Shebat, 4901

*shelo' lekach genivat gabbea' veto'evah u-begadin tzeva'im
vesefen tefillot 'avodah zaah ve-kol meshamsheyah mashum
sekenah.*

[one should] not buy a stolen chalice or cross or ecclesiastical
garb, or prayer books of foreign worship or any of the ritual
implements, because of the danger.
—*Takkanah* of R. Jacob Tam

$\mathcal{Y}$ou have a visitor," Eliazar's wife, Johannah, told him. "I've put him in the entryway."

"A visitor? Now?" Eliazar asked. "But it's almost *Shabbat*. And you didn't ask him to join our Sabbath meal? Is he Christian?"

"You know I keep special dishes for our Christian guests," Johannah reminded him. "I would not be so rude as to send them away without at least offering to share our meal. No, it's Natan again, with his oily hair and beard and that smile that makes me want to lock up all the serving girls."

Eliazar laughed. "Charity, my dear. He is one of us, and we owe him an invitation, even if his appearance doesn't please you." *Or me*, he added to himself.

"But if you hurry your business with him, he can be out well before sundown and celebrate *Shabbat* with his own family," Johannah said. "Go on now."

She gave his shoulder a gentle push. With a sigh, he rose from his chair and went down to greet his visitor.

Johannah was not so unmindful of her duty as a hostess to simply leave Natan shivering in the entry. She had set him down next to a brazier of hot coals set on an iron tripod and given him a measure of warmed spiced beer. All the same, the man was not happy about being left outside the main part of the house. He stood as soon as Eliazar came down, and not out of respect.

"What sort of welcome is this?" he demanded. "Am I, a brother, to be left here in the cold? You wouldn't even treat an Edomite beggar like this."

Eliazar spread his hands in apology. "What can I do, Natan? When Johannah starts cleaning for the Sabbath, even I am forced to do business in the street."

Privately, he was glad he had such a strong-willed wife. In the times Natan had eaten with them, he had criticized the purity of the food, the quality of the dishes and the conversation. His beard and hair were shiny with perfume and oil, like the men of the court whom he imitated. His surcoat was embroidered with sleeves slashed in the latest fashion also. These manners had been brought to Paris four years ago, along with the new queen from Aquitaine, Eleanor, and were considered terribly sophisticated in some circles.

Eliazar had no use for those who aped the behavior of the south-erners. In this he was not alone. There had been numerous sermons by the Christian priests against the frivolity of the court, not least those preached by the influential abbot of Clairvaux, Bernard. But the sale of perfume and scented oil continued to rise all the same.

Eliazar smiled at Natan. "I know you are only stopping by on your way to your own home. I don't want to make you late. What news have you brought?"

"News?" Natan sounded annoyed. "I have no news. I've been traveling constantly for the last few weeks and have had no time to spend trading stories."

Then he, too, forced a smile, as if remembering that he was the guest. "You misunderstood, my dear friend," he said.

Eliazar reflected that the oil in his beard had penetrated to his voice.

"I've only come to ask a small favor. Of course, I will be only too happy to give you something to express my gratitude."

"That won't be necessary," Eliazar said coldly.

"Of course not," Natan answered. "An upright man has no desire for reward. And it is only a small request."

He looked down. Eliazar followed his glance. At Natan's feet lay a sack. He bent over and took a box from it. The box was wooden, about three feet long, six inches or so wide and about as deep. It was nailed shut and then tied with rope.

"I have to go away again for several days and I'd like you to keep this for me in your treasure room," Natan said.

Eliazar squinted at the box in suspicion. "Why can't you have your nephew, Haquin, keep it?" he asked.

"Haquin doesn't have the security you do," Natan said. "He's only a draper. His shop can be entered too easily."

"Clearly this thing has great value, if you won't trust it to your own kin," Eliazar said, intrigued in spite of himself. "I thought you dealt in animals. Where did you come by something of such worth?"

"I traded for it honestly!" Natan insisted. "I saw an opportunity to better myself and I took it. Do you have any objection to that? You never did before. It seems to me that your family were once nothing more than fishmongers in Rouen."

"I only wish we could be so again," Eliazar answered. "So, what is this treasure you had the luck to acquire?"

Natan hugged the box to his chest like a favorite child. "You don't need to know that," he said. "Just put it in a dark corner of your storeroom and forget about it."

Eliazar shook his head. "I can't do that, Natan. I need to know what is in the box so that I can give you a receipt."

"I trust you, Eliazar," Natan insisted. "That's why I've come to you. I don't need a receipt."

Eliazar's eyes opened wide and his hand flew to his own beard in astonishment. "That settles it," he said. "I will not keep this unless I see for myself what you have in this box and give you a detailed list of the contents, along with a copy confirmed with your seal."

Natan started backing toward the door. "I told you that wouldn't be necessary!" he shouted. "If I'm willing to trust you so well, why can't you give me the same respect?"

"Because I know you, Natan ben Judah," Eliazar answered. "Your father was a good man who honored the commandments and wasn't ashamed of being poor. You smear mud on his name with your velvet tunics and Gentile manners. If you had a tenth part of his integrity, you would tell me at once what you've brought to me and how you came by it."

"How dare you insult me!" Natan said, stuffing the box back into the sack. "I would have paid you well for nothing more than a bit of space. But you treat me worse than you would a leper sitting in his own filth. Have you forgotten what you owe me? You will pay for your arrogance, Eliazar!"

He put his cloak on with a sweeping gesture that nearly upset the brazier.

"Yes, no doubt I will pay," Eliazar nodded, guiding him to the door. "Don't you think you should go before you're caught carrying that thing on the Sabbath?"

He only meant to remind Natan of the prohibition against carrying anything on the day of rest, but the man reacted as if he had been struck.

"You hypocrite! You knew all along!" he shrieked. "You were trying to deceive me into sharing the profit with you. Now you'll get nothing, nothing from me, ever. Who told you? It was Solomon, wasn't it? That nephew of yours is half a Christian already. He heard of it from them, didn't he?"

They were outside in the courtyard now and Natan's voice carried up and down the narrow street.

"No one has said anything to me," Eliazar said quietly. "I know nothing of your business."

"You're lying!" Natan shouted. "You want to steal it. You want to kill me and steal it!"

"Natan, you're mad," Eliazar told him, fearing it was true. "Go home, eat, rest. Come talk to me in a few days, when you're able to speak reason."

He opened the gate. Natan backed through it, still yelling accusations at Eliazar, who finally lost his temper enough to slam the thick outer door shut and drop the bar with a satisfying thud. But Natan could still be heard.

"You'll see! One day I'll be rich and you and your family will come as beggars to my table," he screamed. "You'll live to regret treating me like this, Eliazar ben Meir."

"No doubt," Eliazar muttered as he gratefully closed the inner door.

He took off his cloak and put it on a hook. His hands were cold; he had forgotten to put on his gloves. The air was redolent with the aroma of meat and bread. The Christian servant, Lucia, was just finishing laying the table. He closed his eyes and let the tranquillity and order, the small, familiar sounds, restore his humor.

He would go to the synagogue to greet the Sabbath and, when he returned, Johannah would have said the blessing over the candles. It would be just the two of them tonight. Yes, he was glad that Natan had not joined them. It was a rare Sabbath that they had no guests to share their meal.

"You know, my dear," he said as his wife came in to oversee the preparations, "your price truly is above rubies."

"I should hope so," Johannah answered. "Now, hurry. That Natan has made you late for services."

* * *

At about that same time, Catherine's servant, Samonie, was bringing her dinner up the narrow stairs to the women's rooms.

"Here's some stew, Lady Catherine," Samonie announced as she entered. "I'll reheat it on the brazier for you."

Catherine sniffed. "That's the rabbit stew from yesterday," she said in horror. "I can't have that. It's Friday."

"You need to get your strength back," Samonie said. "Even I know people are not required to abstain from meat when they're sick."

"But I'm not sick," Catherine said. "Only sad and tired and still a bit sore. I can't eat this. I'm sorry."

"Catherine LeVendeur, you shall eat every bite and lick the bowl."

Both women started. They hadn't heard Edgar come in.

"Don't worry, Samonie," he said. "I have permission to visit. Catherine, even in the monasteries, people recovering from illness are given meat. You need it."

He took the stew from Samonie and sat down next to Catherine, spoon in one hand, bowl in the other. "I'll feed you if I have to," he threatened. "Please, Catherine. They won't let you out of here until you're stronger and I'm so tired of sleeping with a bunch of farting men-at-arms." He bent over her and whispered, "You do it with so much more elegance."

"Edgar!" Catherine gasped. "Don't make me laugh! You have no idea what that does to my stomach."

They both glanced over at Samonie, only to find she had made a discreet exit.

"Now eat your stew," Edgar said, "while I tell you about a very odd proposal your father has made me."

Catherine took a bite. She swallowed. No lightning struck. No voices reproved. She took another.

"Father?" she asked, pulling a bone splinter out of her mouth. "What does he want you to do now? If he's sending you off to the antipodes the way he does Solomon, I won't have it . . . unless I go too."

"No, it was more strange than that," Edgar said. "Keep eating. He wanted to know if I knew anything about working in metal."

"What kind of metal?" she asked, peering into the bowl. "Do you think this white thing is a turnip?"

"Gold and silver, I think," he said. "Stop examining the food. Just swallow it."

"Do you?" she asked, swallowing cautiously. It seemed to be a turnip. "Work in metal, I mean?"

"Not much," he admitted. "You need to be a real apprentice to learn the techniques. I've only been able to work seriously with wood and stone, picking up lessons here and there. I'm not sure I'd be very good at metal, although I'd like to try. I used to watch the armorers at our castle. They made some beautiful stirrups and bridle pieces."

"Don't they make carved molds for molten ores?" Catherine suggested. "You could do that, I suppose. But why would my father encourage it? He doesn't approve of your doing manual labor any more than your father did."

"He wouldn't tell me," Edgar said. "Now what are you doing?"

"This bit is definitely not a turnip," Catherine said, poking at a lump with the edge of her spoon. "Didn't he even give you a clue?"

"Eat it anyway," Edgar told her. "Not really. He was very close about his reasons. Asked a lot of questions about the time I spent working on the sculptures at Saint-Denis. Did I really do the work or was Garnulf covering for me? How did I adapt to being treated as a workman?"

Catherine snorted and ate around the suspicious lump. "I can answer that," she said. "You were the most arrogant apprentice sculptor I ever met."

She leaned back on the pillows. Edgar put the almost-empty bowl on the stand by the bed. He smoothed the curls on her forehead.

"And you were the least spiritual novice nun I ever met."

They smiled at each other, remembering.

Edgar found himself thinking that he was not going to last the forty days required before resuming marital relations. "So," he said. "What do you make of it?"

"What?" she asked. Her mind had also wandered from the subject at hand. "Oh, Father. I can't imagine. But, whatever it is, promise you won't do it without me."

"I already have," he said.

* * *

Eliazar was not surprised that Natan was not among those at the synagogue for Sabbath prayers. The man was hardly a strict observer of the Law. That didn't matter so much in a community the size of Paris, where there was always the number required for prayers. He was surprised and delighted, though, to find his nephew, Solomon, among the men. Solomon was not particularly observant, either. With him was Baruch of the community at Saint-Denis. There were not enough adult males in Saint-Denis to make a *minyin*, so they were considered part of the Paris community, even though Saint-Denis was under the secular lordship of Abbot Suger and the Jews of Paris answered only to the king. Still, it was not often, especially in winter, that the men of Saint-Denis could attend Sabbath services.

As he hurried to take his place, Eliazar thought he saw another man, seated deep in the shadows. One of the Christian scholars, perhaps. Many of the students of theology had expressed interest in understanding the Hebrew language and Jewish customs. There had been loud debates about letting the Gentiles in, but finally it had been decided that it would only increase suspicion as to the nature of their rituals if the scholars were forbidden to watch. Eliazar was never comfortable when they were there, though. Once one of the students had decided to convert. The trouble that had caused! The man's superiors immediately sent him away to study his own religion, but all the community had been threatened with severe punishment for proselytizing. Eliazar shuddered at the memory and hurried to his seat.

The visitor made no sound during the service, and Eliazar forgot about him. It was only when they were leaving that the man rose and started toward them.

"Brother!" Eliazar exclaimed. "Hubert, what are you doing here? Why didn't you join us?"

Hubert hugged his brother but didn't answer until they were outside. "I've wanted to come for years, but was ashamed, and afraid that I would be discovered," he sighed. "Solomon convinced me to at least attend and watch. But it's too late for me, Eliazar. I don't remember anything, not even all of the *Shema*."

"It doesn't matter, the Holy One hears your heart," Eliazar said. "I've told you before, a splash of water doesn't change what you are.

And now that your wife has gone to live with the nuns, why shouldn't you come home?"

"Just what I've been saying," Baruch added, as he and Solomon joined them.

Hubert shook his head. "Not yet, perhaps not ever. There's too much else to worry about. The state of my soul will have to wait."

Eliazar lifted his eyebrows at that, but didn't press the argument. His brother's lot was hard enough. "What else is it?" he asked. "Your family? Your Catherine?"

"Stillborn daughter, a few days ago," Hubert said gruffly. "She'll be all right. Hard on them, all the same."

"And you. I'm sorry," Eliazar said. "Johannah will grieve for her."

"That's not what I've come about," Hubert added. "But that business is no subject to speak of in the street."

The four men walked the short block home in silence. When they entered the house Johannah greeted them with delight, mentally redividing the dinner and thinking what could be prepared from the larder without breaking the Sabbath.

"*Shabbat shalom* to you all," she said, kissing each of them in turn. "It's good to have guests tonight."

They spoke of trivial matters during the meal: the unusual cold, the quality of the last grape harvest, the growing antagonism between King Louis and Thibault, Count of Champagne.

"That boy needs a strong hand," Baruch said sadly. "Even if he is the king. His wife's sister is living openly with a married man old enough to be her grandfather and he does nothing."

"We all know Queen Eleanor leads him around by a halter," Eliazar said. "He listens to no one else."

"What she needs is a few children to keep her busy," Hubert added. "Oh, forgive me, Johannah. My mind is much occupied with such things now."

Johannah patted his hand. "Don't worry, Hubert. I'm not offended. If the Holy One, blessed be He, didn't see fit to send us children of our own, he still gave us a fine nephew in Solomon. And I'm sure dear Catherine will be granted another child. But the Queen," she sniffed. "The way she dresses and goes about. She goes hunting, riding hard and leaping fences just like a man; I've seen her. It's no wonder she hasn't even gotten pregnant in four years, and she nearly nineteen, now."

"There are those," Solomon interjected, "who say it's not her fault. Young Louis seems to be more of a monk than a king and insists on abiding by all the religious rules for sexual abstinence."

"Well, her convent training doesn't seem to have had that effect on Catherine, I'm glad to say," Hubert added. "She and Edgar both know their duty. King Louis should tend to his."

They all nodded agreement. The one thing the Capetian kings had managed to do for the past hundred years was produce a son to succeed to the throne. The people had ignored many of their other flaws in the light of this virtue. No one wanted France to go through the turmoil that England and Normandy were now suffering with the disputed succession. Civil war was terrible for business.

Baruch must have been thinking of that as he set down his cup and folded his hands. Everything had been cleared away and the lamps were burning low. He cleared his throat importantly.

Eliazar gave him a sardonic smile. "Ah, finally," he said. "You're going to tell me what brought you here over seven icy miles. Your piety is beyond doubt, friend, but I know that it would not be enough to bring all three of you to Paris on such a night."

Baruch bridled at the insult and then relaxed with a shrug.

"There is a matter for concern." He hesitated. "I must ask you something first. Please promise not to be offended, but we need to know. It has been said that you are doing business with Natan ben Judah. Is it true?"

Eliazar looked decidedly uncomfortable. He studied a spill of meat sauce on his tunic for a full minute, rubbing the grease in with his finger. Finally, he nodded.

"I did have some dealing with him last year," he said. "I regretted it almost immediately but had to see the matter through. Since then, I've refused to have anything to do with his trade."

Unconsciously he rubbed the left side of his chest, where the scar was still red from a knife attack the year before. Hubert watched him with growing apprehension.

"You told us that you didn't know who stabbed you last year," he said. "Was it Natan?"

"No." Eliazar's hand formed a fist. "It was a Gentile, I'm sure. And not one I knew."

"But you think Natan was responsible, don't you?" Hubert prodded.

Eliazar sighed. "I fear so, although not directly. He has many contacts among the lawless of the Christians. He even buys and sells among the *ribaux* who roam the forests and answer to no lord. I didn't know that when I first agreed to deal with him. But I should have. I paid for it."

"You paid, yes, but Edgar might have been killed also." Hubert was surprised at his rising anger. He hadn't realized he was fond of his son-in-law. "He was attacked in the streets last spring because of you, wasn't he? He was followed from your house. And you never warned him. The man who did it could be anywhere, preparing to strike at him again."

"No, I'm sure he won't!" Eliazar insisted. "All that is done with. There's been no more trouble since then."

Baruch shook his head. "The boy should know about this before he agrees to our plan. It seems he owes you nothing, now. You saved his life only to put him in greater danger."

"What plan?" Eliazar said. "What has that *mesel*, Natan, been doing now?"

Hubert answered. "We believe that there's a group in Paris trading in stolen church objects. Several objects have been traced this far, then lost. These people melt down the gold and reset the jewels, then sell them. We want Edgar to try to discover who they are and what channels these goods are flowing through."

"Why Edgar?" Eliazar asked. "For that matter, why you? What is it to us if the Edomites are stealing from their own god?"

"It's a great deal if some of us are helping them," Solomon answered. He was looking at his uncle as if he were a stranger. "We aren't, are we?"

Eliazar covered his eyes. "Oh Solomon, how could you even ask?"

"You and Uncle Hubert have traded in enough treasure for the abbot of Saint-Denis," Solomon answered. "I should know; you've sent me to Kiev and back for his trinkets. You've never kept any part of your business from me, until now."

They all looked at Eliazar, waiting.

He glared back at them. "I've told you all I can," he told them. "I needed something done. Natan seemed the best man to do it. I was mistaken. That's the end of it."

"We need to know, brother," Hubert said. "At least enough to be sure that, if Natan is taken before the court, you won't be called to stand with him."

Eliazar's chin went up and he glared at them all stubbornly. "My business was mine alone. It didn't concern you or anyone else in the community. I have done nothing counter to the spirit of the Law. But even if I had, I would not counsel you to give up your plans to protect me. If you believe there are those among us who are endangering the community through their actions, it's your duty to find and stop them. As for my connection to Natan, I can only ask you to trust me. You still haven't answered my question. Why should your English son-in-law be involved in this?"

"Because he is English and we think that's where most of this trade may be coming from," Hubert answered. "And because, according to Solomon, he has the skill to pretend to be an artisan. He may be able to insinuate himself into the group that is actually reshaping these things."

"And you think Natan is working with these people, too?" Eliazar said. It was hardly a question. He knew the answer.

"Natan is an embarrassment and a danger to all of us," Baruch stated. "He should have been placed under *herem* years ago."

"None of his clients have ever brought a complaint against him before the community," Solomon said. "I never understood why. I would have borne witness against him after I found he'd bought the sheep those brigands stole from the village of Saint-Marcel two years ago."

"That wasn't our affair," Eliazar said. "I'm not certain this is."

Hubert looked at his brother in astonishment. "What has Natan done to you?" he asked. "You know that if the Christians discover him with one of their stolen holy objects, we'll . . . you'll all be blamed for it."

"Or we'll have to turn him over to their justice," Baruch added. "And much as I despise the man, I don't like abandoning him. It provides a bad example."

Eliazar slowly nodded agreement. "So. What do you want me to do?"

"Nothing," Baruch said. "We will handle the matter, now that we know you're not involved."

"Do you mean you came all this way simply to assure yourselves that I wasn't a thief and dealer in idols!"

Since that was what they had done, they all immediately assured him that it was never a consideration.

"We needed to come to Paris anyway," Hubert said. "The abbot wants to establish another special feast for the monks when they're given something extra at their meal. He thinks cloves in hot wine would be nice, but he needs more cloves. I held some back from the last shipment for just such a possibility."

"I came to help him carry them back," Solomon said with a straight face.

"And I wanted only to be with my brethren to observe the Sabbath," Baruch added, daring Eliazar to contradict.

Eliazar gave them a look of deep sadness. "I had hoped that my own kinsmen and my friend of forty years would have more faith in me," he said. "There is no more to be said. I will have beds made up for you by the fire. Good night."

The other three watched in gloomy silence as he went up the stairs. Johannah had excused herself and gone up long before. When they heard the door close, Hubert turned to Baruch.

"Are you satisfied?" he asked.

"No," Baruch answered, "but I think we should continue in the plan, all the same. You will speak to Abbot Suger about it?"

"Yes," Hubert said. "I'm sure he'll agree. This activity is much more upsetting to him than to us, don't you think so, Solomon?"

Solomon was still staring up toward the ceiling as if he might manage to look though the boards and into his uncle Eliazar's heart.

"What?" he said. "Oh, yes, the abbot. I'm sure he'll help. I only wish I knew what sort of business a man like my uncle could possibly have had that would make Natan ben Judah the best man to accomplish it."

The ceiling remained solid and Solomon was left to wonder.

It was not quite dawn of Septuagesima Sunday. The air was gray with mist. The streets of Paris were empty. Ice had formed over the

trough in the center of the roads where rain, wash water and emptied night waste collected. Natan stepped carefully on the frozen
mud as he made his way up the rue du Port Saint-Landry. The bag he
was carrying was heavy and seemed to grow heavier the closer he
came to his destination. He didn't like the place he was heading for
but the choice had not been his. Something in the bag had come
unwrapped from its cloth and was digging into his back, just inside
the shoulder blade. Natan tried not to think about what it was. The
objects he was dealing in were not of his choosing, either.

All the same, he reasoned as he walked, it wasn't expressly forbidden. Even if he suspected the goods had been stolen, he had no
proof and it wasn't as if they were truly sacred. He would never steal
a *Torah*, no matter how valuable the casing. He would die for it, just
like the martyrs of Mainz, he told himself smugly. And with the
profit from this transaction he would himself pay for a new copy of
the sacred books to be made.

So, warmed by the glow of piety, Natan reached the little alleyway
that led to the door in the cloister wall. With a sigh of relief, he set
the bag down and pushed against the latch. As promised, it had been
left unhooked.

Someone had taken every precaution. The door swung open
smoothly. Even the hinges were silent. Picking up the bag again,
Natan crept in and edged along the inner wall until he found the
steps leading down. They were slippery and he began to doubt the
accuracy of his instructions.

But at the bottom was another door and through the crack under
it came the glow of lamplight. Natan knocked and the door opened
to admit him.

Four

A small room off the staircase at the keep at Vielleteneuse, Feast of Saint Agatha, virgin and martyr, Tuesday, February 5, 1141 / 26, Shebat, 4901

. . . et quae adhuc desunt in utensiliis domus Domini ad explendum aggredere toto mentis conamine, sine quibus divina misteria et officiorum ministeria non valent consistere. Sunt enim haec; calices, candelabra, . . . sanctorum pignorum scrinia, . . . Quae si vis componere, hoc incipias ordine.

. . . and prepare to undertake with all the effort of your mind [to create] that which is lacking of the utensils of the house of the Lord, without which the divine mysteries and the service of the Office cannot take place. These are: chalices, candlesticks, . . . cases for the sacred relics, . . . If you wish to make these, this is how you begin."
—Theophilus, *De Diversis Artibus* Book III, preface

I'm perfectly well now," Catherine insisted. "And I'm going with Edgar."

"I can't do this unless she's with me," Edgar said. "It's not unknown for journeymen to bring their wives when they go to a new job."

Hubert had anticipated her determination but had hoped Edgar would support him. "Do you want Catherine to live in the sort of place they put journeymen?" he countered. "Sometimes it's no more than a pallet in the workshop."

"We can rent a room from Aunt Johannah," Catherine said. "She has four buildings, two on the Île and two more in the bourg Saint-Germain l'Auxerrois."

"She does?" Hubert was doubtful. "Did she tell you that?"

Catherine nodded. "They were part of her dower and she rents them to students and artisans and people like that. She told me so. No innkeepers or procurers or soapmakers. Nothing smelly or disgusting. We would be fine there."

Catherine didn't say it, but she thought it would be wonderful to have a whole room to themselves, even if she would have to buy most of their food from the bakehouse. And they would be in Paris again. While Edgar learned whatever there was to know about silversmithing, there would surely be a chance for her to stroll down to the Île and listen to the lectures of the masters. Now that she was a proper matron, with her hair covered, there was no reason she shouldn't. She could always carry a basket and do some shopping on her way home, in case anyone asked where she had been.

But matters didn't appear that simple.

"Edgar will have to spend several weeks working with Baruch in Saint-Denis first," Hubert said. "And remember, Edgar, if he doesn't think you can learn enough to convince genuine craftsmen that you're really a silversmith, even a failed one, then we'll forget the whole thing."

Edgar considered that. "And if I can?" he asked quietly.

Hubert paced around the tiny room, stopping to check that no one was waiting and listening on the stairs. The farther he got into this thing, the less he liked it. Especially the part about Catherine.

"Baruch thought you could go to Paris, pretending to be a silver-smith with no master to speak for him," he said at last. "Without a recommendation, even if you showed some skill, few people would take you on. You could seem to be desperate enough to take any sort of work. All we want you to do is keep your eyes and ears open. See if there are any rumors of jobs in the craft for those who ask no questions, especially about where their payment comes from."

Edgar seemed disappointed. "Is that all?" he asked.

"Of course it is," Hubert said. "Would you even consider taking Catherine along if it were more dangerous than that?"

Edgar got up and started pacing as well. Catherine pulled her feet in close to her stool to avoid being stepped on. The men went around each other like two dogs deciding whether or not to attack.

"I thought you wanted me to do something important," Edgar muttered. "Something only I could do. Anyone can wander about picking up gossip."

"I could do that," Catherine piped up. She was getting tired of sitting hunched against the wall while the beasts prowled.

Both men glared at her, more in panic than anger. They knew very well from past experience that she was likely to act on anything she heard rather than simply report it.

"Well, I could," she repeated. "And don't start lecturing me about danger. What I've just gone through was more dangerous than anything that ever happened to me before. What more have I to fear?"

Her deep blue eyes challenged them to refute her. They both looked away.

Hubert's eyes filled. Edgar stared hard at the cobwebs in the cor-ner of the ceiling. The only emotion men of his family were allowed to show was anger, and that well chilled.

"My beloved child . . ." Hubert began.

Catherine stopped him. "Father, tell us what needs to be done," she said calmly. "You know we'll be safer together, as well as hap-pier, so we should begin from that premise and build our plan from it. Edgar, please come sit down. You're making me queasy going round and round like that."

Edgar took her hand, but remained standing next to her. He faced his father-in-law. "When I married Catherine, I gladly gave up my parents' plans for me to enter the priesthood and follow my uncle into the bishopric," he said. "But in these last few months you have never been willing to discuss just what I am to do with my life. You've kept me occupied with errands, as you do Solomon. I can't believe that's all you expect from me. If it's still your wish, I'll go to Montpellier, or even Bologna, to study law. However, I'd rather continue my education in Paris."

"Well, possibly." Hubert wasn't ready to commit himself until he learned where this conversation was going.

"In your plotting, you've forgotten that I'm known in Paris," Edgar told him. "I lived there for four years. But that doesn't need to make me useless for this. If I came back with Catherine and announced that my parents had disowned me for marrying her and I needed to work with my hands to survive, it would be perfectly believable. Any lack of skill could be placed to my not having been trained in the guilds."

"Edgar, you would do that?" Catherine said. "Your friends would all scorn you, or worse."

"Not all of them," Edgar said. "Anyway, don't you think that I would do that much for you, if this tale were true?"

Catherine knew that he would, but even more, she was well aware that he was desperately eager to. There was no point in letting her father know that.

"I think that's very noble of you, *carissime*," she said. "And I think it's an excellent idea." She smiled.

"So, as a poor student forced to support a wife," Edgar went on, "I would be just as likely to fall in with those with unlawful business as if I were a journeyman, and there would be fewer questions asked."

"It's always better to stay as close to the truth as possible in these matters," Catherine added, causing Hubert to wonder how many times he'd been deceived by a tale of hers that was almost true.

"How would you explain your skill?" he asked instead.

"I've been mocked enough for cluttering the floor with wood

shavings," Edgar answered. "My friends consider it a harmless madness. They might find it more likely that I'd sell wooden trinkets, I
suppose, instead of working in silver."

"Oh, yes!" Catherine interrupted. "Let's do that, too. We could
set up a stall at the *Lendit*! I've always wanted one, with a banner
flying from the tent pole."

"NO!" Hubert told her. He ran his hands through his rapidly
greying black hair. This child of his would drive him insane one day.
He'd end up sitting in the middle of the street, giggling at the passers-
by and catching coins in his teeth. It was only a matter of time. "I
haven't worked for thirty years to see my daughter sitting like a
common *fame vilaine* bringing cabbages to market!" he shouted.

Catherine folded her hands in her lap and looked at him with de-
mure respect. "Very well, Father," she said. "No stall. Just a nice,
clean room on the Île. Now, when do we leave?"

Hubert sighed. He knew she had won again. "Baruch is willing to
let Edgar begin his training tomorrow," he said. "Catherine, you
will be churched on the first Sunday of Lent. If Baruch thinks
Edgar's knowledge enough and if you are fully recovered, we'd like
you to leave the next day for Paris."

Catherine got up and kissed him. "We'd be happy to help," she
said. "You know you can depend on us."

Hubert nodded in resignation.

That afternoon Hubert and Baruch made their way down the rue de
la Boulangerie in Saint-Denis. On one side was the high wall of the
abbey cloister, on the other a row of shops. The smell of fresh bread
surrounded them.

"Can you imagine what that aroma does to the poor monks on
fast days?" Baruch chuckled. "Even I can pity them. A bakery next
to a monastery is a cruel trick."

"It could have been worse," Hubert said, smiling. "It might have
been a brothel."

They had composed themselves by the time they reached the corner where the abbot's house stood. Hubert lifted the solid iron
knocker. He hesitated before dropping it.

"Abbot Suger is a very sensible man," he said to reassure them
both. "He'll give us no trouble about this."

"Certainly," Baruch answered with a touch of acidity. "He'll likely reward us for our honesty. Get on with it, Hubert."

The clank was answered immediately. A slot in the door slid open and closed quickly and then the door was opened by one of the monks, so hooded and wrapped against the cold that he was no more than a black shape ushering them in.

"We've come to see the abbot," Hubert said. "We are expected."

The shape nodded and beckoned them to follow. Hubert had a sudden memory of a story told by a traveling player, about a man led into the nether world by just such a figure. He tried to remember the end of the tale, but it wouldn't come.

They were led only as far the entry room of the abbot's quarters, where their guide left them with another bow. Baruch shuddered.

"I never get used to their silence," he complained.

"It's not their fault," Hubert said. "Knowing Suger, I'd imagine they don't get much opportunity to speak. Who would interrupt the abbot?"

"Good afternoon, my friends."

Both men started like guilty schoolboys. Abbot Suger stood in the doorway to his receiving room. They knelt to greet him. The abbot said the blessing over Hubert, then hesitated when he came to Baruch.

"May the Lord God bless and keep you," he said, but refrained politely from making the sign of the cross.

"And may the Almighty One protect you, as well," Baruch answered. "We are honored that you can grant us a few moments with your many duties, Lord Abbot."

"Of course," Suger responded. "Come in, sit down. Prior Hervé will be with us momentarily. He's told me something of your business. A matter of grave concern to us all."

They all went into the receiving room. The walls were bright with embroidered hangings and the chairs were solid and wide, a tasseled pillow on each one.

The men eased into them gratefully.

"Some wine?" Suger asked, raising the pitcher.

"No, thank you kindly," Baruch answered.

"Ah, yes, of course not. You only drink your own wine. 'Credat Judaeus Apella, non ego,' " the abbot quoted, pouring his own cup full. "Like Horace, I am not bound by your laws, so I will have some. Hubert?"

Hubert looked guiltily at Baruch, then nodded and drew his cup from the pouch at his waist.

"You are very thoughtful, my lord abbot," he murmured, wishing that the prior would come soon so that they could get down to business.

They sat sipping in polite silence until they heard a humble scratch on the door.

"Enter," Suger called.

Prior Hervé came in. His ears and nose were still red from the cold and he accepted the wine with alacrity.

When the prior was settled, Abbot Suger set down his glass and folded his hands.

"Now, I understand you men have a plan to help stem this dreadful practice of trafficking in the holy objects of the church," he said. "I applaud this, of course, but am puzzled as to how I might help in this laudable endeavor, aside from refusing to accept any suspicious materials brought to the abbey."

He looked at Prior Hervé, who hastened to add, "As we have always done."

"Indeed," Hubert said. "We are well aware of that and have certainly made every effort to know the provenance of any such object that we might come across in our travels so as not to make you the innocent supporter of this activity."

"It is honest Christian merchants such as you whom I trust to protect the abbey from such embarrassment." Suger smiled at Hubert, who lowered his head, hoping that the abbot would think the movement one of humility rather than of the shame he felt.

"Unfortunately," Baruch added, ignoring the implied insult, "not everyone is so conscientious. Among these is the man, Natan, who visited you recently. We of the Jewish community of Saint-Denis and also that of Paris wish to assure you that we do not countenance his behavior. Natan does not have a reputation for honest dealing even among those of his own people who have made transactions with him. He has been warned more than once by the elders."

"Do you wish to have him brought before me for judgment?" Suger asked.

Baruch was horrified. "No, of course not. He is a brother, an erring one, perhaps, but ours all the same. We will deal with him."

"He could cause great trouble for all of you if he were caught with stolen church property," Suger reminded him.

Baruch leaned forward. "If one of your brothers went astray, would you turn him over to secular justice or would you try to correct him yourself, even if his continued presence in your community were an embarrassment?"

Suger nodded. "Of course I would attend to the matter myself. One does not hand one's own into the hands of the secular authorities. I understand completely. However, that still leaves me wondering what you need from me."

Hubert cleared his throat. He had touched on this with the prior earlier, but he was still nervous.

"It is just as you said, my lord abbot," he began. "Each of us prefers to deal privately with the straying sheep from our own flock. When the utensils used in the Holy Mass are involved, it's possible that clerics are, also. You are not only the head of the greatest abbey in France, you are also the spiritual leader of many clerics, both in your dependent houses and the parishes of the area. If we discover any such men under your authority who have gone astray, we hope that we can rely on your probity and discretion to handle the matter."

Hubert's voice had dropped by the end of his plea. It wasn't easy to tell such an important man that all they were asking for was the assurance that he would do his job and not try to protect malefactors who also might be members of his spiritual family. A priest had been murdered, but one was missing as well. To Hubert that indicated a plot.

Abbot Suger smiled slightly. His eyes were distant. Hubert wasn't sure if he was considering the request or searching his memory for another quote. Finally, the abbot put his cup down.

"Bring me the evidence," he said, "and I assure you, the man will be punished, even if he's my dearest friend."

With that, he stood. Baruch and Hubert knew the interview was over. They also rose. The abbot was slight, not even five feet tall, with a delicate frame, but the power of his office and his personal charisma added to his appearance so much that Hubert was always surprised to find himself looking down to meet Suger's eyes.

They took their leave with many expressions of gratitude. Baruch was silent during the walk back to his home. When they were inside Hubert turned to him.

"I thought it went very well," he said. "What are you brooding about?"

Baruch made a sour face. "I just realized that now I have to spend the next month teaching your damn scholar son-in-law how to work silver!"

The black mud of Paris was thawing in the morning sun. Natan ben Judah swore richly as his velvet tunic was spattered when a cart he was passing suddenly lurched to life, the wheels slipping as the driver urged his horses forward.

"May all your daughters be walleyed whores!" he shouted at the carter, shaking his fist.

The driver only laughed. "They already are," he called back. "And still too good for you!"

Natan clenched his teeth and turned away with scornful dignity. He couldn't think of a riposte. Just wait. One day he'd ride through Paris in a sedan chair, carried by brawny Northmen, with pack-horses full of treasure following him. Then that *avoutre* would be begging him to fondle his daughters.

He cheered himself with this as he plodded down the rue Saint-Christophe to the old church of Saint-Étienne. He hated meeting in these places, but a man who still only dreamed of riches wasn't in a position to set terms.

Soon, Natan reminded himself. *Very soon.*

He knew what they thought of him. He noticed how they were careful to avoid even touching his robe, as if one could catch Juda-ism like leprosy or plague. Natan despised every one of them, all the cowards and hypocrites, Samaritans and thieves. They were as bad as that Eliazar, using him for their own dirty little jobs, then snub-bing him in public. No, he reconsidered; Eliazar was worse. Much worse. He didn't even have the excuse of being a idolater. He'd pay, too.

Natan was so engrossed in coming glory that he ran directly into someone walking quickly in the opposite direction. The other man had pulled his hood far down over his face and was only looking at the ground. Both of them rebounded and fell into the mud, thereby completing the ruin the carter had made of Natan's tunic.

"By the pitch-boiled body of Saint Julitta!" the man exclaimed as he unstuck himself from the street. "Are you hurt, my lord?"

Natan had been prepared to bury this young cleric in profanity but, hearing himself addressed as a nobleman, his whole demeanor changed. He allowed himself to be helped from the mud and inexpertly but thoroughly brushed of muck.

"I beg your pardon," the young man said. "I wasn't watching where I was going. I deserve all your anger. I'm afraid, if I've spoiled your clothing, my lord, that I have no money to replace such fine material, but I will recite the psalms for the good of your soul for the next month, if it will help recompense you for my clumsiness."

Natan realized that this was only some country cleric, probably in Paris on the smallest of benefices from his parish. He wasn't much more than a boy, twenty or so, his accent uncultured and his cloak of the roughest wool. There was no hope of getting even the price of his torn hose from this lad.

"That's quite acceptable, my boy," Natan said grandly. "It was clearly an accident on your part. I forgive you completely. Be on your way now and watch your step!"

The cleric skidded again in the mud in his effort to bow his thanks and move away before he did any more damage.

"Yes, my lord," he said. "Thank you, my lord. I won't forget. Psalms for a month. Who shall I say they're for, my lord?"

Natan froze a moment, then raised his eyebrows in surprise. "Do you think Our Lord won't know?" he said.

The cleric turned bright red. He pulled his hood over his head again in confusion. "Of course," he mumbled. "I . . . I didn't think. I'm sorry, my lord."

Natan waited with benign noblesse as the young man fumbled his way on down the street, turning the corner toward the *petit pont*. Natan readjusted his damaged apparel and, in much better humor, hurried on to his appointment. The thought of the psalms being said for him by this Christian gave him a moment's worry, but after all, he reflected, they were written by Jews. It wasn't like a Mass. That would be an abomination. But a few psalms, what could it hurt?

Natan entered the ruins of the church of Saint-Étienne. The gate to the crypt had been left open. *Why,* he wondered, as he went down the stone steps, *do they always insist on meeting underground?*

Edgar stood in the middle of the workshop and gazed about in awe. On one side of the room was a large window, under which a table had been set into a pit in the earthen floor. The workmen sat on the floor, their legs dangling as they twisted or pounded the silver.

Against the windowless wall an oven had been built of fresh clay mixed with equally fresh horse dung. This provided both a fireproof kiln and a comforting stablelike aroma that covered the more acrid fumes of the metal.

On the tables and hung upon the third wall were a myriad of tools: hammers and tongs and pincers of all sizes and shapes, molds and chisels, rasps and files and things Edgar had no name for. But he was going to learn the names and how to use every one of them. Best of all, he wasn't here in secret, worried that his father or teacher would discover him and give him a thrashing for messing about below his station.

"What should I do first?" he asked Baruch.

Baruch noticed how Edgar's hands were already twitching, eager to begin. He laughed. "Today, you will learn the names and uses of as many of the implements as you are able," he began.

Edgar started for the table.

"But you are to touch nothing," Baruch continued, "until I say you may. Do you understand?"

"Of course," Edgar answered. He crossed his arms, his hands in his sleeves, to resist temptation.

"Don't worry," Baruch said. "You'll have the chance to maim yourself soon enough."

He held out his own hands. They were strewn with scars, burns, nicks, calluses. Baruch looked at them proudly.

"This is really why your class isn't to do manual labor," he said. "It wouldn't look right for these hands to wear your fine silks or to touch your pale soft women. Are you sure you want to go on with this?"

Edgar nodded his head. "My father and brothers have been warriors all their lives and are as scarred as you. The women of my land are as pale as I am, it's true, but they don't seem too soft to be repelled by rough hands. I don't think Catherine will be, either."

"Not from what I've seen of her," Baruch admitted. "Very well . . ."

He was interrupted by a knock at the door.

Before they could respond, the door swung open and a little boy ran in. He was about eight years old, with big brown eyes and a shock of flaming red hair.

"Baruch, I have to pee," he announced.

"Good boy." Baruch got a narrow-necked pitcher from a table near the kiln and handed it to the child, who proceeded to urinate in it as Edgar watched in complete confusion.

When the boy had finished, Baruch sent him to the kitchen for his payment. Then he corked the pitcher and put it back.

"What . . . why?" Edgar began.

Baruch laughed. "A craft secret. The urine of a small redheaded boy is the best element for tempering the iron tools we use to cut the precious gems for jewelry."

"I see," said Edgar. "What happens if there is no redheaded boy?"

"Then that of a goat fed on ferns," Baruch told him. "But that's a nuisance as the goat isn't always cooperative."

"I see," Edgar repeated. He was beginning to wonder if he hadn't underestimated the complexity of being a craftsman in metal. But through his doubt was a great excitement. His first day and he had already learned two trade secrets.

"Now," Baruch said, rolling up his sleeves, "we begin."

Catherine's aunt Johannah bustled about, making sure the household was settled for the night. The fire had been banked and nothing combustible left near it. The pans had been scrubbed. All the windows were shuttered and barred. Eliazar had already seen to the outer doors. She was just about to take her candle and go upstairs when she heard a sound in the pantry.

"Not another rat in the barley bin," she muttered. "I thought we had stopped up the hole they were getting in by."

With a sigh, she pushed open the door quietly, hoping to catch the rat and find out how it had entered. The door swung inward and hit something. There was a stifled shriek.

Johannah squeezed her way in.

"Lucia!" she said. "What are you doing still here? I thought you were going home tonight."

The maid was sitting up on a makeshift bed, the blankets pulled up around her chin.

"My mother has cousins visiting from Melun," she explained. "When I went home, all the beds were full. So I came back and made myself a bed in here. I'm sorry, Mistress. I didn't wish to disturb you and I didn't think you'd mind."

"No, of course not. But how did you get in?" Johannah asked. "I thought Eliazar had locked up already."

"The back gate was unbarred," Lucia said. "He must have forgotten."

"That's most unlike him," Johannah said. "But he has been preoccupied lately. I'll remind him to be more careful. Did you put the bar in place after you came in?"

"Of course, Mistress," Lucia told her.

"Thank you." Johannah turned to go. "Are you sure you will be warm enough?"

"Yes, thank you, quite warm," Lucia answered. She smiled. "Good night, Mistress."

"Good night." Johannah took her candle and left. She was glad it hadn't been a rat, but there was something odd about it all the same. Something in the room was out of place. She couldn't remember. Oh, yes, the trapdoor to the cellar was uncovered. Now why would that be? Well, perhaps Lucia had simply moved a box or two to make room for the trestle bed. It was late; she was tired. She would check it in the morning. Johannah went upstairs to bed.

In the pantry the trapdoor slowly opened. A small oil lamp appeared. Lucia took it so that Natan could climb the rest of the way out.

"Good girl," he whispered, patting her. "You can think on your feet. If you hadn't called out I might have been caught. You deserve a reward for your cleverness."

"A new linen shift?" She smiled. "This old one is so worn. See, it's all holes. You can put your finger right through them."

"So I can," he said. "And the drawstring is all frayed."

He untied it and the shift dropped to her feet.

"The mistress won't be down again tonight." She began loosening his leather belt. "Isn't there something else you'd like to give me before you go?"

"You're certainly eager enough," Natan said as she lifted his tunic and began fumbling with the *braiel* that held up his *braies*. "Doesn't Eliazar keep you warm?"

"That dried-up old man?" She pulled at the knot in the *braiel* with her teeth. "He doesn't even know I'm a woman. Or maybe he isn't a real man. Do those priests of yours ever have an accident with their knives?"

"I've never heard of one," Natan told her. "And, as you can see, they did me no damage in that area."

"Mmmm," she agreed.

"That's enough of that," he said. "I can't stay here much longer."

"Very well." Lucia slid back onto the bed, pulling him on top of her. "But someday, Natan, I want to see what you look like with your boots off, too."

On the first Sunday of Lent Catherine followed the rest of the household to the chapel in the keep for her churching after child-birth. Veiled and carrying a lit candle, she was greeted at the door-way by the family priest, Father Anselm. She repeated the psalm *Laudate pueri, Dominum.* He then blessed her and sprinkled her with holy water, reciting a benediction. Then, taking her by the hand, he led her to the altar, where she prostrated herself and was blessed again with holy water and incense. Then she was once again allowed to receive the sacrament and be a full member of the congregation.

That night she and Edgar were given their old bed back, in a cur-tained alcove off the Great Hall. As she climbed in, Catherine poked at her stomach again.

"It's still rather cheeselike," she said sadly. "Are you sure you want me?"

"Get under the covers before you freeze," Edgar answered. "And I'll show you how much."

"Well, these past two weeks, you haven't seemed as impatient as before and I thought . . ." Catherine started.

She was given no chance to finish her sentence.

*   *   *

The rattling of beds being dismantled for the day woke them. It was well past dawn. Catherine didn't want to get up. It was the first time she had been warm since . . . she didn't want to think about it. Everyone told her not to brood. Edgar slept on. She knew now it hadn't been lack of interest but exhaustion that had kept him in check. These lessons in silversmithing must be harder than swordplay. His poor hands were cut and burned from the hot metal and sharp tools. There was another burn on his cheek from a mold that had broken in the oven and shot molten metal at him. It had just missed his eye. She kissed it softly. He opened his eyes.

"What's that racket outside?" he asked. "Are we being invaded?"

"We're being packed to go to Paris," Catherine said, snuggling against him. "Are you ready?"

"I'd like to put my clothes on first," he said.

"Must you?" she asked. "I suppose so, but what I meant was, ready to pass as a craftsman."

"I think so," Edgar said. "There's much more I want to learn, but Baruch told me to come to him with any commissions I may be given. He'll show me how to do them properly."

"Your old friends will laugh at you for being so insane as to marry," Catherine said. "If you are giving up the Church, you should at least do it for an heiress."

"You're looking for reassurance, aren't you?" Edgar said. "In what form would you like it rendered?"

"Edgar! Everyone is awake. They'll hear!"

"I'll reassure you very quietly."

Suddenly the curtains were pulled aside. Guillaume stood there, grinning at them.

"Hurry up with that," he said. "Father wants to get started before noon."

Catherine hid her face but Edgar stared up at him coolly.

"I never hurry," he informed his brother-in-law. "Come on, Catherine. We may as well get dressed. Guillaume, would you draw the curtain again? We'll be out in a moment."

Catherine was blushing to her ankles. "A room of our own," she said firmly. "With a door. Oh, Edgar, I can hardly wait to be disinherited."

Five

A small room in the bourg Saint-Germain l'Auxerrois, on the Right Bank of Paris, Feast of the Chair of Saint Peter at Antioch, Saturday, February 22, 1141 / 12, Adar, 4901

. . .multos hypocritas sub habitu monachorum usquequaque dispersit, circumeuntes provincias, nusquam missos, nusquam fixos, nusquam stantes, nusquam sedentes, alii membra martyrum, si tamen martyrum, venditant.

. . . a number of hypocrites, in the garb of monks, wander about everywhere, circulating through the district, sent from nowhere, belonging nowhere, lingering nowhere, abiding nowhere. They sell some parts of the martyrs, if they are martyrs.

—Saint Augustine
De Opere Monachorum

*T*heir furnishings were nothing special, a bench, two wooden trunks for clothes and bedding, a table, a bed frame that could be folded up in the day or double as a couch, and a couple of three-legged stools. Someone had nailed a shelf to the wall for bowls and platters. There was also a curtain hung on a rope across the corner for the chamberpot, which Catherine dumped out the window early every morning before the street became too crowded. During the day they went down to the communal privy in the back court.

Johannah had apologized for the room when she brought Catherine to it. It was right over the street and all day one could hear the carts and the peddlers going by. Voices of people, dogs, sheep, pigs and crows rose in a polyglot melange. One of the window frames had warped and rags had been stuffed into the space to keep out the cold. Because the building was wood, the only heat came from the little charcoal brazier, set on tile squares, and from the room below, where the rhythm of the day was set by the thump of a weaver's treadle. The room was dark most of the time, because the windows, covered with waxed cloth, were shuttered against the winter.

"I don't know what your father will say," Johannah had told her. "I can't believe he agreed to this. Are you certain you'll be warm enough here?"

"Aunt Johannah, you've never lived in a convent or a castle," Catherine said. "This will be fine."

"I'll give you some linen for wall hangings," Johannah said. "I usually rent this room to students; it's not really nice enough for you."

"I like it," Catherine assured her. "We don't even have to go outside to buy dinner. When I hear the *talemelier* calling, I can just lower down a basket for the *nieules* and meat pies. It will be fun."

Johannah smiled at her. It must seem like a game now. Her childlike delight showed in naming the sweet first. But how long would Catherine enjoy it? Children could end their games and come home.

Why had Hubert agreed to this? A cramped room above a weaver's workshop was not the sort of place she'd have thought he'd let his daughter live. He had mumbled something about letting them set up their own household and see what it was like, but what was wrong with Hubert's house on the Grève? Now that Madeleine was in the convent, there was no reason Catherine shouldn't live there. And certainly he could afford better for his daughter, whatever he thought of the man she had married.

Johannah had promised herself that she would ask no questions, but she had eyes and ears and forty-seven years of watching and listening. They were up to something, including Catherine. She only hoped Eliazar wasn't part of it.

So she gave Catherine the key to the downstairs door and a bucket of moss for the latrine so she wouldn't have to use those little bundles of straw, which were much cheaper but also much rougher.

"Now remember, dear," she said, patting Catherine's cheek. "You can come to me for anything. You know that, don't you?"

"Yes, Aunt Johannah." Catherine kissed her. "Thank you."

After her aunt left, Catherine had danced around the room. It was the first time in her life she'd had a room of her own. Well, it was Edgar's, too, but that made it even better.

The euphoria had lasted until he came in from his first day of pretending to be a disgraced younger son, hunting for manual work. Her happiness evaporated as soon as she saw his face.

"Edgar? What's wrong?"

He didn't answer but went to the water basin and washed his hands. He splashed his face, too, and then sat at the table, leaning forward to bury his face in his arms.

"Do we have any wine?" he asked.

"Yes, I brought some from Vielleteneuse," Catherine answered slowly, getting out the cups. "Edgar? You're frightening me. What is it? Has someone died?"

He straightened up and took the cup she was holding out to him. Then he looked up into her stricken face and smiled. "No, of course not," he said. "I didn't mean to frighten you."

He drank the wine too quickly. Catherine waited.

He smiled at her again, this time with embarrassment. "I wanted to play a part," he said. "I thought it would be fun. Also, I wanted to prove that my carvings weren't just something for a winter evening, to pass the time and clutter the floor." He took the pitcher from her and poured another cup. "Catherine, no one would take me on, not at any price." He drained the cup. "They looked at my wood and ivory pieces and the silver brooch and things I made with Baruch and they just shrugged and told me to be off; they didn't need anyone; they didn't hire foreigners; what had I done to be masterless?"

"But that was the plan," she reminded him.

"I know." Edgar laughed in a way that frightened Catherine even more. "It's succeeding marvelously. In a week or two I shall be ready to take anything offered me."

"Then what's wrong?" She covered his hand as he reached for the pitcher again.

He took her hand in his and turned it up, studying it as if there were an oracle in her palm. "As I was going from place to place," he spoke hesitantly, "somewhere in the day, I forgot it was only a ruse. I began to feel that, if I didn't find work, we'd be thrown out on the street. Catherine, what if it were true? How could I feed us, and clothe us? With no family, no craft guild, no lord responsible for us, what would we do? And children, how could we care for them?"

"We could set up a tent at the *Lendit*, travel the fairs," she answered promptly.

"You know better than that," he said, refusing to be reassured. "You have to pay for a stall, be a member of the association. Everything has a fee, even just wandering the street with your wares hanging around your neck. Catherine, as I was rejected and turned away over and over, I started to believe that I would never find anything, that we would starve."

Catherine kept her hand in his as she circled the table and sat next to him on the bench. She took his other hand and held them tightly.

"Edgar," she said, "I don't believe you would ever let us starve, no matter what. But if there were nothing else left to us, then I would rather starve with you than be secure and well fed in the king's palace."

"I know that," he said. "That's what makes it so terrible."

They looked at each other, not moving.

There was a pounding at the door below.

"Hey, English!" a voice called. "Open up. You have visitors!"

*   *   *

In a small room at the upstream end of the Île, Natan ben Judah peered into his cup.

"What did you say this was flavored with?" he said as he eyed the flecks floating in the foam.

"Just a few herbs." His companion laughed. "Rosemary, I'd guess. What difference does it make? It's not the taste, it's the effect, right?"

"It could use a stir with a hot poker," Natan decided.

The other man reflected that Natan could do with the same. Nevertheless, he took an iron from the fire and let it sizzle in Natan's mug.

"There," he said. "Is that better?"

Natan sipped, grimaced and then drank the beer. He looked at the third person in the room, waiting for instructions.

"Just once more?" his friend begged. "We'll pay double this time."

"Very well," he said grudgingly. "I'll carry one more load for you, but that's all. Find one of your own to take the risks. I'm sick of it."

"Going back to safe jobs, like dealing with the *ribaux?*" the first man laughed.

"At least they steal honestly." Natan's voice rose. "Ride through, pick up a few stray sheep, eat them, sell the skin. All out in the open. Not like here, all hot and smoky. Might as well be in *Sheol.*"

"We'll all be in Hell soon enough," the other one said. "Natan, where are you going?"

"I need some air," Natan gasped. "I don't feel well."

He stumbled out. The other two waited a moment, listening to the retching in the passageway. Then the first one got up, shut and barred the door.

"Unfortunate, Natan," he said as he settled down by the fire. "You chose the wrong way out."

At least, Catherine reflected, their worry that all Edgar's friends would desert him had been proved baseless. Every evening there was someone there. The English and Scottish students came to give him gossip from home and to stare at Catherine. They learned too quickly that she understood their Latin vulgarities and switched to their own language, which made her resolve to learn it at once.

Others came to visit, old friends of both of theirs. Solomon balanced on the rickety stool many nights and shared the food Johannah was always sending them. Berengar, who had once been a student of Abelard's, came to rant about the treatment the master had received at the council at Sens the year before. He usually brought a jug of beer or a loaf along with the scratched-over tablets on which he was preparing a scathing denunciation of those who had condemned his teacher unheard.

To give them credit, Catherine was forced to admit that they all brought something to share. They didn't seem to despise Edgar for marrying. Even John, the serious scholar who appeared to do nothing but fast and study, told them that he felt that for those who couldn't be chaste it was better to marry than to burn.

"My own brother, Robert, is a parish priest in England, with a wife and son," he said. "He's devout and conscientious in his duties, more than I can say for some others who are continent in sexual matters and negligent in all others."

"Has the war come near him?" Edgar asked.

"The war is everywhere," John answered. "My other brother, Richard, is a canon at Exeter and was much grieved during the siege there. But Robert's village has been spared so far. Salisbury is, the last I heard, in the hands of the empress. King Stephen's men came through last year and looted the cathedral at Sarum, may they all be cursed for their sacrilege. But no one I know was hurt."

"May God continue to preserve them," Edgar said. "I heard something last summer about Salisbury. Perhaps you know the truth of it. I was told that, when the canons opened Bishop Roger's treasury to King Stephen, after the bishop died, it wasn't just his hoard of gold and weapons that was taken."

John looked uncomfortable. "I've heard all sorts of tales," he said, "none of them from sources I would consider reliable. What's the news of Master Abelard?"

Edgar accepted the abrupt change of subject. If John wouldn't speak of it, then there must be something to the rumors. Edgar could wait to find out.

"The master has been given a refuge at Cluny," Edgar told him.

"Abbot Peter even managed to arrange a meeting between him and Abbot Bernard. They've reconciled, it is said."

"But Master Abelard's work has still been declared heretical by Pope Innocent," Catherine said angrily. "He was allowed no more hearing in Rome than he was at Sens. Abbot Bernard had messengers there and back before the Master even reached Cluny."

"I know," John said. "It seems to me that Abbot Bernard truly believes that Master Abelard's teachings are dangerous, but it was wrong all the same to condemn him unheard. I wish Abelard had at least tried to refute the charges. He could have easily. Abbot Bernard is no match for him in logic."

Catherine agreed. "For a long time, I couldn't understand why he had walked out of the assembly, without defending himself. Perhaps it was his illness. But I've also remembered a sermon he once preached at the Paraclete, on Susannah and the Elders."

"He saw the abbots and bishops of France as lecherous judges?" Edgar asked.

"We all know Master Abelard; decide for yourself," Catherine answered. "The sermon was about how to respond to an unjust accusation. The only answer, he says, is silence."

"But he appealed to Rome," John pointed out.

"Susannah appealed to God," Catherine said. She didn't add that other sermons on the trial of Jesus had implied that Abelard also compared his own persecutions to Christ's.

"Master Abelard might have been better off doing that," John suggested. "There was no Daniel waiting in Rome to defend him. So, he's still at Cluny?"

"As far as we know," Edgar told him. "His health is not good. Astrolabe saw him at Christmas and said he's become very frail."

"Poor man," John said. "It's odd, he's younger than Master Gilbert but I think of Abelard as aged and Master Gilbert as in his prime."

"Is Master Gilbert still lecturing?" Catherine asked. "I'd like to hear him."

"You should go, both of you," John said. "He has many connections in Paris and at Chartres. He might know someone who could find work for you, Edgar. He lectures at the Bishop's Hall twice a week. The place is as packed as Saint-Denis on the saint's day. I have no idea how many of those who attend can follow the lecture, but half Paris is determined to try.''

He picked up his cup and wiped it out with a cloth he had tucked into his belt. From his sleeve he pulled out a small packet wrapped in oilcloth. A gold liquid was oozing from it. He laid it on the table.

''I've given up honey for Lent,'' he said, not looking at them. ''I'd be grateful if you would save me from temptation.''

''John . . .'' Edgar began.

Catherine took the package and set it in a wooden bowl. ''It's very kind of you,'' she said. ''*Gode s . . f . . fsances.*''

John laughed. ''*Thanc thu,* Catherine.''

''Yes,'' Catherine gave up. ''What you said. I want to learn Saxon but those blowing noises are impossible.''

''Never mind,'' John said. ''You have a nice accent. When the Normans try to speak Saxon, they sound like seals sneezing.''

They all laughed and he bid them good night.

Edgar looked at the honey. ''We can't take charity we don't deserve,'' he said.

''We can take a gift from a friend,'' Catherine answered. ''Or I can take it to Aunt Johannah tomorrow and she can use it to make cakes for that festival of theirs she told me about.''

''Which one is that?'' Edgar asked.

''Something to do with the Book of Esther,'' she said. ''Tomorrow they fast and the next day they celebrate.''

''Very well,'' he said. ''I'll walk you over and then perhaps visit Master Gilbert. I don't know how long your father wants me to go on with this. It's been a week and I've learned nothing except that a man without a master can't find work.''

Johannah was up to her elbows in dough and delighted to see Catherine and the packet of honey.

''Set it on the stone counter over there,'' she said. ''Then you can help me.''

''I can?'' Catherine said. ''I thought you didn't want Christians touching your food.''

''Some Christians, some food,'' Johannah answered. ''Lucia touches almost everything. I supervise to be sure she does it properly. There aren't enough of us to have servants of our own faith.

And who has time to do all the cooking and cleaning and attend to business, too?" She gave the dough one last pounding and tipped it into a bowl to rise. "But today is Sunday and Lucia is home with her family," she continued. "So I thought I'd make some *Purim canestel* for Eliazar."

"What can I do?" Catherine asked.

Johannah pursed her lips, surveying her work. "I need to prepare the beans for tomorrow," she said. "Esther ate only beans in the king's house so she wouldn't break the dietary laws, so we do, too, along with the cakes. Can you take this basket down to the cellar and fill it for me? Then we can sit and talk by the fire while we shell them."

"Of course, Aunt."

Catherine put the basket over her arm, picked up a little oil lamp and went down the stairs.

Edgar found Master Gilbert's house on the rue de la Porée on the other side of the river, in the bourg of Saint-Geneviève. He hesitated when asked his business.

"My friend, John, suggested I come here," he said. "I was once a student of Master Abelard's and also of Master Robert at Melun."

"Master Gilbert lectures twice a week," the doorkeeper said. "He has no need of new students."

"Yes, I know but . . ." The door was shut in his face.

He raised his hand to knock again, explain further, but he couldn't do it. He wasn't a beggar. *Godes micht!* He'd been a fool to come here in the first place. It was bad enough asking strangers, artisans and craftsmen, for work. It was too humiliating to come before a master, with those who used to be his fellow students standing around, and admit he needed charity. That was taking the game too far.

Edgar pulled his woolen cloak more tightly around his throat. The day had turned raw, with a damp wind that cut through everything but the fur-lined cloaks and *pellices* of the rich.

He felt for the bag around his neck. It was lighter than he could ever remember. Of course, a poor scholar without a prebend couldn't have a heavy purse. He felt inside. Four deniers, enough for some wine. In another bag at his belt, he had the examples of his work that no one had wanted. Perhaps he could trade a wooden comb for a mug or two and save the coins.

He was even thinking like a poor man.

The tavern was one he had often gone to before he and Catherine had married. It was no more than a smoky hole scooped between two stone walls and roofed over. Edgar remembered to step down upon entering. Strangers usually were thrown flat, to the general entertainment of the room.

The only light was a lamp at the table, where the owner sat and checked the color of the coins. Edgar went over to her.

"I haven't any money today, Laudine," he said. "Will you give me a *henap* full in trade for this?"

He showed her the comb. It was of yew wood and still had the soft scent of the tree. The end was carved with swirls and bird's eyes. He was rather proud of it, but no one else had been impressed.

Laudine turned it over in her hand. "What's the matter, Edgar?" she asked. "Your girl throw it back at you?"

"No, I made it," he told her. "I have some spoons, as well, and a pepper box. Would you like to see them?"

She laughed. "What happened to you, boy, that you've turned peddler? I thought your father sent you plenty."

Edgar shrugged. He had told the story so many times now that he had no trouble sounding sincere.

"We've had a falling out," he explained. "I've taken a wife here in France and he's not pleased about it."

"A wife!" Laudine's laugh became a snort. "You foreigners are such innocents! What happened? Her brothers catch you with her in the fields? Insisted you salvage her 'honor'? Edgar, that's the oldest trick in Paris!"

"I'm not so green as that," Edgar said. "She comes from a good family and has given up her own inheritance for me."

Laudine gaped at him. "By the rough hands of Saint Radegunde!" she said. "You're not green; you're mad! The two of you will starve within the year! You're lucky her dowry was all you lost!"

"So I've been told," Edgar said.

He started to put away his handiwork but Laudine stopped him. "Avoi! Gaudry!" she called to a shape sitting across the room.

"Come look at this." She patted Edgar's hand. "I've always been too kind to lunatics."

The shape moved into the light and became a man of medium height, shorter than Edgar but broader in the shoulder. Laudine showed him the comb and pepper box.

"What do you think?" she asked him. "Weren't you saying the other day that you needed someone to do some woodwork for you, but you didn't want to pay the guild prices?"

"Keep your voice down, you old *bordelere*," Gaudry muttered and added loudly, "That was just talk. Where can you find a workman to trust unless you get him through the guilds?" He threw the things back on the table. "Anyway," he said, "I don't need pretty work; I need some forms made, plain but exact. Not this sort of thing."

"I can do that, too, sir," Edgar said softly. "I've had some training in making molds. I worked for a silversmith for a time."

Keeping his back to the room, Edgar took out the spoon he'd made. The bowl fitted well into the handle, which was ornately decorated. He also showed him the pepper box. It was plainly carved but even, a perfect cube. Gaudry looked from it to him.

"Idiot got married," Laudine explained. "The pair of them were thrown onto the streets. Got no more idea of how to survive than new-hatched chicks."

Gaudry considered. "I don't work by the bells," he said. "No leaving at Vespers. If you're willing, I'll give you a try. But if you're some scholar who thinks he can mold silver because he read about it in Boethius or some such, you'll be sorry you wasted my time."

Edgar held up his newly scarred hands. "I know how to make a mold," he said. "What will you pay?"

"Two sous for every properly made piece," the man answered. "I don't care how long it takes you; that's the price."

"Very well," Edgar said. "Where is your workshop?"

"It's on the Île," Gaudry answered. "You won't find it on your own. Be waiting tomorrow at the court of Saint-Étienne. I'll meet you and take you to it."

So he could tell no one where to find him. Edgar hesitated, then nodded.

"Good. Be there at first light." Gaudry tossed a denier in the air. Edgar caught it. "You have my word."

He bought a cup of wine with the coin so as not to seem ungrateful to Laudine. He could hardly wait to tell Catherine. Finally, he was earning his own way.

Catherine kept her hand against the wall as she went down the steps to the storage cellar. Even in summer it was cool down here. In the winter it was bone-cuttingly cold. The house had been built above it, but the cellar was just a dead end in an ancient maze of tunnels that wandered under the Juiverie and beyond. They had saved her life once.

She reached the bottom and set the lamp on an earthenware tun where Uncle Eliazar stored his wine. Then she took the basket and began to fill it with beans, dry and crackling in the shells.

There was a wind in the door. Catherine heard the creak and felt the sudden draft just before the lamp went out.

"Aunt Johannah?" she squeaked.

There was something down there with her. An animal, like a bear, lumbered toward her. Catherine tried to make her voice obey.

"Aunt . . . Jo . . . han . . . nah," she squeaked again.

The thing was snuffling, gurgling, coming closer. it smelled like a cross between the mouth of hell and a soapmaker's. Catherine backed away. It was between her and the stairs. The monster made a mad plunge at her. This time she managed to scream.

The thing roared horrible hellish syllables as it fell upon her. "Whadavudonwitit! Whadavudonwitit!"

There was a horrible rattle and Catherine found herself pinned to the floor by a weight that was twitching convulsively. It must be a bear. It was covered with fur.

All at once it was still. Catherine put her hands up to push it away. Then she felt and smelled something else.

"Oh, no!" she shrieked. "Holy Mother, Dear Savior, God in Heaven! Somebody! Get this thing off me!"

This time her screams reached the floor above.

Six

*asarah devarim qashim nivre'u ba'olam. har qasheh barzel
mechattekho; barzel qasheh 'ur mefa'pe'o; 'ur qasheh mayim
mekhabbin 'oto; mayim qashim'avim sovelim 'otan; 'avim qashim
ruach mefazzartan; ruach qasheh guf sovelo; guf qasheh pachad
shovero; pachad kasheh yayin mefigo; yayin kasheh shenah
mefakkachto; umitah kashah mikkulam.*

Ten strong things were created in the world. A mountain is
strong, but iron can cleave it; iron is strong, but fire can melt
it; fire is strong, but water can extinguish it; water is strong,
but clouds can carry it; clouds are strong, but the wind can
scatter them; wind is strong, but the body can carry it; the
body is strong, but fear can break it; fear is strong, but wine
dispels it; wine is strong, but sleep lessens its effect; but
death is stronger than them all.
—Babylonian Talmud, *Baba Batra* 10a

$\mathcal{N}$atan ben Judah. Of course. Who else would be so inconsiderate as to die under our roof without even being invited in?" Johannah had no sympathy for the deceased. "As well as what he did to you while he was dying. Are you feeling better, *enfançonette?*"

Catherine sat by the fire, wrapped in a swath of coverlets over a clean *chainse*. Her hands shook and the pewter cup she held rattled against her teeth. She was recovering from the shock but she wished the bathhouses weren't all closed for the night. A shallow tub in the kitchen wasn't enough to make her feel cleansed. Johannah sat next to her. Eliazar and a neighbor had gone down to see to the body.

The bell at the front gate jangled. Johannah got up to open it.

Catherine tried to compose herself. If that was Edgar, she didn't want him to see her so disquieted. Death happened every day, after all.

At least in your case, it seems to.

Catherine sighed and took another gulp of the mulled cider. Then her lips trembled, thinking of their baby. This man, this Natan, had lived, at any rate. And from what Aunt Johannah said, he hadn't spent his life in a state of grace.

Now you feel you must find out what he was doing in the cellar, besides soiling your best woolen bliaut as well as the chainse and the pellice underneath.

Well, of course I must, Catherine thought back. *Clearly this is what was intended when the man fell on me. Fate wishes me to take an interest in the matter.*

She was accustomed to debating her life with these voices in her mind, although they had been less intrusive since she had had Edgar to debate with.

Before they could respond, Johannah returned, Edgar following close behind.

"You see," Johannah finished a conversation that had started at the gate, "Catherine is unharmed, only frightened. Anyone would be if a strange man fell on them in the dark and then died."

Edgar knelt beside her and pulled at a dark curl that had gotten stuck at the corner of her mouth. His look was concerned, but underneath that was exasperated amusement.

"Oh, Catherine," he said. "Not again!"

Catherine decided not to remind him that the first time she had become involved with murder was only minutes after they had met, when she had nearly been crushed by a body thrown from the tower at Saint-Denis. She still said prayers for poor Garnulf.

"At least this time it wasn't anyone we knew," Catherine retorted.

"Good. Then it's no business of ours," he said firmly, but there was a question in his eyes. "How are you?"

"Much better, now that you're here," Catherine answered, leaning against him. "I feel a little shaky. It was so dark; I had no idea what was coming at me. I thought it might be a demon or a monster."

Edgar could feel her trembling still. Her hands were icy, her lips pale. Why did these things always happen to her? Before he met Catherine, the only corpses he saw were created by quite usual means: battle, sickness and accident. Since then, it had begun to seem to him that people died unnaturally just to confound her. She didn't look for bodies. They simply sprouted up wherever she went.

Edgar sighed. "Let me take you home," he said.

Johannah gave him a cup of the cider. "I'm sorry there are no cakes," she said. "But can you wait a few more minutes? If Catherine can manage it, I think Eliazar would like to ask her about what happened."

"I think that my mind is stronger than my legs at the moment," Catherine said. "We can stay here as long as you need me."

"Are you sure, Catherine?" Edgar asked, but only for form's sake. He knew how curious she was. To himself he admitted that he wanted to know more, as well.

They soon heard the sound of splashing as Eliazar and the neighbor, Joseph, washed off the contagion of death. Eliazar came in alone.

"Joseph has gone for Natan's nephew, Menahem," he said. "As the nearest relative, he'll have to arrange for the burial."

He looked at Johannah, who was slightly built and barely came to his shoulder in height, and shook his head in wonder.

"How did you ever manage to move the body?" he asked.

"Catherine helped," Johannah answered. "I couldn't leave her there trapped under that thing, could I?"

"Of course not," Eliazar said. "You should have called me."

"I didn't think of it," Johannah snapped. "Next time, I will."

Eliazar wiped his forehead. "I'm sorry," he told her. "The two of you should never have had to endure such an experience. "I'm angry with myself, not you."

"Did you send Natan to our cellar?" Johannah demanded. "Did you know he would be there when Catherine went down? Did you throw him against her?"

"I should have known," Eliazar said, pulling at his beard.

Edgar started to ask why, then decided to wait. He had learned enough from Hubert and Baruch to realize that Catherine's uncle was hiding something from them. If so, he was unlikely to reveal it before his wife and niece.

"Uncle, what killed him?" Catherine asked. "And how did he get there?"

"The door to the tunnels was open," Eliazar said. "It should have been barred and hidden behind boxes. Did you open it, Catherine?"

"No, of course not," said Catherine. "I only went through that door once before and don't even remember where it is. The room was still when I went down. I didn't notice the door at all. I think the draft from its opening was what blew out the lamp."

She shuddered again and Edgar put his arm around her.

"It's only that I couldn't see," she repeated. "I didn't know what it was."

"Do you know how he died?" Edgar asked.

Eliazar shook his head. "Poison, we think, or perhaps some sort of fit," he said. "The elders will have to be told. Someone must investigate this."

Catherine started to raise her hand. Edgar tightened his grip on her arm.

"But Eliazar," Johannah said, her voice rising in worry, "why did he come to our house?"

They all looked at him. Eliazar hesitated, then shook his head. "I don't know," he said. "He had no reason to be here. I wish I knew who had left the tunnel door unbarred."

There was a lot more that Catherine wished she knew. Where had

Natan come from? What was he looking for? Why had he smelled like that, even before he died? Most of all, who was he that his death should be a cause for annoyance rather than grief?

"Poison?" Edgar said. He was wondering, too, why Eliazar had named the unnatural cause of death first.

"His limbs were twisted and his face in a rictus," Eliazar told them with distaste. "His skin was an odd blue color. At least it looked so in the lamplight." He broke off his description and sat down abruptly next to the hearth. "How long does it take a man to run up the street and tell another to come get a body?" he grumbled.

"Who would have wanted to poison this man?" Edgar asked.

"Almost anyone who knew him," Eliazar said. "Although I'd have preferred to wring his neck."

"Husband!" Johannah said. She turned to Catherine and Edgar. "He doesn't mean it. We are all very upset. Natan was unpleasant, but I'm sure no one would poison him."

"Of course," Edgar assured her. "Of course, it may have been a fit, or an accident."

"Or even demons come for their own," Johannah decided. "I would believe that easily."

"There was a strange odor about him," Catherine said slowly. "It was smothered in oils and perfume but there was something of it that reminded me of a blacksmith's. That's why I thought I had come to the mouth of Hell. And something else, a metallic emanation from his breath."

Edgar suddenly sat up straighter. He loosened his hold on Catherine. "Eliazar, where do those tunnels lead?" he asked.

Eliazar threw up his hands. "Who knows them all? Some connect the houses of the community to the synagogue. There's one that goes to the storeroom under Saint-Christophe."

Edgar nodded. "I remember."

"We filled it with provisions during the time after the Christians collected their armies to invade the Holy Land," Eliazar said. "After we saw what happened to our brethren in Mainz and Speyer. Fortunately, we haven't needed it as a refuge."

"Are those the only ones you know?" Edgar asked.

"I explored a little, when I was a boy," Eliazar admitted. "My family lived in Rouen, but I was sent here to study and live with my teacher. We boys used to dare each other to go around one more corner in the darkness. But there always seemed to be another one."

"So this Natan could have come from anywhere on the Île?" Edgar said.

"Yes, of course." Eliazar grasped at this thought eagerly. "Anywhere. He may have simply stumbled against the door and it opened. He might not even have known where he was."

But then why was the door left unbarred? Catherine wondered again. Eliazar seemed to have dropped that question entirely. She didn't say it aloud, though. She wanted to think this over a while, preferably in her own bed. All of a sudden, she was exhausted.

The bell rang and Johannah went to let in Natan's nephew, Menahem, the draper. Eliazar got up to greet him in the hall.

Edgar and Catherine heard the murmur of their voices, but caught no words until Haquin's voice rose querulously.

"Christian!" he shouted. "What was a Christian girl doing in your cellar?"

"That's silly," Catherine whispered to Edgar. "The Christian servant is down there all the time."

"He's upset, Catherine," Edgar said. "He's afraid you'll make trouble for them."

Johannah came back in. Menahem is going down to see to his uncle," she told them. "It would be better if you left now, if you feel up to it, Catherine."

She had brought their cloaks and gloves. As they put them on she stood watching as if undecided what to do next.

"Aunt Johannah?" Catherine said. "Doesn't Natan's nephew know about Father?"

"No, dear, that's exactly the problem," Johannah said. "You see, Menahem thinks that you two are simply visitors, business acquaintances of ours. Not many people are aware that your father and Eliazar are brothers. It's not safe for either of them to have such a thing widely known."

"We understand," Catherine said. "Neither of us will mention it. Will someone from the Jewish community want me to appear as a witness to this?"

"It's possible," Johannah said. "If they decide that Natan was poisoned. Women are allowed to give evidence in . . . such cases. But since you aren't one of us, I don't know what the ruling would be."

"We can worry about that when we need to," Edgar said. "Catherine, do you feel strong enough to walk, or shall we ask Eliazar for the loan of a donkey?"

Catherine had a sudden image of them fleeing into Egypt. "It's not far," she said. "I'll be fine."

They said good night and Johannah bustled them out apologetically but as quickly as she could.

They reached their room well after dark. Edgar had spent the time after they crossed the *Grand Pont* looking over his shoulder, wishing he had owl eyes. He told himself that no one was following, but thought he could hear footsteps keeping pace with them all the same.

The next morning Edgar woke suddenly and sat bolt upright. How late was it? The room was dark as Judas's heart but outside it could be light already. He scrambled out of bed, waking Catherine as he extricated himself from her arms and the leg that she'd wrapped around his. Even asleep, she needed to reassure herself that he was there, that there was someone between her and the door.

"What's wrong?" she asked in sleepy alarm.

He groped around for a taper, lighting it by blowing on the banked coals in the brazier, then found and lit the lamp.

"In the excitement last night, I forgot all about it," he told her. "I finally found work, I think, and of the sort we were hoping for. I met a man in a tavern. He told me to be at Saint-Étienne at first light. If I hurry, maybe he'll still be there waiting for me."

"At Saint-Étienne?" Catherine sat up, pulling the blankets around her so that the warmth wouldn't escape. "I don't remember any gold- or silversmiths over there. Where did he say his shop was?"

Edgar had been afraid she'd ask that. "He didn't say, only that it would be too hard for me to find alone."

His voice was indistinct, coming from beneath the tunic he was pulling on over his head. When his top half was covered, he looked around for his pants.

Catherine didn't move. Edgar tried to ignore her silence with bustle as he searched. Finally, she spoke.

"Your *braies* are in the chestnut box," she told him. "You'll want the leather ones if you're going to work all day."

He got them out and put them on, then pulled on the thick woolen hose that kept his boots from chafing.

"Gaudry told me that he doesn't work by the bells," he said carefully. "You mustn't worry if I'm late."

She nodded.

He stopped midboot. "Catherine," he said, "this is what we wanted. I'm following the plan."

"Yes, I know."

He tried again. "Catherine, one thing I've learned since I married you is that whenever you become monosyllabic, I'm in trouble. I know you don't like my going out alone with someone who might be dangerous to a place I have no directions for."

She began fussing with a fingernail, avoiding his eyes. "In the search for truth, there are always risks," she said. "We knew that when we agreed to come here."

That did it. He stomped his boots on the floor and glared down at her.

"You're plotting something," he said. "Don't look at me like that and, for heaven's sake, don't lower that blanket. You'll freeze and I'll not be able to leave at all. Now, what are you going to be doing today?"

She kept the covers at her neck and smiled at him. "I thought I'd clean the room and then I might go over to the Île and see who is lecturing. Adam of the Bridge doesn't seem to mind the cold when he expounds. Or I could go see if Aunt Johannah needs my help. She never did get the cakes made."

He was still suspicious. "And that was all?" he asked.

"I'll stop by the bakers and get some cabbage pies for dinner," she added.

"Are you feeling well enough after last night?" he asked.

Catherine shivered. "Yes. I'm not trembling anymore. It was so horrible that it seems more like a nightmare. I'm trying not to think about it. Truly, it's better for me to be out with people around me than sitting here and brooding."

He was unconvinced. Having a body fall on her the night before wasn't enough to make Catherine so tractable. But he could think of no means to make her tell him what she was really up to. He glanced at the window. It was still dark, but there were sounds in the street now. He had to leave. He bent over and kissed her, resisting the urge to get back in bed.

"You'll keep the pie warm until I return?" he asked.

"Of course," she answered. This time there was no deception in her tone. "I'll mull some ale for you as well. Be careful."

He hurried down the street and across the bridge to the Île. There were few people out in the frozen dawn. A man staggered by under the weight of a crate of noisy chickens. The milk peddler and his wife pulled their cart along the road to the *pierre o let,* an ancient monolith that had become the center of a market area. They were all wrapped in as many layers as they could wear, red, runny noses sticking out over their scarves. Edgar sniffled as well.

When he reached the courtyard of Saint-Étienne, it was empty. The wind whirled from the river on his right, carrying a fine icy mist that penetrated through all the wool he was wearing. He looked around. Was he early, or too late? Perhaps Gaudry had changed his mind, had only agreed to take him on to appear charitable before Laudine.

"You the new metalsmith?" a voice asked at his elbow.

Edgar jumped, then looked down. The man must have been waiting for him in one of the alleyways, out of the wind. He was shorter than Edgar, but appeared even smaller than he was. He had the perpetual hunch of a person who had spent every day since childhood bent over a table.

"I am," Edgar replied. "What is the name of the man who sent you?"

"Gaudry, as you know well," the man answered. "But it never hurts to be cautious. I'm Odo. I'm to take you to the workshop."

He set off. Edgar followed. He had expected that they would turn down one of the many narrow streets that emptied into the square, but his guide headed for the church itself. Six hundred years old, roofless and unused, it had yet to be deconsecrated and was therefore respected and left in mournful ruins. They entered through a side door and down the northern transept. Odo went boldly into the choir, stepping over fallen beams, and then to the vestry. Edgar hesitated. He had no business in this part of the church, in use or not; it was only for clerics. Odo didn't look back. With a silent prayer for forgiveness, Edgar hurried to catch up.

They went through another door and came out in the space between Saint-Étienne and the little church of Notre Dame. They turned right and entered a windowless shed built against the wall of the canon's cloister.

The door shut behind them, leaving them in darkness. But Edgar had had time to note that there was nothing in the shed but stores of hay. He felt for his knife, sure that he had walked into a trap.

He tensed himself for the attack, but it didn't come. Instead he heard a scrabbling as the hay was pushed aside and then a grunt from Odo.

"Give me a hand with this," he said. "The wood has swollen in the damp and it's stuck."

Edgar felt for the door and nearly tripped over Odo, who was kneeling and pulling at a ring set into the floor.

"What sort of shop is this," he asked, "that one must follow a treasure map to get to it?"

Odo grunted as the trapdoor opened. The steps below it were moss-covered at the edges but well trafficked in the center. Edgar could see the way because there was a light farther down the tunnel, too far away for him to judge the source. If this Gaudry wasn't doing something illicit, then he was secretive to the point of madness. One thing Edgar was certain of: no innocent apprentice would go further without hesitating.

"Why should I follow you?" he asked Odo again. "No one puts a metalworks underground but trolls. You may be leading me to my death."

Odo turned around to back down the steps. His face was in shadow, but Edgar sensed that he was grinning.

"Who would kill the likes of you?" he countered. "Are you hiding a treasure beneath that tunic? Perhaps you think we polish our silver with human blood."

That hadn't occurred to Edgar. He wished it hadn't been mentioned now. Between the Saxon tales of his childhood and the sermons against heretical sects of his school days, he had heard of a number of rituals that required blood to be diverted from its usual course, often taking place in underground caverns. He pulled his gloves up farther over his wrists and tightened his scarf.

"Go on!" Odo commanded. "Don't be such a coward. You'd think there was a dragon waiting down there."

Since that had been one of the thoughts flitting through Edgar's mind, he felt obliged to make up for his lapse into pagan superstition at once. He entered the tunnel. Behind him he heard the scrape and thud as Odo pulled the trapdoor shut behind them both.

After Edgar had left, Catherine dressed herself hurriedly, hose and slippers first, to ward off the cold seeping up through the floor. The weaver had not come in yet from his rooms in the back and there was no heat below to warm their room. It wasn't much colder than the convent, she reflected, except at the Paraclete one never slept naked but fully dressed, to be prepared to get up for the night Office.

Of course, the nuns each had their own little bed, with nothing but a blanket and faith to keep them warm. On the whole, she preferred her present arrangement.

Before she left, Catherine made sure the coals were still glowing beneath their coat of ash and that there were enough to last until she got back. Then she put the leather money pouch around her neck and tucked it under her *chainse*. There were enough coins in it for pies and ale, she hoped. She wondered if this man would pay Edgar by the day, by the piece, or only with promises.

In her whole life, Catherine had never been obliged to wonder where money came from. She had done accounts for her father and for Mother Héloïse at the convent, but those had been mathematical exercises. Someone else had always fed and clothed her. Now she was astonished at how quickly the thin quartered coins vanished from her purse and how slowly new ones appeared. Like Edgar, she was suddenly forced to consider what life must be like for those with no father or monastery to care for them.

With her mind flipping between plans to find out more about this Natan who had so embarrassingly expired in her arms and half-formed schemes to bring in a few more coins, Catherine was not particularly attentive to the traffic. She managed to get to the end of the rue Saint-Germain l'Auxerrois without mishap, but there hesitated. She had planned on turning right onto the rue Saint-Denis and crossing the Grand Pont to the Île and on to Eliazar's home. But the cutting wind reminded her of a fur-lined cloak she had left at her father's house on the Grève. It was unlikely that he would be there now, but there should be a servant who could let her in to get it.

She started across the main road from Paris to Saint-Denis without looking. The next moment she found herself sitting in the gutter in the middle of the road under a shower of curses from a cart driver who had narrowly missed running her down.

A pair of strong arms reached down to help her to stand. Catherine heard the rasp of chain mail on leather. She looked up into the face of her protector. His grip loosened as they recognized each other.

"Jehan." Catherine swallowed. *"Diex te saut.* Thank you. I wasn't looking."

"That is obvious."

Now that she was standing on her own, the knight released her. He seemed more than eager to do so. Catherine guessed that he was regretting stopping to help her at all. Her previous encounters with Jehan had been far from cordial.

However, they seemed to be going in the same direction. Catherine managed to get to the far side of the road and set out toward the Grève. Jehan followed her, then caught up. Whatever he thought of her, Catherine knew he was duty-bound to protect her as Hubert's daughter. Although he was usually in service to Thibault, Count of Champagne, Jehan was occasionally loaned to Hubert as part of an armed guard to defend the merchants as they traveled. It was always possible that the count would be displeased if he learned that Hubert's daughter had come to harm through his inaction.

Both of them sighed. They walked in silence for a few moments, but lack of conversation made Catherine nervous.

"Is Count Thibault in Paris now?" she asked.

"No," Jehan answered.

"Countess Mahaut?"

"No," Jehan repeated.

Catherine refused to be defeated. "You are still attached to their court?"

"Yes," Jehan said. He gave another deep sigh and spoke without looking at her. "Count Thibaut is in Blois. The countess is at

Troyes, I believe. I am in Paris to bring a message to the king from the count."

"I thought they weren't on speaking terms," Catherine said. "Because of Raoul leaving the count's cousin for the queen's sister."

"I don't indulge in gossip," Jehan replied. "If I did, I might have something to say about women who leave convents to marry foreign nobodies and shame their families. And I might suggest that they think more about what they've done to their own sisters and not worry about the queen's."

Catherine was stung by the accuracy of his dart. "What about my sister?" she asked. "Is something the matter with Agnes? Is she ill?"

He looked at her now, his face hard with anger. "You know all about Petronilla and Raoul and nothing about Agnes, and you care less," he said. "You wander about leaving maimed souls behind as you go and you never once bother to turn back and give them your help. You destroyed my friend, Roger. He was your own uncle and he loved you, but you let him die."

"You don't understand . . ." Catherine began, but Jehan had been started and he was bound to finish.

"You somehow managed to turn Raynald of Tonnerre into a weeping recluse," he went on. "And now you've abandoned your sister to care for your mother as her own chances for a good marriage vanish."

"Agnes must have explained about Mother," Catherine said. "And the nuns at Tart are caring for her now. Agnes is free to marry, if she wishes."

"Then why won't she?" Jehan countered.

"Why won't . . . ?" Catherine was nearly as tall as Jehan and wearing her shoes with thick, wooden soles. She moved so she could look into his eyes. He turned away.

She didn't say anything more. *We have had cause to remind you of the consequences of an idle tongue,* her voices said smugly.

Catherine took the reprimand as well deserved. Her pointless questions had brought too many revelations at once. She had purposely forgotten that Jehan had been a friend of her uncle Roger, now dead. She did remember that Jehan had never been fond of Edgar. She was also aware that Jehan blamed her for every bit of bad fortune in his life for the past two years. But it hadn't occurred to her that part of his resentment involved his feelings about Agnes. Jehan must have come into some property at last if he was thinking of marrying. Or perhaps part of his bitterness was that he was thinking of marrying and no fortune had come his way.

They reached the Grève and both turned toward Hubert's house. Catherine began to wonder about the welcome she would receive there if her sister were home. But it didn't seem likely that she would be. Agnes hadn't been in Paris since last spring, when she had learned the truth about her Jewish ancestry. She had told their father she would never live under his roof again. Catherine wondered how Agnes felt about Jehan. Whatever her feelings, she would probably not have told him about Hubert's incomplete conversion. Would that secret be a reason for her to refuse him?

Guilt flooded Catherine's heart. In her desire for Edgar and in her joy at finding in Eliazar and Johannah a loving family of any faith, she had left her sister behind. She'd rarely even thought of her. While Catherine was in the convent, Agnes had been the one to cope with their mother's growing attachment to the saints to the exclusion of the living. And, when Catherine came home, that had only made matters worse.

They had reached the gate. Jehan pulled the bell cord and they waited. Catherine wanted desperately to turn around and run. Who would answer? What could she say?

The servant who answered the bell recognized Catherine. She couldn't remember his name, but smiled and asked after his health.

He coughed richly in reply.

Catherine turned to Jehan. "Thank you for accompanying me," she said. "Would you care to come in? There must be soup or something to drink."

"I was coming here anyway," Jehan answered. "I also have a message for your father."

They were brought into the main hall, the only room with a fireplace. Agnes sat near it, a length of sewing on her lap. Her face lit as she rose to greet them. Catherine started toward her, relieved that her sister was no longer angry with her. Then she realized that Agnes hadn't even noticed her. The smile was for Jehan.

Then Agnes saw her. The smile was withdrawn and replaced by a cold stare.

"You have not been invited," she said softly. "I am now the mistress here. Please leave the house at once."

She turned her back on Catherine, took Jehan's arm and led him to the fire.

Catherine stood awkwardly at the doorway. She wondered if Ishmael had ever tried to come home from the wilderness and if Isaac had looked through him as Agnes had looked through her now. And what did her sister mean, that she was mistress here? Was she now reconciled with their father? Had she forgiven Hubert, but not Catherine, for keeping his ancestry secret? Catherine wished with all her heart that she were back in her drafty room, waiting for Edgar to return. One thing was certain: she had to be anywhere but here.

The cloak forgotten, Catherine left the house she had been born in. All she wanted now was to go home.

Edgar inhaled the now-familiar odor of dung and hot metal. The tunnel had come up into a normal workroom, much like Baruch's. The windows were too high to see from, so he still had no idea where he was, but they provided good light to work by.

Edgar bent to the task he had been given. First he had wet some ashes, put them in a crucible and held it over the coals until the dried mixture had adhered to the surface. Then he had placed the crucible in a hole made by scooping out some of the coals. Finally he added silver and lead and put coals all around to melt them. Now he was blowing carefully on a firebrand to release the lead from the silver. Most of it had been skimmed off already. Baruch would be proud of him.

All of a sudden the silver began bubbling in the crucible. It foamed and threatened to overflow. Edgar took the tongs and pulled it from the furnace.

Gaudry's head came up at once. "Eh! *Mesel!*" he shouted. "Can't you even refine silver? Wasn't that in your book?"

Edgar put the crucible down on the beaten-earth floor. "This has brass in it," he said. "I need some ground glass to keep it from boiling over again."

Gaudry grunted and pointed to a ceramic mortar and pestle. "The broken glass is in the box under the tool table."

Edgar hated grinding glass. The sound made his hair stand on end and his teeth ache. But he did it without comment. He had been put to the test by Gaudry all morning and, so far, his training had held. He felt a tremendous pride in this achievement. His ignoble talent had some use after all.

Even more, this accident with the silver had been his first clue that he had fallen into the right place. Brass was normally mixed with silver to make niello, which was used in the decorating of fine pieces, like chalices. This silver might not have been melted down from stolen church property, but, considering the unorthodox way he had been hired and led to the workshop, it was a distinct possibility.

Edgar hummed contentedly as the glass screeched. He was so involved in the work that he completely forgot to worry about what Catherine was doing. When he thought of her at all, it was not in connection with ecclesiastical intrigue. Mainly he reflected on a full stomach, laughter and a warm bed.

But not necessarily in that order.

Seven

The room over the weaver's, Paris, the Feast of Saint Matthais, the thirteenth Apostle, Monday, February 24, 1141 / 14, Adar, 4901, the first day of Purim

Modus legendi in dividendo constat. Divisio fit et partitione et investigarione. Partiendo dividimus, quando ea quae confusa sumt, distinguimus. Investigado dividimus, quando ea quae occulta sunt, reseramus.

Analysis takes place through separating into parts or through examination. We analyze through separation into parts when we distinguish from one another things which are mingled together. We analyze by examination when we open up things that are hidden.

—Hugh of Saint-Victor
Didascalion, Book VI, Chapter 12

*C*atherine sat on the bed and cried. First she cried because Agnes had hurt her so and ignored her for Jehan, a man who hated her. Then she cried because she had let Edgar leave without even knowing where he was going. Then she cried some more because she was lonely and frightened and sorry for herself for being so inept that she couldn't even give birth properly.

Crying solved none of these problems, but, when she had reached the stage of hiccoughs and nose-wiping, she felt much more clear-headed. She rinsed her face and adjusted her scarf so that her hair was covered, except for a curl that snuck out unnoticed over her left ear. Then she sat down again and calmly considered what she should do next.

The bells began: Saint-Leufroi, Saint-Jacques, Saint-Opportune, Saint-Germain and, from farther away, like an echo, Saint-Magloire, Saint-Merri, Saint-Jean. She couldn't hear the response from the churches on the Île. The wind was from the north and so the ringing was being blown south, toward Orleans. The bells of Paris spoke to Catherine as old friends, telling her secrets, reminding her that she was home.

It was only Tierce. The day had barely begun.

Below she heard someone speaking to the weaver. He answered in the rasping rhythm of the loom. Then there were footsteps on the stairs, coming to her door. Catherine hoped the visitor would be someone too well-mannered to mention how red her eyes were.

Fortune was not being kind to her today. Catherine answered the knock. There stood her cousin Solomon.

"Either you were drinking all last night," he greeted her, "or sobbing all morning. Edgar started beating you already?"

"Of course not!" she answered. "I just felt like crying."

He nodded. "Good idea. I often feel like crying myself. Especially when I come all the way to see you and can't get past the doorway."

Catherine moved back to let him in. "I'm sorry," she said. "I'm not thinking too clearly today. A man died on top of me last night."

Solomon put his hand to his mouth in mock horror. "Catherine! Is that the sort of thing you should boast of? Especially to your poor, unmarried cousin, to whom such pleasure comes rarely?"

Catherine's eyes narrowed. She pushed him hard enough for him to land on the stool, laughing at her.

"Solomon, why do you always tease me so?" she asked. "You know about it already, don't you?"

He nodded. "Aunt Johannah sent me over to see how you were. I know it's a terrible thing to have happen but somehow . . ." He shrugged apologetically.

"I know," she said. "It's me. And some things are so horrid that one must mock them to keep one's sanity. But I wasn't weeping over the death. I was frightened then, but now I'm angry. I want to know why this man died."

There was no point in telling him about Agnes. It was much better to worry about a dead stranger than a live, bitter relative.

"Did you know this man Natan?" she asked.

Solomon grew serious at once. "I knew him," he said. "He was a thief and a hypocrite. No one mourns him."

"Not even his nephew?"

He shook his head. "Menahem is an honest man who works hard. Natan was his mother's brother. His nephew allowed the man to stay with him for her sake. But Menahem disliked him, too. Natan bragged that his clothes were made in Spain and he had no need to buy from a simple Paris draper. Natan was sure he was better than anyone."

"Was he rich?" Catherine asked.

"Who knows?" Solomon said. "He dressed like a courtier from the south and anointed himself with scented oil. He may have been rich or spent all he had on his raiment. Haquin says he left no money for his burial. None that can be found, anyway."

Catherine caught the doubt. "Do you think Natan has left a hidden treasure?"

Solomon got up. He hadn't bothered to take off his cloak. "I don't know, Catherine," he said. "But I do know that there's a lot going on that no one is willing to share with me. I want you and Edgar to help me discover what it is. Where is he, by the way?"

Catherine opened her mouth to answer, then stopped. Was Solomon part of the search for the stolen church property? She couldn't remember. Too many plots; too many secrets. She hated not knowing what she could say, even to the people she trusted most. Oh, yes, her father had told her; Solomon had started it. Something about a chalice.

"Edgar has found work with a man who claims to need a silversmith and doesn't want to go to the guild," she said. "We think he may be a link to this trade in church property."

"It's possible," Solomon spoke slowly. "There are many men who don't wish to adhere to guild rules, but it's as hard to avoid them as to get a boat past Paris without belonging to the water merchants. Edgar's new master may be one who was forced out of a guild or was never allowed in. In that case, working for him could be dangerous."

"I know," Catherine answered. Her fears were now clearly ordered in her mind. Edgar came first. "The man wouldn't tell Edgar where the shop was, likely to protect himself in case Edgar was a spy for the guild. At least I hope that was the only reason. But that means we have no way of finding him."

"He should have told me about it," Solomon said. "I could have followed him. What was he thinking of, going alone? That's the sort of thing I'd expect you to do. I thought Edgar had more sense."

"Oh, thank you," Catherine answered. "And who was it who nearly got himself killed walking alone at night from Vielleteneuse to Saint-Denis?"

"I was driven out by your pious brother!" Solomon was standing now.

"Guillaume wouldn't have sent you away, not after dark!" Catherine shouted. "It was just your stubborn pride!"

"Too proud to be treated like a dog at his table, you mean!"

They were nose to nose, yelling at the top of their lungs like street peddlers. Almost identical, with black curls and Roman noses, except for their eyes, his green, hers blue. They were well matched in temper, as well. Catherine took a breath to shout a rebuttal.

They both jumped as the floor shook beneath them. The weaver was pounding on the ceiling.

"*Damledex!* Stop that noise!" he shouted. "I have a customer down here!"

Catherine caught Solomon's arm as he prepared to stomp a reply.

"You always tease and we always fight," she sighed. "Now, how are we going to find Edgar?"

"Did he give you any sort of clue as to where this place was?" Solomon asked.

"He said he was to meet the man on the Île, near Saint-Étienne," she said. "But there's no guarantee that the workshop is anywhere near there. It seems likely to me that it isn't. That whole end of the Île is the property of the bishop. It's no where near the street of the goldsmiths."

"A man who didn't want to attract the notice of the guild would hardly put his shop under their noses," Solomon said.

"I know, but how else could one mask the smell of the kilns?" Catherine said. "Edgar used to wash every night before he left Baruch's and there still was a scent of metal about him."

"Nevertheless, we need to start somewhere." Solomon started putting on his gloves. "Do you want to come with me?"

"Of course."

The day had warmed a bit, the sun watery through the clouds. The court of the church of Saint-Étienne was more crowded now, with students hunting a quick, cheap meal and with those hoping to sell them one. Catherine felt a stab of yearning as she caught tags of conversation, bits of lectures repeated and pondered, Latin accented with all the languages of Christendom. Someday she would come back here and sit at the edge of the *schola* and once again listen and ponder on her own. Other women did; Mother Héloïse had. How desperately she missed the joy of unraveling a passage from Augustine or Jerome and finding the kernel of truth at its heart.

"Do you see Edgar?" Solomon asked.

She shook her head. "It's not yet Sext. I doubt he will be let go before Vespers. He told me the master doesn't mind the hours, but I don't see how they can continue working by candlelight."

She scanned the faces of the students, all ages, nations and status. There was no one she knew. These were mostly cathedral scholars. Master Abelard's old students tended to stay on the Left Bank, or study with the teachers on the *petit pont*.

"Solomon! *Shalom!*" The voice was loud and cheerful.

Catherine turned to see a big, blond man with a ruddy face clap

Solomon on the back with a force that made him wince. Solomon rolled his eyes in resignation at Catherine and then smiled at the man.

"Brother Andrew!" he said. "*Salve!* How good to see you again. Catherine, this is Brother Andrew, a canon of Saint-Victor. Andrew, this is—"

"Your sister," Andrew assumed as he inclined his head toward her.

"*Frater Andreas, ave,*" Catherine said. "*Catherine, filia Huberti mercator, amicaque Salomonis.*"

The canon blinked. He had been prepared for Hebrew, or at least French.

"Perhaps you prefer Saxon?" Catherine continued, still in Latin. "I have lately begun a study of the language of my husband, but my grammar and pronunciation are far from perfect."

Solomon kicked her discreetly. Catherine winced, but took his meaning. She stopped showing off.

"Catherine's father and my uncle are occasionally business partners," Solomon explained. "Before her marriage, she was a student at the convent of the Paraclete."

"Of course." Brother Andrew's face indicated that no further explanation was needed, either for her Latin or her desire to express herself. With a look of relief, he returned to Solomon. "I was just on my way to visit your uncle," he said. "There is a passage in Numbers that I need his advice on." To Catherine he added, "Eliazar and his friends have been very helpful in teaching me the Hebrew language and in explaining the interpretation of the Heptateuch in the *Hebraica veritas.* I am convinced that many of the difficulties we have in reconciling the Old and the New Testaments can be eliminated if we discover and adhere to the original meaning of the words in, of course, the original language."

He didn't ask if she agreed. "By the way," he added to her, "I'm not Saxon; my family came to England from Normandy with Duke William, so I'd prefer it if you speak French."

Solomon took his arm and gestured to Catherine to follow them. "It's fortunate that I met you, Andrew," he said. "You would find my uncle's house empty today. Everyone is in the synagogue for morning prayers."

"They should be over by now, certainly," Andrew said.

"In your studies, I can see that you haven't included our feast days," Solomon answered. "Even the women and children go today to hear the *Megillah* read and cheer Haman's defeat through the courage of Esther. They won't be back until after Sext, I should think, and then there will be a feast, as yesterday was a day of fasting."

Brother Andrew was disconcerted by this news. "Of course, I have no wish to intrude in one of your festivals," he said. "Although I would be very curious to see how it is performed. Why aren't you with them?"

"I intend to be there when the food is served," Solomon answered. "But I had unavoidable duty this morning. Catherine's husband, Edgar, asked me to accompany her on her errands as he cannot and they have no servants."

"Edgar?" Andrew asked. "Tall fellow, Saxon from Scotland?"

"That's right," Catherine answered. "You know him?"

Andrew sighed. "Yes, we met many times at various lectures. I always liked him, despite his leanings. I tried to warn him of the danger of following Peter Abelard, but he wouldn't listen. Such a good family, too, even though they are also all wrongheaded and stubborn. I had hoped he would mellow with ecclesiastical advancement."

He glared at Catherine. "But now you've married him and doomed his career, if not his soul. And you came from the Paraclete. I might have guessed. The poison of that man Abelard spreads, just as our Abbot William of blessed memory said it would."

"The truth that Master Abelard spoke will not be silenced, if that is what you mean." Catherine's jaw quivered with anger.

Brother Andrew looked her up and down with his own cool anger. Then he bowed to Solomon. "I have a great respect for the Jews," he said. "But I have none for heretics, or their concubines. Please inform your uncle that I will visit him on Thursday for our regular lesson."

Brother Andrew hurried away, brushing his cloak as if the heresy of Peter Abelard might have affixed itself to him. Solomon watched him go, shaking his head.

"I should have hit him for insulting you that way, Catherine," he said.

"Of course. You may insult me, but no one else is allowed to," Catherine answered.

"If I were Christian, I would have defended you," Solomon insisted.

"Assaulting a cleric would have been just as stupid if you were Christian, unless you were a greater cleric," Catherine said. "The canons of Saint-Victor have always disliked Master Abelard, and the feeling was returned. The master had no use for Abbot William of Champeaux and his old style of teaching."

"Why do you speak of Abelard as in the past?" Solomon asked. "He's still living at Cluny, isn't he?"

Catherine sighed. "Yes, of course. But he seemed so frail when he left Sens. I suppose that I feel that if he has truly embraced the monastic life this time, he is no longer of this world. I'm glad Edgar wasn't here. He *might* have hit Brother Andrew, and not on my account."

The crowd was clearing as the clerics went their ways, either to say the Office or sleep until the afternoon lectures. Catherine continued looking for Edgar, but she suspected that there was no way to find him. She could only pray that he would return safely.

"What should we do now?" she asked Solomon.

"How do you feel about honey cakes and lentils in goose broth?" he asked. "Don't worry, the lentils aren't from the cellar. Aunt Johannah borrowed them from a neighbor so that the Purim dinner would be complete."

The question reminded Catherine that she hadn't eaten yet and it was past midday. "Do you allow heretics to eat at your table?" She grinned at Solomon.

"Only if they remember not to wipe their mouths on their sleeves," Solomon answered.

"I'm a well-mannered heretic," she assured him.

Edgar wasn't aware of the passage of time, or of the winter day outside. He was dripping with sweat and had tied his hair back with a strip of cloth to keep it from falling into his eyes. His leather *braies* were spotted with cinder burns and specks of metal. There was a knot between his shoulder blades that he knew would ache all night. As he hunched over the table, he wondered how long it would take before he became as stooped as Odo.

Gaudry had been setting him tests all day. Edgar doubted that anything he had done would survive the afternoon. He wondered if the artisan distrusted him or just wanted to be sure he had some skill before giving him a real piece of work. This test was the most difficult so far. Baruch had explained to him how the *organarium* worked, but there had been no time to even practice with it.

It was a device for turning a long strip of silver or gold into beads. Two hinged iron pieces, the bottom one fixed to a block of wood for stability, were set up so that the metal could be placed in a groove between the iron. When it was positioned properly, Edgar gave the top piece a sharp blow with the broad end of his hammer, then carefully turned the silver and hit again. He opened the mold and took out a bead the size of a pea. He set it in a wooden bowl next to him. Then he moved the metal another space and repeated the process.

"There." He showed them to Gaudry. "Ten silver beads, not a crack in them."

Gaudry looked at the collection with no sign of interest. "Took you long enough," he said. "A bit lopsided, as well. Still"—he forestalled Edgar's denial—"they'll do. Can you twist wire in the English fashion, say to rim a chalice with?"

Edgar nodded. "I know the patterns. But I have never fixed them to other metal."

"I'll do that part, if you can twist the wire without breaking it." Gaudry looked around the small workroom, as if hunting another task to test him with.

There was a knock on the door.

"Ah, about time," Gaudry muttered. He turned to Edgar. "Clean up your bench. Scrape all the bits of silver into the bowl and then wash the ash off them. I know the weight of my goods, young man, so don't try carrying anything off with you. I'll take you on by the day, tell you each night if I'll need you again. Two sous a day, instead of by the piece, one for the work and the other to keep your mouth shut."

His openness startled Edgar.

"I'll say nothing," he assured Gaudry. "I want no trouble from the guilds."

The pounding at the door grew more insistent. Edgar bent again over the table, swiftly putting the handful of deniers Gaudry had given him into the bag at his neck. Gaudry opened the door.

"Where have you been . . . ?" he began. "Oh, it's you. What are you doing here? Where's that blasted peddler?"

Edgar couldn't hear the response. Gaudry had gone out into the passage with his visitor and shut the door behind him. There was silence for a moment; then the door was flung open and Gaudry shouted at Odo's retreating back.

"By the burning furnace and roasted pig's feet of Saint Blaise, I don't care what happened!" he roared. "You find it at once or we'll all be ruined."

Edgar bent to his work and tried to appear deaf to anything else. As he scraped up the silver bits he wondered what was lost and who the missing peddler might be. Could it have anything to do with the chalice Solomon had found? Had Gaudry been hired to make a re-placement for it without knowing why? Or was he even more deeply involved in the trade in church regalia? On the other hand, none of this might have anything to do with his mission. The peddler could be one who traded in jewels and precious stones. His failure to de-liver his goods could mean a commission not finished in time. That would be enough to anger Gaudry. Still, this was the only lead Edgar had discovered so far and, he reflected, it was the only job he had been offered.

He would be back tomorrow, whether Gaudry needed him or not.

Johannah's greeting to Solomon and Catherine was subdued.

"We had intended to celebrate the holiday with our neighbors," she said. "But it seemed inappropriate considering what has hap-pened, so we are alone today. I'm glad you came. It's good to have family with us in times of trouble."

They followed her into the main hall. Eliazar sat by the fire, star-ing into the flames. He looked up when they entered and gave a sad smile.

"A poor feast it would be," he said, "if there were no one to share it with us. Purim should be a joyous time, when we remember how one young woman saved her people. I'm sorry you came instead to a house afflicted by such a death."

"We came to help," Catherine said, kissing him.

"And to eat," Solomon added.

"Of course," Eliazar said, adding, "I'm not sure that a man who hardly ever shows his face at the synagogue should be allowed to share the feast."

Solomon wasn't concerned. "I was taking care of Catherine," he said. "And saving you from a visit from Canon Andrew."

"Oh, no! That would have been all I needed." Eliazar wiped his forehead in relief. "That man torments me with his questions. Very well, you have done a good day's work on both counts. You've earned your keep."

Just as they were sitting down to eat, there was a commotion in the kitchen and Lucia burst through the door.

"What is this about a man being murdered in your cellar last night?" she demanded.

Johannah rose to calm her. "We don't know that he was murdered, dear. A man did die there, but we've done all the purification we can and the body has been removed, of course. He came in through the tunnel door, which had been left unbarred. You didn't happen to leave it that way, did you?"

Lucia looked bewildered. "Tunnel door?" she repeated. "Do you mean there's some underground passage down there? And you let me make up a bed in the storeroom without telling me? Saint Cecilia's angelic lover! I could have been raped!"

"The door is normally barred, Lucia," Johannah said. "Nothing could have harmed you. We still don't know how Natan got in."

"Natan?" Lucia went pale and grabbed at the nearest object, which happened to be Catherine's shoulder. "Natan," she whispered.

Her fingers dug through Catherine's wool *bliaut*, causing her to wince at the pain. Lucia felt the movement and released her at once.

"Do you mean the man who visited here last year?" she asked, her voice still shaking. "I thought he had finished his business with you."

"He had," Eliazar said. "His death has nothing to do with us."

"Then why was he in your cellar?" Lucia asked.

They all looked at Eliazar.

"I tell you, I don't know," he answered. "I mean to find out, however."

"How did he die?" Lucia asked.

There was a pause. Johannah finally answered. "We don't know for certain. He may have had some sort of attack, something he ate, perhaps."

"Poison," Lucia said. She crossed herself hurriedly.

"We're not sure of that," Eliazar said firmly. "But even if it were, he didn't eat it here. Now, Lucia, will you serve the meal?"

"I will not," she answered. "I don't want to work in a place where people die without warning. And I especially don't like it that I had to hear this from the milk peddler, instead of from you."

"Lucia, I apologize," Johannah told her. "We are all very upset by this, as you can imagine. We hoped to spare you. Now, please, bring in the dinner. If you like, you may go home afterwards. Catherine and I will do the cleaning."

Lucia considered a moment. "Very well," she said. "But I can't promise to be here tomorrow. I need to ask my mother about this."

Johannah managed a smile. "That's a good, dutiful girl. I'm sure she'll understand that Natan's death was an unfortunate accident and that you wouldn't want to give up a good place too rashly."

"I don't know what she'll understand," Lucia warned. "I'm already berated enough for working for Jews." She turned and went back to the kitchen.

Catherine leaned over to Johannah and whispered, "Do you think she'll really leave?"

Johannah shook her head, although she seemed worried. "I pay her three times what she would get in a Christian establishment; I don't think her mother will let her give that up. I hope not. It's not easy to get anyone to serve in a Jewish home."

Lucia brought the meal in silence and it was eaten without appetite. Even Solomon couldn't summon any enthusiasm, even for honey cakes.

As she cleared away the last platter, Lucia faced Johannah. "I've thought it over," she said. "If Mother will allow it, I'll stay. But I'm not going into that cellar and if I hear or see anything strange, any howls or cold fingers on my neck, I'm leaving."

"If that happens, Lucia, I may leave, too," Johannah assured her. "Thank you."

After the servant had left, Catherine and Johannah found themselves with the greasy pots and platters.

"You don't have to help," Johannah insisted feebly.

"I don't mind at all," Catherine said. "I'll go draw some water."

The light in the courtyard slanted toward sunset, but Catherine judged that it would be a while yet until sundown. Better to keep busy here than wait and worry for Edgar alone in their room.

She had just reentered the kitchen, carrying the full bucket, when there came a thumping from the cellar.

"Mother of God, protect me!" Catherine cried and dropped the bucket.

"Let me in!" a voice called.

Johannah and Catherine looked at each other, Johannah's hand moving quickly in the sign to ward off evil. The water splashed across the wood floor unheeded. Finally, Johannah found her voice.

"I think this time we should call your uncle," she said. "Go fetch him."

By a supreme force of will, Catherine made her legs move her into the hall.

"Solomon, Uncle!" she gulped as they looked, puzzled, at her wet skirts. "Something, down there!"

They were past her and down the stairs at once.

Johannah and Catherine followed, each armed with a candle and a crockery pitcher.

"Eliazar, open the door!" the voice called again.

This time Catherine recognized it. "Father!" she called.

Solomon unbarred the door to Hubert. He stood in the passageway, holding a torch.

"I wasn't sure this was the right door," he said. "I don't see how Natan could have found it last night, ill and without light."

"Hubert, how did you learn of this?" Eliazar asked.

"Edgar," Hubert said. "He found me down at the quai and told me what happened. I took the passage that comes out under the Grand Pont. I made more than one wrong turn before I found markings I thought I knew. Did you show Natan the way here?"

"No," Eliazar said decidedly. "I always made him come through the gate when he visited. Of course, he may have found his own way. He grew up here, too."

"When did you see Edgar?" Catherine asked.

"A little after Nones," Hubert said absently. He shook his head. "I don't understand why, if Natan were ill, he would try to come here. Why not his nephew's home?"

"Why take the tunnels at all?" Eliazar said. "Natan was a man who always refused to take the straightest way. He had as many twists as the Seine. It's like him to confound us even by his death. We may never know the truth of it."

The torchlight distorted Hubert's face but Catherine thought she saw fear in it. That chilled her more than the thought of ghosts and demons.

"I think we should try to find out," Hubert said. "The labyrinth down here is nothing, I fear, to the one we've become tangled in out in the world. I've had a number of visitors in the past few days, from Saint-Denis and beyond. May I come in?"

As they moved to let him by, Hubert noticed something.

"Why is there water dripping down the staircase?" he asked.

Edgar hadn't intended on seeing Catherine's father. When Gaudry had released him, he had hurried home to her, with thoughts of various warming activities speeding his path. The disappointment he felt at finding the room empty amazed him. She hadn't even left the pasties warming over the coals. Where could she have gone?

Edgar sighed and put his gloves back on. Unknowingly, he echoed Catherine's thought that any activity was better than waiting.

He had found Hubert supervising the unloading of wine casks from a raft tied up at the Grève. At first his father-in-law had answered distractedly, but when Edgar mentioned Natan's death, Hubert immediately gave him his full attention.

"Is Catherine all right?" Hubert gave a short, humorless laugh. "I seem to ask you that every time we meet."

"With good reason," Edgar sighed. "Yes, she was when I left her this morning."

"Good. Now tell me again about Natan," Hubert said.

Edgar repeated the story, keeping only to what he knew and leaving out any speculations. When he finished, Hubert called to one of his men to take over the work.

"I don't like this," he said. "I don't like it at all. I have to talk with my brother. Will you and Catherine be in tonight?"

"I suppose so," Edgar said. "We generally go to bed soon after dark."

"As do we all," Hubert said. "I want to speak with both of you. I'll come as early as I can. Oh yes, and I also would like to speak with

that friend of yours, the man from Salisbury who studied with Abelard. I see him now and again, over by Sainte-Geneviève, sometimes
with Master Gilbert or Master Robert."

"You mean John?" Edgar asked.

"Yes, John, that's right." Hubert seemed annoyed at forgetting
the name. Edgar had not been aware that he knew John at all. "Can
you ask him to meet me at your room?"

"If I can find him, I will," Edgar said.

So now he was combing the streets, looking for his friend John as
well as keeping an eye out for his wife. He hoped he'd find one of
them soon. It was growing dark and he was cold and hungry. While
he felt obliged to fulfill Hubert's commission, Edgar rather hoped it
would be Catherine he found first.

Although he disliked admitting it, especially to himself, Edgar had
always been a little in awe of John. It didn't seem logical; Edgar's
family had pretensions of royal blood and John's were only country
people, servants of the Salisbury canons. But Edgar had always
known that while he was just a student, John was a scholar. Also,
unlike most of Edgar's friends, John took his clerical status seriously
and kept his vow of chastity. It was only John's sense of humor and
their shared attachment to their English roots that allowed them to
be friends.

It was on his second crossing of the Petit Pont that Edgar noticed
John, bundled to the nose, his wax tablet on his lap, sitting in a corner out of the wind to listen to Adam of the Bridge expound on
Aristotle. When there was a pause in the lecture for debate, Edgar
slid in next to his friend.

"Just as I thought," he said. "The tablet is just for effect. Any
notes you made today would crack the wax to slivers."

John's eyes crinkled with amusement. He pulled his scarf from
over his mouth.

"You've found me out," he laughed. "I don't think Master Adam
realizes it, though. He'll wonder all night how I plan to refute him
tomorrow. How are you?"

"Well enough," Edgar told him. "Are you teaching your noble
ninnies this afternoon or can you come home with me? Catherine
has promised cabbage pie and mulled ale."

"I did my teaching this morning," John said. "Mulled ale sounds like heaven. I believe I've lost all feeling in my toes." He stood and shook his feet, stamping them until the warmth returned. "Actually," he said as they headed across the Île, "I wanted to discuss something with you. Did you know that the empress captured King Stephen at Lincoln last month on the Feast of the Purification?"

"No, the news hadn't reached me," Edgar admitted. "It's a Norman war; I don't pay much attention. Has the king been ransomed yet?"

"Not that I've heard," John replied. "And I do follow the events at home. But I have learned something else that touches on what we were speaking of at my last visit."

"What was that?"

"About the time Stephen was in control of Salisbury," John said. "You were right, his candidate for the bishopric took a few souvenirs away with him. And now I understand that some of these things have made their way to France. The canons of Salisbury want them back. One thing in particular. But there is a problem. Philippe is reported to have lost it. Will you help us recover this object for Salisbury?"

"Of course," Edgar answered. "What is it that's missing?"

John refused to say. "When we are inside," he warned. "I may have already said too much."

He looked over his shoulder. Edgar did as well. A beggar held out his bowl to them.

"A crust for God's mercy?" he pleaded.

John stopped and threw him a coin. They continued on.

A moment later something made Edgar turn around and look again.

The beggar was gone.

Eight

The room above the weaver's, the same day, just past Vespers

Collecto itaque copioso decentissimae militiae cuneo, . . .
pulchram illam et delectabilem circa Salesbiriam omniumque
bonorum refertissimam provinciam exterminare aggreditur; captis
quoque et direptis quaecumque eis occurrerant, in domibus et in
templis iniecerunt. . . .

So with a collection of many well-armed knights, . . . [King
Stephen] attacks and destroys the lovely and fine area around
Salisbury, full of all good things; they fell upon and
plundered everything they found, set fire to homes and
churches . . .
—Gesta Stephani

*C*atherine had forgotten about the ale and cabbage pies. It had been that sort of day.

First she and Johannah had stopped to mop the floor; then Hubert had politely suggested that Solomon take Catherine home while he and Eliazar discussed the matter at hand. Neither Solomon nor Catherine approved of this plan. Catherine also wanted to know about Agnes and why she was in Paris. But Hubert refused to speak about anything until he had talked to his brother.

"I promise, Catherine, I will tell you all about it tonight," he said. "But now I need to understand from Eliazar what has happened. You already know. Please go."

"I don't know enough," Catherine muttered, as she and Solomon wrapped up for the walk back to the bourg Saint-Germain.

"This is what they used to do to us when we were children," Solomon grumbled as they left. He was carrying a pot of the lentils and had been warned against spilling it. "Don't they realize that we're grown?"

"I don't think they care," Catherine said. "I'm sure Father only let me marry Edgar so that I would have a keeper."

"Well . . ." Solomon started.

The discussion that escalated from that was what made Catherine forget the pies.

They arrived at the room without spilling the lentil pot, at least. The weaver was just closing when they came in.

"You'll need more food," he said. "Your husband, if that's what he is, has brought a friend home."

Catherine sent Solomon up with the lentils. Then she hurried to the baker's in the hope of getting whatever was left at a reduced price. The selection wasn't that good: cabbage and turnip and something that the baker swore was pork but which Catherine suspected was cat meat. She took the vegetable pies.

When she got back, she found that the men had taken a pitcher down to the tavern to fill and now were busy adding honey to the ale and heating it. The lentil pot was precariously placed at the edge of the brazier, which had been stoked with charcoal and was now glowing brightly.

"What took you so long?" was Edgar's greeting. "I made John promise not to say anything important until you arrived. He's been uncommonly silent."

It took a few more minutes for everyone to settle with a cup in one hand and a pie in the other. When there was a hand free, the lentil pot was left open on the table to allow each person to scoop up a spoonful.

"Now, who begins?" Catherine asked, licking her fingers.

"John," Edgar said. "He's the only one of us who gets up in the middle of the night to pray. We should let him go early."

"I expect to share information," John said. "Not donate it for free. But I'll tell you what I know. Didn't you say Catherine's father was coming here tonight?"

"So he told me," Edgar said. "But many things could have prevented him. Start now. Catherine is falling asleep on my shoulder."

"I am not." She yawned and pulled herself up to pay alert attention.

"I'm sorry that your father isn't here, Catherine," John began. "In his dealings with other merchants, he might have learned more about this than I know."

Nevertheless, he settled in to tell his story.

"Do you remember last year, when King Stephen tried to make Philippe d'Harcourt bishop of Salisbury?" he asked.

Edgar nodded. "After Bishop Roger finally died. I've heard talk about that, too. They say Stephen chained Roger up in a cow barn and left him to starve."

"I've heard that, as well," John said. "But I find it hard to believe that any ruler would so humiliate a prelate of the realm. At any rate, Bishop Roger died and Stephen, or more likely his adviser, Waleran of Meulan, decided that Philippe would be a good candidate for the see. He was already dean of Lincoln and Stephen's chancellor."

"But the canons of Salisbury wouldn't have him and Henry of Winchester wouldn't let him be consecrated. I know all that," Edgar continued. "It makes one wonder how well the king and his brother, Henry, are getting along."

"Henry knows his first duty is to God, even before his family. Stephen should remember that. But that's of no importance to my story." John dismissed the speculation. "It seems that Philippe came to Salisbury, though, with Stephen. I know they kept Christmas there. My brother told me. I think that, by then, Stephen knew Philippe couldn't have the bishopric. After he realized that, Philippe decided, either with the king's permission or without, to take a few mementos from the cathedral treasury."

"I thought Stephen had already confiscated all Roger's property," Catherine asked, to prove she was still awake.

"This wasn't from Roger's personal treasure," John said. His normally calm tones became angry. "These were holy relics from the church of Salisbury itself."

"How could he dare?" Edgar asked. "The saints protect themselves, we know. Thieves are struck with paralysis or blinding headaches."

"Unless the saint wishes to be moved," Catherine added. "Perhaps to punish the community for a lack of piety."

"I can't believe this is the case," John said. "Although there is much about the matter that puzzles me greatly."

"What did Philippe take?" Solomon asked. He found relics a distasteful subject, at best, and preferred the conversation to continue without tales of miraculous intervention.

"Some small things," John said. "A chalice, I think, some other implements of the Mass."

The other three sat up straighter. Solomon opened his mouth to mention that Abbot Suger had already suggested that the chalice might be from Salisbury, but John went on before he could speak.

"It's said that there is something else missing." He was almost whispering in his horror. "I have heard that when the canons went to display the sacred relic given to Saint Osmund of blessed memory by Abbot Warin of Malmesbury, they found the silver reliquary empty."

Catherine felt Edgar go still next to her.

"How could the canons have permitted such a sacrilege?" Edgar spoke with an intensity that frightened her. "I would have died before I let any Norman touch him."

"The canons didn't know it was gone," John said. "Philippe took the relic out of its coffer and put it in another one, a gold-plated box, it is said. It wasn't until the relics were to be placed on the altar to celebrate the return of cathedral land by Matilda that someone noticed that the reliquary containing Saint Aldhelm's arm was empty."

"Saint who?" Catherine asked.

Solomon was grateful that he wasn't the only ignorant person in the room.

"Aldhelm." Edgar smiled fondly. "He is a true Saxon saint. He lived over four hundred years ago, when our people were still largely pagan. He was the first great Latin scholar, even before Bede. I'm surprised you didn't read his work on virginity at the Paraclete. But I love him because he wasn't ashamed to be Saxon."

John continued the tale. "He studied at Saint Augustine's in Canterbury and became renowned for his erudition, but he returned to be a monk in Dorset and began preaching in the little church on his land. It's still there; I've seen it. The roof is gone and yet rain never falls within it. The shepherds go into it for protection during storms. But few people came to Aldhelm's church in the beginning and those who did only understood the Mass and the gospels imperfectly. Instead of giving up, Aldhelm took his preaching to the bridge leading into the town. He stood there on market day, every week."

"And he didn't just shout at them to abandon the old gods or Christ would destroy them," Edgar interrupted. "He told them the stories of the Evangelist in a way that they could understand, in Saxon poetry, which he wrote and sang himself."

"He's an important saint to us," John finished. "Abbot of Malmesbury and first bishop of Sherborne, scholar, poet and defender of orthodoxy. Are you certain you've never read his work?"

Catherine shook her head.

"Well, it seems Philippe d'Harcourt has," Edgar ended grimly. "Why else go to so much trouble to abduct him? What does he think he can gain?"

"But, John," Catherine said. "I still don't understand what this has to do with us. If Philippe took Saint Aldhelm, isn't that a matter for the bishops of England and Normandy to deal with?"

"It will be eventually, I hope," John answered. "But I think that Saint Aldhelm has decided to return home on his own."

"Yes?" Catherine waited.

"I have learned that even before Philippe returned to Normandy, the men he entrusted with his treasure were robbed. One poor priest of Evreaux was brutally killed, martyred in his effort to protect the holy relic." John paused for effect, not knowing that they were already aware of this. "It is said that one of the things taken was the box containing Aldhelm's arm. *And* I also have reason to believe that it was brought here, to Paris."

Their reaction to that was all he could have desired. Edgar was upset that a chalice and jewels had been stolen from Salisbury, but they were only things. Aldhelm was a part of his heritage, as a Christian and a Saxon. He jumped up at once, spilling Catherine off his lap, and proposed gathering all the English students and masters in Paris to begin a house-to-house search. The others managed to convince him that this was impractical.

"Then what are we to do?" Edgar demanded. "Saint Wilfrid's wicked stepmother! The Normans have taken our land, John. Will we let them steal our saints, as well?"

"I think, Edgar," John said, "that you are already doing something. Tell me again about this Gaudry and his workshop."

Hubert left his brother's house long after dark. He thought about going to Catherine's, as he had promised, but decided against it. Tomorrow would have to do. He understood that his daughter and Edgar shared a bed; he'd bought it for them. But he still didn't feel comfortable rousting them out of it or thinking about what they did in it. He wanted grandchildren, of course, but preferred to dwell on their arrival, not their begetting.

As he passed the watch on the Grand Pont Hubert sighed, remembering his other daughter, now sulkily ensconced at home. Agnes was the beautiful one, the ever-dutiful child, who had given up dreams of a home of her own to care for her mother, poor Madeleine, going slowly mad, overwhelmed by religion and guilt. He loved Agnes with a sort of wonder that he never felt about Catherine or Guillaume. There was nothing of him in Agnes, he believed. She was small and fair, with honey-blonde hair and hazel eyes. She looked like the heroine of a love song. She looked like her mother had on the day he had first seen her.

And now she averted her eyes when speaking to him and only

spoke when it was necessary. Hubert wasn't sure whether she hated him for being born Jewish, for not telling her about it or, most likely, for letting poor Madeleine spend her days in obsessive prayer, consumed by her guilt at marrying an apostate. He didn't know which; Agnes wouldn't discuss the matter.

"I will stay with you, as mistress of the house," she had informed him coldly, "until you are able to arrange a suitable marriage for me. Unless, of course, you would rather have Catherine take care of you."

Hubert had agreed. He loved Catherine dearly but feared that she was completely capable of trading every pot in the kitchen for a new book. She kept accounts like one of Henry Beauclerc's tax collectors but he didn't feel she would be happy or extremely competent in the role of lady at the high table. But even more, this would keep Agnes with him for a time. Perhaps one day he could convince her to forgive him.

This was not the day.

The stableman let him in through the side door with a warning.

"Your daughter is waiting up for you."

Hubert thanked him and squared his shoulders for whatever might come.

Agnes was sitting by the banked fire, wrapped in a fur blanket. Her face was just a white blur in the darkness. She recognized his step and rose.

"You didn't need to wait up for me, *ma douce*," he said.

"Yes, I did," she answered. "I wanted to talk with you when no one else was around. You had a visitor tonight. One of your people."

"My people?"

"He said his name was Menahem and he refused to eat or drink anything I offered," Agnes said. "I presume he is Jewish."

"Menahem? What did he want?" Hubert asked.

"Something about your other daughter," Agnes answered. "At first he seemed to think that I was the one who consorted with infidels. He wanted to know what 'Natan' had said to me before he died. I told him he was mad and sent him away, but now I'm sure it has something to do with Catherine. She was here this morning. I sent her away, too. Jehan says she's an *engigneresse* who creates destruction. Who is Natan? Did Catherine destroy him, too?"

"He's no one you need to concern yourself with," Hubert answered. "I will deal with Menahem. He had no business coming here. But, Agnes, you should not speak so of your sister, who loves you very much."

"She is no longer my sister," Agnes said. "She abandoned her place in the convent and deserted our mother. If you speak of her again, I will leave."

Hubert knew there would be no more discussion tonight. He waited until Agnes had gone up to her room, to the bed she had used to share with Catherine. Then he sat for a moment, too worn to attempt the stairs. He noticed a clay bowl nestled in the ashes and covered with a flat board. He fished it out carefully with the tongs and found a broth of herbs and barley, kept warm for him.

She never forgot. However deep her bitterness, Agnes always made sure he had his posset before bed.

Hubert cradled the bowl between his hands and salted it with his tears.

"You have three new burns on your thigh," Catherine said to Edgar just before she snuffed out the lamp. "Do you need some salve?"

"You could just kiss them and heal me," Edgar suggested.

"I think salve would be more effective," she replied. "But I could try that first."

It seemed to be enough. Edgar got into bed and arranged the covers. He settled gratefully into the hollow of the mattress. Every muscle in his body ached. He closed his eyes.

"Edgar?"

"Unh?" He was nearly asleep.

"I suppose that means you also have three new holes in your only leather *braies*."

"Unh."

"Good night, *carissime*."

"Mmmmmph . . ."

Morning proved Catherine was right. But the holes in the leather were small. She could patch them. She was more concerned with where Edgar was going.

"I'm beginning to believe that more happens under the Île than on it," she complained. "You say this place is below ground?"

"No," Edgar answered. "But we go under something to reach it and come up inside. It's hard to keep one's sense of direction with all the turns, but I think it's still on the east end, near the bishop's palace."

"That doesn't make sense."

"I know," Edgar answered. "You'd think someone there would notice the smoke and the fumes."

She watched him pull his clothes on. He didn't seem inclined to talk.

"Edgar, about this saint of yours," she started.

"He's not mine," Edgar said. "But he doesn't belong in France."

"Even if he wants to be here?" she asked.

Edgar gave her a look of derision. "Why would Saint Aldhelm want to come to France?" he asked.

"You came to France," she reminded him. "Why did you?"

"To study, of course," he answered. "To drink wine and be seduced by beautiful French women. And don't you dare make some sacrilegious comment, Catherine. This isn't a joke to me."

"I know that, Edgar," she said. "But you aren't thinking in terms of religion. You only see a Saxon being kidnapped by a Norman. Aldhelm isn't in England or France really; he's in heaven. No one here can make him do anything. If he has allowed his arm to be taken from Salisbury and then stolen from Philippe d'Harcourt, you might try to imagine what his purpose is."

Edgar didn't answer. She could almost see his mind turning her statement inside out, looking for a flaw in the logic.

"And," she added, "you might ask what part he wants us to play."

To her surprise, he grinned at that.

"I was worried," he said. "It isn't like you to suggest that we be patient and allow heaven to move according to its own design."

"Do you think it's prideful to believe we have a place in divine order?" she asked seriously. The sin of pride was the cause of most of her penances.

"No, I don't," Edgar said. "Everything else has a place, why shouldn't we? But sometimes I wish we lived in the days of the prophets when signs from heaven were much more frequent and easier to understand.''

He put on his cloak and picked up his gloves. "I promised to show Solomon where the route to the workshop begins,'' he said. "He's going to try to discover where it comes out.''

"I would feel better if we knew where you were,'' Catherine said. "Almost all the artisans are on this side of the river. I still don't see why or how Gaudry could have put his atelier on the Île. Do you think he's working on his own?''

"I haven't seen enough to guess,'' Edgar said. "That's why I'm going back.''

Catherine swung her legs out of bed. Edgar paused to watch. She laughed and pulled her *chainse* over her head.

"Of course you are,'' she said. "Tell that to John. I know very well that you love every minute you spend there. I only keep the secret because I want you to learn enough to fashion me a pair of silver earrings.''

When Menahem, the draper, returned from morning prayers he found Hubert waiting for him.

"You are never to enter my home again,'' Hubert began without greeting, "unless at my express invitation. Moreover, under no circumstances are you ever to speak to my daughters, either of them. Do you understand?''

Menahem backed away, into the door of his shop. Hubert followed.

"I repeat,'' he said, and he did. "If you come near my daughters, I shall see that you suffer for it.''

"You misunderstand.'' Menahem held up his hands in supplication. "I have no intentions toward your daughters. I hoped you would be there, that is all. I only wanted to know more about my uncle's death. I meant no disrespect, sir. I will walk round the city to reach the other side of the street if that is the only way to avoid them in future. I swear it!''

Hubert watched the man cringing before him, terror making him shake. What was the matter with him?

It came to Hubert in a thunderclap. Menahem assumed he was Christian. Hubert had gone to great pains that he should. The draper's terror was not just for his own life as a man who had been threatened with dishonoring another's daughter. He feared for the whole community. If Hubert should decide to punish one Jew for his effrontery, then the others would suffer. It was always so.

The thought made the bile rise in Hubert's throat. It shamed him to be thought just like the great lords, who would burn a whole town to revenge themselves on an enemy. But it also shamed him to know that this servile thing before him was what his people had to become in order to survive.

"Stand up, man!" he ordered. He took a deep breath. "I apologize for my anger. But it would still not be wise for you to come to my home. It was not my daughter, Agnes, who was there when your uncle died."

Menaham cautiously lowered his arms. "So I guessed from her answers," he said. "Although I feared she might be lying to get me out of the house."

"Agnes wouldn't lie; she would simply refuse to answer you," Hubert said with a sigh. "It was my daughter, Catherine, who was visiting Johannah. I don't want you questioning her, either. If you wish information, come to me. What is it you are looking for now?"

Menahem bent to open a wooden chest and began taking out lengths of cloth, which he laid on a table.

"I'm expecting a customer from the king's court today," he explained nervously. "He wants rough wool to send to a monastery he has endowed. Says he doesn't trust the prior to spend the money as directed. Everything needs to be ready to show him."

Hubert wasn't interested. "Agnes told me you wanted to know what Natan said before he died. Why?"

"A man's last words are always important," Menahem answered, fiddling with the cloth. "He might have had a final request or received a vision. It would be my duty to act upon such information."

Hubert's eyebrows raised at the image of Natan receiving a divine vision. "I have heard that Natan left nothing for his burial," he said. "And yet, it's rumored that he was a wealthy man."

The draper's fingers became more agitated as he smoothed out invisible wrinkles and plucked at unseen bits of fluff in the wool. "Ah, well," he said at last. "My uncle was a trader, not in as grand a manner as you are, of course. But I'm sure you know that it's an insecure profession. One lost shipment and all can be lost. That must have been what happened. The coffer he kept with me held only a few small coins. Perhaps he had been ruined by shipwreck or bandits. Possibly his mind was so affected by the loss that he took the poison himself, may he be forgiven."

Hubert watched Menahem closely. The man was keeping something back, of course, but what? The idea that Natan had been driven to suicide was preposterous. He was the sort who drove others. But the part about not finding any treasure, that sounded honest. Why else would Menahem have dared come to his home, alone, so insistent to speak to the one person to whom Natan might have told his hiding place?

"Had he said anything to you about losing a shipment?" Hubert asked.

"He never discussed his business with me," Menahem answered too quickly.

Hubert didn't press any further. He knew that Menahem would never tell an outsider about such things, even under torture. He respected him for that. It was a marvel how cowardice and courage were so mingled in a man.

"Very well," he said. "I'll ask my daughter and tell you if your uncle said anything to her regarding a cache of goods. But if you bother any member of my family again, I will go to your elders and have them place the *herem* on you. See how long you stay in business if no one will associate with you."

"You know nothing about it," Menahem replied. "They wouldn't cut me off from the community on your word."

"They might if they thought your behavior endangered their families, as well," Hubert answered. "Do you want to take the risk?"

"I have already told you I'll not go near your daughters," Menahem grumbled. "May I be planted like an onion, head first in the earth, if I break my word."

"I'll dig the hole myself," Hubert assured him.

Having discharged that duty, Hubert considered what to do next. A visit to Eliazar would be useless, he decided. Their conversation the night before had been full of evasions. Even though they had been raised apart, Hubert could sense when his older brother was keeping something from him. Eliazar had insisted that he had no idea how Natan had found his way to the cellar, had repeated that he had done some business with him last year and regretted it and that they had not had any dealings since then. It hurt Hubert more than he could say that his own brother didn't trust him with the truth. He had said as much.

"It hurts me also," Eliazar had answered, "that my own brother has no faith in my honesty."

They had parted with a kiss of friendship, but Hubert had left with a feeling of lonely grief that was almost more than he could bear. And then he had come home to Agnes. He was almost afraid to go see Catherine. If she rejected him, he might be tempted to take poison himself.

Poison.

Menahem had been quite sure that poison was the cause of Natan's death, not a fit or some other natural cause. Why? Had the body been examined by a physician? If so, what had been found? Perhaps Menahem had just decided that, knowing Natan, the unnatural cause was the more likely.

Now, whom could he ask to help him find out?

Hubert smiled and made his way out of the Juiverie to a tavern he knew of. The room above was the school, the room in back, a brothel. The woman who owned the building made a good living from both. As an extra, her tavern sold the best beer in Paris. At this time of day the odds were quite good he would find Solomon there.

Hubert spotted his nephew as soon as he entered, seated at a corner of the long table in intense conversation with a woman who had her back to him. After his recent encounter with Menahem, Hubert hoped Solomon had more sense than to negotiate with a Christian prostitute. Or, if he did, to be sure the light was out before he dropped his *braies*.

Solomon nodded to him and the woman turned around to see who was there.

"Catherine!" Hubert roared. "Are you insane? What are you doing in a place like this?"

"Hello, Father." Catherine rose and gave him a kiss and a smile. "I'm waiting with Solomon for John to finish teaching so that we can all go hear Master Gilbert speak."

"You could find no better place to take her than this?" Hubert accused Solomon.

"She's been very entertaining," Solomon told him. "Bietrix has already gone out for another bundle of rushes after Catherine commented that they were a bit thin on the floor and greasy. They then had a long conversation about some form of cosmetic, I believe, after which a student came in and made a proposal to Catherine in Latin—why, I don't know. Her response was brief, I'm glad to say, but the boy left at once, blessing himself repeatedly. She won't tell me what she said."

"I merely suggested that he not use the subjunctive mode until he had mastered it completely," Catherine said.

Hubert could tell she'd been having a wonderful morning. He sat down next to Catherine on the bench and sniffed at the liquid in her cup.

"Pear cider, Father," she told him. "All the way from Normandy, the woman said." Then she leaned closer to him and whispered, "Vinegar, water and honey. I can tell. You taught me the difference."

"Thank you, my dear," he said and felt the muscles in his neck relax. She put an arm through his and leaned against him. At least he had one child left.

"You should wait, also," Solomon told him. "Have a cup of beer. John wanted to speak with you. From what he told us last night, I think he may know something about the other end of the journey for that object I found."

They looked around. They saw no one else in the room. The tavern keeper, Bietrix, had gone into the back. But walls were thin and no one could be sure what lay on the other side of them.

"What does he think I can do?" Hubert asked.

"Apparently it was only one of several objects," Solomon said. "He hopes you might help him find the others."

Catherine leaned closer and whispered in his ear, "We're going to rescue an abducted Saxon saint." She kissed his cheek. "Doesn't that sound like fun?"

At that moment the tavern keeper returned and saw Catherine nestled against Hubert.

"And I believed you were a lady!" she said. "None of your trade in here, *jael*. We have our own guild, you know."

Catherine and Solomon tried to hide their laughter but Hubert had had enough for one day. He got up and faced the woman.

"I have a trade, too," he said heavily. "I am of the *marchands de l'eau*. Would you care to have no wine or grain sold to you for the next year or would you prefer to apologize to my daughter?"

He was most proficient at playing the powerful lord. Hubert had become more a part of his world than he realized.

"Your daughter, is she?" Bietrix said. "Then you should watch her more closely. I have a daughter, too, but she isn't allowed to linger in taverns, even this one."

"I have more confidence in my daughter's good sense," Hubert said. "Now, bring us a ewer of beer."

As he sat down, Catherine was tempted to ask if he had meant what he said about her good sense, but she was afraid the answer would be no.

Hubert had used his altercation with the tavern keeper to take the time to consider what Catherine and Solomon had just told him. He wondered if this was what Prior Hervé had meant when he had warned that the abbey might require him to "help" the saints in their peregrinations. He hadn't liked the sound of it then and it was just as discordant to him now.

Did the prior already know where Solomon's chalice had come from? Did it have something to do with the pearls Natan had tried to sell? If so, was his brother, pious Eliazar, somehow involved with this dangerous trade? Why, and how, had Natan died? Was he sending Edgar into the same peril?

There were only two things he was certain of. The first was that he didn't want Catherine becoming entangled in this web.

The second was that there was no way she would let him keep her out of it.

Nine

At the corner of the rue de Juiverie and the rue des Marmousets, just in front of the synagogue, Friday, February 28, 1141 / 18, Adar, 4901

Adeo, praeter illud quod de illo Beda in Gesti Anglorum tangit, semper infra meritum jacuit, semper desidia civium agente, inhonorus latuit.

Outside of what Bede wrote about him in the *Deeds of the English*, he [Aldhelm] has always received less attention than he deserved, through the apathy of the public, he has always been neglected.

—William of Malmesbury
Gesta Pontificum Anglorum
Book V, *Vita Aldhelmi*

*S*pring was coming to Paris. That meant it was wet and muddy. Eliazar had left the house late for morning prayers, his hood pulled down over his face, and didn't see Menahem standing in the porch of the synagogue until the draper stepped in his path, blocking the doorway. He was also hooded but Eliazar recognized the cloak, a particularly intricate weave of yellow and green.

"*Shalom*, Menahem," Eliazar said.

Menahem didn't move.

"May the Almighty One bless you." Eliazar smiled, taking off his hood now that he was under cover.

Menahem still didn't move.

"Menahem? What is it?" Eliazar was becoming annoyed. "The others have all gone in already. Have you been struck dumb?"

Menahem reached up and took off his hood. Eliazar gasped in pity and horror. The man's face had been battered as if kicked by a mule. Both eyes were black, the right one swollen shut. His lip was split, his nose crumpled. There was a cut along his chin and a bruise in the center of it that plainly showed the pattern of a heavy ring.

"Oh, Menahem!" Eliazar said. "How horrible! You shouldn't be out, but home in bed. What happened? What servant of the devil has done this to you, my poor friend?"

"The servants were of your old friend and partner, Hubert, my friend. He has done this to me," Menahem croaked. "I wanted you to see, before you went in to pray."

"You must be mistaken, Menahem," Eliazar said. "Hubert would never do such a thing. You're feverish and confused by your pain. Come, let me help you home."

Menahem swallowed as if fighting nausea. "I am not mistaken," he said fiercely. "He threatened me and then he sent his *ribaux* to beat me. He told me he knew nothing about Natan, but he lied, as you lied. Natan left me no treasure, not a denier. But someone believes he had one and they think I know about it. This is what comes of his sort of business, and yours."

"Menahem, please." Eliazar tried to calm the man. "There must be some mistake."

"Only the one I made the day I let my mother's only brother stay under my roof," Menahem answered. "You know more about this than you've said, Eliazar ben Meir. If you wish to tell me the truth, come see me when you've finished your pious duty. No! I don't need your arm. My wife and my son will help me home."

Eliazar watched him go, leaning heavily on the shoulders of his wife and his eldest son, a child of ten. He decided not to try to help. They needed only to cross the street and go a few more steps. Menahem's shop was the third one down on the street of the drapers.

But still he stood in the doorway, his heart and mind no longer prepared to worship in the proper spirit. Should he go home? Find Hubert and demand to know what was going on?

Inside he heard the voices rise and fall. The morning benedictions were almost over. The *Shema* would be recited next.

For all of his life, Eliazar had prayed, every morning, every evening. Even in the wilderness on long journeys when there had been no synogogue and only a few brethren with him, he had never once forgotten.

His mind was full of consternation and his spirit in great turmoil. He feared that it was through his actions, not Hubert's, that Menahem had been subjected to such abuse. It horrified him that something he had considered an act of courage, a deed that would find favor with the Almighty, seemed to be bringing such disaster on others of the community, after all he had done to protect them. How could he have been so wrong in his judgment? Eliazar felt lost and alone.

Wasn't this the time, above all, when he needed to obey the Commandment and trust in the Lord? "Hear, O Israel . . ." The voices rose.

Eliazar took off his cloak and went in to join the affirmation.

Edgar arrived at the workshop just after dawn, as ordered, soaked through and shivering. He soon warmed. Gaudry set him to work almost before he had removed his cloak.

"I need to cast silver today, enough to make a large drinking vessel," he said. "Use the block you refined yesterday. The wax and molds are on the shelf there."

"Where is the salt box?" Edgar asked.

"Next to the tongs, man," Gaudry snapped. "Do I have to show you anew each day?"

Edgar prepared for a long day and a fresh set of aches in his arms and back. The silver would have to be melted and cast, perhaps more than once. Then it would need to be dipped in a solution of clear lye and salt, reheated and dipped again. He wondered if Gaudry would let him shape the cup.

"Will the work be plain," he asked, "or ornamented?"

"That's not your concern," Gaudry told him. "Just do as you're told. I'll complete the piece. Do you think I'd trust the delicate work to some slack-jawed foreigner, trained God knows where?"

Edgar reminded himself that he was here to locate stolen objects, to find a lost saint, not to increase his artisan's skills. But he would have liked to try etching a pattern in the silver or setting in a pattern of precious stones and gold wire, as Gaudry had implied that he might. With a sigh, he began to assemble the materials. He looked around. Something was missing.

"Where's Odo?" he asked casually.

"Sent him on an errand," Gaudry answered. "Stop babbling. This isn't one of your classes in grammar. Hold your tongue and do your job, if you want another day's wages."

Edgar held his tongue and got on with the work. He reflected sadly that he was unlikely to get any information from Gaudry as a result of friendly conversation between master and apprentice. It wasn't the same as being Master Abelard's student. The master had never been too proud to share a mug with his followers. He was ruthless in disputation, of course, and could draw blood with his sarcasm. But when he had cut you to ribbons, he could often be persuaded to pay for the drinks.

It didn't seem that Gaudry would even give him time to eat the hunk of cheese Catherine had packed. The man was in a state about something. He moved from one job to another with no pattern, leaving tasks undone, neglecting to put tools away. Everything Edgar did was wrong. He was made to cast the silver twice and even then Gaudry wasn't satisfied.

"Too brittle," he insisted. "It's sure to crack before it bends."

"Let me hammer it out and see, Master," Edgar asked as humbly as he could manage.

Gaudry's reply was the back of his hand to the side of Edgar's head.

Edgar picked himself up. With a superhuman effort, he swallowed his anger and his pride and returned to cast the silver once again.

Toward midday Odo finally appeared. He brought nothing with him, so Edgar assumed that the errand had been for information. He hunched over the crucible, trying to appear oblivious to anything else in the room.

Odo was obviously bursting to tell something. Gaudry made an attempt to muzzle him until he could be pushed back into the passageway.

"This isn't just street talk, Master," Odo said as he moved backward through the doorway. "I spoke with a man who'd seen the body. He's dead, for sure."

Gaudry shut the door behind them. Edgar set the crucible on the edge of the oven and crossed the room. He put his ear against the wood but heard nothing more than muffled sounds, Gaudry low and worried, Odo high and excited.

Edgar went back to the kiln. He resalted the metal and set the crucible on the coals once more. The door creaked and opened a crack. Gaudry's voice came through more clearly. Edgar held the pot steady with the tongs and held his breath.

"There must be more to it," Gaudry said. "Go back and ask again. No one would be stupid enough to kill him without knowing what he'd done with it. Someone's lying. Find out who."

He came back in, barely glancing at Edgar as he removed the crucible one more time.

"Pour it," he ordered. "And don't lose a grain. Then you can see that all my etching tools are prepared. After that, scrub and sand the worktable. After that, I'll think of something."

Edgar stifled a sigh. He wondered what Catherine would say about the new holes in his leather *braies*.

Catherine was at that moment wedged into a corner of the Bishop's Hall. The large room was full of people, come to hear Master Gilbert de la Porée give his views on Boethius' views of the trinity. Most of the listeners were male, clerics of all sorts and all ages, but

there were a few other women, discreetly veiled. Catherine wondered if one of them were Queen Eleanor. While the queen's taste
seemed to run to epics and the poetry of the south, she occasionally
came to more serious lectures and debates.

Catherine had seen Eleanor many times as she rode with her re-
tainers out to hunt or on one of her incessant journeys. The bright
colors and sparkling jewelry, the laughter as they passed, were from
another world. There were those who derided her opulent apparel
and openly condemned her love of pleasure, but to Catherine it was
like catching a glimpse of something magical. Even though Hubert
trafficked in the jewels and ointments that Eleanor loved, they were
simply parcels to Catherine. The queen transmuted them to the
realm of legend.

None of the ladies were sparkling today. They were all quietly
dressed and attentive. Catherine turned her own attention back to
Master Gilbert.

At first she was somewhat annoyed, as his discourse was aimed at
refuting Peter Abelard's assignment of attributes to the different
persons of the Trinity. On the other hand, Master Gilbert seemed
also to be refuting Saint Augustine's theories. That took courage,
not to mention intellectual confidence to the point of hubris. She
forgot her resentment and settled in to follow the argument. It took
all her concentration. Master Gilbert's distinctions were subtle, indeed.

When the lecture had concluded, Catherine waited for John, who
had offered to escort her back home. When he found her, he had
another man with him. He was about Edgar's age and wearing a
patched and threadbare robe. His brown hair was carefully tonsured
and his eyes were an indeterminate light brown. His cheekbones jut-
ted over hollow cheeks. Clearly the man did not get enough to eat.
Catherine wondered if the reason were asceticism or poverty.

John answered the question for her. He took her aside and whispered, "Are you and Edgar too poor now to give alms?"

"Of course not," Catherine answered at once. "I hope we never
will be."

"Then may I bring Maurice with me tomorrow?" John nodded at
the young cleric. "He's just come up from the Orleanais. From what
I can tell, his prebend allows him to eat three days out of seven. He

won't beg, but I fear he may starve. He's fallen in love with Paris, I believe, and would rather die here than leave. When his stomach is not gnawing at him, he's good company."

"You could bring him if he were mute and stupid as a rabbit," Catherine assured him. "He'll no doubt fast today, anyway, as it's Friday, and I only have bread and flaked fish for the evening meal, but tomorrow there will be pease porridge with a bit of cabbage and, perhaps, a little meat. I'll set the peas to soak tonight and put in an extra spoonful."

John thanked her and then went over and spoke to Maurice, who glanced at Catherine and nodded thanks, giving her a shy smile before he wandered off into the crowd.

When John and Catherine were outside and on their way back to the Right Bank, John confessed that his desire to have Maurice dine with them was not only charitable.

"He has a bed with one of the canons of Notre Dame at the mo-ment," John explained. "That means he can come and go within the cloister as he wishes. From what Edgar said, this metal shop may be near, or even within the bishop's walls."

"Will he help us?" Catherine asked. "If the workshop is in there, how could the bishop be unaware of it? Maurice would be in danger of losing the little he has if anyone caught him spying on them or if he brought scandal to the house that sheltered him."

"I would never ask him to spy," John told her. "Edgar and I will simply question him gently about anything unusual he may have seen—"

"Or smelled," Catherine interrupted.

"Or smelled," John went on. "In the vicinity of the cloister."

"That seems harmless enough," Catherine agreed, her conscience assuaged. "Until tomorrow, then," she added. "*God ceapeth thu.*"

'God protect you, as well," he laughed.

The door at the top of the stairs was standing open. Catherine stopped. The weaver had said nothing about a visitor. She should go back down and ask him.

Instead she stood at the threshold and peered into the semidark room. There was someone sitting on the bench. She turned to run back down, but the man saw her.

"Catherine," he called.

She spun around. How could she have not recognized him, even in the gloom?

"Father!" she cried as she hugged him. "We thought you would come yesterday. Where were you? Is anything wrong?"

"Eliazar and I talked far into the night," he explained. "And then he came to see me again this morning. He's both worried and frightened and won't tell me why."

Hubert shook his head in sorrow. Eliazar was treating him like one of the Edomites. There had never been a wall between them before. It grieved him as much as Agnes's rejections. And the story Eliazar had brought about Menahem upset him even more. What if the men who had attacked the draper believed Catherine knew where to find Natan's hoard?

"But Eliazar did have a question that he wanted me to ask you," he continued. "He wants you to try to remember exactly what happened, just before Natan died."

"I'm not likely to forget it," Catherine said.

"You might," Hubert said. "Truly horrible events tend to blur in our minds. Perhaps it's heaven's way of protecting us from living them over and over. Now, tell me, what happened first?"

Catherine thought. "There was a sudden gust of wind," she said slowly. "The lamp went out. I heard a noise, a shuffling and snuffling. I thought it was a bear or worse. It came closer. I tried to scream and I couldn't." She paused. "He must have seen me before the light was blown out. He came directly toward me."

"You're sure?" Hubert asked.

"I think so." Catherine frowned. "Yes, I'm sure. You know how crowded it is down there. I didn't hear him bump into anything and nothing but the lentil barrel behind me was spilled."

"Very well," he said. "Then what happened?"

She didn't want to remember. She shut her eyes tightly and willed herself back into the darkness.

"He growled at me," she said finally. "Then he grabbed me and fell, pinning me to the ground. He made horrible noises. I was sure it was a monster."

Hubert put his arm around her. "I know, *ma douce*," he soothed. "But it was only a man. Remember that. It was a man. Now, those sounds he made, were they nothing but growls, or were there words mixed up in them?"

Catherine considered. Until Aunt Johannah came down with a light, she had been certain she had been attacked by a demon. Now, if she began with the premise that the thing had been human, then would the sounds she had interpreted as those of a beast acquire rational signification? She concentrated.

"Growl, rumble . . . rah . . . hwat . . . avu . . . donwit . . . " she murmured.

"What are you doing?" Hubert asked.

"That's what I think I heard," she told him. "Does it make any sense? Perhaps, if he was speaking, it was in Hebrew."

"I hope not," Hubert said. "Try again, more slowly."

Catherine repeated the growls.

"Wait!" Hubert stopped her. "Repeat the last part."

"Hwat . . . avu . . . donwit . . . hwer . . . isit," she obliged.

"Where is it!" he said.

"What?" she asked.

"That's it!" he told her. " 'What have you done with it? Where is it?' That's what he said."

Catherine couldn't share in his delight. "I'm sure you're right, Father," she said. "But I don't see how that helps us. What have I done with what? Natan apparently didn't know where it was and didn't tell me what. Do you know the answer to either?"

"No," he admitted.

He wouldn't tell her how relieved he was that Natan had given her no information. After what Eliazar had told him of the attack on Menahem he feared for the safety of anyone who knew much about Natan. He would go back and tell the draper that his daughter was ignorant of all Natan's doings and that Menahem would have to look elsewhere for the knowledge his assailants had demanded. That is, if he could convince Menahem that he himself had had no part in the attack.

"Is that all you came for, Father?" Catherine asked. "I think we have some ale left, although the honey has congealed. I can warm it."

"Yes, a cup of ale would be good," he sighed.

Catherine put the pitcher in a bowl of water over the brazier. "How is Agnes?" she asked too casually.

"She's well," Hubert answered in the same tone. "She says your mother seems very happy with the nuns. They're letting her observe the anniversary of your ascension. Everyone is very kind to her."

"Except me," Catherine said. "I let her think I had gone to heaven when I had really run away to Paris. There didn't seem much choice at the time, but Agnes won't forgive me."

"She hasn't forgiven you as yet," Hubert admitted. "Or me for deceiving her. But someday."

"Someday." Catherine couldn't imagine it. "Has Jehan asked you about a marriage?"

"Jehan?" Hubert seemed confused by the abrupt change of subject. "Why should he ask me about anything? He's Count Thibault's man."

"Oh, well, I may be mistaken," Catherine said. "But I think he wants to marry Agnes."

"WHAT!" Hubert's bellow nearly upset the pitcher. "That's nonsense! The man is a younger son of a younger son. He owns no more than his horse and armor, if that. He has no right even to think of her."

"She may be doing most of the thinking," Catherine warned.

Hubert stared at her. "You learned all this in one visit?"

"I looked at her. I looked at him," Catherine explained. "I looked at her looking at him. There is a possibility that my conclusions were incorrect."

"I certainly hope so," Hubert said.

The ale had begun to steam. Catherine poured a cup for Hubert. The rest she saved for Edgar.

"Is anything more known about Natan's death?" She asked. "What do they think killed him?"

"The physician isn't certain," Hubert told her. "He was very annoyed that Johannah had washed or burnt all your clothing. Even more when he found that Menahem had done the same to the things Natan was wearing. He wanted to test the excrement for poison."

Catherine grimaced. "We didn't think of such things at the time," she admitted. "All either of us wanted was to remove the filth as quickly and thoroughly as possible. I'm afraid I wasn't following the rules of logic. Was there any other sign to indicate what happened?"

"The general feeling is that it was certainly poison," Hubert told her. "The physician believes Natan may have eaten something from one of the *solenum* plants. What, we don't know, or how he came by it. With Natan, one does tend to think that someone else killed him, if only because so many had good reason to wish him dead. But he may have simply eaten a bad piece of meat."

"I never heard of rotten meat doing that to a person," Catherine said. "Unless it had a very unusual sauce."

Sauce. There was something else she nearly remembered. Something to do with food.

"There was another smell, Father," she said. "It was mixed in with his unguents and the metallic scent. Or it might have been along with it. It was something bitter, like one of those horrible emetics Sister Melisande used to give us. I wish I could place it."

Hubert patted her hand. "You've done splendidly, daughter. Don't worry about it. A man like Natan was bound to make a bad ending. The community will decide if it needs to be investigated further."

"What if they think it doesn't?" Catherine asked. "Will we never know what happened? That's not right. There must be a way to discover more. Was there anything in the storeroom? He could have dropped something in the dark. Has it been searched?"

"I don't know," Hubert admitted. "Johannah had the rituals of purification done but I don't think she's had time to empty and scrub out the room. Her servant won't help her. The girl refuses to go down there at all."

"I can understand that," Catherine said. "But I prefer to face my fears. I think I'll go see if I can help. Will you walk me to the bridge?"

Johannah admitted to Catherine that she had yet to completely scour the storeroom.

"There's been too much happening since then," she told Catherine. "People coming and going, both above and below. And still Lucia and I have to prepare for *Shabbat*."

Catherine could smell the preparations and wished she could stay to sample the food, but she wanted to be home to share the Lenten dried fish and bread with Edgar.

"I don't want to be in the way," she began. "But I'd like to go down for a few minutes. I keep having nightmares about the room. I'm sure I could dispel them if I just saw it again in a good, strong light."

"Not much chance of that, my dear," Johannah told her. "There are always shadows in the storeroom. But I'll let you have a few candles, if you're careful, and you can poke in all the corners if you think it will help. Lucia, get out the two pronged candlesticks."

Lucia fetched the candles as well and set them in the brass holders. She shook her head as she did so. Catherine noticed.

"You don't think I should go back to the storeroom?" she asked the servant.

"It's nothing to me," Lucia said. "I suppose a lady like you, who reads Latin and studies with the men, knows better than I do."

Catherine was surprised. "How did you know I studied?"

"You're Master Hubert's daughter, aren't you?" Lucia said. "Your father is always telling Master Eliazar about you. How quick you are and good at your books. To listen to him, you only lack one thing to be pope."

"Saint Catherine's scrolls!" Catherine said. "He says that?"

Lucia nodded. "So I'm sure you know what you're doing, going back into that hole where poor Natan met his fate."

"Perhaps not," Catherine told her. "It may be pointless. But I'm going to do it all the same. Can you open the trapdoor for me and hand me the other candles when I'm down the stairs?"

Lucia moved the box in the pantry and pulled the door open. A musty smell rose from the darkness and Catherine nearly reconsidered her decision. But she held one candlestick firmly in her right hand, put out her left to steady herself and started down. At the bottom she set the candle on one of the wine barrels and reached up for the other one.

Lucia hadn't waited for her, but had left the second candlestick balanced on the top step. Catherine took it and moved it down to the middle step. No light came down from the room above. Lucia must have closed the pantry door. Catherine shrugged and set about examining the storeroom.

It had been cleaned cursorily, the hard earth in the center of the room scraped and the soiled layer removed. The lentils had been thrown out with the dirt.

Perhaps it was only the memory of what had happened there, but there was something disquieting about the room. The walls were raw boards put up mainly to keep the earth from falling in. White roots slipped between the cracks like sepulchral fingers. The air was damp and laced with odors of mold and sour wine. She was glad to note that the door to the tunnel was shut and barred and that a stack of boxes now blocked it. Nothing human could enter today.

Catherine started in the farthest corner, under the steps. Natan hadn't come anywhere near it in his stumblings but she intended to search thoroughly. She lifted the candle holder to peer behind a pile of boxes.

A rat ran over her foot.

Catherine gave a startled squeak. Her hand shook and hot wax spilled onto her fingers. With a cry of pain, she dropped the brass holder. One candle went out at once. The other, perversely, stayed lit even as it rolled toward a packing box padded with straw. Catherine grabbed at it, missed and sprawled across the floor. She was up on her knees at once and this time got the candle before it reached the tinder.

She sat in the center of the floor, licking the wax from the burns and cursing herself for being so clumsy.

There was something on the floor, sticking out from between the boxes, that was catching the light. It gave a shimmer of metal. A brass hinge, perhaps? Catherine pulled on it, but it was wedged in tightly.

Checking to be sure the candles on the steps were steady, she blew out the one she was holding so that she could use both hands to push the boxes apart. There wasn't much space for them to move. If she could just get one to slide a little . . .

She bent a fingernail painfully on the wood before she was able to move one of the boxes a scant inch. With the other hand she pulled on the metal strip. It came partway out but seemed to be caught on something. Catherine bent over to see what it was but then her body blocked the light completely. Nervously, she fitted her fingers in the narrow space.

Yes, the metal had a jagged edge. "Don't cut yourself, *inana*," she muttered. It wasn't stuck in the edge of the box. There was something else attached. Catherine felt carefully. A hook or a chain of some kind. She wiggled it. Whatever it was came loose and she pulled out a thin strip of metal about as long and half as wide as her hand. One end of it was rough, as if it had been cut or even torn somehow. Hanging from the ragged cut was a section of silver chain, linking together some wooden beads. This, too, was broken.

Catherine looked at them both, puzzled. She had no idea what the metal was for. The beads, now—they didn't look ornamental. The carving was crude and the chain links roughly done. They looked like part of a set of prayer beads, the sort that devout but illiterate people carried to count paternosters on. But what were they doing here, in the storeroom of a Jewish home?

Her first thought was to take them upstairs and show them to her uncle. He had been acting so strangely lately. Although it shamed her to think it, Catherine feared he would simply take the objects, thank her and tell her that he would see to it. But would he? It was awful to be unable to trust a person one loved. But Eliazar was hiding something and until she knew what it was, Catherine decided that it was better if she investigated this discovery herself.

Had Natan dropped these things when he died? Catherine thought back. He had come straight for her. She had been standing over there by the bean barrel. No, he hadn't come near this side of the room.

These things had to have already been in the storeroom. For how long? she wondered. Who had left them there? Could they have anything to do with why Natan had found his way here to die?

Nothing spoke to her. There was no revelation. The bit of metal glinted as she turned it in the light. It was scratched as well as bent, but she could see no sign that the scratches meant anything. No secret message etched with a fingernail and smuggled out of a dungeon. The beads weren't worth repairing. They may have been meant for the midden.

But Catherine could think of no reason for them to be here. Carefully, she tied the metal in her right sleeve and the beads in her left. She wanted to ask Edgar about them.

Gathering up all the candles, she went back up to the pantry. When she opened the door to the kitchen, Lucia was there alone, polishing Johannah's silver Sabbath platter. She gave Catherine a nod.

"Did you find what you were looking for?" she asked.

"I don't know what I was looking for," Catherine told her. "But I felt no sudden gusts of heat or cold and no ghostly fingers touched me. It's just a room. There's no evil lurking in it. You needn't be afraid."

Lucia bent her head over the platter. "I won't go down there, ever again," she said.

Her face was turned away from Catherine, but it was reflected in the silver. She was crying.

Catherine made her good-byes and left at once.

As she walked home she considered how strange it was that, of all the people she had spoken with, only Lucia had shown any sign of pity for the dead trader. "Poor Natan" she had said. Was her comment simply the proper respect one showed for anyone who died, or was she genuinely sorry? Were her tears for this Natan ben Judah, who, even in death, was despised by all who had known him?

Or did Lucia just hate polishing silver?

Once Edgar had washed and they had eaten, Catherine showed him the things she had found.

"What do you think it's from?" she asked as he examined the metal.

"I can't tell," he said. "It's gold, I'm sure. Hammered this thin, I would guess it would be for plating something. A box, perhaps, or something of a baser metal."

"And the beads?"

"I agree with you," he said. "A poor man's prayer counter, or part of one. It does seem a strange thing to find at Eliazar's. Certainly it has no value, even whole."

Then he noticed her hand. The burns were long red streaks from the web of her thumb up her forearm.

"Oh, Catherine!" he said.

"It's not bad," she assured him. "I put goose grease on my hand as soon as I got home."

"I can see that." He gave an embarrassed smile. "But I wanted some sympathy for *my* aches and burns."

Catherine laughed. "I'll give all you need, *carissime*." She kissed him. "Where would you like me to start?"

Ten

Catherine and Edgar's room, Saturday afternoon, March 1, 1141 / 21, Adar, 4901

Ore bones gens, or covient que vos prenés garde de vos meismes en ceste sante Quarentaine; . . . Va, "Sathana! Jo n'en fraindrai mie ma geüne, ne jo ne managerai mie ne ne bueverai trop, ne rien ne ferai que tu m'amonestes."

Listen, good people, now promise that you will watch out for yourselves during these holy forty days; . . . Say, "Satan! I will not break my fast, neither will I eat or drink too much. I will do nothing that you have tempted me to."

—Maurice de Sully,
Sermon for the first Sunday of Lent

*E*dgar liked John's friend, Maurice. He was well mannered, enjoyed his food, told a good story and had no intellectual arrogance, a welcome change from most of Edgar's acquaintances among the students.

"I've been in Paris since last spring," Maurice explained to the others, when he came up for air after his meal. "My family are tenants of the lord of Sully. My lord allowed me to go to the monks at Fleury to learn my letters and then they sent me here. I've never been so far from home before."

"It must all seem very different," Catherine prodded.

"Not what I expected, I'll admit," Maurice said. "There is a tremendous variety of people here. Somehow I thought that Paris was only the court and the cathedral, with the abbeys of Saint-Victor and Sainte-Geneviève keeping watch on them. But there's so much more, all the shops and merchants and crafts. And foreigners! Oh, I beg your pardon!" He looked from John to Edgar in alarm.

"The first thing I noticed, myself," Edgar said. "Paris is full of foreigners. Don't you think so, John?"

John poured some more beer. "Normans, Picards, Lotharingians, Gascons, even Burgundians," he sighed. "It's a good thing we all speak Latin or the place would be another Babel."

"I believe I even saw a Syrian lord the other day," Maurice said solemnly.

"Did you?" Edgar asked. "That is rare. What makes you think he was Syrian?"

"He was very dark and dressed like the traders from the south," Maurice said. "His beard and hair were perfumed and oiled. He spoke French very well, though. You would have thought he was born here."

"How interesting," John told him. "He may have been from Spain, but I doubt as far as Syria. There has been more trade since the Holy Land was reclaimed, but not many of their merchants come this far."

"I suppose," Maurice said slowly. "But there was something about him that made me think of the Levant. Of course, that's nonsense. Catherine, here, has that look about her, too."

"My father is from Normandy," Catherine said. "My mother from Blois."

"You see?" Maurice said, eyeing the scrapings in the porridge bowl. "I must have been mistaken. Perhaps it was because of the bag the man was carrying that I assumed he was a trader from distant parts."

As Maurice ran his spoon around the edge of the bowl, Catherine and Edgar exchanged glances over his head. Edgar raised his eyebrows. Catherine mouthed, "Maybe. Ask him."

John tapped Catherine's arm. "Ask him what?" he whispered. Maurice looked up.

"This Syrian," Edgar said. "When and where did you meet him?"

"Two or three weeks ago," Maurice answered. "Before *quinquagesima*, I'm sure. It was very early in the morning and I wasn't watching the path. I was walking along the north side of the cloister, just outside the wall. I knocked him over, right in the mud. He dropped his bag and stained his hose and cloak. He was very gracious about it. I said psalms for his soul for a week afterwards."

" 'Gracious'?" Catherine said. "It must not have been Natan, then."

"You know this man?" Maurice asked.

"I thought we might," Edgar told him. "But from all we've heard, he would not have been forgiving to someone who upset him in the road."

"Did you see what was in the bag?" Catherine asked.

"No, it was tied shut," Maurice said. "Although it clanked when it hit the ground, as if it were full of pots or metal dishes."

"You didn't see where he went afterwards, did you?" Edgar asked.

Maurice shook his head. "I hurried on as quickly as I could. I was almost late for Prime." He licked the last of the porridge off his spoon and smiled at them in grateful repletion. "And now John and I must go, too." He stood up. "We're planning on reciting the night Office with the canons of Saint-Victor."

John pushed his stool back from the table. "I only hope we don't yawn all the antiphons, after this very satisfying meal," he said. "Thank you both and good night."

Catherine stacked the plates and leftover bread high on a shelf so the mice wouldn't reach them before morning. Then she prepared for bed, her forehead creased in thought. Edgar noticed her worried expression.

"Do you think it was Natan that Maurice met?" he asked.

It took her a moment to pull her attention back to him. "What?" she said. "Oh Natan. It does sound like him. But what would he have been doing there? Do you think he tried to sell his pearls to the bishop?"

"Why not?" Edgar answered. "If Prior Hervé wouldn't buy them. Although it would have made more sense to go to someone of the court. Lords don't often ask how one came by something, if they want it."

"Yes, I suppose," Catherine said absently. She continued rebraiding her hair.

Edgar sat next to her and began to play with the side she hadn't yet combed. "If it's not Natan, what are you worrying about?" he asked.

She sighed. "The night Office. At the Paraclete I used to get up every night to say it. Sometimes I was so tired I could barely follow the responses, but some nights, when everything was still outside and the moon had set, it was like being suspended in the seventh sphere, almost to heaven."

He rubbed his face against her shoulder. "It wasn't something that was often expected of me," he admitted. "But I think I know what you mean. Now, didn't we vow not to regret our choice of a secular life?"

She turned her head and her hair slid like silk across his cheek. "Yes, we did," she said. "I ask your pardon for my lapse."

He smiled. "Lay people can go to heaven, too, Catherine. Even Augustine said so."

He kissed her and Catherine reflected that he was probably right. And, anyway, like her mentor, Abbess Héloïse, she knew she would rather go to Hell with Edgar than to heaven alone.

* * *

Solomon sat in the kitchen watching Lucia sweep the floor. He liked the way her hips moved in counterpoint to the rhythm of the broom.

"Do you need someone to walk you to your home tonight?" he asked.

"One of my brothers will come for me soon," she answered.

Solomon was sure no one had to wiggle like that to move a broom. He sighed. "I suppose your brothers are all strong as Charlemagne and eight feet tall."

She laughed. "My brothers are strong enough to protect me from unwanted attention. One of them is named Samson."

"Samson? The brewer?" Solomon tilted forward on his stool. "He's got arms like oak logs. I didn't know he was your brother."

Lucia's smile was taunting as she wielded the broom over into the corner where he was sitting.

"My other brother is a carter," she said. "He and Samson hope to work together one day, making beer and selling it to all the local villages. His nickname is Goliath."

"Ah, well," Solomon conceded, "you should have no trouble reaching home in safety, then."

"I never have." She bent directly over him to sweep under the carving table. Lucia wore no perfume but there was a natural musky odor about her that made Solomon's eyes cross in the effort to keep his hands to himself.

There was a knock at the kitchen door. Lucia went to open it. Solomon allowed himself to relax.

"I hope you're finished here," Samson greeted his sister. "Mother needs your help tonight, dishing out the soup and filling the mugs."

"Yes, I'm done," Lucia told him. "Let me get my cloak."

Samson stepped in and noticed Solomon. "What are you doing here, Solomon?" he demanded, eyes narrowing. He turned to his sister. "What's he doing here, Lucia? Does your mistress know?"

"I live here," Solomon answered.

"Since when?" Samson asked.

"Practically all my life," Solomon answered.

"I never saw you here before," Samson said.

"I've been traveling a lot the past few years," Solomon answered. "I'm only in Paris now and then."

He braced himself for the next question. It came.

"You a Jew?" Samson made it more of an incredulous snort than a question.

"Yes," Solomon answered.

Samson's face worked as if he were trying to think of another meaning for the word *yes*. "You never said you were a Jew," he countered.

"You never asked," Solomon said.

"But you drink my beer," Samson challenged. "And you swear by the saints."

"That's true," Solomon said. "You make excellent beer. And as for swearing, the saints are as good as anything else. Do you want me to stop buying my beer at your mother's tavern?"

Samson thought. "No, you're a good customer," he admitted. "And it's not like you're the only one of your race that buys from us. Come when you like. But . . ."

Lucia came back, wrapped in her cloak. Samson fairly pushed her out the door.

"But," he repeated, "don't let me find you anywhere near my sister again." He slammed the door as he left.

Solomon rocked back and forth on the rickety stool in deep contemplation. Just once in his life, he would like to meet a girl with no uncles, fathers or brothers.

A few days later Eliazar received a visit from the seven elders of the community. As soon as they entered, he knew that something was wrong. They declined Johannah's offer of refreshments as well as his attempt to have another bench brought in so they all could be seated.

"Very well, my friends," he said. "Then tell me your reason for coming here, if you don't wish to break bread with me or sit for a sociable conversation."

Abraham ben Simson was usually the spokesman for the group by virtue of his learning and his family vineyards, one near Saint-Victor and the other on the Right Bank, which he had managed to keep despite pressure from the various seigneurs of the area to sell them. He was respected both for wisdom and the ability to compromise. Abraham had been Eliazar's first teacher of the Talmud. Now the old man was gazing at him with a look of deep distrust.

It frightened Eliazar more than anything that had happened to him in his life. Abraham cleared his throat. "Menahem ben Nehemiah came to see me last night, just after I said *havdolah*," he said.

"How is he faring?" Eliazar asked.

"He's healing slowly," Abraham answered. "The beating those men gave him was severe."

"May the Almighty One protect him from further harm," Eliazar said.

"It is for that reason that we have come to you, Eliazar ben Meïr," Abraham said. "Menahem believes that his suffering was because of his uncle's death. Those men who attacked him insisted that poor Menahem knows of a treasure that Natan hid. He says that he begged you to tell him what you know about it, but you wouldn't help him. Menahem has told me that if you continue in your stubborn refusal, he will have no choice but to interrupt daily prayers and demand that you either reveal what you know or face the *herem* of the community."

Eliazar bowed his head. His heart was in torment. Even the threat of such a ban horrified him. But how could he convince them that he knew nothing of Natan's death without betraying the one who had trusted him?

"Please." He faced the men. "You all know me. You can't believe I would deny poor Menahem his rightful inheritance. If I knew who those men were or what they were seeking, I would tell him at once. It's true that Natan wished to leave a parcel with me, but I refused when he wouldn't tell me what it contained."

"And yet it is known that he was a frequent visitor to your home last spring," Abraham said.

"That matter has nothing to do with this," Eliazar wondered how many times and to how many people he would have to repeat it. "I was mistaken to have employed Natan. I regretted it. I told him so the last time he visited. The next time I saw him was when I found him dead on the floor of my storeroom."

"But why did you employ Natan at all?" Abraham's voice was hard. "You knew his reputation."

Eliazar closed his eyes. "I cannot tell you," he said quietly. "I was helping a friend. I promised him that I would never speak of this to anyone. To do so would put both of us in grave danger."

One of the other men whispered something in Abraham's ear. The old man nodded.

"Eliazar," he said, "your argument with Natan was heard by your neighbors."

"How could they not have heard?" Eliazar said. "The man was mad, screaming at me. But it was because I wouldn't do what he wanted."

"This business that you won't discuss with your friends and brethren," Abraham began. "It was something Natan did know about, is that correct?"

Sadly, Eliazar nodded. "I didn't tell him at first, but you know how he was. He guessed the truth."

"And this truth that Natan ben Judah knew," Abraham continued, his voice growing louder, like a threatening wind, "this thing so terrible that you hide it from your own people, might it not have been information that Natan ben Judah would feel worth selling to others? Or demand that you pay him not to tell?"

Eliazar thought about that. It was strange. The oddest thing of all, really, considering the kind of man Natan had been. "He never asked me for money to hold his tongue," Eliazar said. "Even in his wild temper, he never threatened me with that. Perhaps Natan had his own sort of honor."

Abraham looked sorrowfully at his former pupil. "Before Natan was buried, Elhanan, the physician, examined him," he said. "He is quite certain that the death was from poison, although he is unsure of the type. Some form of *solenum*, he fears. The man died in your house, Eliazar."

"Yes!" Eliazar shouted. "I know that! But he didn't eat here. I don't know who killed him or how he made his way to my storeroom. I have no answers for you. Do you intend to accuse me of murdering him? Perhaps you'd like to hang me next to the road for all the Christians to see?"

Eliazar's neighbor, Joseph, stepped forward. "None of us believes you could murder anyone," he told Eliazar firmly. "Even one such as Natan. But you have a Christian partner and his daughter is often in your home. This is dangerous enough, but we understand. Many of us have friends among the Edomites and we all have to live in their midst. Now Menahem has been attacked and threatened and he says it was by Christian men. What are we to think?"

"Whatever you like," Eliazar said wearily. "I've told you all I can. But may I be forced to spend the rest of my life among monks if Hubert had any part in what happened to Menahem. He is an honest man."

"I don't know if that will satisfy Menahem," Abraham told him. "But I am inclined to trust you for now. What do the others say?"

He turned to the men behind him. They nodded, some more reluctantly than others. Eliazar knew he had only been given time, not exoneration.

"I will go to Hubert at once," he told them. "He knows what calumny such as this can do. He'll wish to find out who really sent those men to Menahem's."

"If this business of yours has dragged us into the quarrels of the Christians," Abraham warned, "you may find that only the monks will have you."

That same afternoon Hubert was standing on a quai near the monastery of Argenteuil, several twisty miles down the Seine from Paris. He was arranging for the shipment of wine from last year's pressing. Abbot Suger was particularly fond of the red wine made by the Cistercians from their vines at the source of the river Vouge. The barrels had to be transported overland to Dijon, then to Troyes, then down the Seine, passing through enough different lands to more than quadruple the cost by the time all the tolls and travel expenses had been paid. Hubert admitted, though, that whatever the trouble it took, the abbot never questioned the price.

The wine was usually unloaded at the Port Saint-Denis, where the Croult emptied into the Seine. But Hubert had been instructed to bring some of the barrels here to Argenteuil, another long loop down the river, for the use of the monks there. The priory of Argenteuil had been a convent from the time of the Merovingians, but was now occupied by monks from Saint-Denis. Catherine had more words than Hubert cared to hear about the manner in which Suger had acquired Argenteuil and all its property. But it did provide a convenient place to unload goods for the abbey that were being brought upstream from Rouen.

Hubert was very sorry that Héloïse and the other nuns had been forced to find new homes when Suger had pressed the abbey's claim, but he had heard rumors at the time that the sisters had not been living chaste and holy lives and therefore deserved the expulsion. And as for Catherine's insistence that the charters the abbot used to prove his ancient rights were forgeries, well, that was for scholars to decide. If the pope believed them genuine, then who was he to argue?

The cellarer of Argenteuil was a most meticulous man who didn't seem to mind standing about for hours in a damp wind checking the mark on each barrel and sampling to be sure the contents matched the mark. Hubert might have felt more sympathy if he had thought the man a secret tippler, but Brother Jonas only sniffed and sipped the wine. The red in his cheeks was from the cold, which he must feel even more than Hubert, as he was wearing only a woolen cloak over his habit and sandals with no hose.

Finally the monk replugged the last spigot, put his own mark on the last barrel and announced to Hubert that he was satisfied.

"As I'm sure the prior will be, and Abbot Suger, when he visits," Hubert said. "I'm surprised that his own cellarer isn't here to supervise. Brother Michael usually prefers to take care of the shipment himself."

"Brother Michael is in the abbey infirmary." Brother Jonas sniffed disapprovingly. Hubert wasn't sure it was because the question might be construed as an insult or if the monk was contemptuous of those who gave in to the weakness of their bodies.

"This is a hard time of year," Hubert said. "Paris resounds with the noise of coughing. I've taken to wearing a bag of herbs to ward off the sickness myself. I pray Brother Michael will soon recover."

"That's as God wills, of course," Brother Jonas answered. "But I understand his condition is not serious. He should soon be able to resume his duties."

"It is kind of you to take them on, in addition to your own." Hubert knew he had offended the man and tried to make amends.

"I do as my abbot requests," Brother Jonas said. "All my work is an offering to Our Lord, no matter what form it takes."

"Of course," Hubert said, but the answer puzzled him. Was the man saying that manual labor was as good an offering as prayer and ritual? Hubert knew that. The priests of Paris seemed to take that theme for half their sermons. But the emphasis Brother Jonas had placed on the last sentence seemed to imply something that he thought Hubert should understand. No matter what?

Hubert took a deep breath and let the cold air clear his head. He'd been brooding too much on secrets lately, until every sentence appeared to have at least three meanings. Why should Brother Jonas's words be more than they appeared?

He bid the monk farewell and went to the ostler's to get his horse. He had accompanied the wine from just above Paris, paying and negotiating its way downriver. Now that the carting of it was no longer his responsibility, he planned to ride as quickly as he could to Vielleteneuse and spend an evening playing with his grandchildren.

Guillaume had sent two of his men to guard Hubert on the journey. Hubert appreciated his son's thoughtfulness but felt it was not really necessary. The road from Argenteuil to Vielleteneuse was well protected by the dependents of the abbey.

So he was not at all pleased to find a third man waiting to accompany him.

"Jehan!"

The knight had been lounging against the wall of the stables but stiffened immediately at Hubert's voice.

"What brings you here?" Hubert asked. "Who sent you?"

"No one sent me," Jehan answered, annoyed. "I was visiting Guillaume and heard you were coming. I thought you'd be glad of an extra sword."

Hubert tried to control his anger. After all, he only had Catherine's impression that there was something between Jehan and Agnes. It wasn't right to assume the worst and treat the man accordingly.

"Yes, of course, very good of you," he muttered. "I would be honored if you would ride with me. I'm sure you know all the news from Champagne and Blois. You can tell me what Count Thibault intends to do about his brother's imprisonment by Empress Matilda."

Jehan smiled and bowed politely and, after a meal of hard bread crumbled in broth and a mug or two of beer, they set off. Hubert and Jehan rode in front; the other two guards followed at a great enough distance that they could trap anyone daring to attempt to leap from the woods and attack an unarmed merchant.

Since the trees were still leafless, the likelihood of anyone doing this without being seen well in advance was remote. The men relaxed and passed a skin of beer back and forth to relieve the chill. They fell farther and farther behind Hubert and Jehan.

Jehan noted this. He resolved to mention their laxity to Guillaume later. But for now, it was useful to him. There was a matter he needed to discuss with Hubert alone.

Hubert seemed determined to learn all the news of England and Normandy first. "They say Geoffrey of Anjou is leaving a trail of ashes in his conquest of Normandy," he was saying. "Is the devastation that bad? They also say Stephen is on the point of ceding it to the empress as his ransom. Can that be?"

Jehan shrugged. "I haven't been north in months," he told Hubert. "Certainly Stephen has made enemies of his own people and Geoffrey has exploited that. As far as I know, no terms have been set to ransom the king. Nor has anyone approached Count Thibault to contribute to it."

"Odd," Hubert mused. "I've never understood why Thibault refused the duchy of Normandy when it was offered him. He could have controlled the entire north of France and squeezed the Capets like a cluster of grapes in a press."

This was an old question and Jehan didn't feel like pursuing it. He had no idea what was in the count's mind. It wasn't his job to. He simply went where he was told and fought whomever his lord was battling at the moment. And tried thereby to earn the reward of a piece of land of his own or even a castellany. Originally, he had hoped for an heiress to come with the property, but lately he had been trying to devise a plan that wouldn't include such a drastic step. After all, Agnes would not be dowerless.

"Master Hubert," he began.

At that moment a man leaped upon him from a branch overhanging the road. Jehan felt the weight on his back and the knife at his throat and cursed himself for ignoring a lifetime of training. He should have been automatically scanning the hedges and trees. Instead, his mind had been on Agnes. It seemed that both he and her father were about to pay for his lapse. He tried to reach for his own knife, but it was too late.

Eliazar looked around nervously as he crossed the open space of the Grève, but no one seemed to be following him. Still, he couldn't escape the feeling of being watched as he pulled on the bell rope at

Hubert's door. The slot in the door moved and a pair of young blue eyes stared up at him.

"Good day, Ullo." Eliazar was relieved that someone he knew was tending to the house this afternoon. "I've come to see your master. Is he in?"

The boy moved the slot back and opened the door. Instead of letting Eliazar in, he leaned out.

"Master's gone downriver with the wine for the abbey," he explained. "Be back in two or three days, most likely. There's no one here now but my Lady Agnes."

"No one watching out for her?" Eliazar asked.

"Me," Ullo answered indignantly. "And she has her maid and Anna, who comes in by day to cook."

"Ullo, who is it?" Agnes's voice came from somewhere above.

"It's Master Eliazar, come to talk with Master Hubert," Ullo shouted up the stairs. "I'm telling him when to come back."

There was a moment of silence. Then Agnes appeared at the top of the steps.

"Ask Master Eliazar if he would like a cup of something warm to drink before he leaves," she said.

Eliazar looked up in astonishment. He could only see her feet and the hem of her robe. He wished he had a view of her face. What was she thinking of? Both Hubert and Catherine had told him of Agnes's reaction to the news of her ancestry. Well, he would find out nothing by refusing her offer.

"Please tell your mistress that I would be most grateful for her hospitality," he said to Ullo.

He wondered if she would now have him sent round to the kitchen like a beggar. But no, Ullo was leading him up the stairs to the main hall. The fire in the hearth was bright and welcoming. Agnes went in and seated herself at a small table next to it. She motioned him to a stool on the opposite side.

"Do your boots need drying?" she asked. "I can have someone attend to that while you have your drink. You may hang your gloves on the hook there. Do you prefer spiced cider or ale?"

"Ale, if it's convenient," Eliazar answered. "My boots are dry enough, thank you."

She picked up a small bell from the table and rang it. Eliazar studied her as, he supposed, she was studying him.

She wasn't like Hubert at all. Or Catherine. Agnes was small and fair with a delicate nose and chin. It crossed his mind that perhaps Hubert had had nothing to do with the making of her, that Madeleine had deceived him. It might be a comfort to Agnes if she found out she was a bastard rather than the daughter of a Jew. Then she raised her chin and stared straight into his eyes and he knew she was in some way part of his family. It was just the look his own father had worn when he caught his children playing quoits when they were supposed to be studying their verses.

Eliazar smiled. Agnes didn't.

"You know who I am," she said.

Her hands were laced tightly together in her lap, her knuckles white with the pressure.

"Of course," he said. "The daughter of my old friend, Hubert. I haven't seen you since you were a little girl, so I'm sure you don't remember me."

"No, I don't" she said. "I do know that my father has had business dealings with you and that you have been partners in several of his trade journeys."

"That's right," he answered warily.

Ullo entered and Agnes ordered him to bring the ale.

"Shall I tell Humberga to come in and sit with you?" he asked.

"That won't be necessary," Agnes told him. "She's busy airing the mattresses to take with us to Vielleteneuse." She turned back to Eliazar. "We plan to spend Eastertide with my brother, Guillaume," she explained. "Do you know him, as well?"

"We have met," Eliazar answered. He felt her tension but knew of no way to help her.

Her fingers twisted in her lap. She studied them a long time. Eliazar waited. Finally she seemed to come to a decision. She looked up at him.

"I suppose you are some sort of relation of mine," she said. Her eyes dared him to try to lie to her. He could do it no more than he ever had been able to lie to his father.

"You are my niece," he said softly. "Your father is my youngest brother."

Her face didn't change, but her hands suddenly stopped moving and rested, palms up, limp in her lap.

"My father always told us his family were all dead," she said evenly. "That he had been taken in and raised by an elderly mer-chant of Rouen, who had no children."

"Did he tell you how this family died?" Eliazar asked.

"No, but last year, Catherine did." Agnes's lips tightened. "She said they were murdered by the soldiers who had taken the cross to free Jerusalem. They reasoned that it was foolish to kill the infidel in the Holy Land and allow the infidel in their midst to live. I hadn't known that happened in Rouen. I had only heard of the incidents in Germany."

Eliazar closed his eyes, remembering anew the devastation he had felt when the messenger came to Paris with the news. His mother and three sisters, all slaughtered. It was years before he learned that poor Hubert, a child of five at the time, had been taken in by old Milon, who had had him baptised and raised as his son.

"My sister, Jochabed, was about your age then," he said quietly. "She had just been betrothed."

"I don't want to hear about her," Agnes said. "She was a fool. She could have chosen baptism and life, both here and hereafter."

Eliazar rose. "Jochabed died a martyr in sanctification of the Holy Name. She is one of the righteous. Did you ask me up here to sneer at her sacrifice? Do you think only Christians are prepared to die for their faith?"

Agnes stood also. "We die for the true faith," she said. "You let yourselves be killed because you're too stubborn to see what is obvi-ous to the rest of us. You die blindly in the darkness. Your sister is in Hell."

Eliazar stepped toward her, his hand tensed to strike. She glared at him with defiance. She wanted him to hit her, he realized, so that she could prove she was as brave as Jochabed had been.

Perhaps she was. Eliazar lowered his hand. Breathing as if he had just fought for his life, he stepped back and took his gloves from the hook over the hearth. He told himself that it wasn't her fault. This was how she had been taught. The real miracle was Catherine, who loved him in spite of her upbringing.

With all his heart Eliazar tried to pity Agnes, but all he could feel was abhorrence. "So do you now intend to destroy your father, by denouncing him to Bishop Stephen?" he asked.

Agnes's eyes opened wide. "I hadn't thought of that," she said. "I couldn't. The shame would be too great. No, I couldn't betray my father, even though he has betrayed me. No. No, of course not."

She sat down again, suddenly a lost and frightened child. Eliazar could think of no comfort to give her. He wasn't sure he wanted her to have any.

He mumbled his thanks for the drink he hadn't tasted, put on his gloves and left.

The man shivering in the alley across from the house gave a sigh of relief and went after him. He was careful not to be seen, but it didn't matter. Eliazar was too upset to notice.

Eleven

The tavern owned by Lucia's mother, late afternoon, Monday, March 10, 1141 / 28, Adar, 4901

Meum est propositum in taberna mori, Ut sint vina proxima morientis ori. Tunc cantabunt laetis angelorum chori, "Sit deus propitius huïc potatori.

It is my intention to die in a tavern, and let the wine be near. Then the choir of angels will sing with joy, "May god be gracious to this drunkard.
—"Golias," *Carmina Burana*

*S*olomon sat again with Catherine in a corner of the tavern. She was amusing herself picking the flakes out of the beer while they waited for Edgar.

"Why don't you just strain them between your teeth like I do?" Solomon asked.

"I prefer knowing what's going into my mouth before it's too late," Catherine said. "Bietrix, do you know what herbs your son put in the beer?"

The proprietor left her seat at the vat and came to sniff Catherine's cup.

"Woodruff, I think," she said. "Samson uses it in the mead, too. Of course, it might be borage, or bog myrtle. Hard to tell, once it's all mixed in. Why? Don't you like the taste?"

"No, it's fine," Catherine lied. "It's just that I—"

They were interrupted by a shriek from the back room. Bietrix hurried to see what the problem was. Solomon wiggled uncomfortably.

"Your father may be right," he told Catherine. "This isn't a proper place for you."

"I'm with you, aren't I?" She answered. "No one has shown any interest in me at all. I wouldn't come here alone. I do have *some* sense."

Solomon thought about responding to that statement, but decided that she had enough to aggravate her at the moment.

The shutters of the tavern were open a crack to let in the brisk spring air. Catherine got up and looked out, noting how the sunlight was already gone from the narrow street. When she came back to her seat, she didn't say anything, but her inner turmoil showed in the way she pursued the bits of herbs around the rim of her cup.

"Don't worry," Solomon said. "He'll be here soon. The silversmith has never made him work past sundown yet."

"I know," Catherine told him. She continued fussing with the beer.

"I wish I could find out where that workshop is." Solomon was becoming concerned, too. "It's almost two weeks now and all I can figure out is where it isn't. I've been around the wall of the cloister a dozen times and there's no sign of a kiln. I wish I could get inside."

"Edgar wants to ask Maurice to hunt for it," Catherine said. "But we're not sure yet how well we can trust him. He seems honest, but he's also very grateful to the canons for taking him in."

"Why would the canons of Notre Dame want or need to have a clandestine metal shop?" Solomon asked. "They can set one up quite legitimately to provide for the church."

Catherine considered straining the herb flecks through her sleeve. It couldn't make the beer taste any worse. This was not Samson's best effort. She compromised by using the tip of the sleeve to skim the worst of whatever it was off the top.

"I don't know the answer, Solomon," she said. "I'm beginning to believe that we'll never discover what Gaudry is making there or if he has anything to do with the relics stolen from Salisbury."

She took another sip of the beer. It was beginning to taste better; the sleeve did help.

"At least Edgar is enjoying himself," Solomon said.

In spite of her worry, Catherine smiled. "He's burnt holes in every piece of clothing he owns," she said. "His arms and back ache all night. His eyes are always red from the fumes. The work is never done to suit. He's happier than I've ever seen him."

"It's unnatural." Solomon swirled the last bit in his cup and drank it, flecks and all. He went to get some more.

What was keeping Edgar?

At about that same time, Eliazar was standing in the walled garden behind his house, head tilted up, searching the sky for the new moon, which would signal the beginning of the month of Nisan. He tried to keep his thoughts on the One who had created the moon, immutable, yet ever changing. How much he regretted not having the gift to understand the deep, mystical meanings behind the laws of the universe. He had tried to study the *merkabah*, the vision of Ezekial, and the books of the *Hekhaloth*, but he could not understand how a thing could be both large and small at the same time, nor find the meanings hidden in the words of the creation. In his study of the Torah, he only saw the *peshat*, the literal meaning of the words. He had not been granted the enlightenment needed to understand the mystical messages. In teaching men such as Brother Andrew, the *peshat* was all that was safe to expound, but Eliazar wished he had the gift to communicate more of the hidden, true sense.

He sighed. Perhaps not. There was danger in that as well as he had found to his sorrow.

Somewhere someone was pounding on a door. Why didn't anyone answer? The knocking was most insistent. Finally Eliazar realized that the reason no one opened the door was because the visitor was at his door and there was no one to answer. Lucia had gone home and Johannah to the *mikvah* to bathe. He hurried in through the house and flung the door open without bothering to look through the slot.

A woman stood before him, heavily veiled, accompanied by a boy of about eleven years of age whom Eliazar recognized at once. It was Ullo, Hubert's page and errand runner.

He stared at the woman in astonishment. "Agnes?"

"Do you intend to humiliate me further," she asked, "by keeping me standing here in the street under the eyes of all your neighbors?"

He stepped out of the way and Agnes entered, followed by Ullo. She lowered the veil and spoke before he could collect himself enough to offer her food or warmth.

"I have just had a messenger from the monastery of Argenteuil," she said. "He told me that my father was attacked on the road shortly after leaving them yesterday."

"Heaven protect us!" Eliazar exclaimed. "Is he badly hurt? Where were his guards?"

"He's alive," Agnes said. "Or was when the messenger left. As for the guards, I don't know. He only said that Father had been hurt. The monks sent both to me and my brother, Guillaume, bidding us come at once."

Her voice broke at the end. Eliazar was gratified to know that, despite her anger, she still had some feeling left for Hubert.

"Of course," Eliazar said gently. "And you must do so. But it's nearly dark. You can't go tonight. I'll find someone to take you at first light tomorrow. No, I'll take you myself."

"I have made my own arrangements," Agnes told him. "That's not why I've come here. It's Catherine."

"Catherine?" Eliazar asked. "She doesn't know?"

"There was no way to tell her," Agnes said. "I have no idea where to find her. I don't even know where she's living now."

"It doesn't matter." Eliazar reached for his cloak. "At this time of day, she'll be at Bietrix's. Wait here and I'll fetch her."

"I will not wait here," Agnes told him. "Tell me where this place is. Ullo and I will find her."

Eliazar reminded himself that she was young and frightened. He answered her gently.

"It's a tavern not far from here that the students frequent," he explained. "Hubert would not approve of my letting you go there with only a child to protect you. The streets are dark now, the shops closed. You'll be safe here. My wife will be back soon to see to you."

"I do not wish to stay in your home," Agnes said. "Nor do I want your wife anywhere near me. You people have nothing to do with me." Her voice had an edge of hysteria.

Eliazar gave in. "You will then have to bear my company for a time, at least," he said. "For you cannot go alone. Catherine and Edgar can see you back to your home."

It was well past dark when Edgar finally arrived. Catherine and Solomon had already started on a bowl of soup. They were dipping crusts in it and sucking them when he walked in.

He slumped onto the bench and stared at the food, too tired to reach for it. Catherine took a piece of the soaked bread and held it to his mouth.

"*Leoffedest,*" she whispered. "What have they done to you?"

He wrapped his hand around hers and bit on the bread. Then kissed her greasy fingers.

"Hauling clay and charcoal all day," he muttered. "Not to mention the buckets of horse dung. Up and down, from the river to the shop, through those cursed tunnels. He's building a whole new oven. I'm surprised you knew me with this coating of dust and soot."

"I recognized the *braies,*" Catherine said, running her fingers through his soot-streaked hair.

"The river?" Solomon leaned across the table, keeping his voice down. "Do you know what quai he's using and where the tunnel comes out?"

"Yes, on the north side, above the bishop's mill," Edgar said. "We came up outside the cloister wall, but there are so many twists inside that I still can't tell how far we really are from the workshop. Saint Winfrith's death ship! I'm an artisan, not a pack mule. And those damn tunnels are so low! I must have cracked my head a dozen times against the beams in the roof. No wonder Odo is perpetually hunched."

He pushed aside his hair to show the bruises on his forehead. Then he grinned ruefully.

"I'm not sure I really want to be an artisan, after all," he said. "Unless I can start as master in my own studio. I think a pack mule must have a better life than I did today."

"You don't have to continue this," Solomon told him. "We haven't come any closer to finding the answer. It may be that Gaudry has nothing to do with the missing altar vessels or with this Saxon saint."

Edgar took a drink from Catherine's cup. The three of them huddled companionably over the soup bowl.

"I think he does," Edgar insisted. "We were supposed to be crafting a chalice, much the same size as the one you found, Solomon. And Gaudry has orders for several other things, including something that requires gold leaf and fine glass, almost clear. Catherine, your cup is empty."

Remembering how tired he was, she went and refilled it.

"Drink this one more slowly," she warned him. "This brewing is bitter but very strong. Now, what happened?"

"Nothing," Edgar said. "We had everything ready to begin when, as far as I can tell from Odo, who says little, and Gaudry, who mostly yells commands, something went wrong. Someone died suddenly. Without him, they can't continue. He had something they need and now it's lost. Not much to make a deduction from, is it?"

"Do you think the dead man is Natan?" Catherine asked.

Edgar shrugged. "They haven't said a name. It might not be. He couldn't have been the only man to die in Paris that week."

"But we know he had a parcel that he wanted Uncle Eliazar to keep for him," Catherine said. "And we think it was he that Maurice knocked over by the cloister. The man was carrying a bag that clanked. We know Natan had recently begun to deal in jewels and gold, and that his earlier trading had involved stolen goods."

"The assumption is reasonable," Edgar said. "But not conclusive. Is there any more soup?"

This time Solomon got up.

Catherine dipped the tip of her sleeve in the cup again. Edgar pulled it out with barely controlled annoyance.

"I don't like the flavoring," she explained. "Now what was I thinking of? You distracted me."

"Sorry," he said. "You play and I'll fill my own cup."

They had just settled down again when the door opened. None of them looked up. Most of the customers this time of night went directly back to the brothel.

Catherine smelled her perfume first. For a second, she thought it was her mother standing next to her. The scent was the same. She looked up.

"You are disgusting, Catherine!" Agnes greeted her. "Our father may be lying at the point of death and here you are, carousing in a tavern. Do you work here, too?"

"Agnes!" Catherine stood and reached out for her. Her sister pushed her away. "What's this about Father?" Catherine asked. "What's happened?"

"He's been hurt, attacked on the road. We have to go to him at once," Agnes said. "Despite what he's done, he's still my father and I know my duty. Do you?"

Solomon and Edgar stood, prepared to leave at once. Agnes regarded Edgar's layers of filth with revulsion. Then she saw Solomon. She blinked. He smiled at her. He had a charming smile. Agnes didn't return it. She looked back and forth between him and Catherine, noting the likeness.

When she spoke it was from between clenched teeth. "If you tell me this man is my brother," she said, "I'm going to start screaming and I'm not going to stop."

Hubert woke up in bed at the guesthouse at Argenteuil. He blinked several times in confusion. Hadn't he been there yesterday morning? For a few seconds he wondered if the day before had been a dream. He remembered it in that fragmented way most dreams are recalled.

He tried to lift his head, then changed his mind. The effort sent arrows of pain through his neck and jaw. A hand touched his fore-head.

"Don't try to move, Father," Guillaume said. "You'll tear the bandages."

"Guillaume, why are you here? What happened?" Hubert asked. "Where's Jehan? '

"You were attacked by a couple of starving *ribaux*," Guillaume told him. "The idiots only had short knives. It appears that they planned to fall onto you both from the trees simultaneously, but only one hit his target. The other missed you entirely, landed in the road and broke his back."

"And the first?" Hubert asked.

"You don't remember?" Guillaume said. "He landed on Jehan and prepared to cut his throat. You stabbed him in the side with your meat knife."

"I did?" Hubert said. It didn't sound like something he would do.

"You saved Jehan's life." Guillaume chuckled. "Of course, he may yet die of embarrassment. When his friends learn that the man he was to protect defended him, he'll be unable to show his face at a tournament for months, perhaps forever. "The guards I sent are going to be digging middens and hauling firewood for some time, as well," he added. "They never should have let you get so far ahead of them. If those villeins had been any smarter or less hungry, they could have slit both your throats before help arrived."

"It would have been pointless," Hubert said. "I was carrying nothing of value."

"Father," Guillaume sighed, "You are wearing a gold chain of membership in the *marchands de l'eau*, as well as two rings, one with a fairly good ruby, and a fur-lined cloak and boots. They would have killed you for the last alone."

"I see. Well, I'm glad they didn't. Now, why do I ache so?" Hubert asked.

"Your horse wasn't pleased by all the noise, as far as I've been able to learn from Jehan," Guillaume answered. "You struck Jehan's assailant, the man turned to strike back at you, both of you over-balanced. At the same time, your horse decided it was time to run. He threw you in the road, where you landed on top of the thief. The monks thought at first that you'd broken your arm, but it seems merely to be bruised and swollen."

"What happened to these clumsy thieves?" Hubert wanted to know.

Guillaume snorted. "My brave knights finished them off. Since both were by then unarmed, one shrieking in agony from the pain in his back and the other squealing from the sticking you'd given him, I can't consider it a brave deed. Father Anselm asked me to consult with the prior while I was here about appropriate penances for them."

"Starving, were they?" Hubert asked.

"It's been a hard winter, Father," Guillaume said. "But they were outlaws already or they would have come to the abbey or to one of the castellans for alms. Don't concern yourself with them. My men should do penance for making them die unshriven, but they would have ended on the gallows anyway."

Hubert sighed. He supposed so and good riddance to them. Half his expenses were to protect his goods from robbers on the journey. But he would have felt more heroic if the villeins had been more evil and less desperate.

The infirmarian from the priory came in to see how Hubert was doing. Guillaume started to leave, then turned back.

"I should warn you, Father," he said, "that the prior sent word of your accident to Paris as well as to Vielleteneuse."

Hubert groaned. "Then Catherine knows of this? She'll be worried. Did you send someone to tell her I was fine?"

"They didn't go to Catherine, but to the house on the Grève," Guillaume explained. "The prior didn't know that Mother no longer lived there. Agnes sent a reply that she was coming at once. But I doubt she can be here before tomorrow morning."

"Agnes is coming here?" Hubert said. "Do you think she's forgiven me?"

"Since I don't know what you did that she wouldn't forgive, I have no idea," Guillaume told him. "Neither one of you will talk about it. I don't know why I should be left out of a family fight."

"Agnes feels I didn't treat your mother well," Hubert equivocated.

"Nonsense," Guillaume said. "I believe Agnes is angry because you haven't married her off yet to a count or a duke. Get the girl a husband, Father. There's nothing wrong with her that can't be cured by a firm hand. I'll help you look."

With that the infirmarian took Guillaume's arm and guided him from the room, leaving Hubert to reflect upon his injuries and what he might have done to deserve such an interesting variety of children.

It had taken a few minutes to calm Agnes and get all of them out of the tavern. At Catherine's urgent plea that her sister was about to have a fit and might possibly start foaming at the mouth, Bietrix had brought some wine she kept for the occasional wealthy visitor and administered it. While Agnes sipped, Eliazar explained what he knew about Hubert's mishap.

"He may be dying! Poor Hubert." Eliazar wrung his hands. He suddenly wondered if Menahem had somehow managed to exact revenge for being beaten, but how? He was a simple draper, with few contacts outside Paris.

"If Agnes will permit it, we'll stay with her tonight so that we lose no time in the morning," Catherine said, looking warily at her sister, who seemed to be responding to the calming effect of the undiluted wine. "When she's ready, will you take us home?"

"I can take you home!" The voice was exasperated.

Catherine looked around Eliazar, then down to where the page sat on the dirt floor. "Ullo! I'm sorry, I didn't see you. Of course you can take care of us, but it's dark tonight with only a slivery moon. Did you bring your crossbow or your sword in case we are set upon in an alley?"

Ullo scowled and owned that he hadn't. Edgar took pity on him and drew him aside.

"My wife and the Lady Agnes take a deal of protecting, as I know too well," he explained. "I would prefer the largest force possible to see them across the river. Of course, you could lead it."

Ullo knew he was being condescended to and appreciated it. Most of the time he was just ignored. Even though Edgar was at the moment as grubby as his father's pigman, Ullo remembered that he was some sort of English lord and accepted him as such. A lot of the tales he listened to in the hall and at the fairs concerned knights dressed as serfs. They always triumphed in the end and rewarded those who had been kind to them while in disguise.

"Have you found the magic sword and horn yet?" he asked.

Edgar seemed startled, then looked at his tattered clothing and laughed. "Not yet," he said. "I hope I do soon, before I have nothing left to wear."

Eliazar had brought a lantern for them to find their way through the narrow streets. He tried to get Agnes to agree to come to his home first, but she adamantly refused, so he, Edgar and Solomon accompanied her to Hubert's house on the Right Bank.

"Will you permit me to stay here tonight and go with you tomorrow?" Catherine asked Agnes when they had arrived.

"I came for you in the hope that you would," Agnes said stiffly. "You are the elder daughter and the responsibility is yours. Is your husband staying as well?"

"Of course," Catherine said.

Edgar caught her arm. "I can't go with you," he whispered.

Before Catherine could answer, Agnes decided that her duty as a hostess included making everyone sit and have a hot drink before leaving.

"I can't believe you've never been here when I visited," Solomon said as he followed her up the stairs to the hall. "Are you sure you don't remember me?"

Catherine and Edgar stayed behind in the entryway.

"I have to be at the workshop tomorrow," Edgar said. "Gaudry will be furious if I don't appear and I have no way to let him know. I should go back to our room tonight. It would ruin our story if someone saw me leaving here in the morning. Your father is supposed to have disowned you."

Catherine swallowed the whine she felt rising in her throat. He was right. It wouldn't do to ruin the plan now, after so much trouble.

"But you agree that I must go to my father," she said.

"Of course."

"I don't like being away from you." She hadn't meant to say that. He knew it well enough.

Edgar took her hands. "The bed will be very cold without you. If you haven't returned by Sunday, I'll come to Argenteuil. Solomon can go with you tomorrow and you can send a message back by him."

"Yes, I suppose that would be best." Catherine sighed and released Edgar's hands. She rubbed her own on her skirts. "My dearest, even if you don't stay the night, I think we should try to prevail upon Agnes for some soap and water before you touch anything else here."

Agnes did not offer to let Catherine share the bed with her, as they had all through their childhood. Instead she had a cot made up in the little counting room where their father kept his papers and records of transactions.

"You were always happiest here, anyway," she said.

"Agnes," Catherine tried, "what kind of Christian are you that you can't forgive me?"

"Have you repented?" Agnes asked.

"Repented what?" Catherine demanded. "Leaving the convent? It would have been a sin to stay when my heart was out here with Edgar. Deceiving Mother? I regret that every day. I want to see her so much that it aches, and everyone tells me it would only make her condition worse. Don't you think that's penance enough?"

"It's a beginning," Agnes said. "But not enough. What about what you've done to me? How you left me to run off with your strange-looking lover. How I was deceived. You knew what Father was; you're friends with these people. You never told me. Instead you went to them. You abandoned Mother and me, that was bad enough. Oh, Catherine, have you also abandoned Our Lord?"

"Never!" Catherine cried. "I am Christian to the core of my soul! But Agnes, 'these people' are our blood kin. I've grown to love them. Why should I abandon them in their darkness? Did it ever occur to you that I might be able to convert them by my example?"

For the first time, Agnes wavered.

"No, I hadn't thought of that," she admitted. "That is the way the priests tell us is best, especially for women, although I find it difficult to imagine you preaching to that Solomon or him listening."

She rubbed her fingers along the edge of the writing table and checked them for dust. Catherine waited hopefully.

"Can't we be friends again?" she asked. "You're my only sister. I miss you."

Agnes's lower lip trembled and she blinked rapidly.

"Not yet." She shook away the tears. "I'm taking the lamp with me. There's too much in here that can burn."

She left Catherine alone in the dark.

What did you expect?

Catherine moaned. She was not about to add an argument with herself to all else she had endured today. But the voices were insistent.

"I expected her to come to me in tears and beg me to accompany her so that we could care for Father together, as sisters and friends," she admitted. "Do you think he's seriously hurt?"

Your reasoning ability has clearly faded since you left the Paraclete, they sniffed. *You forget that your sister is as proud as you are. As for your father, that's in the hands of God, whom you appear to have forgotten in spite of your recent avowal.*

Catherine took the rebuke and, in part to drive the voices from her mind, knelt by the bed, crossed herself and began reciting from the book of Lamentations.

"Plorans ploravit in nocte, et lacrymas eius in maxillis eius; non est qui consolatur eam, ex omnibus charis eius."

Perversely, it comforted her to think of someone else crying alone in the night with no one to give her consolation. Then she thought of her father again and her prayers became less affected and more heartfelt. She fell asleep in the middle of the psalm *Conserva me, Domine,* "Protect me, Lord, for you are my refuge," and slept all night without dreams.

Twelve

The workshop of Gaudry, the silversmith, Tuesday, March 11, 1141 /
First day of Rosh Hodesh, 1, Nisan 4901

Incipium autem disciplinae humilitas est . . .

"The beginning of discipline is humility . . ."
—Hugh of Saint Victor
Didascalion Book 3, Chapter 13

*E*dgar stepped back and looked with pride at the kiln he had constructed. The coals had been burning all morning; the inside glowed white with the heat, but there was no sign of cracking. He felt something inside himself glowing, too. For the first time since his marriage, he was confident that he and Catherine would never starve. He could do something that people would trade food for. It was a shame he would never be master in his own shop as his father was master in his own castle. Fleetingly, Edgar wished he had been born into a class that appreciated his talents.

"I pay you to work, not worship." Gaudry's voice came from directly behind him and made Edgar jump.

The smith moved around Edgar to see the kiln better. He squatted before the coals and nodded once. "It's not bad." He spoke grudgingly but not without admiration. "This will do."

Edgar suppressed a desire to whoop with delight. Instead he tried to make his comments as matter-of-fact as the master's. "Now that we've made it, what are we going to refine in it?"

"Gold," Gaudry told him. "Rich red gold. But first I need a box carved from wood. You did say that was your first talent."

"I can shape wood more skillfully than metal," Edgar admitted. "I've been doing it since I was a child. What sort of box do you need?"

Gaudry hesitated. He seemed to be considering the best method of explaining something he didn't want to talk about at all.

"It's this way," he began. "I've been given a commission by an important churchman. He needs a good copy made of a certain reliquary."

Edgar's first thought was, what for? One didn't make a new reliquary unless the old one was considered too humble to honor the saint. Abbot Suger was constantly adding to the adornment of the containers for the bones or possessions of the saints of Saint-Denis. There was no point in copying the same design; it had to be better.

However, this didn't seem the time to challenge Gaudry.

"A copy?" he asked instead. "How exact a copy do they need? Am I to work from the original or a sketch?"

"Neither," Gaudry told him. "The original is . . . not available. I'll give you the dimensions of the piece and you'll work from those."

"Which saint is to be honored by this reliquary?" Edgar asked. "I'll need to know who it is so that I can carve appropriate scenes on the box."

"No, you won't," Gaudry said sharply. "You just make the damn box the way I tell you to. I'll cover it with gold leaf and do the decoration myself. Do you understand?"

Edgar nodded. "But any cabinetmaker can fashion you a box, sir," he added.

Gaudry's face returned to its habitual look of annoyance. "Do you want me to hire a cabinetmaker?" he asked. "If so, then I can see no reason to keep you on."

"No, sir, of course not," Edgar said. "I'll do it. I simply was confused."

"That's because you keep trying to think," Gaudry snorted. "Your head is still full of that useless drivel the masters spout. I've heard them shrieking out that Latin nonsense as I cross the bridge. In this world, boy, there are no prebends or benefices for most of us. If a man has neither, then he does the work his master sets and asks no questions. Now, for the last time, is that clear?"

"Yes, Master Gaudry," Edgar said. He looked down so that the master wouldn't see the anger. Perhaps it was just as well he had not been born to a family of artisans.

"Now," Gaudry continued, "I want you to choose a block of wood that can be hollowed and hinged. It needs to be in the shape of an arm, the left, fingers included, up to the elbow. Is that too difficult for you?"

"No, sir!" Edgar said. He was so startled that he sounded eager and willing enough even for Gaudry.

Aldhelm! It had to be. It was Aldhelm's left arm that Abbot Warin of Malmesbury had given to Saint Osmund for the cathedral of Salisbury. Edgar didn't know what the original reliquary had looked like, but he remembered John saying that Philippe had put the arm in a gold-plated box. A box in the shape of an arm? It was a strange way to smuggle a relic secretly, in a box that could be for nothing else.

Also, if they were planning on receiving a ransom for Saint Aldhelm, why would the thieves need a new reliquary? If the arm were returned in a new container, there would always be questions as to its authenticity. Miracles would have to flow from it like milk to convince the people they hadn't been tricked.

But what if the original reliquary were returned? That must be it. Edgar went cold with fury. Someone was planning to fool Philippe or Salisbury or both, by returning the old reliquary with a false relic and keeping the real one. Edgar's fists clenched. Those *eolderdeofol-cynn*! Did they think that the sainted bishop would work miracles for those who had stolen him? Edgar was determined that he'd have nothing to do with such sacrilege. Saint Aldhelm was English and he belonged in England.

But how could he help to ensure that this saint of his people went home? Edgar had little hope of ever living in England himself. His family had made their choice to go north after the Saxon defeat at the battle of Hastings and their home was now Scotland. Even with their civil wars, Edgar had no hope that the Normans would ever leave. But he knew that he must do whatever it took to return Aldhelm to the place where he had once been bishop, even if it meant trusting the Normans who now controlled Salisbury.

"*Halig* Aldhelm," he prayed. "I will do whatever I can to fulfill your desire and I hope that it is to return to Salisbury. But, if you want me to help you, a little guidance would be much appreciated. And if you're of a mind to manage a small miracle, that would be even better."

Catherine clutched Solomon around the waist and reflected on how much less comfortable riding was since the days when she had criss-crossed Francia perched behind her father on his horse. She leaned against her cousin's back, grateful that he had insisted on coming with them so that she wouldn't need to ride astride so soon out of childbed.

It had, however, deferred any possibility of a reconciliation with Agnes. Catherine's sister rode ahead, alone and astride, her bright yellow hose showing above her boots, no matter how often she pulled the skirts of her *bliaut* over them. Solomon watched her with appreciation Fortunately she refused to turn around and notice.

They reached Argenteuil about midday. The bells for Tierce had not yet rung. Guillaume was waiting for them in front of the priory hostel. He hugged Agnes and Catherine, assuring them that their father seemed to be recovering rapidly. Solomon was greeted with a cold stare.

"I'll see to the horses while you visit your father," he told Catherine. "You know how I feel about monasteries. Find out when he'll be able to travel. If it's only a day or two, I can stay in the village and accompany him back to Paris, unless he prefers to go to Vielleteneuse."

"Will you have a place to stay?" she asked. "I don't remember any Jewish families in Argenteuil."

"There's one old man, a trader," Solomon told her. "He used to sell wine to the nuns. The new prior won't buy from him, but he manages to find work in town. I know he sells fish to the peasants. I believe Uncle Hubert gives him a commission now and then. He'll have a bed for me."

Catherine looked at him closely. "I don't suppose it's occurred to you that this man might have taken a commission from Natan, as well," she asked.

Solomon rubbed his nose and grinned at her. "Fantin doesn't get many visitors," he said. "I'm sure he'll be eager to tell me all the gossip, especially as to how difficult it's become to earn an honest living surrounded by monks and other Edomites."

"Just be sure you remember every word to tell me," Catherine said.

Solomon grew serious. "Of course I will. And you be sure to find out all you can about what happened to your father. When Natan died, I thought the only pity of it was that you were assaulted in such a manner. But now people in the community are saying that it wasn't an accident that he came to Uncle Eliazar's cellar."

"They don't believe our uncle had anything to do with Natan's death, do they?" Catherine said, alarmed. "How could he have?"

"Rumors don't need to follow rules of logic," Solomon told her. "And Uncle doesn't help by refusing to explain the nature of his business with Natan. Yes, I'm afraid there are those who believe

Natan was killed to keep him from betraying Eliazar's secret."

From the doorway, Guillaume shouted for Catherine to come with them.

"I'm coming!" she called back. "Solomon, you should have told me this sooner. I'll do what I can and meet you here this afternoon, before Vespers."

He nodded. "'Go on. Your brother looks ready to flay me alive just for speaking to you."

"Guillaume has become terribly pompous since he was made a castellan," Catherine sighed. She raised her voice. "Yes, I said I was coming!"

"Saint James the Dismembered!" Guillaume greeted her, holding open the door to the hostel. "Your father lies inside on a bed of pain and you stand in the road in full view of everyone chattering with that Jew. I don't care if you've known him all your life; it's scandalous!"

Catherine passed through the doorway in front of him. For a wonder she held her tongue. But she was thinking how sad it was that Guillaume had been sent to their mother's family in Blois for fostering and training as a knight instead of traveling the fairs with their father. She suspected that he was ashamed to be related to either Hubert or her. Heaven only knew what he would do if he discovered that Solomon was also a relative. She suspected that his reaction would make Agnes's seem mild.

Then she saw her father.

He lay quietly in the narrow bed, his head and shoulder bandaged. One of the monks had given him a shave that morning. Without his usual dark stubble, Hubert looked very pale. Catherine hurried over and knelt by the bed, taking his hand.

"Don't worry, *ma chère*," he told her. "I'm fine, truly. I only fell from my horse, nothing more. They shouldn't have sent for you."

"Yes, they should," Catherine told him. "It isn't right to leave you in the care of strangers. Is there anything you need? What have they fed you? Can you sit up yet?"

Hubert gave her hand a squeeze. He looked at Agnes, sitting stiffly on a stool on the other side of the bed. She hadn't touched him. She kept her eyes fixed on the crucifix over the door to the cloister.

"I have been well fed," he told them. "I can sit up, but my head spins when I try, so they've advised me to lie still for another day or two. The only thing I need is the love of my children."

Agnes wouldn't meet his eyes. Hubert reached out for her. She didn't take his hand, but neither did she move away. Guillaume watched her with undisguised curiosity.

"Agnes," he said, "whatever it is, it can't be worth abandoning the honor and affection you owe your father, can it?"

He clearly wanted an answer. Catherine held her breath. Hubert let his hand drop. He closed his eyes.

Agnes sat as unmoving as the statues at Saint-Denis. She appeared as unmovable. At last, she took a deep breath and looked up at Guillaume.

"I know my duty," she said. "But nowhere have I heard that affection must accompany it. I was not taught dialectic or knightly codes, only the things proper to a woman of our class. You and Catherine may lecture me from your superior education, but I shall follow the teaching of our mother."

Finally, she took Hubert's hand. His eyes flew open in hope, but he found none in her face.

"I have no wish to shame or dishonor you," she said. "Or our family. I intend to obey the commandment. Does that satisfy you?"

It didn't, but Hubert slowly moved his head, wincing as he jarred his hurt shoulder.

Agnes released his hand and got up. "Guillaume, where have you arranged for us to stay?" she asked. "I didn't have time to have a bed dismantled and brought with us."

"There is a section of the hostel for women," Guillaume told her. "I'll show you the way. Catherine?"

Catherine didn't move. "I'll stay with Father until you return," she told them. "I know I'm not very dutiful, but I can do this for love."

The look Agnes gave her was harder than a blow, but Catherine didn't care anymore. Agnes's holy indignation was irritating her beyond sympathy.

When the room was empty, she leaned over and kissed Hubert on the cheek.

"Uncle Eliazar and Aunt Johannah send their love and concern," she whispered. "Solomon came with us and will be happy to do any errands you may have. Are you sure you're all right?"

Hubert smiled at her, then sniffed. "You look so like your grand-mother," he said. "It breaks my heart that you never knew her. Now, don't worry. I'm fine. I was very lucky that those thieves were inept."

"Father, you are certain they were thieves?" Catherine asked. "This attack had nothing to do with what is happening in Paris, did it?"

"It would be foolish to assume so," Hubert said, after considera-tion. "It does bother me that the men Guillaume hired to protect me let themselves be taken off guard, but the road is normally safe enough. They had no reason to expect an attack in daylight."

"I suppose," Catherine said. "It was very lax of them, all the same."

Hubert smiled. "Of Jehan, most of all," he said. "I don't think we'll be hearing any more about his seeking a bride from my house-hold."

"Jehan! He was there? No one told us," Catherine said.

"That's not all." Hubert told the tale of his own questionable heroism with some relish. Catherine did her best not to laugh.

"Yes, that should end Jehan's attractiveness as far as Agnes is con-cerned," she said. "She told me once that she only wanted a man who could protect what was his. A man who needs to be rescued by her father . . . I can almost pity him."

"You would, if you saw him," Hubert said. "He came last night to beg my pardon. He looked like a man waiting to know the nature of his torment in Hell. I promised him that I wouldn't boast of his dis-grace. You mustn't do so, either."

"No, I won't," Catherine promised. "At least, I'll try not to. But I must tell Edgar. He's suffered more than once from Jehan's scorn. Poor Agnes, where will she look for a husband now?"

Later that evening, Solomon stretched his legs contentedly before the fire in Fantin's hut by the river. It was only one room, and the hearth was made from packed clay, but here he could relax, knowing he was welcome. Still, it must be a hard life for the old man, who had made a good living buying wine and catching fish for the nuns before Suger had driven the women out and replaced them with his monks.

"Why do you stay?" Solomon asked. "You have family in Melun and Paris. They would take you in."

Fantin picked up the dinner bowl and the cups, wiped them out and put them on the shelf over his one clothes chest. He looked around, seeming to take inventory of his possessions.

"It must appear a poor place to you," he admitted, "after the grand homes of Paris. But I need little. My only sorrow is that I have no way to study the Law here, no one to pray with."

"A good reason to move to a place where there are brethren," Solomon said.

"Ah, but then who would give you a safe bed and a fish that is clean?" Fantin asked. "Who would *you* recite morning and evening prayers with?"

Solomon wiggled uncomfortably. His daily prayers generally consisted of a mumbled acknowledgment that he still trusted in the God of Israel. And as for food, it was better that neither Fantin nor Aunt Johannah ever found out the composition of the meals he had consumed on his travels. All the same . . .

"I'm grateful to you and glad you're here," Solomon admitted. "It's good to be able to sleep without wondering which of the other people in the room might want to slit my throat."

He took back his cup. Fantin still had access to some remarkable wine, from the vineyards of Abraham of Paris, he guessed.

"So far, I haven't been threatened," Fantin assured him. "The Christians seem to find me a curiosity and Abbot Suger considers me under his protection, along with the families of Saint-Denis. The mayor of Argenteuil is a nephew of his, so the abbot's wishes are honored. And," he added with slight embarrassment, "I have friends here. I sometimes take a pitcher and have a game of tric-trac with Lazarus, the shoemaker. They named him that because, when he was born, he cried and then stopped breathing. They got him started somehow and he says that the whole thing frightened him so that he'll never stop again. He's the only man in town older than I am."

That reminded Solomon of something. "I'd forgotten how long you've lived in Argenteuil," he said. "You must have been here when Héloïse was prioress."

"And before that." Fantin smiled fondly. "I remember when she first came to the convent for schooling. Such a pretty, happy little girl. She'd climb trees and sit on the branches laughing at the poor old nun who had her in charge. She grew up too bright and beautiful to be hidden away from the world."

"Or perhaps that was the only way to keep her so." Solomon had learned a few things from Catherine.

"I haven't seen her since the monks came," Fantin said. "Ten, twelve years ago it was. That was after Abelard, of course. She was still beautiful but the sadness in her would break your heart. I always wondered what happened to her baby."

"Astrolabe?" Solomon had a hard time thinking of him as a baby. "He still lives mostly with his father's family in Le Pallet. But I saw him last year, when they condemned Abelard again. Astrolabe is a good man. I like him. He was very disappointed in the decision of the council."

"Ah, well, it was hard for him, I imagine," Fantin said. "To have his father shamed like that. But it does keep the Edomites from worrying us, when they go after their own."

Solomon could see the logic in that. He had never understood what the argument between Abelard and his accusers was about, anyway. It was difficult for him to become excited about the nature of a trinity he didn't believe in, just as he found it hard to share Edgar's passion for the bones of some dead Saxon priest.

The next morning Solomon went with Fantin to the dock on the off chance that someone had hired men from the town to attack Hubert.

"It doesn't seem likely, though," he said. "He was only bringing a wine shipment for the abbey. Hubert has made the trip a hundred times. He's well known. Who from here would bother him?"

"But if someone wanted to," Fantin replied, "they would have no trouble in finding him."

As they approached, they could hear the sounds of serious disputation. One man was standing on the wooden quai, the other in a small boat tied to the post at the end. The one in the boat seemed to be unhappy with the amount of the toll.

"There's nothing I can do about it," the man on the dock was saying. "All fees are set by the town and the abbey of Saint-Denis. It's my job to collect them. Would you have my family starve because I neglected my office?"

"If they look anything like you, starving would do 'em good," the man in the boat said. "I'll be fried in hot oil before I pay that; it's twice what it was last year."

"It's been a hard winter; we had to raise tolls to repair the dock and the road," the first man said.

Solomon stopped dead in the middle of the street. He grabbed Fantin's arm and pulled him behind the shelter of a garden hedge.

"That man!" he said. "The one collecting the tolls, who is he?"

"Gerard, mayor of Argenteuil," Fantin told him. "And if that poor fool in the boat thinks his saints will help him win, he can stop praying. Gerard holds the *tonlieu* from the abbot of Saint-Denis, who is also his uncle. He won't decrease it a sou."

"Saint John on a platter!" Solomon said, despite Fantin's reproving stare.

"You shouldn't swear by their saints," he cautioned. "It only makes them angry."

Solomon didn't care if he meant the Christians or their saints. He had to get back to see Catherine, get her to take a message to Hubert. He exhaled explosively. This was a true revelation and a wicked dilemma. It made him feel better to know that the peasant he had taken the grain and chalice from wasn't in danger of starvation, whatever he might tell people. But he didn't want to be the one to tell Abbot Suger that his nephew was trafficking in wares stolen from the church.

Even more so if it turned out that the abbot already knew.

Catherine woke to the warmth of a soft body pressed against her back. She snuggled into it, then opened her eyes with a start. That wasn't Edgar. Most definitely not. Where was she? Who was in her bed? She twisted around.

There lay Agnes, just as she had for all the years of their childhood, one golden braid still wrapped around her head, the other fallen loose, caught under her shoulder. She was sound asleep and looked as innocent as the angels in the frescoes at Notre Dame.

Her appearance in the bed was as amazing to Catherine as if she had been one of the angels themselves. She remembered quite clearly that Agnes had haughtily refused to even share a room with her and settled on a bench in the hall instead. For a sleep-sodden second, Catherine wondered if the person beside her was an incubus, come in the form of her sister to destroy her.

Agnes slowly opened her eyes. "Have I missed breakfast?" she mumbled.

Catherine decided it probably wasn't an incubus. "It's Wednesday in Lent, Agnes," she said. "Breakfast won't be until afternoon."

With a groan, Agnes burrowed into the blankets. Then she realized where she was. She sat bolt upright.

"What are you doing in my bed?" she asked.

It took some time, but Catherine finally convinced Agnes that she was the intruder.

"Oh, yes," she said, rubbing her head. "I was cold and the bench hard. I decided there was no reason to be uncomfortable because I was angry with you."

"And they say I'm the logician of the family," Catherine said.

"Well, there wasn't," Agnes said. "Now, I left my clothes in the bag in the hall. I can't get up until someone brings them to me."

Catherine reached for her shift and shoes. "We certainly don't want Sir Jehan finding you almost in a state of nature," she laughed. "I'll get your things."

"Jehan?" Agnes squeaked, looking around as if he might pop out from a cupboard. "I thought he had returned to Blois. What's he doing here?"

"Trying to heal his wounded pride, I would guess," Catherine told her. "Ask Father. Or better yet, ask your brave knight."

Gracious! her voices intruded. *You are becoming a most uncharitable, unforgiving person!*

Catherine sighed and admitted the fault, but she didn't go back and apologize. She was surprised to find that, like Agnes, she wasn't ready to reconcile, not yet.

Edgar didn't relish going back to a cold, empty room that night. Without Catherine in it the place reverted to a student hovel, like a thousand other drafty, noisy rooms in Paris. He'd lived in them for the past five years. It was only watching Catherine's delight in the freedom and privacy that made it tolerable. Well, perhaps simply having her with him was enough to make anything tolerable.

So he stayed longer at Bietrix's tavern than usual, staring into his beer mug and wishing he hadn't been so short with Catherine about her propensity for examining each fleck and lump in her food. It was true that the habit annoyed him, but still, it was much more entertaining than eating alone.

"Edgar? That you?"

Edgar looked up. "Maurice!" he said. "What are you doing out so late? Come, sit with me."

Maurice took the offered half of the bench, balancing his mug of fish soup. It was as full as Bietrix could make it. She had a soft spot for hungry clerics.

"I shouldn't be out at this hour," he admitted. "But I was sent on an errand. The lord gave me a coin for my trouble. I tried to refuse, but he insisted. He said that I was to get my dinner with it as I'd arrive too late to eat with the others."

"That isn't the same 'Syrian' lord you were telling us about, is it?" Edgar asked.

Maurice shook his head. "No, a Norman. One of the canons sent me with a message for him. I haven't seen that other man again. He must have returned to his own country."

Edgar was relieved to hear that. It would have ruined his half-built theory if it could be proved that the man Maurice had run into wasn't Natan.

"You didn't get any beer," he said. "Are you abstaining, or wasn't the coin enough for soup and drink?"

Maurice seemed embarrassed. "I have only the one cup," he said. "And I don't need anything more."

Edgar guessed that Maurice was either saving the rest of the money for another hungry time or, more likely, intended to give whatever he had left to the first beggar who held out his hand. He went over to the table where Bietrix watched over the barrel and the soup pot.

"Here's a quarter sou." He put the ragged bit of silver on the table. "I'd like the loan of a cup and as much beer and bread as that will buy."

Bietrix picked up the coin and laughed. "If that were any thinner, you could see the light through it," she said. "Here, if you're not too proud, you can have the loaf ends some lordling students left this afternoon. Already softened and soaked with a nice bit of pork fat. They didn't seem to mind it was the Lenten season."

Edgar looked over at Maurice, so thin one could almost see light shining through him. He could have used the fat.

"Don't play temptress, Bietrix," he said. "The usual flatbread and a cup of beer. We will try to keep the Lenten season, at least."

"Ah, that's why you've sent your wife away?" Bietrix asked as she filled the wooden cup to the rim. "Can't keep to the rules with her right there in the bed?"

This was closer to the mark than Edgar liked. He and Catherine had endured enough of that sort of abstinence during the last months of her pregnancy and the required forty days after. Since then they had been fairly lax in obeying the rules for proper time and place. He had worried about it, but Catherine had decided that it was better to heed the commandment to be fruitful and multiply while they were still young enough to do so. Edgar had needed little convincing.

"Illness in the family; she'll be back soon," he mumbled.

He took the bread and beer to the table and made Maurice finish it, despite his protest.

"Actually, I've been wondering something," Edgar said. "You might be able to help me."

"Anything," Maurice answered through the soup.

"You know I've been working with a metalsmith for the past few weeks," Edgar said. "But it worries me that my master is not attached to any of the guilds. I was curious, do the canons of Notre Dame have their own smithy, somewhere on the grounds?"

Maurice stopped eating long enough to screw up his face in thought. "No," he said at last. "I suppose there's no need. We can get anything necessary here in town. Who would want the smell right under the window of the cloister?"

"Yes, and most of the metalsmiths are on the Right Bank, over by the butchers and the tanneries and the other objectionable trades," Edgar said, mostly to himself.

"That's not too far to go," Maurice said.

He dipped the last of the bread in the last of the soup, delighted that it came out even.

"I must be back before Compline," he told Edgar, "so I'll take my leave now. Many thanks. I hardly gave you much company in return for your generosity."

"Give me a paternoster," Edgar suggested. "I need all the intercession I can get."

Maurice promised he would give the state of Edgar's soul earnest consideration during his prayers. He hurried off to do so at once.

Edgar remained at the table, staring into his beer, until Bietrix suggested that he either go home to his own bed or rent one from her, complete with companion. Edgar put on his cloak and left.

Where could that blasted Gaudry have his shop, then? As Edgar made his way through the narrow, twisting streets, he tried to imagine a place on the Île where the sharp distinctive smell would be unnoticed. The east end of the island was the cathedral and the bishop's property; the west end, the palace of the king. In the middle there were only a few blocks of shops, mostly cloth or other finished goods and the houses of some of the Jews. Most of the Jewish butchers and other businesses were on the Right Bank. Then there were a number of shabby buildings like Bietrix's that served as housing and classrooms for students and their masters as well as tending to other needs of those young men who were far away from home and family supervision. But Edgar could think of nothing that might mask the smoke and stench of the kiln. And he had just built a second one! Why hadn't anyone noticed?

Feeling his way through the dark passageways, Edgar reflected that he might indeed have been tricked into doing work for the devil himself. What if the forge and kiln weren't in the tunnels of the Île, but really part of the vast, unmappable regions of Hell?

He crossed himself with a shiver and prayed that Saint Aldhelm would keep him safe as he descended once again into the pit.

Thirteen

Argenteuil, Thursday, March 13, 1141 / 2, Nisan, 4901

Multa de acquisitis, plura de quibus ecclesiae ornamentis quae perdere timebamus, videlicet pede decurtatum calicem aureum et quaedam alia, ibidem configi fecimus.

Many of our acquisitions and more of those ornaments of the church that we feared to lose, for example a chalice of gold with an engraved foot and other such things, we ordered to be fastened down.
—Abbot Suger
De Aministratione, part XXXIII

$\mathcal{B}$ut why would the abbot's nephew be wandering about the countryside in the dark with a stolen chalice?" Catherine asked. "It can't have been the same man."

She thought it a reasonable statement. Solomon felt his honor was being challenged.

"Of course it was the same man!" he insisted. "I recognized the voice. He even used some of the same words. I'd like to see this underfed family of his. They seem to be his excuse for any outrage he commits."

"But the chalice he had wasn't taken from Saint-Denis," Catherine said. "We don't know for certain where it came from. It may not be the one taken from Salisbury. It may not even have been stolen at all."

"What do you mean, not stolen?" Solomon tried to remember not to shout but he felt Catherine was being purposely obtuse. "Perhaps Mayor Gerard bought it out of the tolls he's collected and was going to donate it to the priory and he put it in a bag of grain to keep it from being dented. Do you think because he's related to the abbot that he cannot sin?"

"Of course not!" Catherine tried not to shout back. "I'm not that credulous. You should know me better by now."

Solomon gathered up the reins of his anger. "Yes, I do know you, as you do me," he said more quietly. "So will you grant that I'm not mistaken about the voice?"

"Yes, I will," Catherine conceded. "However unlikely your story. You have a good memory for such things. And if it was Mayor Gerard you met on the road, then he must have acquired the chalice illicitly or he would have complained to the abbey at once that you had taken it and demanded that Abbot Suger lead the search for you himself."

"That was my thought," Solomon said. "Now, what do we do?"

They were sitting beneath an enormous oak tree not far from the

Seine but out of earshot of any buildings. Mindful of her father's recent experience, Catherine had checked the branches for lurking ruffians before she sat down.

"Do?" She thought. "First, you should go tell Baruch of this development. I'll talk with Father. Let them decide what to tell Suger. They have more experience with the abbot than we do. But I suspect they'll want something more in the way of proof before they bring an accusation like this before him."

"Yes, that's reasonable," Solomon said.

Catherine gaped at him. "You admit that?"

He held up a warning hand. "Don't mock me in this. It's a serious matter. A man has been murdered."

"And Gerard tried to murder you," Catherine said. "I don't forget that."

Solomon honestly had. "I was thinking of Natan," he said. "I can't help feeling that Gerard's theft is tied to his death."

"Now that I won't grant you," Catherine said. "That's a leap of logic with no intervening steps."

Then she started thinking. Perhaps the steps were there. Natan had tried to sell his pried-out pearls to the abbey. At almost the same time, Gerard was near the abbey, with his probably purloined chalice. Both objects might have been from the same hoard. And what of the things she had found in the cellar, the beads and metal strip? Could they have come from Salisbury as well? They seemed too humble for a rich cathedral, but she shouldn't leave them out.

The most important question was still whether Gerard and Natan had been working together. Catherine didn't know enough about either man to make a decision. There must be a way to find out more.

"But Natan was killed in Paris," she said.

"It took you half a day to ride from Paris," Solomon reminded her. "And if I were trying to smuggle goods from Normandy into France, Argenteuil would be a good place to take them from the river, especially if I were friends with the man who held the *tonlieu*."

The idea was becoming more plausible to Catherine.

"If we could only place Natan in Argenteuil in January, as well as at Saint-Denis," she said. "Did you ask Fantin?"

"Yes," Solomon said. "He knew Natan, but not well. Natan thought the hut was too humble for a man of his status. It's like him.

So Fantin can't be sure when he was here. He thinks Natan may have stopped by during the winter, but he isn't sure when or how many times he may have visited."

Catherine got up and brushed off her skirts to release her exasperation. There were too many things they didn't know. The problem was that she couldn't be sure if they were looking at one connected set of events or a dozen unrelated ones. Where had Gerard's chalice come from? Where did Natan get the pearls he tried to sell Prior Hervé? Were either of them involved in the theft of the arm of Saint Aldhelm from Philippe d'Harcourt, who was himself a thief? Most of all, who had killed Natan, and why? Was any of it related to the job Natan had done for Uncle Eliazar? Eliazar had implied that it was that work that had led to the knife attack on Edgar the year before and to Eliazar's own, nearly fatal, stabbing soon after.

And above all, how much danger was Edgar in at this very moment?

Solomon had been worrying, too.

"I think it's time for me to get back to Paris," he said. "Now that we know your father is recovering. Uncle Eliazar needs me more. I'll stop at Saint-Denis and tell Baruch what I've learned about Gerard."

Catherine was torn between her duty to her father and her concern for Edgar. And, she admitted, she didn't want to do anything that would cause Agnes to feel more martyred than she did already. Returning to Paris while their father still required their care would only increase her sister's contempt.

They were walking back to the priory, both occupied with their own thoughts, when Solomon stopped and caught Catherine's arm.

"There he is," he said. "Gerard, the mayor of Argenteuil. There, over by the fence, talking with that priest. Have you seen him before? Don't stare, just look quickly."

Catherine did as they strolled by. "He doesn't look familiar," she said. "I'd never have taken him for a relative of Suger's. He's taller and much rounder." She took a second look. "That's odd. The priest Gerard is speaking with does remind me of the abbot. I wonder why?"

"A lot of clerics have 'nephews' all over the surrounding countryside," Solomon guessed. "Maybe the abbot was not so abstemious in his youth as he is now."

"Suger?" Catherine almost laughed. "Strewing bastards about the region? I don't believe it. He's too devoted to the reputation of Saint-Denis. He was an oblate there from childhood. He would never risk shaming the abbey. No, the priest is probably some more distant cousin. That must be why he seems familiar to me. Or perhaps I've seen him before, somewhere else."

She shook her head, releasing the worry. There were enough problems to deal with.

Hubert was sitting up when Catherine came in, clearly feeling better. "I think I could ride if someone gave me a hand up," he said. "I have too much to do to lie about all day. Also, I don't like to impose on the hospitality of the monks."

Catherine was doubtful. "You'll be too jostled by the gait, I'm sure. We could get Guillaume to send a cart."

"A cart!" Hubert was appalled. "Like a criminal? The only way I ride in a cart is inside a coffin."

Agnes entered in time to hear his last pronouncement. "You aren't going anywhere," she said. "I shall stay and nurse you until the infirmarian says you are fit. But, after that, I want you to arrange for me to go to Grandfather's."

Hubert fell back onto his pillow. "To Blois? Why go there? Your home is in Paris. I thought we had an agreement."

"It's obvious to me that you aren't able to keep your part of it," Agnes said. "You are too concerned with your trading and your other family to find me a suitable husband. Grandfather will see that I am properly taken care of. For all I know you'd marry me off to a Saracen, if it brought you profit."

"Agnes!" Catherine intervened. "Stop that. You're only making him feel worse. And you're doing it deliberately. Is that your idea of duty? You should know Father would never sell you into marriage. That's what the great lords do. We don't have to."

Agnes was relentless. "Father, can you deny that you'd marry me to another merchant if you thought the alliance would improve your business?"

Hubert closed his eyes. He should have taken Agnes with him, as well as Catherine, on his journeys, but Madeleine had wanted her home, especially after little Roger died. He should have, should have . . . too many things; but he hadn't and this was the result.

"My golden child," he said, "all I have ever wanted is your happiness and security. I don't deal in slaves, especially within my own family. If you think your mother's father can do better for you than I, by all means, go. Ask your brother to arrange an escort and send a messenger to Blois so that they will be expecting you."

He turned his face away from them. Catherine put a hand out to Agnes. Her sister pushed her away angrily.

"This is your fault," she sobbed. "All of it. You ran away from the convent. You abandoned God. Everything started to go wrong from then. Now we're all being punished! I hate you!"

She stormed out.

Catherine should have been used to these outbursts by now, but she simply couldn't believe that the Agnes she loved could have changed so completely.

She believes that you are the one who has changed, her voices reminded her.

"But I can't go back now," Catherine told them. "It's too late."

"Of course it is, Catherine," Hubert answered her. "We can only go forward. I learned that years ago. I only wish I knew which direction forward is."

"I can't leave you here in her care," Catherine said. "She'll only cause you greater suffering."

"I think you should," Hubert answered. "First of all, you have a duty to your husband, which comes before what you owe me. Secondly, Agnes may be more amenable to reason if you aren't here. She's confused and resentful—and with some reason."

"I know, Father," Catherine admitted.

"Also, I need you in Paris to help defend your uncle," Hubert continued. "From what Solomon said, the elders fear his actions may have endangered the community. They'll excommunicate him if it proves true."

"Is that the *herem?*" Catherine asked.

"It comes under that term, although there are forms of the *herem* that are more like a ban," Hubert said. "But in this case Eliazar would be denied the use of the synagogue and the protection of the community. He might be physically driven out and a letter sent to the other communities, asking that he not be permitted to live among them."

"They would drive him from his home?" Catherine was horrified.

"If they felt there were good reason," Hubert said. "So you see, you must return. There has to be a way to uncover this secret of his."

"And what if he has done something deserving of excommunication?"

"Then I will take him into my home," Hubert said. "He's my brother and the ties of family are stronger than those of any community. It's no use, Catherine. Forgive me. In my heart, I am still a Jew. I cannot abandon Eliazar, no matter what."

Catherine understood the seriousness of what he proposed. By admitting his apostasy to the world, Hubert would lose his standing in the Christian community, his membership in the merchants' guild, perhaps his life. Christian society was hard on those who left the Faith. Even if Abbot Suger were willing to protect him, Hubert might well be killed by outraged neighbors. Catherine wasn't ready for a future that desolate.

"I can forgive you, Father," she said. "Although I will pray that you may one day receive the grace of true belief. You mustn't risk your own safety. Give Edgar and me a little more time to discover the truth. I love you and I love Uncle Eliazar and Aunt Johannah and even Solomon. None of you must be hurt, not if I can help it. If there is a way out of this thicket, I promise we will find it."

Edgar and John were sitting at the table in his room, hunched over a crude map Edgar had made on a wax tablet.

"I know all the turns now," Edgar said. "And roughly the distance between each one. What I'm not certain of is the angle of each corner. I turn left, but I don't think it's ever at a right angle. Somewhere between sixty and one hundred degrees, I'd say. That's not good enough."

"Stop beating yourself," John suggested. "And let's see what we can make of this. Here's the entrance to your tunnel in the old crypt of Saint Étienne." He pointed to an X in the wax.

"Yes, and from there I'm sure we go under the parvis of Notre Dame, but not all the way to the church," Edgar said. "For one thing, the foundations there are too deep. They block off all of the old tunnels. Then there must be a left turn, or we'd be in the river. The next is a right, which is why I thought we were under the cloister, but that passage runs a long way and then there's another left. That's to the new workshop. For the old one, we went right again."

John lightly scratched buildings over Edgar's path. "What about the other route, from the river?" he asked.

Edgar slapped his forehead. "*Dwolenlic ceorl!*" he berated himself. "I'm not thinking clearly. Of course, we could triangulate on that."

He drew a few more lines from the other side of the island. John studied them approvingly.

"So, that's not too bad," he said. "The workshop appears to be somewhere between the church of Saint-Pierre au Boeuf and the cloister wall."

"There are a hundred buildings there, mostly made up of student rooms and shops," Edgar said. "There aren't any artisans of any sort, at least not the sort that would be creating a stench strong enough to cover that of a forge. I must be wrong."

John disagreed. "You've been taking that route every day for two weeks now. You couldn't be that far off. We're missing something obvious, that's all. Tomorrow, I'll take this and follow it as best I can. I may arrive at a true revelation."

Edgar laughed. "John, just keep your eyes open and don't expect any visions. You aren't the type."

"I've been told that before." John grinned. "Did I ever tell you about my first master?"

"Abelard, wasn't it?" Edgar said.

"No, the very first, an old priest near Salisbury," John said. "I was sent to him for reading and writing, basic computation, that was all. I was just a boy. It wasn't until later that I realized that the old man was a magician, an alchemist, perhaps."

"Really?" Edgar's eyes widened. He suspected that John was playing with him. "And what did this old necromancer cleric teach you?"

"Reading, writing, basic computation," John answered. "But every afternoon, he would set me at a table and bid me stare into this great glass full of water and then ask me what I saw."

"And you saw . . . what?" Edgar prompted.

"My own face turned upside down," John laughed. "And the room behind me distorted as a curved glass will make it seem. That was all."

"I should have known," Edgar said. "You are the most literal-minded man I've ever met. So you never learned magic?"

"No," John said ruefully. "Not a whiff. I had fun making faces in the glass, but my master threw me out and told my father I had no talent for learning. Soon thereafter I began my studies at the cathedral school. They were more meaty, but not nearly as diverting."

"I think you made the right decision," Edgar said. "You wouldn't look dignified, somehow, in a flowing robe all tattered from acid, with your sleeves tied full of mandrake root and frog's toes."

"That's true, Edgar." John smirked. "That's more your style."

Edgar had to admit that his clothing had suffered from his recent work. "Catherine has offered to mend them for me," he told John. "But she does convent sewing and keeps wanting to stitch little rabbits and birds across my ass. I don't think I'm strong enough to endure what Gaudry would say to that, not to mention my friends."

"When will she be back?" John asked.

"Soon, I hope," Edgar said. "She sent a message that her father was healing. She also said she's discovered something in Argenteuil that might help us here."

"Something about Saint Aldhelm?"

"I don't know. She wouldn't have told a messenger that," Edgar said. "I wish she'd hurry back so we can hear it all."

"Of course," John said as he rose to leave. "I can't imagine any other reason for you to want her to return."

"Oh, there is," Edgar said, smiling. "Catherine is better than either of us at geometry. She could triangulate the map."

Catherine was doing her best to return to Paris. For a place that did so much trade with the city, it was odd that so few people were going that way from Argenteuil in the next few days. There were barges being hauled upriver and she might have found passage on one of those, but the Seine meandered so that it took three times as long to take that route, especially fighting the spring current.

Solomon could take her as far as Saint-Denis, but he planned to spend the Sabbath with Baruch. That would mean she would lose a day and have to travel on Sunday. It appeared that the only person in the world who was heading back to Paris was the one she most dreaded traveling with.

He wasn't any more thrilled than she.

"But this is a way to redeem yourself, Jehan," Hubert assured him when he offered Jehan the assignment. "I'm trusting you with my elder daughter's safety. That's a sign of my continued faith. You can tell Count Thibault so. It won't delay you. She's packing her things now. You can leave at once."

Jehan stood by the bed, twisting his gloves with his strong fingers until the leather squeaked. Agnes sat next to her father, preferring to look out the window than at either of them. It occurred to Hubert that this mission might well be the damnation Jehan had feared.

"Will you take Catherine to Paris?" He repeated.

Jehan tried in vain to get Agnes to look at him. What did she want him to do? Was there any way he could win back her respect?

"Very well," he said at last. "Whom do I deliver her to?"

"I imagine she'll tell you," Hubert said. "She's staying near Saint-Germain l'Auxerrois. One thing," he added firmly. "Whatever she says, don't leave her at Bietrix's on the Île."

Jehan knew the tavern well, and the back room. It seemed to him a perfect place to leave Catherine. She would deserve whatever might happen to her there. However, he promised reluctantly that he would deliver Catherine to her husband.

Outside the priory, Jehan indulged in some vicious cursing before he was able to feel up to the task.

So now he and Catherine were riding down the crowded rue Saint-Denis in bright, springlike weather, surrounded by merchants, pilgrims, soldiers, peasants and occasional noblemen. The only danger they were in was from each other.

Catherine persuaded herself later that she had been unduly tempted by a loose demon of the lower ether. Why else would she have given in to the impulse to taunt Jehan? She set herself a week on bread and water to atone. Her contrition was real enough. Unfortunately, it came too late.

"Have you heard that Agnes is going to Grandfather's keep in Blois?" she asked Jehan. Since she was riding behind him, her face pressed against his mailcoat, there was no way he could pretend not to hear her.

"To Raoul?" he replied. "I didn't know the old bastard was still alive."

"Very much so," Catherine told him. "Despite the earnest prayers of half the family."

She waited, but Jehan seemed content with his own thoughts. Later she realized she had failed her second spiritual test. She ought to have stopped talking then.

"Grandfather still has enough connections in Blois and Anjou to find Agnes a powerful husband," she went on. Her face was tilted up to Jehan's shoulder to be sure every word was clear. She could feel his muscles tensing. "He'll find her someone with land of his own, a castle, perhaps a family monastery she can be patroness to." Catherine shoved the words at him like a cattle goad. "She needs a man who can protect her, take care of her. Someone she can be proud of."

He whipped around and pushed her so quickly that she was on the ground before she realized what was happening. As she sat in the road, staring stupidly up at him, Jehan threw her bag down on the ground beside her.

"You *meseleuse bordelere!*" he shouted. "*Engineuse! Jael! Filles d'Aversier!* You cursed woman! I'll not go another step with you. Not if your father paid me in Venetian gold! Find your own way home. I hope you have your throat cut! You deserve worse, you *lice tornadereuse!* May you be raped a hundred times by leprous Saracens!"

Catherine was too stupefied to answer.

A priest passing by with a basket of onions stopped and tapped Jehan's leg.

"My lord," he began, "whatever this woman has done, you have no right to admonish her on a public road in this manner. As the Apostle says—"

"Stay out of this!" Jehan yelled, kicking him away.

The onions spilled out across the road and the priest scurried after them. There was an angry shout and a screech of wheels.

Jehan didn't bother to see what had happened. Fury had overcome a lifetime of training. Throwing a last oath at Catherine, he set off down the road at a trot, causing those on foot to jump quickly aside to avoid being run down.

Catherine still sat where she had landed in the middle of the road. She felt soaked by invective, half expecting her clothes to be drenched in obscenities. How could he have done such a thing? He had sworn to protect her. Jehan must have gone mad!

Someone took her by the elbow gently.

"Are you all right, my dear?" It was the priest. He was holding his empty basket in one hand.

"I think so. Thank you for trying to help," Catherine said. She noticed the basket. "Oh, he spilled your load, as well! I'm so sorry! Let me help you pick them up."

The old man shook his head. "There's nothing to pick up. The other travelers got them all."

"Then I must give you something to recompense you for your loss." Catherine fumbled about under her cloak for the bag tied around her neck. "I have only a coin or two, but you're welcome to them."

"Since the onions were to give to the poor of my parish, I will accept them gratefully," the priest said.

He leaned over to help Catherine to rise. As she did so, she cried out in sudden pain. "Oh, Saint Barnabas's blistered bunions! I've sprained my ankle."

For the first time, the consequences of her impulse to torment another were made manifest to her. Apart from shock at Jehan's storm of oaths and horror at his betrayal of his duty, she hadn't been much concerned when he left her. It was bright daylight and only another three or four miles to Paris on a crowded road. She could have walked it easily. She had done it often before. Now, she had no idea what was to become of her.

Ahem, her voices said smugly. *May we remind you what a haughty spirit goes before?*

"No, you may not" Catherine muttered.

The priest let go her arm.

"Oh, forgive me, sir," she said. "I didn't mean you. Could you help me over to the side of the road? I believe that this man wants to get his cart through."

She hadn't actually seen the cart, just the ox pulling it. It stood peacefully blocking the road, chewing on an onion. The carter held another onion by the stalk and was also munching contentedly. Neither appeared that eager to continue their journey.

As Catherine hobbled out of the way, the man driving the cart called out to her. "Did that *avoutre* toss you out without paying?"

Catherine pulled herself up and started to make a scathing reply to this when she realized that the man wasn't being insulting, but concerned. His indignation was for a knight who would take something without paying for it, not for a woman who would sell. Still, she felt obliged to correct the carter's misapprehension.

"The man had agreed to take me home to my husband," she explained. "But he changed his mind," she ended lamely.

The man took another bite of onion. "Just as I thought," he said. "They always do."

Catherine sat on a Roman milestone and tried pulling off her boot without screaming. The priest pulled at the heel for her and it finally came off. The ankle was swollen to the size of a cabbage. The only thing she could think of to wrap it with was her woolen stocking. She managed to peel it off without showing too much leg, for she was acutely aware that the carter hadn't yet moved but was watching her with the same steady gaze as his ox.

"There's no room on the seat," he said, when she had tied the stocking as securely as possible. "But if you want, you can ride in the back with the barrels. I'm going to my mother's house on the Île."

The old priest was obviously torn between getting back to his church and making sure that none of Jehan's wishes for Catherine's future came true.

"Perhaps I could come with you and then walk back," he suggested.

Catherine bit her lip. She would be glad of his moral protection but didn't want to inconvenience him any more than she already had. She looked at the carter.

He was an extremely solid man. Large, broad-shouldered, thick-necked, stolid. She wondered if he and the ox were related.

"Where on the Île are you going?" she asked.

"Near Saint-Christophe," he told her. "My mother keeps a tavern there. My brother makes the beer for her. I take the extra to Auberville and La Villette to sell. I still have half a barrel left. You can have a cup."

Hope was beginning to grow in Catherine. "Your mother wouldn't be named Bietrix, would she?"

The man blinked. "Yes! Are you one of her girls? I don't remember you."

"No, but I know her," Catherine explained. "She makes a wonderful bean and pigeon soup. If you take me there, my husband will come for me. He'll pay you for your trouble."

The carter didn't seem to care either way. Catherine decided to take the chance.

She thanked the priest, who continued his journey with a look of relief. When the man climbed down to lift her into the cart, Catherine had brief second thoughts but kept her mind on being with Edgar again before evening. At the same time she tried to think of a saint particularly interested in protecting women who traveled alone. The only one she could think of was the Magdalen, although her early life was the example Catherine was at the moment trying to avoid.

"Please, Saint Mary," she prayed. "Get me home safely and I promise I'll go to Vézeley and light a candle at your tomb. I beg you, just get me home!"

She settled into the cart and tried not to let the empty barrels roll toward her. The one she was leaning her back against sloshed. She remembered the man's offer. At first, thinking of the usual quality of the beer at Bietrix's, she thought not. But she was thirsty, and her ankle hurt tremendously. So she untied her cup from her belt, found the spigot and managed to fill it without spilling much.

She drank it, flecks and all. This batch used a different flavoring. It was slightly bitter, but not bad.

"Excuse me?" She poked at the carter. "Thank you for the beer, and the help. I'm sorry, I don't know your name."

"Goliath," the man said. "At least, that's what everyone calls me. My Christian name doesn't fit anymore."

"Thank you, Goliath."

As Catherine settled back, it occurred to her that there were two things her father would be even more angry about than Jehan's behavior. She was traveling in a cart and she was going to Bietrix's tavern.

Catherine sighed. Sometimes one must simply bow to fate.

Lulled by the steady pace of the ox and the effects of the beer, Catherine relaxed and went to sleep.

The sun was setting when the placid ox finally pulled the cart past the Grande Chastelet and across the bridge to the Île. The cart was too wide for most of the streets, even now when the vendor's stalls had been shut for the night. Goliath had to take a circuitous route, past the palace, across to the rue de la Calanore, then across the courtyard between the churches of Saint-Christophe and Saint-Étienne and then, very carefully, down the narrow alleyway behind the tavern.

Goliath leaned over to be sure Catherine was still there. "I need to unload the barrels for my brother but I'll take you first," he told her, climbing into the back of the cart. "We'll have to go through the brewery, either that or the brothel."

Catherine was too tired and her ankle was throbbing too much to care which. She let Goliath pick her up and carry her in through the back gate of the building. The garden was stacked high on one side with the barrels. The smell of yeast was overpowering. Goliath kicked at the door. To Catherine's astonishment, it was opened by Lucia.

"Lady Catherine!" she exclaimed. "Goliath! Put that woman down this minute!"

"Lady?" Goliath struggled to understand this. "You mean she isn't a whore?"

"He can't put me down, yet, Lucia," Catherine said at the same time. "I've hurt my foot and can't walk. Your brother very kindly brought me home."

"I'm sure that explains everything," Lucia said.

She asked no more questions, though, but led them through the brewing room and opened the door to the tavern so that Goliath could take Catherine in.

On Saturday evening the room was packed with people, both men and women, local tradespeople as well as the students. As she had hoped, Catherine saw Edgar at the end of the table by the window, sitting with John and Andrew, the Norman canon from Saint-Victor.

"You can put me down now," she told Goliath. "That's my husband over there."

But to Goliath, a delivery meant to the owner, so he pushed his way across the room, Catherine dangling from his arms, until he stood next to Edgar's table.

Edgar looked up. He closed his eyes, opened them again. She was still there. John started laughing. Catherine smiled.

"*Diex te saut*, Edgar," she said. "I'm back."

Fourteen

Paris, Gaudry's workshop, the feast of Saint Joseph, carpenter and loyal husband, Wednesday, March 19, 1141 / 9, Nisan, 4901

Mens humilis, studium querendi, vita quieta,
Scrutinium tacitum, paupertas, terra aliena
Haec reserare solent multis obscura legendo.

A humble mind, a questioning desire, a quiet life
Silent investigation, poverty, a strange land.
These will resolve the problems of many.
—Bernard of Chartres

*E*dgar had found a block of yew, split it, smoothed it, hollowed it out with slow care, using chisels of different sizes to make the curves. He spent so much time shaping the interior that Gaudry complained.

"If you can't work faster than that, I'm going to pay you by the piece," he threatened. "It's only the inside of a box. There's no point in smoothing and oiling it. No one will see, anyway."

"I thought it was for a reliquary," Edgar said.

"That's what I was told," Gaudry answered.

"Then this is where the bones of the saint will rest." Edgar continued rubbing at the wood with a cloth dipped in oil. "It would dishonor him if I allowed his remains to lie in a roughly hewn box."

Gaudry thought about that for a moment. "Yes," he said finally. "That's true. Whatever those others are plotting, it's our duty to create something that we can display with pride on the Day of Judgment. Very well, take all the time you need, Edgar. You'll still be paid by the day. But don't let me catch you taking advantage of my pious nature, or I'll knock your teeth out."

Edgar nodded and returned to work, pleased that Gaudry had included him in the company of those who honored the Lord with the work of their hands. As each day passed he felt less like a foreign lordling come to Paris for an education and more like a member of another band entirely, one that was as fiercely proud as his own. It grieved him that he could never truly call himself part of that group. Gaudry's grudging praise gratified him more than any he had ever received from the masters of the Paris schools.

Gaudry was busying himself fining the gold and pounding it into sheets the thickness of spring leaves. The men worked in silence for a time, except for Odo, who was sharpening the tools. He hummed the same two lines of a hymn over and over as he rotated the stone against the metal. This was punctuated by the rhythmic thud of Gaudry's hammer. For Edgar it was the closest to heaven that he ever expected to be. It was a shame to disturb such peace, but he knew he would have to.

He dipped the cloth in the oil again. "Others?" he said to Gaudry. "Do you mean the ones who ordered the reliquary? What sort of plotting could they be doing? I don't want my work used for sacrilege."

"Once we're paid for it, that's not our concern," Gaudry said.

But the rhythm of his mallet became more of a stutter. Finally, he put it down and leaned against the bench with a worried expression.

"The canon who ordered this told me our work was to replace a reliquary that had been damaged," he told Edgar. "His partner was supposed to bring it to me to repair. But the man never came and Odo heard he was found dead somewhere. Now this canon wants a whole new reliquary. I keep telling myself it's not my business. I take the payment and shut my eyes. But there's something about the whole matter that smells. I don't mind deceiving the bishop, the pope even, but I don't want to offend the holy saints. There's no telling what could happen. They take their revenge in the hereafter as well as the here."

Edgar was astonished. It was the most Gaudry had said to him in the whole time he'd been there. The smith must be more unsettled than he had pretended to be concerning the nature of their task.

"Who is this canon who gave you the job?" Edgar asked. "Do you know what church he's from? Is he an agent of Bishop Stephen?"

"He never said where he was from," Gaudry admitted. "I figured Notre Dame, because it's so close. But he might be from Saint-Victor, or even farther. He wouldn't give me his name. I only saw him once and he stayed in the shadow as much as he could. He was thin and of middling height, like a thousand other men. He seemed nothing more than a minor cleric, a bit timid, even. I thought he might have been entrusted with the relic, accidently broken the case and be wanting to have it repaired before the bishop noticed."

"But you don't believe that anymore now that we're crafting an entire new reliquary," Edgar said.

"No, and not now that the other man is dead," Gaudry said. "I saw him several times. An oily minor lord, looked from the south, though he spoke good French. He brought us other things before the reliquary was mentioned, broken church vessels that he wanted reshaped or melted down altogether. He told me they weren't his, he was simply the courier for the churchmen."

"Did you believe him?"

"Yes," Gaudry answered with certainty. "He had the air of one doing a distasteful job as quickly as possible. He wasn't the one giving the orders. For all his fine dress and manner he didn't have the . . . I don't know, the lordliness, perhaps. You know how they look, like they know they'll always have food on the table and someone else to serve it. This man didn't have that. I thought he might have been forced into being the courier because of something he'd been caught in."

"Like a lady's bed?" Edgar smirked.

In the corner Odo chuckled. "I'd believe that of him; probably the real reason he's dead."

"Maybe," Gaudry said. "But I think it's more likely he tried to cheat his employers or threatened to go to the bishop about these 'repairs' of church property and had to be killed to keep him quiet."

"But you don't know who any of these men were?" Edgar asked. "You never asked for a name?"

"I work outside the guild," Gaudry said. "I don't give them my name, either."

Edgar returned to his work. The description matched. Both Maurice and Gaudry gave the same characteristics for the man who brought the goods to the smith. It sounded as if Natan had gone too far into the business of the Christians. Everyone said he had been greedy. Could he have been so foolish as to threaten the people he was working for? Or perhaps they had decided he was no longer of use to them. If he had been poisoned, then he may have eaten whatever it was thinking that he was among friends.

But what could he have eaten, and with whom? And which of the thousand canons living around Paris had told Gaudry to make a reliquary that could fit the arm of Saint Aldhelm? And how had they come by the arm at all? The unraveling of this knot was going as slowly as his carving.

Edgar gave up on identifying one canon in a city of clerics. His mind went back to how Natan could have been poisoned. How observant a Jew had he been? Solomon ate all sorts of things, except pork, although he preferred food made according to the Law. Eliazar and Johannah would only eat what was prepared in a Jewish home. But what of Natan? Edgar decided to ask Catherine to find out when he saw her tonight. It should make her happy to be given a task. Not being able to move about quickly seemed to be unbalancing her humors. After the consternation her arrival at the tavern had caused, her disposition had not been equable for the past few days. It was his duty as a husband to save her from melancholia.

Edgar was uncomfortably aware that it was also his duty to challenge Jehan for his behavior on the road. There would be a certain satisfaction in feeling his knuckles connect with the man's chin, but Edgar was too rational not to know that the next thing that would happen would be his own chin hitting the dirt. Knowing that in abandoning Catherine Jehan had destroyed his own hopes for any preferment in the future didn't make Edgar feel better. If he had been raised to fight as his brothers had, Edgar would have been duty-bound to challenge Jehan, to defeat him in open combat and strip him of all he possessed. That's what he should do, even now.

Edgar made an altogether too vicious jab at the wood, creating a dent. He was startled to realize that he had not cast aside all the attitudes of the nobility after all. Silently, he apologized to Saint Aldhelm for his temper, adding a prayer that Jehan might be afflicted with boils.

With Agnes and her maids gone and no one left at his home on the Grève, Hubert had suggested that Ullo stay with Eliazar. Johannah was delighted to have a child in the house and had a hard time remembering that he was Christian and only a visitor. He, in turn, found it a novel experience to be listened to and given sweets every time he showed his face in the kitchen. His only tasks, it seemed, were to fetch things for Lucia from the cellar and to take the donkey to Saint-Germain l'Auxerrois morning and evening so that Catherine could ride over.

That spring morning he was seated on a high stool at the kitchen worktable, happily cracking walnuts for a pudding while pretending they were Saracen heads. Catherine sat next to him, picking the seeds from dried fruit. Oddly enough, she was humming the same hymn as Odo, but she knew more than the first two lines.

"*Verbum bonum et suave, Personemus illud Ave, perquod Christi fit conclave, Virgo, mater, filia,"* she sang, and Ullo pronounced the words in tune although he didn't understand their meaning.

"I thought that was a song for Advent," Lucia said, coming in with a basket of fresh herbs, the first shoots of spring.

"We should only praise the Virgin in one season?" Catherine asked.

Lucia set down the basket and went to the cupboard for a wooden bowl and curved chopping knife to mince the herbs for a meat sauce. "Forgive me," she said. "I forgot I was speaking with an expert in doctrine, my lady."

Catherine opened her mouth to apologize, but stopped. That would be even more condescending than giving Lucia a lesson in religion.

Lucia gave no sign of caring whether Catherine apologized or not. She stripped the fresh leaves into the bowl and began chopping them. After a moment, she stopped and looked through what remained in the basket.

"*Avoi!*" she said. "Not enough chervil. Ullo, do you know what dried chervil looks like?"

"Of course," Ullo said.

Lucia rolled her eyes. Another arrogant petty lordling.

"Then go down in the cellar and get me three stalks from the dried bunches hanging from the ceiling," she said.

Ullo went happily. He couldn't reach the herb bundles without pushing the boxes to stand on. He would be Roland, caught in the pass, at the last minute climbing the rocks to sound his horn, just before death overcame him. Or maybe Godfrey of Boullion, scaling the walls of Antioch, just before death overcame *him*. Ullo was not at all bothered by the idea that Natan had stumbled into the cellar just before death overcame him.

"I hope you don't want those herbs immediately," Catherine said. "He can spend an afternoon down there."

"Just so I don't." Lucia shivered.

Catherine prodded at a recalcitrant plum pit. "Yes, I can understand how you feel," she said. "But I don't think Natan's spirit is lingering nearby."

"No," Lucia said, savagely ripping borage. "I'm sure you don't. You think he's roasting now in Hell, with imps making him swallow molten gold so that red-hot coins drop from his bottom. Don't be sympathetic to me. I've heard you all. 'Natan was a bad man. A bad Jew. He aped the Christian lords. He cheated and stole.' No one shed a tear for Natan!''

Catherine got up and limped to where Lucia stood. In her wrath, the maid was in danger of cutting off one of her own fingers with the knife. Catherine laid a hand over hers.

"Someone did," she said.

Lucia stopped the chopping. She looked directly at Catherine, her eyes wide and glistening. The pain hit Catherine as if it had been her own.

"You grabbed my shoulder when you learned who the body was," she reminded Lucia. "Your nails left marks in my skin. He wasn't a stranger to you."

Without moving, Lucia seemed to crumple from within. "No," she whispered. "I knew him."

Even though Catherine had guessed, she was startled by the depth of Lucia's grief. It was true. No one, not even Menahem, Natan's own nephew, could find a good word to say for him. Death could not change the fact that he was despised by all who had known him.

But if he had been so evil, how could Lucia love him? If he had been so heartless, then why did she weep?

And she did. Lucia was bent over, sobbing out her loss. There was nothing Catherine could do but hold her. The weight was too much on her good foot and the two of them sank to the floor, Lucia with her head in Catherine's lap, crying out the grief no one shared.

Catherine could think of nothing to do but sit and stroke her hair until the passion subsided. As Lucia quieted, Catherine leaned over her and asked softly, "Do you need help? Are you pregnant?"

Lucia almost laughed. "No. I wish to God I were. Then there'd be a piece of him left on the earth."

"Yes," Catherine said. "I understand that. I'm sorry, truly I am. Would it help to say that I intend to find out who killed him?"

Lucia pulled herself together and got up from the floor. She straightened her scarf and wiped her eyes. "No," she said. "It wouldn't." She held out a hand to help Catherine rise.

"Will you help me find out, all the same?" Catherine asked as she struggled to her feet.

"Yes," Lucia said. "I want someone to pay."

When Ullo returned, having also conquered Jerusalem with Godfrey's brother, King Baldwin, Catherine and Lucia were just where
he had left them, busy with their tasks.

There was another group of English students sharing their table that
night, so it wasn't until they were in bed that Catherine told Edgar
what she had found out from Lucia.

"She was in love with him?" Edgar found that hard to believe.

"Both Maurice and Gaudry assumed he was a Christian lord,"
Catherine reminded him. "He must have had a certain exotic
charm."

"But Lucia knew he was Jewish," Edgar said.

"That's true," Catherine said. "Of course, I knew you were English. Perhaps she thought she could convert him."

"You want me to turn French?" Edgar was horrified.

Catherine shook her head sadly. "I haven't a hope. Not with the
way you eat. Although, you know, listening to the others tonight, I
realized that you've almost lost your accent."

"I shall endeavor to regain it at once," he said firmly. "Now about
Natan. We know he worked with Christians. Was he the kind of
man who would ingratiate himself by eating their food?"

Catherine tried to remember what she had overheard. "I doubt
it," she said finally. "From what Solomon and Uncle Eliazar said, he
was very particular about his food. Unlike some people who don't
even stop to see what it is before they fill their mouths."

Edgar was stung. "I didn't know it bothered you."

Catherine laughed. "It doesn't. Well, not anymore. Actually, it's
rather satisfying to watch you shoveling food in with such enthusiasm. All that fuel has to be expended eventually."

She was awake enough to suggest how. But Edgar was still puz-
zling over how Natan could have been poisoned.

"It would have to be someone he trusted," Edgar said. "No, don't
stop. I can think about this while you do that."

"Then I must not be doing it properly," she answered.

They were quiet a moment.

"Someone could have bribed one of the Christian servants to put
something in Natan's dish," she suggested. "But that doesn't seem

very likely. It would have to be done at the table without anyone
noticing. We don't even know where Natan ate that night, do we?"
    Silence.
    "Do we?" she repeated. "Edgar, what do you think? Edgar? What
are you . . . Edgar!"
    She must have been doing it properly after all.

When Catherine arrived at her aunt's and uncle's on Thursday, she
was surprised to see Andrew, the canon from Saint-Victor, waiting
in the hallway.
    "I've met you, haven't I?" he asked. "With John in the street and
then the other night in a tavern. What are you doing here?"
    Catherine grappled for a plausible answer. She thought of none
and so decided to attack instead.
    "What are *you* doing here?" she asked.
    "Old Eliazar teaches me Hebrew and explains passages of the Pen-
tateuch in the original for me, remember?" he said. "Master Hugh,
may his soul now rejoice in heaven, instructed me to seek the truth
of the New Testament in the words of the Old."
    "I see," Catherine said. "I was also grieved to hear of Master
Hugh's death. I'm sure his erudition lives on in his students."
    Andrew studied her for signs of sarcasm. Catherine looked back
at him, her eyes wide, sincere and disturbingly blue. He blinked.
    "Are you also here to study Hebrew?" he asked more politely. "I
recall hearing that Abbess Héloïse was a student of the language."
    "Yes, she taught us some at the Paraclete," Catherine answered,
glad he had come up with an excuse on his own. "Eliazar's wife is
helping me so that I don't forget it."
    Andrew was honestly confused. "But you've left the convent.
What possible use could you have for Hebrew now?"
    "I don't know," Catherine answered. "But if an occasion arises, I
would not wish to be found wanting."
    What a tangle of lies and half-truths she was creating! She had
never progressed much in Hebrew beyond the *aleph bet* and that was
so that she could do accounts for her father using the letters as numbers. Solomon had taught her a few phrases and she had picked up a
little more from Johannah. Now Catherine wished she had taken the
time to learn. Héloïse would have taught her more, if she had asked.

Andrew was dubious. Then his face lit with understanding. "Oh, of course. I know why you've really come here. You don't need to be embarrassed. John told me that your families had disowned both you and Edgar. I can't blame them, considering your rash marriage, but in your situation, I might be forced to do the same."

"I beg your pardon?" Catherine had no idea what he was talking about.

At that moment Johannah entered the hall, followed by Lucia with a plate of cheese and cups of wine for Andrew and Eliazar.

"It's all right," the canon whispered. "I'll tell no one I saw you here." He followed Lucia up the stairs.

Johannah greeted Catherine with a hug. "What was that about?" she asked.

"I can't imagine," Catherine said. Then she realized. "Oh, of course!" She almost laughed. "That *stultus* thought I was here to pawn my jewelry to you, now that I've been cast out by my family to starve."

"He should have known I don't lend money," Johannah sniffed. "Though I'll say nothing against those who do. The Christians make it harder every year to survive any other way. Andrew's been coming here long enough and asked enough questions to realize that I don't need to do such work. But he can't see beyond his own beliefs. I liked his friend better."

"His friend?"

"There used to be two of them who would come each week for lessons," Johannah explained. "Brother Andrew and Brother Thomas. They were both good enough boys, for Christians, but Thomas was more open-minded in his questions. Andrew often refuses to look at the *peshat*, the simple meaning of the text. Everything for him has to somehow predict his Messiah. Although I think that Eliazar has managed to convince him of his error once or twice."

"That the Messiah has not yet appeared?" Catherine said, shocked.

"Of course not," Johannah said. "Nothing will convince him of that. Eliazar has only made him admit that sometimes your scholars see predictions of your Christ in the Torah that simply aren't there. But Thomas was different. He would listen and smile and ask intelligent questions. He was very respectful. For a while, he even came twice a week, once with Andrew and again on his own. But then, about a year ago, he stopped."

"What happened to him?" Catherine asked.

"I don't know," Johannah said. "Perhaps he went to another city, or home to his family. No one ever told me."

Something was worrying Catherine. There was a connection forming that she didn't want to make. Leaning on her aunt's arm, she went with her to the kitchen, where Lucia was scrubbing out all the cupboards in preparation for Passover.

"I have some bread that we won't use before the holiday," Johannah said. "It's in a bag on the table. Why don't you take it home with you?"

Catherine suspected that her aunt had bought too much on purpose but accepted the gift gratefully.

There was a clattering sound from the cellar and a cry. Lucia screamed and bumped her head on the inside of the cupboard. Catherine dropped the bag, scattering crumbs on the floor. Johannah sighed, knowing it would now have to be scrubbed again.

At the same time she rushed to the trapdoor, which was propped open. "Ullo!" she called. "Are you hurt?"

"They'll never take me alive!" a high defiant voice called back.

"Just don't destroy all our provisions in the heat of battle," she warned.

Johannah came back to the table, where Catherine sat laughing. Lucia was muttering curses under her breath. If even one of them came true, the defender of Jerusalem would suffer an ignominious end.

"Let the child play," Johannah said. "His young eyes will find the smallest bit of *chametz* whatever he pretends it is."

"The smallest bit of what?" Catherine asked.

"Leaven," Johannah told her. "There mustn't be a trace of it anywhere. We'll have the ritual hunt later, but I like to be certain. Of course, I simply told him to move all the boxes and sweep around the barrels, that we were cleaning for the holiday. I believe he thinks I mean Easter."

"Ullo's head is so full of *gestes* and legends that I doubt he notices where he really is or who we are," Catherine said. "Or else he takes your customs for granted. He's the son of a friend of Father's from Rouen."

"Ah, yes, the community there is fairly large," Johannah said. "Our ways might not be that strange to him."

The sound of battle clanked from below for a few more minutes. Then Ullo came back up the stairs, broom under one arm and the spoils of war in a basket hooked over the other. He handed the basket to Johannah with a bow.

"You're sure you got everything that was on the floor?" she asked. "Even in the corners?"

"I swear," Ullo said. "I held the lamp into the darkest shadows and the demons fled from me."

There was something about him, so innocent and certain. Catherine wanted to protect him, that he might never meet a demon he couldn't send running.

Johannah saw her look. She patted Catherine's hand.

"Put away your grief, child," she said. "You and Edgar will have many more children, I'm sure."

Catherine smiled and nodded. That was it, of course. As Edgar knew well, being immobile was bad for her. It was too easy to brood and fall into the sin of despair. What she hadn't told Edgar was that her melancholy was overlaid by mortal terror of enduring another birth like the last one. She shook herself. This was foolish. She had chosen her path: nettles, thorns and rocks. Now she had to walk it and there was no logic in complaining.

Johannah was digging through the basket for anything of value that might have been dropped by accident. Catherine leaned over in idle curiosity.

"What's this?" Johannah held up a torn piece of parchment. "There's writing on it. How odd. Not French. Is it Latin?"

She handed it to Catherine, who squinted to make out the smudged letters.

" 'Laurentius bonum opus operatus est, qui per signum crucis caecos illuminavit,' " she read. " 'Laurence performed a good deed, he who through the sign of the cross gave light to the blind.' It's an antiphon for the saint's feast, I think, perhaps from a breviary."

"How could a thing like that have come to be in our cellar?" Johannah wondered.

"I have no idea," Catherine said. "May I keep it?"

"Certainly," Johannah said. "It's of no use to me."

"Ullo," Catherine asked, "do you remember where this was?"

"Oh, yes," Ullo said. "It was caught on a crack between the stones of the fort."

Catherine sighed. "I'm not familiar with the geography, Ullo. Which fort?"

Ullo sighed back. "The boxes against the wall opposite the stairs," he said in disgust.

"Thank you, Ullo."

Catherine folded the bit of parchment carefully and tied it in her sleeve. She tried not to show her worry. That was the place where she had found the beads and bit of metal. Three things that seemed to have belonged to a Christian, all of them broken. They frightened her.

She had to find a way to make Uncle Eliazar tell her what had happened last year. But first she needed to know everything she could about what Natan had been doing and with whom.

"Lucia," she said, "would you like to eat with Edgar and me to-night? We're having bread and soup left from the jug we took back from your mother's last night. It's not much, but you're welcome."

"You've worked hard today," Johannah agreed. "If you wish it, you may leave when Catherine does. I'll take care of Eliazar and Ullo."

Lucia did not look delighted at the invitation, but responding to Catherine's pleading expression, she agreed.

They left soon after. Catherine was too obsessed with her new speculations to wait any longer.

So there had been another cleric, Thomas, who didn't come any-more. There were a dozen possible explanations for that. He may have become bored and given up the study or been given a new as-signment by his superiors. He may have gone home to care for his mother. Catherine could imagine many reasons for Thomas to have stopped visiting Eliazar.

But the bits she had found were just the sort that a poor canon might carry: beads and a prayer book or breviary with thin metal clasps listing the verses and responses for the daily Office through-out the year. But why would these shreds be in her uncle's cellar?

Catherine refused to believe the answer that tried to leap into her mind. She didn't want to think it. But she had been trained to take all information, organize it and form a logical conclusion. One can't ignore the facts simply because the answer isn't palatable. Catherine forced herself to list the questions.

What if Natan had not been the first person to die in the cellar?

What if someone had decided to dispose of a young canon of Saint-Victor and Natan knew about it?

What if that someone was her dear Uncle Eliazar?

Catherine flinched at the thought. *These are not conclusions*, she told herself, *merely propositions. But they must be considered.*

Catherine prayed that Lucia would prove her wrong.

Fifteen

That evening, Edgar and Catherine's room

Et quoniam magna ex parte huius libri explanationem quantum ad sentiarum summam spectat, secundum alios qui ab Hebreis sicut et nos litteralem sensum pentateuci edocti sunt nullis penitus mutatis supra posuimus, nunc littere quam illi indiscussam reliquerunt insistamus.

The explanation of this book is given for the most part without any changes, as far as the main idea is concerned, according to others who, like ourselves, have been taught the literal sense of the Pentateuch by the Jews. Now let us take up the letter which they have left undiscussed.

—Andrew of Saint-Victor
"Notes on Leviticus"

*A*lthough Lucia had agreed with reluctance to go home with Catherine, she settled in comfortably once they arrived. Catherine could tell that the small room with its crude furniture surprised her but, beyond a puzzled look, Lucia gave no indication that it wasn't what she had expected.

She helped Catherine heat the soup and arrange the bread ends on a platter. Not exactly a meal from Arthur's court, but when Edgar arrived with the lidded pitcher full of cider, it was more than adequate for three people.

Especially when one of them showed no inclination to eat.

Lucia emptied her cider bowl quickly but spent more time than Catherine did examining and stirring her soup. Edgar was finding it difficult to remain patient. Under the table Catherine took his hand. He squeezed it and forced himself to wait.

"I'll tell you what I know about Natan's business," Lucia said finally. "But I want you to use it to find the one who killed him, not to protect your own friends. You must swear this or I will say nothing."

She tore a corner off the bread and crumbled it into the soup. The bowl in front of her was already filled with a gelid mass of crumbs and broth that Edgar was tempted to save for plastering the cracks in the window frames.

"We need to find the truth," Edgar said. "Right now, there are people who think Eliazar arranged to have Natan poisoned. We don't believe it, but if we find that is what happened, we won't conceal it. I promise you that."

"I don't know that I can trust you," Lucia sighed. "But no one else seems to care at all."

She glared across the table at them both. Her glance fell to their clasped hands. Catherine let go. She felt as if she had stabbed the woman. Lucia wiped her eyes with her wrist and dug savagely at the soup with her spoon.

"Why does Natan's death matter to you?" she asked. "Either of you? What difference does it make if some greasy Jewish trader is murdered? The only person I've heard of who has any interest is that nephew of his. And he only cares because he thinks Natan left a hidden legacy somewhere."

"Could he have?" Edgar asked. "Not that it's important to us, of course. We have no claim on it. But Catherine says Natan was hunting for something when he died. Perhaps he had put treasure in the cellar that he wanted you to have."

"Me?" Lucia seemed surprised, then laughed. "He often said that one day he would drape me in jewels and silk, but that's the sort of thing men always say when they want to get you into bed."

"Did you believe him anyway?" Catherine asked.

Lucia looked down at the soggy bread. She took her spoon out. "He gave me presents from time to time, a bracelet, sweets, a scallop from Saint-Jacques. I always wondered how he came by that. They were enough for me. I don't trade myself for gold."

Edgar understood from Catherine that they would have to be very careful or Lucia would tell them nothing. But he found it difficult not to be impatient. It embarrassed him to hear the tender details of her encounters with Natan.

Catherine knew that Lucia had to talk about those first. Before the world she had to pretend he meant nothing to her. Catherine could only guess how much that hurt. This was Lucia's only chance to grieve with others and part of her comfort was in telling them what he had been to her. Edgar was sitting on the stool with the uneven leg and he was rocking it with an emphasis that was a clear signal to Catherine of his distaste for further teary memories.

"Edgar," she said, "I don't think we have enough coals to last the night. Could you see if the weaver has extra to lend? And then perhaps you could refill the cider pitcher?"

He got up with such alacrity that Lucia was impressed by his devotion. As Catherine tied his cloak for him, he bent and whispered in her ear, "How long should I be? I owe you, *carissima*."

"Not over an hour," she answered. "Don't worry. You'll pay." She went back to Lucia. "Now," she said. "Tell me all about Natan. Did you meet him when he came to Un . . . to Eliazar's?"

Lucia shook her head. "I met him a little before then. He came to the tavern sometimes. I help Mother in the evenings, especially on feast days when business is good. He would have a mug or two and talk with a few people he knew. I think he was a friend of my brother, Goliath. Natan may have given Goliath the loan to buy his own cart a few years ago. I'm not certain. It's not a thing men talk about."

"That's not usually a basis for friendship," Catherine said. "More resentment at having to pay the interest."

"I don't know," Lucia said. "Goliath seemed happy with it, said Natan was a good man, for his kind. Samson told him he was addle-brained to trust a Jew." She laughed. "Goliath told him it was addle-brained to trust anyone, that he had good reason to know Natan wouldn't cheat him."

Catherine shelved that statement along with others that made no sense in this matter. She was sure that if Natan had given Goliath a loan at good rates, he must have had a hidden reason. Was it Lucia? Was that what Goliath meant?

"Had Natan, um, noticed you by then?" she asked.

"I don't think so," she said. "Men generally 'notice' me when they think I work in the back. Mother lets Jews drink in the tavern, if they want, but she won't have them in the brothel. She's afraid the priests will complain at having to use women who've been touched by infidels and she doesn't want to lose such regular customers. So Natan never even looked at me." She smiled. "Or so I thought."

"When did you start working for Johannah?" Catherine asked.

"A little over a year ago," Lucia answered. "No. Longer. I started just after Michaelmas, so it must be a year and a half."

"Was Natan a frequent guest there? Is that how you got to know him?"

"Not at first." Lucia crinkled her face in an effort to remember. "As far as I know, he came to dinner for the first time the following winter, sometime after Ash Wednesday. I think he had been to see Eliazar a few times before that."

Catherine held her breath. "Do you know what sort of business he and Eliazar were doing?"

Lucia shook her head and Catherine exhaled in disappointment.

"It seemed to be a deep secret, but I never understood why," Lucia said. "All Natan did was take some worn clothes and a few other things to sell. Goliath took him to Argenteuil with the beer cart one day and he got rid of the things there. Natan told me later that he'd never do anything like that again unless the return was much greater."

"Old clothes?" Catherine repeated.

"Yes. I never saw them, but Natan said that he couldn't sell them for much. He thought Eliazar was a fool."

"Did he say why?" Catherine asked.

"He said . . . Wait, let me think." Lucia rubbed her forehead.

Catherine wished Edgar would return with the cider. It might help Lucia's memory.

"Oh, yes," Lucia said. "He told me that one can take piety too far and then it becomes nothing but suicide. He thought that's what Eliazar was doing."

"But he never told you exactly what it was?" Catherine pressed.

"No." Lucia shook her head sadly. "I think somehow he admired Eliazar; he just thought the old man was insane to take whatever risk it was." She looked wistfully at Catherine. "There were a lot of things he didn't tell me," she admitted. "And I know he never would have converted and married me. But he loved me all the same, you know. He did."

Catherine swallowed her doubts and assured Lucia that he must have. "Why are you so sure he wouldn't have converted?" she asked. "By all accounts he dressed like a southern lord and associated mostly with Christians."

"I know," Lucia said. "But that was to protect himself and to make it easier for his business. And I think he liked the feel of velvet. He looked very good in gold, I thought. Dark men do.

"But what he really wanted was to be a great leader among his own people, or at least one who was a force in the community. He wanted to be able to support scholars and adorn the synagogue with silver and rare wood. He said that every one of the scholars who sneered at him would one day bow as he passed in the street. He'd make them pay for their scorn. He even wanted to raise an army that would give Jerusalem back to the Hebrew people."

"What?"

Lucia laughed. "I know. It was a ridiculous idea. Even Natan didn't believe it could be done, at least not until the coming of their Messiah. But he wanted it every bit as much as the men who fought to regain the Holy Land for the Christians. No, I'm sure he loved me, but not more than his God."

"Would you have converted for him?" Catherine asked.

"Of course not!" Lucia seemed scandalized by the very idea. "I gave him my body, and gladly, but not my soul. What do you think I am?"

Fortunately for Catherine, Edgar returned and she didn't have to answer that question. They passed another hour or so, drinking the cider and chatting, but Lucia had no more information she wanted to share.

They walked her home in the moonlight, Edgar carrying the lantern. Catherine decided she was feeling well enough to exercise her ankle, although her pace was slower than before. When they reached the tavern it was full. Either Saint Joseph was still being celebrated or the students were anticipating the end of Lent by a week.

"Our rooms are in the building in back, on the other side of the alley," Lucia explained, leading them around the long block and down the narrow passageway.

As they came closer to the rear of the tavern, they realized that the space between it and the house was completely filled by Goliath's cart.

"Now, what's *that* doing there?" Lucia said angrily. "He knows better than to leave it blocking the way. Goliath! Samson! Come move your blasted cart! How am I supposed to get into the house?"

There wasn't even enough room for one of them to edge between and pound on the outer door.

"We'll have to go back around to the front and find them," Lucia said. "I'm sorry. You don't need to stay. I'm perfectly safe."

"We can walk around with you," Edgar said. "To be sure that your mother knows you're home."

As they started back to the front of the tavern, Catherine lagged behind, then stopped. She was sure she had heard something moving in the cart.

"I think I'll wait for you here," she called. "I need to rest my foot before we go home. I'll just lean against the cart."

Edgar gave her a scowl. He never trusted that casual tone from Catherine. But he was torn between two duties and, he reasoned, they would only be a minute.

As soon as they turned the corner, Catherine climbed up to where she could look between the slats of the cart. Her ankle protested at being twisted in this manner, but she ignored it.

At first she couldn't make out anything but the dark shapes of barrels and boxes. Then she heard it again. A rustling sound and a high keening, like a kitten in pain.

She wondered if somehow an animal had climbed into the cart and been unable to get out. It sounded hurt. She pulled herself over the side and stepped in carefully, trying to find the source of the noise.

Her foot touched something soft and the keening grew to a shriek of panic. Catherine knelt in the cart and felt for it. Instead of kitten fur, her hand touched burlap. The animal was trapped inside a sack. She stopped. Perhaps it was some game animal that Goliath and his brother had trapped for food or fur. In that case, she had no right to let it escape. She touched the bag again and whatever it was wriggled in terror.

Her pity for the poor thing was too great. Catherine knew she couldn't leave it. And if she released it, she had better do so quickly before anyone came. But she was experienced enough to know that wild things aren't always grateful to the one who rescues them. Gingerly, she pulled the cord at the neck of the bag and opened it.

When nothing appeared, she bent to lift the other end of the bag to force the animal to run. It was heavier than she expected and a much bigger animal. She was having second thoughts when she saw something appear at the mouth of the sack.

"Oh sweet baby Jesus!" she prayed and quickly pulled at the ropes that were around the child's hands. She got him out of the bag and freed his feet as well, after pulling down the gag over his mouth.

"Who are you?" she whispered as she helped him out into the alley. "How did you get here?"

"Silas ben Menahem," the boy said. "They're going to sell me into slavery. Help me!"

Catherine had just lifted Silas over the side of the cart when she heard voices at the end of the alleyway. Edgar's wasn't one of them. The boy's terror was contagious. Without even looking, she jumped down, pushed him under the cart and followed, crawling between the wheels to the other side. Then gritting her teeth against the pain in her ankle, she took his hand and they ran as fast as they could.

* * *

Edgar and Lucia had found Goliath in the brewery, pouring a foul-smelling mess into an open trough.

"You idiot!" Lucia greeted him. "You know you can't leave the cart in the alley like that. What if there were a fire?"

"What are you talking about?" he asked her, staring at Edgar. "Where's your wife?"

"Waiting for us by your cart," Edgar said.

"My cart is at the stable by the slaughterhouse, where I always leave it," he told them.

"It is, is it?" Lucia dragged him to the gate, which luckily, opened inward. "Then what's this great thing blocking the roadway?"

"Saint Bridget's beery bathwater!" he roared. "Who put that there?"

There was a slapping sound of boots on the wooden planks that lined the alley. Edgar tried to move past Goliath to see what had become of Catherine. He might as well have tried to move a stone fortress.

"Are you saying someone stole it?" Lucia asked.

"Of course not," Goliath answered. "How could it be stolen when it's right here? I'm going to skin that ostler alive if he's been renting my cart out. But why would anyone leave it at my own door? Hey there! You in the alley! Get this thing out of my way so I can wring your necks!"

He grabbed hold of the slats and began shaking. The cart rocked back and forth, banging against the walls on either side.

"Here, stop that!" Edgar said. "You'll frighten my wife. Catherine!"

There was no answer. Edgar called again.

"Perhaps she decided she'd rather wait in the tavern," Lucia suggested. "I'll go look."

"She said she'd wait here," Edgar said. "Catherine!"

There was a space between the top of the cart and the doorway large enough for him to slip through. Edgar pounded Goliath's back until the carter stopped his demolition work long enough to heed him.

"You'll never catch your thieves that way. Give me a boost up," he ordered. "You've probably terrified her. Let me get over and tell her it's not Armageddon, only an earthquake."

But Edgar knew that a little roaring and shaking weren't enough to frighten Catherine. It was with a growing sense of panic that he climbed over the side of the cart and into the alleyway. It was empty.

Where had she gone? Would he have been able to hear if she had screamed? Widsith's bloody sword! What could have happened to her?

Edgar raced to the end of the street, hoping she had decided to follow him to the tavern after all.

He heard the clink of chain mail. He had just enough time for one solid Saxon curse before the blow landed with professional accuracy on the back of his head, knocking him out.

Catherine and Silas stumbled more than ran through the narrow alleyways. Even though the shops had been pulled shut for the night and goods taken in, the route was still cluttered with refuse. Even in daylight it would have been hard to move quickly on the uneven ground. Now, with one person limping to start with and the other stiff from being tied up all evening, it was hopeless to attempt any speed.

After the second turn, Catherine stopped in the shadows to listen for the sound of anyone chasing them.

"I live on the rue de Draperie," Silas panted. "I want to go home. My mother will be worried, especially after what they did to my father."

"I know where you live," Catherine said. "And whoever abducted you does, too. We have to get to Eliazar's."

"No!" The boy tried to pull away from her, but Catherine caught him.

"Yes," she said. "He'll send word to your parents and get you home safely. I promise."

"No!" Those men who captured me were hired by Eliazar's partner, that Christian from Rouen," Silas insisted. "If you take me there, he'll give me back to them. Let me go!"

A shutter flapped open somewhere above them.

"What's going on down there?" a voice called. "I'm trying to sleep."

Catherine put a finger gently on the boy's lips, to quiet but not frighten him further.

"Trust me," she said. "Please." She searched her mind for the word in Hebrew. "*Nave nali*, Silas. Your father is mistaken. Hubert knows nothing of the men who hurt him or those who kidnapped you. Eliazar will protect you. I promise. I've set you free. I won't let anyone take you again."

She couldn't see his face clearly but felt his shoulders sag in resignation. She wanted to hug him as his mother would, giving him her strength and reassurance. But he was old enough that she feared he would be insulted at the implication that he needed such comfort.

She hugged him anyway. It seemed to help.

They had caught their breath now. They were only a street away from Eliazar's home. Catherine listened for the sound of pursuit but heard nothing. All the same, she took the last block slowly, staying under the eaves in the darkness lest the growing moon catch them in its light and give them away.

They had no need to worry about being admitted at Eliazar's gate. Every household of the community was open and people were gathered in the street. There was a knot of men standing in front of Eliazar's. Catherine could hear them shouting.

"Come out here and face us, Eliazar," one man yelled. "It's you who've brought this upon us! Why must poor Menahem continue to suffer for your misdeeds?"

Some of the people in the street shouted their agreement. But others tried to pull the speaker away from the door. Catherine couldn't hear what they were saying but the gestures were those of conciliation. At the edge of the group a figure sat on the ground, his head bent over crossed arms, his shoulders shaking beneath his cloak that, even in moonlight, was bright green and yellow.

Silas broke away from her.

"*Abba!*" he cried. "Papa!"

Everyone stopped and looked in his direction. Menahem tried to rise but was overcome by his relief and simply held out his arms to the boy speeding toward him.

Catherine followed more slowly, unsure what her reception would be from this angry group. Fortunately, Johannah chose that moment to open the gate. Catherine took advantage of the commotion around Silas and his father to slip through without being noticed.

"Aunt Johannah," she whispered, "I must speak to Uncle Eliazar. Immediately!"

"My dear," Johannah began. "With all this worry and the horrible accusations people are making, I don't think this would be—"

"What sort of accusations?" Catherine asked.

"About Menahem. That Eliazar and your father murdered Natan and are trying to make Menahem tell where the treasure is."

Catherine was stunned. "Father? That's what Silas said. What could he have to do with this?"

"Nothing," Johannah answered, shutting the gate behind them. "Neither of them have anything to do with Natan's death. They would never threaten Haquin. They're good men."

She sounded as if she had repeated those sentences too often. Catherine took her hands in her own and held them tightly.

"Please, Aunt," she begged. "I must talk with my uncle, alone."

Something in Johannah disintegrated. She closed her eyes and pulled away from Catherine.

"Thirty years and more I've known him," she said. "Since I was a child and he came here to study. Never before has he kept anything from me. Now he has a secret so terrible he won't tell his own wife." She fixed Catherine with a look.

"You think you know what it is, don't you?"

Catherine shook her head. "I don't believe it. I must be wrong. But what I've discovered . . . No, there has to be another explanation. Where is he?"

Johannah pointed. "Up in his room, praying. He's been there ever since word came that Silas was missing. Go tell him the boy's been found. Then ask him your questions. May you have better luck than I have making sense of his answers."

Edgar awoke to the smell of new beer, and the taste. Goliath had poured a pitcher over his head to bring him around.

"Stop!" Edgar spluttered. "I'm awake. Who hit me? Where's Catherine?"

"I couldn't see who hit you," Goliath said. "I saw your wife running the other way down the street with a child running behind her."

"A child?" Edgar decided there must be beer in his ears, as well.

"Are you sure it wasn't someone dragging her off?"

Goliath was sure. "I saw no one following her, either," he added.

"Perhaps because they stopped to dispose of me." Edgar touched the bump on his head and winced. He tried to rise but the pain and sudden nausea forced him down.

"You're no good to anyone tonight," Goliath said. "I've got to get the ox and take the cart back. I'll take you home, as well."

"But . . . Catherine." Edgar struggled once again to stand.

Goliath waited until Edgar gave up. "When I last saw her, she looked in better shape than you," he said. "She may already be at home waiting. If not, I'll get my brother and we'll rouse the watch to look for her. Will that do?"

It wouldn't, but Edgar had no choice. He let himself be dumped in the cart on top of an empty burlap bag. Through the pounding in his head, it occurred to him that his father would have died rather than allow himself to be borne through the streets in a beer cart.

One more reason to be grateful that he was two countries and a large body of water from home.

"Uncle?" Catherine tapped on the door. "Uncle Eliazar? Please let me in. Everything is all right. I found Silas and brought him home. He's with his father now."

She heard the latch lift and Eliazar opened the door. His clothes were disheveled and torn and his beard glistened with the tears caught in it. The front of his tunic was covered with dust and bits of chaff. Catherine made a note to ask her aunt how often the rushes were changed in here.

"The child is unhurt?" Eliazar's voice quavered.

"He's fine," Catherine told him. "His abductors frightened him but did him no other harm."

Eliazar closed his eyes in relief and murmured a prayer. "Does he know who they were?"

"He says it was men sent by you and Father. I don't think he knew them."

Catherine forced her voice to remain calm. Looking at her uncle's reaction to the loss of a child, she couldn't believe that he was capable of murdering a man. And yet, would he have felt it murder if the man were Christian? She didn't know. He was of her own blood and yet alien. It humiliated her that in the depth of her soul, there would always be the fear of the chasm that lay between her faith and his.

The distance never seemed so great as at that moment. Eliazar stared back at her from the other side of the Jordan and all the waters rushed between them.

He didn't speak, only looked at her with a weariness that finally roused her to pity.

"Silas believes what he has heard from his father," she said more gently. "That you are hunting for a treasure that Natan left."

"I told him I wanted nothing to do with his trade." Eliazar shook his head. "I should have done the job myself. My worst mistake was to ask Natan's help."

Catherine tried to sort out whom he was talking about. "Told who? Natan's help with what, Uncle?"

Eliazar's jaw set in the expression that was all too irritatingly familiar to his friends and relations. Catherine put the question aside but resolved not to allow him to leave the room until it was answered. Temperament must be passed down the generations, for she knew her stubborn nature could meet and rival his.

"Very well, then," she continued. "There is a treasure, isn't there?"

Eliazar sighed. "I don't know."

He could feel her eyes on him. It wasn't fair that she should look so much like her grandmother. Thank the Almighty One Catherine didn't know how impossible it had been for the child Eliazar to dissemble to his mother.

Perhaps she didn't need to.

He looked up and gave her a sad smile. "He had something that he felt was of value," he admitted.

Catherine said nothing.

"I don't know what it was," Eliazar insisted. "A box, so by so." He showed the measurements with his hands. "He wouldn't tell me what was inside and so I refused to keep it for him. I thought it might be stolen goods, maybe even some of the church property he tried to sell at Saint-Denis. I don't want those things in my house. I don't know where he took it and I don't care."

Catherine still didn't speak, simply continued to look at him. Her eyes were lighter than his mother's had been. Catherine's were blue.

Hers had been green, like Solomon's, evidence of an ancestress who had been caught in the path of a Viking raid two hundred years before. But the color didn't matter, only the long steady gaze, full of sorrow.

"It's the truth," Eliazar told her softly.

Catherine nodded. "I believe you," she said. "About Natan's treasure." She paused, hoping he would tell her the rest. She wished she had brought the bits of metal and paper she had found in the cellar.

Perhaps it's better that they are out of his reach, her voices intruded. *Without them there is no evidence that he might destroy.* "Hush!" Catherine drove those wicked doubts to the back of her mind. But they had been there all along and would remain until she knew the truth. She took a step forward and put her hands on his. "What happened to Brother Thomas, Uncle?"

It was as if she were suddenly holding a block of ice. His hands never moved, but all the warmth left them. His face turned gray and she feared she had killed him with her question.

His mouth opened and closed several times before he could force the sound out. "Who? . . . I heard . . . he went . . . on a pilgrimage."

"A pilgrimage?" she snapped. "Where? Conques? Rome? Vézeley? Compostella? Where?"

The words flew at him like arrows from an arbalest.

"Did he get permission from his superior? Did he tell his friend, Andrew? Shall I ask at Saint-Victor for someone who went with him, someone who has heard from him?"

Eliazar had never seen Catherine angry. He had always thought of her as loving and tolerant. Finally, he realized what she was accusing him of.

"You think I killed that poor, gentle boy?" he wailed in dismay. "Oh, Catherine! How could you?"

Catherine let go of his hands. Neither one of them noticed the marks her nails had left on his palms.

"I found pieces of clerical belongings in the cellar, Uncle," she said. "Why were they there?"

"That book of his," Eliazar muttered in annoyance, confirming her fear. "I thought I had found all the bits. And the beads rolled everywhere. I hoped they were lost forever."

"Please," Catherine said. "Tell me the truth. I can't bear the things my mind suggests. If Thomas wasn't murdered, then what happened?"

Eliazar shook his head sadly. "Come, child, sit down," he said. "I didn't kill Thomas. As far as I know, he's alive and well, may the Lord protect him. I will tell you, but I fear that, when you know what I have done, you may prefer me to be a murderer."

The pieces of the puzzle jumbled in her mind and suddenly arranged themselves in a new pattern. What could be worse than murder? The answer hit her all in a rush and Catherine realized that her uncle might be right in that she would rather he had only killed a man. But she sat on the stool by the fire all the same and waited, hands clasped around her knees like a child prepared to hear a fable.

By the time he finished the story, her hands were covering her face as she shook with horror at what he had done and terror at what might happen to him if his crime were discovered.

"Forgive me, Catherine," Eliazar said. "Not for what I did. I know you can't do that. And I need no pardon from you. I would do it again, I'm proud that the Almighty One, blessed be He, chose me for this. But I never meant you to be burdened with such knowledge."

Catherine swallowed. "I forced you to tell me," she said. "You bear no blame for that. As for the other . . . I don't know. I can't think rationally about it now.' But I think you should tell Aunt Johannah."

"And have her incriminated with me?" Eliazar asked.

"She would rather that than be kept outside your heart, which is where she feels you've placed her now."

Eliazar nodded. "You're right. I've hurt my Johannah. I thought it would be best. I was wrong. I've felt for some time that I wasn't protecting her with my silence, but how did you know that was how she felt?"

"There is no truth more horrible than knowing the person you love best in the world won't trust you," Catherine said. "Even I know that."

Eliazar reached over and stroked her untidy curls. "Edgar may not always realize it," he said to her, "but he is a very lucky man."

"So are you, Uncle," Catherine answered. "I will keep your secret and pray that both you and Brother Thomas may one day be saved."

She stood up and shook out her skirts, as if ridding herself of all she had just heard.

"Now," she said. "I need to get home before Edgar believes I've been captured by brigands. And then we are going to start a serious search for this mysterious treasure and for the people who want it so badly."

Sixteen

Gaudry's workshop, somewhere in Paris, vernal equinox, Feast of Saint
Benedict, Abbot Friday, March 21, 1141 / 11, Nisan, 4901

*Neque guttae graciliter, Manabant, sed minaciter, Mundi rotam
rorantibus, Umectabant cum imbribus, . . . Quae catervatim
caelitus, Crebantur nigris nubibus.*

Nor did the raindrops trickle down, but drenched the
spinning world with darkly dropping showers . . . that
thundered in torrents down from the heavens in black
clouds.

—Saint Aldhelm
Carmen Rhythmicum 45–54

*I*t was raining.

Edgar could hear it pounding on the roof of the workshop and sizzling as the water found its way down the chimney of the kiln. He had been told to keep the oven hot today and he winced every time he bent to add more charcoal to the fire. His head ached abominably from the clout he had received the night before. He'd let Gaudry and Odo think he was suffering from an excess of devotion to Saint Joseph rather than explain what had really happened. They were most sympathetic, but a late night spent with an ale mug did not excuse him from work.

He gave the bellows a vicious squeeze. Catherine had appeared shortly after he returned home, with a story of saving a kidnapped child. He had believed her; of course he believed her. The more bizarre her explanations, the more likely they were to be true. But she refused to tell him anything more than that Menahem's son was safe with his family and that he hadn't seen the men who had thrown the bag over him. More upsetting to Edgar, she had seemed almost unconcerned that he had been knocked out and left for dead in an alley.

"Poor dear," she had said absently. "But it's not a very big lump. You'll be fine in the morning."

Then she had curled herself into a corner of the bed and cried until she fell asleep. Nothing he could say or do made any difference. Finally, he had given up and tried to sleep, too.

He awoke to the storm at what should have been dawn. Catherine had crawled out of bed over him and was kneeling at the brazier stirring flat beer into a bowl of porridge for the morning meal. The coals had almost burnt to ash so there was little light for him to make out more than her form.

"This would be better with milk," she said quietly. "I should have bought some yesterday. I'm sorry."

"I don't mind," he answered, wondering if that were all the apology he could expect. "Is there anything left of the honey John brought?"

"A little," she answered. "I'll put that in as well."

Catherine busied herself with this for a few more moments while he dressed, then brought him the bowl and his spoon.

"Uncle Eliazar says that Natan had a box with him on his last visit," she began. "It was big enough, I think, for a reliquary. About the length of an arm."

"We suspected that already," Edgar said as he slurped. "Is that all your uncle told you?"

"No."

Edgar finished the porridge and handed Catherine the bowl. He waited.

Catherine sat next to him and leaned her forehead against his shoulder, inhaling the smell of his body mixed with that of unwashed wool. It was so familiar and comforting.

"Uncle finally told me his secret. It has to do with what happened to the other canon of Saint-Victor. I told you about him—Thomas, the one who used to study with Andrew." She spoke into the folds of his tunic. "The beads and bits of a prayer book that I found belonged to him."

"He was attacked in the cellar? Did Natan murder this canon?" Edgar asked. "Is that why Eliazar is afraid?"

"Uncle only hired Natan to sell the *superpellicium* that marked Thomas as a cleric," Catherine said. "And a crucifix. I'm not sure Natan even met the canon."

"Then how did those things you found get there?" Edgar took the bowl back and laid it on the table. Then he put his arms around Catherine and turned her face up to his. "Why had this canon no further use for his crucifix and surplice? What happened to him? Tell me the truth. Did Eliazar kill him?"

"No, of course not. Uncle would never murder!" Catherine took a deep breath. "But what he did may be worse. Brother Thomas isn't dead; at least his body still lives. As I understand it, he's set out for Alexandria, to join the Jewish community there. Uncle convinced him to apostatize."

Edgar looked down at her in shock. "By the blinding light of the Apostle," he whispered. "Who'd have thought that gentle old man would have such courage? I'm not sure I could take such a risk for my faith."

"Courage?" Catherine said. "He's helped to doom a man to everlasting damnation!"

"Probably," Edgar answered. "I'm not the final judge of that. But don't you wonder about a belief so strong that a man could jeopardize not only himself, but his family and friends, for the sake of one soul? Eliazar must feel he's saved the man from deep idolatry."

"Yes, that's what he said, but . . ." Catherine said.

"I know. It's a terrible secret for us to carry. And it's frightened you." Edgar thought it was time to pause a moment. This wasn't something that could be handled with logic. So he kissed her.

Catherine dropped the sticky spoon.

Edgar could feel an inexorable force pulling them toward the bed, but Catherine's next words cut off all carnal thoughts.

"But someone else does know," she said. "Last year, when you were attacked in the streets after you left Uncle's house, that was the same day Thomas told Uncle Eliazar of his decision and asked for help. He was hiding in the cellar all the time you were there. Whoever tried to kill you must have thought you were helping them."

Edgar considered. "When the knife bent against me, the man who tried to stab me cried out that I was a demon."

Catherine nodded. "Of course he did. To him you were a servant of Satan making another conquest. No wonder he thought you couldn't die." She sighed and put her hand on his chest. "I'm so glad you were bringing my dower in gold coins that could blunt a knife. I never could have forgiven Uncle Eliazar if the man had killed you. Anyway, Thomas left Paris soon after that, in secret. He couldn't get permission from Abbot Hugh to make a pilgrimage or even to leave Saint-Victor. Uncle Eliazar asked Natan to sell Thomas's clerical garb to pay for the journey. Somehow, someone else must have found out about it and decided to take revenge."

"If they wanted revenge, why not simply denounce Eliazar to the bishop?" Edgar asked.

"I don't know." Catherine moved away from him. "I'm guessing now. Uncle told me as little as he could. He loathed disclosing any of it to me. But I wonder if that's why Natan suddenly began trading in other church property. Lucia says he hated doing it, even though he was well paid."

"You think there was someone threatening him with exposure unless Natan helped them?" It was plausible, Edgar supposed, but there was no proof. He shook his head, drawing her to him again. He knew Natan's death wasn't Catherine's main concern now. What bothered her was that a canon of Saint-Victor, someone well steeped in orthodox learning, could be so easily convinced to abandon the faith. Catherine was doubting the strength of her own belief, especially in the light of her affection for that side of her family.

"*Leoffedest,*" he said. "You can't let yourself worry about the fate of all creation. Master Abelard says that it's right for children to follow the faith of their fathers out of respect but that, once we are grown, we must come to belief through understanding. If Thomas was convinced through reason that Christ is not the Messiah, that is his decision, and the state of his soul is between him and God."

"But why was Uncle Eliazar the instrument of such evil?" she asked. "Why does it have to be someone I care about? And why should *you* have been put in danger because of it?"

"Catherine, do I look like the pope?" he answered. "I don't know the why of anything. I just do what seems right at the time and trust that I won't be allowed to go too far into error. And at this moment, I think I should be going to the workshop. But I promise that, if a demon should appear to tempt you to apostasy, you may call me at once and I'll drive him away with pleasure."

Catherine smiled at him. One of the reasons she loved Edgar so was that he could always bring her back from the labyrinth of teleological exploration before she got lost, but without making her feel foolish for entering the maze in the first place.

"Thank you," she said. "I hope you find Saint Aldhelm."

"I hope he wants to be found," Edgar answered. "Can we have boiled tripe tonight?"

Catherine shuddered. Was there nothing the English didn't boil?

"I'll ask at the butcher's," she promised.

The thought of the tripe, boiled and chopped with dried herbs and garlic, was coming between Edgar and the even working of the bellows. Distracted by Catherine's revelation, he had forgotten to bring even a slab of bread to stave off hunger until evening.

Gaudry had almost finished layering the wooden arm with the gold leaf. He then intended to add swirls of silver wire, which Odo was busy drawing out.

"That canon came to see me last night," Gaudry mentioned casually. "He said he might be able to give us some agates, garnets and small pearls to decorate the reliquary with."

"Did he tell you a pattern?" Edgar asked. "If this is to be a copy he must want something similar, at least."

Gaudry looked up from the work. "No. He told me to make my own pattern. Odd, isn't it, when he was so adamant about making something simple before?"

Edgar agreed. What did it mean? Had this work been intended all along for some other saint than Aldhelm? Was this a legitimate commission after all? That didn't make sense. The monasteries had their own craftsmen who could replace a reliquary. Gaudry normally worked in jewelry for the nobility—hairpins, necklaces, cups, occasional ornamentation for a saddle or bridle. Why go to him for such important work if it could be made somewhere else by people trained for it?

No. There was something wrong. Edgar had already guessed that the box Natan had been carrying contained the missing arm. That had to be the treasure that these Christians who attacked Menahem were looking for. That meant that Natan must not have delivered it. So why were they making a new reliquary? What would be placed in it? Gaudry refused to look beyond the job he had been hired for. His only worry was that the payment might not be sufficient.

Edgar couldn't stop speculating. The conclusion he was reaching caused him to pump the bellows more and more fiercely.

"Look out now!" Gaudry shouted. "We need coals, not ash. Slow down."

With an effort, Edgar returned to the steady pressure that kept the heat even. But inside he was boiling. It was clear to him now. They were going to substitute another arm for Saint Aldhelm's and ransom it to Salisbury as genuine.

But how would they convince the canons that it was the same relic? If it couldn't be returned in that same reliquary, then even Philippe would be suspicious. While the number of saints in heaven was immense, the desire of the faithful to have a piece of their remains was such that fraud and substitution were almost commonplace. No one would accept a putative relic without certificates of authenticity.

Or clear evidence of a miracle, of course, preferably in the presence of hundreds of witnesses.

"So, Bishop Aldhelm," Edgar asked as he stared into the glowing coals. "How do you intend to stop this sacrilege? And just what do you want me to do about it?"

Catherine found that, despite her inner confusion, she couldn't keep away from her uncle's house. It shocked her to realize that she desperately needed someone to discuss things with and Aunt Johannah was the only one nearby that she could trust.

For a cowardly hour she had considered running back to the Paraclete and putting the whole matter before Abbess Héloïse. She would know what to do, what comfort to give. The abbess could look at any dilemma without flinching. She wouldn't condemn Catherine for still loving someone she ought to loathe, for embracing those she should fear. Héloïse would tell her what she should do.

It's rather late to remember that, isn't it? The voices were so smug. *You're a grown, married woman now. You can't go running back to the convent every time the world upsets you. That's not what it's for.*

Isn't it? Catherine responded.

Not for you, they answered. *You can't live in two worlds.*

Catherine brushed the rebuke angrily from her mind. She hated it that those voices were so often right. It was as if Sister Bertrada, who had disciplined her more than once, refused to relinquish Catherine to the life she had chosen. How it galled to admit now that the old nun might have actually had her best interests at heart.

Her inner conflict was so great that Catherine had largely ignored the rain. She arrived at Eliazar's door with her scarf wet through and her hair dripping.

Lucia took her wool cloak. "Why didn't you put the hood up?" she asked reasonably.

Catherine shrugged and unwound the soggy linen from around her neck and head. Lucia took it, wringing it out over the stones in the entry.

"Have you found who killed Natan?" she whispered.

"No, only that Eliazar didn't," Catherine answered.

Lucia gave her a sidewise look of doubt. "That's not enough," she said. Then she and the wet clothes vanished into the kitchen.

Catherine stood in the entry a moment, then followed the sound of voices upstairs to the main hall.

Eliazar, Solomon, Johannah and Baruch were seated on cushioned chairs close to the fire. As Catherine entered, they all looked up with expressions of guilt. Solomon recovered first.

"Did you swim the Seine to get here?" he asked, getting up. "There is a bridge now, you know."

That brought Johannah to her feet. "My dear, you're drenched," she observed. "Come sit here and warm yourself. Solomon, get her a tisane. What brings you to us on such a day?"

Catherine looked at Baruch, who smiled at her, the firelight gleaming cheerfully off his bald head.

"Don't worry," he said. "I know who you are. I've known your father for many years."

"It was Baruch who found Hubert living in Rouen, when we all thought he had died," Johannah explained. "He brought your father back to us."

"That may not be a reason for Catherine to rejoice," said Eliazar. He regarded her warily. Now that she knew about Brother Thomas and his own role in leading the man from Christianity, perhaps Catherine would begin to agree with Agnes's opinion of him.

Catherine sat down, unsure herself. Solomon gave her a cup of something warm to drink. She didn't know what it was, but noticed that no bits were floating in it. She looked at him.

"Chamomile. I strained it for you." He grinned.

For some reason this made her eyes fill. That this should be the one time in his life that Solomon would choose to be considerate— it wasn't fair. She drank around the lump in her throat, then turned to her uncle.

"Have you told them?" she asked.

He nodded.

"Do you . . . do you all agree with his actions?" she asked them.

The other three stared at her and she could feel the space between them grow.

"I am ashamed," Baruch said and Catherine looked at him with hope. He continued, "Ashamed that I should have mistrusted my old friend. You are a hero, Eliazar. I ask your pardon for my doubts."

"Well, I'm not ashamed; I'm angry." Solomon sounded it. "How could you use a man like Natan to help you in something so dangerous? Why didn't you ask me? I could have sold your canon's possessions easily. Think of the things I've traded for Abbot Suger! Why couldn't you trust me?"

"Or me?" Johannah said quietly.

Eliazar looked sadly at his wife. "For that, I am sorry," he said. "And I ask your forgiveness, all of you. I was too proud. I wanted to take all the risk to myself or, even worse, put it on a man for whom I had no affection. It was not distrust, but fear, that kept me from telling you." He sighed and went on. "I wanted to protect those I loved best. If there was retribution, I wanted to bear it alone."

"That was very selfish of you, Uncle," Solomon said.

"Do you think that if the Edomites came to punish you, any of us would be spared, even if we knew nothing of what you had done?" Baruch asked. "Or that, knowing, we would betray you to save ourselves?"

"I don't know anymore what I thought, beyond believing that I must keep the secret at least until Thomas was safely on his way," Eliazar said. "After that, I tried not to think of it again. That's all."

"Then you didn't tell them everything, Uncle." Catherine leaned forward. "They don't know that someone did find out. Did you reveal that they tried to stab Edgar and very nearly succeeded in killing you?"

"What!" Johannah leapt to her feet and stood over Eliazar, who cowered in his chair. "You told me it was a robbery attempt, that the man tried to cut your purse and got you instead."

Eliazar put his hands over his face.

"You would have let me be widowed without even knowing why?" Johannah accused. "To think you were the victim of a senseless crime instead of a martyr to the Holy Name? Eliazar, is there no end to your selfishness? I agree with Solomon. Families should die together."

Eliazar's fingers parted and he peered up at Johannah with one eye. He gauged the severity of her expression and quickly covered it again.

Solomon tried to stifle a laugh. "I don't believe I suggested that we all throw ourselves into the flames, Aunt," he said. "Not unless absolutely necessary. Personally, I feel I have a better chance of avoiding martyrdom if I know what's going on."

"Exactly," Baruch added. "Now, Johannah, stop terrifying us all. Eliazar has said he's sorry. That should be the end of it."

"But it isn't." Catherine hated to say it. The words made her feel more of an outsider every moment. "Whatever was started last spring is still going on. Natan is dead and whoever killed him may have done it because he helped Brother Thomas. Did none of you ever wonder why, after years of trading in stolen livestock, Natan suddenly began to traffic in gems and ecclesiastical objects? Isn't that unusual?"

Eliazar shifted uncomfortably. "Yes, I wondered," he said at last. "I suppose I thought that he had found there was more profit in jewels than sheep. As long as he kept me out of it, I didn't care. I didn't like the man. He cheated his own people."

"Would he have betrayed you?" Catherine asked.

Eliazar shook his head. "No. It's strange, but I never once thought he might. Perhaps he might have denounced me to the elders, but not to the Christians. Natan had his own honor."

"But you and Natan were the only ones who knew what Thomas planned?" Solomon understood what Catherine was implying and didn't notice her attempt to stop him from talking. "Could Thomas have told anyone? Andrew, for instance?"

"Thomas knew what the risk was, especially from the other canons of Saint-Victor," Eliazar answered. "They would have had him in a cell doing penance and being preached to night and day until he recanted. Isn't that right, Catherine?"

"I suppose," Catherine said. "I've never known anyone who left the Faith. His superiors would certainly try to convince him of his error."

"And starve him until he did," Baruch sniffed.

Catherine turned on him angrily. "What would you do if a child of yours asked for baptism?" she asked.

"I'd never allow—!" Baruch's repugnance at the thought was

obvious. He stopped and took a deep breath. "Yes. I take your meaning."

"So it isn't likely that Andrew would know what Thomas planned and ignore it," Catherine said. "You know him, Uncle. Do you agree?"

Eliazar nodded. "Andrew studies our faith only to find confirmation of his own. But, apart from that failing, he's a good man. He wouldn't have permitted Thomas to leave Paris, but neither would he have tried to murder me. If he had wished to, he could have done it anytime this past year."

"Then who attacked you?" Solomon demanded. "Was Natan murdered because of what he did for you?"

Catherine thought she heard a gasp from the hall. She started up. How long had Lucia been listening? What had she heard?

Eliazar stared at Solomon, about to answer. Catherine raised her hands to stop him. Swiftly, she got up and tiptoed to the curtained doorway. With a sudden movement, she pulled the curtain aside.

Lucia stood in the passage. She showed no indication of being startled or guilty.

"Come in, Lucia," Catherine said. "How long have you been listening?"

"Long enough to know there's been more evil done in this house than Natan's small sins," she answered, entering the room. "I respected you, Master Eliazar. Natan said you were a good man and he was proud to help you. He was wrong. You used him and then left him out in the dark to die."

Catherine put an arm. around her. "I promised you I'd find Natan's murderer," she said. "No matter who it was. We need your help, Lucia. You told me that Natan went to Argentevil to sell some oil clothes. Did you know that after that Natan began dealing in a number of things stolen from a church?"

Lucia shook her head. "Not exactly, although I wouldn't have cared. My parish does just fine without golden chalices and silk vestments. Our priest says God has no use for such things, so why should the monks and bishops?"

No one offered to disagree.

"Did he ever tell you who he was working with?" Catherine asked. "Someone at Argenteuil?"

"He went there sometimes," Lucia answered. "But there was also someone from Notre Dame. He hated going near the cloister, but the man insisted. I don't know his name. Natan might not have, either."

"That still might help," Catherine said. "If you remember any more, will you tell us?"

"Of course," Lucia answered.

"Thank you," Catherine said. "And what about Brother Thomas?"

"Who?" Lucia looked at them all, as if appraising their worth. She shook her head. "I never heard of a Brother Thomas."

Johannah looked at the maid with new eyes. But she asked none of the questions that rushed into her mind. "Well, then. Have you finished boiling the pans for Passover?" she asked instead.

"Not yet," Lucia answered. "I'll have them done before I go home tonight. I'll light the lamps for you before I go."

Johannah nodded. "I'll be down to help you shortly."

Lucia left.

Solomon looked at Catherine. "What was that about?" he asked. "Why did you let her go? She could destroy us all. And where did she learn about the canon? How well did she know Natan?"

"She just told you that she'll say nothing," Catherine answered.

Solomon still looked doubtful.

"Under my own roof!" Johannah exclaimed. "How could I be so negligent?"

"That well?" Solomon whistled. "And she has very large brothers, too. I did underestimate Natan."

Catherine got up. "Solomon, would you walk me home?" she asked. "I'll explain everything and you can tell me on the way what you intend to do about Abbot Suger's nephew."

"There's not a lot I can do if Gerard wants to run about the countryside with chalices in his pack," Solomon replied. "He could easily argue that I attacked him. Baruch agrees with me. There's nothing more to be done. And if Natan was working with him, there's all the more reason to forget the matter."

He reached for his cloak all the same.

Catherine kissed her aunt and uncle good-bye, but not with the same warmth as before. They all felt it.

Solomon helped her on with her cloak. Her scarf was still dripping in the kitchen so she put the hood over her loose braids. Neither one of them spoke until they were out on the street, heading for the rue de Juiverie.

"Now," Solomon said cheerfully. "Where are we really going?"

Edgar had tried to find out from Gaudry more about the man who had ordered the reliquary, but either the smith didn't know or he wouldn't say. After much prodding, Edgar decided it was the former.

"He's a medium-sized, pinched-faced man," Gaudry repeated. "Looks underfed, although I've heard the canons do fairly well for themselves, out of rents and suchlike."

"But you're not sure he's from Notre Dame?" Edgar reminded him.

"Sure enough," Gaudry said. "I've seen him about the town. Even though he lives in the cloister, he has property he takes rent from, not far from the tavern where I met you."

"But you're certain that you don't know his name?"

"I never asked." Gaudry returned to his work. "And don't start. Neither am I sure where we are right now. I took the directions, but I didn't look to see what was above us. And if you find out, don't tell me. It's always better not to know."

That was clear enough. Edgar knew he would get no more information. They had finished for the day. He banked the coals and then studied the gold-plated box in the lamplight. At the moment, that's all it was, a piece of hollow wood shaped like an arm, its only value the cost of the gold and the skill of the craftsmanship.

But add a piece of bone or a lock of hair or even a shred of cloth that had belonged to one of the martyrs or church fathers and that same piece of work would become priceless. It would be revered, honored, displayed on the high altar on feast days, even brought out and threatened with destruction if the community thought the saints weren't doing their best to protect their people. But what if the saint weren't in the reliquary at all? What if there were no miracles because the box contained the bone of a farmer or the tunic of a bathhouse cleaner? What would that do to the people who prayed and believed they had received no answer?

Like Catherine, Edgar had a sudden urge to run to someone else who would answer these questions for him. He wanted Master Abelard, but Abelard was now at Cluny, under the protection of Abbot Peter. And the Master was ill, perhaps dying, although Edgar feared it was more from discouragement at the condemnation of his life's work than from the sickness that had plagued him the past few years.

No, there was no master he could turn to. But, he remembered, there was a friend.

Edgar washed his hands and face, collected his sous and went in search of John.

Catherine hurried through the streets quickly enough to keep Solomon slightly breathless as he trotted beside her, but not enough to keep him from noticing that she had turned left, not right, and that they were heading back toward Saint-Étienne.

"Are you thinking of getting some cider to take home?" he asked her. "Sounds like a good idea, but you forgot your pitcher."

When they were almost to the court around the churches, Catherine stopped and pulled Solomon into a doorway.

"We've agreed that Natan has hidden some sort of treasure, right?" She went on without waiting for his answer. "There's a canon of Notre Dame involved, or someone who says he is, right? You and Edgar are both fairly sure that this hidden workshop is somewhere near the cloister, if not under it, right?"

She stopped. Solomon was eyeing her with something very near to dread. He backed away.

"No," he said. "Absolutely not. I won't even consider going there and neither will you."

"Solomon! Don't you want to find the truth?"

"Not if it means dying a moment later," he answered.

"Fine," she said and turned to leave.

Suddenly he grabbed her and held her until she stopped struggling. Catherine had no idea how strong her cousin could be, or how impervious to reason.

Not long afterwards the weaver was outraged to have his shop invaded by a man pulling a woman behind him as she protested violently. He debated getting up, even in the middle of a thread, but his second glance told him who the woman was. He recognized the man as a frequent visitor. So he simply glared at them as they passed through, making a note to complain strongly to Johannah about the sort of people she was renting to.

"Let go of me!" Catherine yelled as Solomon dragged her up the stairs by one wrist.

"Not until I've turned you over to your husband!" Solomon yelled back. "You're insane, Catherine. You need to be kept under guard for your own safety." He kicked the door open and threw her in. "Edgar, come take charge of your *meshuganah* wife," he said. "Oh, excuse me!"

Catherine was already halfway up, to give Solomon a bit of his own. She caught his startled look, turned around and blushed scarlet.

Edgar was sitting at the table just as she expected. But next to him, their jaws open in consternation, were John, the student Maurice and another man, younger than either of them but clearly much more important.

"Catherine," Edgar said with a sigh, "may I present Giles du Perche, archdeacon of Rouen? My lord, this is my wife."

Seventeen

Catherine and Edgar's room, a very short time later

Sic enim Christianitas viluit, sic cupidas increvit, ut Sanctorum corpora mercen fatiamus [sic], felicas exuvias venum preponentes. Exhorruit primo Monochus immane facinus.

To such a degree has Christendom been corrupted and to such a degree has avarice increased, that we sell the bodies of the saints, offering our holy relics for profit. Every monk shudders at such a terrible crime.

—William of Malmesbury
Gesta Pontificum Anglorum
Book V Vita Aldhelmi

$\mathcal{E}$dgar, I apologize." Solomon bent over to help Catherine up. "I had no idea you had guests. Catherine, I really wasn't angry."

"I know," she answered, struggling to regain her feet and her dignity. What would Sister Bertrada say if she saw her now? Catherine shuddered.

"I ask your pardon for such an unseemly entrance," she said, giving a half-curtsey.

It was just as well she didn't realize the picture she presented. Her head was uncovered and she had lost the ties from her braids so that her hair had unraveled down her back in a perplexity of curls. Her *bliaut* was stained, with mud-dipped hem. Her boots were covered in street grime. She did not look like the wife of anyone respectable.

Catherine knew she had committed a terrible social sin and that her appearance was not that of a well-bred lady, but that was no reason for these men to stare at her so. They might have at least risen to greet her. Where were their manners? She took off her cloak and put it on the hook by the door. As she did she glanced toward the corner of the room, relieved to see that the curtain hiding the chamber pot was closed. She couldn't remember if she'd emptied it this morning.

"Edgar, is there anything I can get for your guests?" she asked. "Solomon and I can go for soup . . . or something."

She didn't need any voices to tell her that she looked a complete fool. Edgar must be writhing in embarrassment.

It was John who saved her. Suddenly remembering himself, he stood. Quickly, the other two followed.

"Giles arrived last week from Rouen," John explained. "His uncle, Archbishop Hugh, has entrusted him with the very delicate matter of retrieving the items stolen from Chancellor Philippe."

Catherine gave a startled glance at the well-dressed boy. The archbishop's nephew, Giles du Perche. Oh, dear. Of a very distinguished family from Normandy, as she recalled. Catherine wished the floor would part like the Red Sea and allow her to slip away to safety.

Behind her, she could sense Solomon edging for the door. She reached back to stop him.

"Too many clerics for me," he muttered in her ear. "Tell Edgar I'll talk with you both later, luckily for you. Be prepared to repeat to me everything they say."

He nodded to the group and made his escape.

"A friend of yours, as I recall?" John said pleasantly, gesturing toward Solomon as he retreated.

Catherine relaxed. "Yes, an old family friend. But that does not excuse our behavior. Please forgive me."

John could control himself no longer. He exploded into laughter. "Only if you will forgive me for telling you I haven't seen anything so funny in years as Edgar's face when you burst in here."

Edgar felt a flash of irritation at both John and Catherine, but the absurdity of the situation was too great. He gave in and smiled. "Sit down, *carissima*," he said. "We have everything we need. John and the archdeacon here have enlisted Maurice to help us."

"To find the workshop?" Catherine asked.

"Partly," John told her. "But we are fairly certain now that one of the canons is involved in this theft. It is of the utmost importance to discover which one."

"You are quite sure this smith said it was a man from Notre Dame?" Archdeacon Giles asked. "Meddling in the affairs of another archdiocese is a very delicate matter. It would be unpardonable if we made an accusation we couldn't prove."

"I'm sure," Edgar said. "But that's what we need Maurice for. I've never seen the man who commissioned the reliquary. The master silversmith has but doesn't know, or won't reveal, his name. All I have is a general description, but Maurice will know if there is anyone at Notre Dame who fits it."

"Would Gaudry identify the canon if the man were found?" John asked.

"Perhaps," Edgar said. "But Gaudry is not a member of the guild. It would be worth his livelihood, maybe even his life, if he admitted to keeping this workshop, even if the canon would vouch for him, which seems most unlikely."

"So Maurice will try to find a canon who wanders the tunnels instead of going out the gate like an honest man?" Catherine asked.

"Good, then I can tell Solomon he doesn't have to go in with me."

"Catherine, you weren't!" Edgar sputtered.

"It occurred to me that the missing arm might have been hidden somewhere beneath the cloister," Catherine said. "Or even inside it."

Giles gaped at her again. "You intended to enter the bishop's cloister?"

"Oh, no," Catherine assured him. "Just discover where someone else could have."

Giles took a long moment to think about this. "I don't believe any of this is covered in the instructions my uncle gave me," he replied at last.

Edgar grinned and was about to speak, when John gave him a kick under the table.

"It's well known that Archbishop Hugh trusts your judgment implicitly." John smiled at the young man. "I'm sure that's why he chose you for this mission."

Giles still seemed uncomfortable. "Originally, I was told only to go to Saint-Denis, where we had heard that a chalice had been found resembling one taken from the church at Salisbury. Prior Hervé showed it to me and has kindly agreed to keep it safe until my return."

"Was it the same one?" Edgar asked.

"It matched the drawing I was given," Giles admitted. "The prior suggested that I continue on to Paris and ask John if he could make a positive identification, since he once served at Salisbury. Then I learned that the arm might also have been found."

"I told the archdeacon about your search for Saint Aldhelm, Edgar," John explained. "He insisted on coming to see you."

He said this by way of apology. John knew how Edgar felt about Normans. Edgar wasn't satisfied.

"With respect, my lord, I'm not sure how you can help us," he said. "We believe that, for reasons beyond our understanding, Saint Aldhelm has allowed his arm to be transported to Normandy, then stolen and taken to France and finally lost by the very thieves who dared to commit such sacrilege. I suspect that no one alive now knows where he rests."

"I will do whatever possible to help," Giles said. "My only duty is to assist those who are searching for Saint Aldhelm and see that he is returned."

"Returned to whom?" Edgar asked. "To the canons of Salisbury? The last I heard, Empress Matilda was in control of that area and had King Stephen in prison in Bristol. I also was under the impression that your uncle was a fervent supporter of the king."

"That's correct," Giles said.

"Then would he return property to Salisbury while Matilda still held it?" Edgar challenged him. "Or give it instead to Philippe d'Harcourt to bargain with as the price of the bishopric?"

"Edgar," John warned.

"No." Edgar waved him off. "I won't risk my life just to put another damned Norman in a Saxon see."

Giles may have been trained as a diplomat, but he was also young and proud of his Norman blood. He reached across the table and pulled Edgar up by the knot at the neck of his *chainse*.

"The Saxons were no more than slaves of the Danes long before we came to England," he shouted as Maurice and John tried to unhook his fingers. "Duke William was the savior of Britain. And you come from a race of weak-winded, vulgar cowards."

Instinctively, Edgar reached for a sword. It shocked him to remember that he'd never worn one. His hand seemed to know the way so well. Instead, he grasped hold of the table to prevent himself for going for the archdeacon's throat.

"Get out of my house," Edgar said quietly, looking straight into his eyes. "Or I'll kill you."

With some difficulty, John and Maurice convinced Giles to leave with them. Maurice offered to take the archdeacon to the cloister for a proper meal and a warm bed in the guesthouse. Catherine was sure both would be far better than Maurice was used to.

Edgar waited until the door closed and the sound of their voices had faded. Then he released his hands from the tabletop. Catherine sat in unnatural silence. She could see that his nails had broken with the force of his grip. She had never realized how strong his hatred was for the people who had driven his ancestors north. Perhaps that was why he had no energy left to despise Jews.

He flexed his hands several times, stretching his long fingers until the joints cracked. Finally he looked at her.

"It seems that neither of us made a good first impression on Lord Giles," he said. "I don't suppose we'll be invited to Rouen any time soon for dinner with the archbishop."

Catherine tried to smile. "I've nothing appropriate to wear, anyway," she answered.

She got up and began fumbling with their few dishes. Edgar watched her.

"Catherine?"

"Yes."

"It doesn't matter. John will calm him down. If necessary, I'll even apologize for insulting a guest. At least the archdeacon knows that I'd rather have Aldhelm lost forever than be used as a simoniacal purchase."

"Yes."

"Catherine, what is it?" Edgar asked. "Do you think I should have agreed to help that bastard?"

"Not if you felt it was counter to the wishes of Saint Aldhelm."

She dropped a clay cup. It cracked.

"There's something more, isn't there?" he said softly. "Tell me."

She moved the dishes around a few moments longer. "I've never seen you angry before," she said at last. "Annoyed, often, but never angry. I thought you might try to kill him. You frightened me."

Edgar stretched out his hands again, studying them. "You have one sort of pride, Catherine, which is all your own. I have no idea where it came from. I have another that was born in me and was fed to me every day of my life with every meal and every family prayer. This rage is that of my father and his brothers and my mother's kin, as well. They intended me for the church, as you know. But not the contemplative life. I was to be another sort of fighter in the struggle to regain our land.

"These last few years in Paris, I thought the fury had dulled. It's been seventy-five years since the conquest, after all." His hands curled back into fists. "I was wrong. It might as well have been yesterday and the blood of my fathers still fresh on the ground. I'm sorry I frightened you."

Catherine knelt by the chair and took his hands, smoothing them out over hers. "It's good to be able to feel passionately," she said. "I would want you to be strong enough to defend the Faith, or our . . . children, or even your own people, if any of them were in danger. But not to provoke a boy who believes in his own family and people as much as you do and who may very well be part of Saint Aldhelm's plan. Also," she added as she felt him tense, "I'm frightened that someday I might transgress one of those beliefs and draw your anger to myself. If that happens, I hope you kill me quickly because I couldn't bear living with a man I feared."

"Catherine! I will never hurt you; I promise."

His injured innocence broke the spell. She smiled.

"Of course you will. We're not saints. Our behavior this afternoon is certainly proof of that."

Edgar grimaced. "I wonder if John will want to speak to me again."

"Probably," Catherine said. "He has a forgiving nature."

The oil lamp flickered. It was almost empty.

"It's not dark out yet," Edgar said. "Do you want to get something to eat?"

"No," she answered. "I'm not hungry. I want you to hold me."

"Yes," he said. "I need to hold you." His fingers moved to untie her *chainse*. "By the way," he added, "did you notice that your hair's come undone? No," he added, as she felt for it. "Leave it like that. I'll help you comb it out in the morning."

"Shall I put on my sleeping cap?"

His fingers moved through her curls.

"Not yet."

Solomon didn't expect to be overtaken by Edgar's guests only minutes after his leaving. They didn't notice him as they passed. The archdeacon, Giles, marched stiffly down the road with John on one side of him, expostulating with eloquent gestures, and Maurice on the other, looking nervous.

What had happened? Solomon was tempted to turn back and find out but decided instead to follow the trio. They all seemed to be heading in the same direction, back to the Île.

He followed them as far as the cloister gate. Maurice knocked and they were admitted.

Solomon stood at the corner of the rue de Boeuf feeling foolish. Twice in one day was too much. Where had he expected them to go?

Had he thought they would lead him to a secret meeting with this mysterious canon? He realized that he believed that the men already knew which canon it was and were hiding the truth to protect the probity of the order. He sighed. He wouldn't learn anything more standing here. It was almost dark. He turned to go home, then brightened.

There was a warm light shining through the cracks in the shutters of Bietrix's tavern. Someone was singing. Solomon jingled the coins in the bag at his belt. Plenty for a bowl of beer. Perhaps he would have just one before returning to his uncle's house. Poor Uncle Eliazar! Even with Pesach approaching, there would be little music in his heart this year.

Vowing only to stay the length of time it took to down a mug, Solomon pushed open the door and went in.

The air was smoky from the hearth at the rear of the tavern that backed onto the oven in the brewery. The room was almost empty. In one corner a man in brown was sitting and staring into his cup with the intensity of a soothsayer. Solomon assumed he didn't want company. Against the far wall lay a beggar, a child with a twisted spine. Bietrix let him sleep in the tavern when the nights were cold. Solomon looked around. Where had the singing come from? The sound had been so clear from outside.

The curtain to the brothel was still. Bietrix was no where to be seen and Solomon did not like the idea of hunting for her in the back room. He knew his money wasn't welcome there.

Now he was curious. He was sure the music had come from here. He went over to the door to the brewery and knocked. No answer. He put his ear to the wood. There were definitely sounds coming from the other side. Perhaps they hadn't heard him. Solomon pushed at the door and it opened.

Lucia was standing over a trough containing a disgusting mass of bubbling liquid, wearing a loose *chainse* with a tunic over it that must belong to one of her brothers. She had belted it with a piece of rope. The paddle she used to skim the froth was heavy enough to need both hands and she was singing as she worked.

"*Hu et hu et hu et hu!*" She emphasized each word with a thump of the paddle on the side of the vat. "*Jo l'ai veü. La jus soz la coudroie. Hu et hu et hu et hu! A bien pres l'ocirroie.*"

She sang so fiercely, about a pair of lovers interrupted by a thief, that Solomon decided she didn't want any interruptions, either.

Yet, it was so nice just to watch her. Even with her hair covered by a cap and sweat dripping down into her dress, she was lovely, Solomon thought. He shook himself, remembering the size of Goliath's fist. Lucia looked up.

The singing stopped.

"What do you want?" she asked.

"To listen to you sing," he answered without thinking. "I mean, I came in for a beer, but your mother isn't at the table."

"Fill your cup, leave a coin on the counter," Lucia answered. "I can't leave this."

"Do you want help?" Solomon asked.

"I can do it," she answered shortly.

Solomon came closer to peer at the mess in the trough. "Please don't tell me that I drink something made from this," he said.

"Not without paying first," she answered.

"What's in it?" He sniffed.

"Malt, barley, yeast, water and gruit," she answered.

"Gruit?" he asked. It sounded like a regurgitation. Smelled like it, too.

"Makes it taste better." Lucia handed Solomon the paddle. "Here, you hold this. I want to add a bit more."

She went over to a large ceramic pot, lifted the lid and scooped out a handful of dried herbs and berries. She threw this into the trough.

"Just a little for now," she said. "We add most of it when it's in the keg, to flavor it. Now this has to sit for a few days. Since you're here, you could help pour it into the barrel."

Solomon looked around nervously. "Isn't that something your brothers do?" he asked.

She laughed. "They took the cart today to deliver the last brewing before Holy Week begins. If I don't get this into the kegs there'll be nothing left for us to drink on Easter."

"You mean it will be ready by then?" The frothing mass of liquid did not resemble anything he remembered drinking. No, that wasn't right. There was that fermented milk drink he'd had in Kiev once. Solomon gagged at the memory.

Lucia seemed confused by his questions. "Haven't you ever seen beer made before?" she asked.

"Not really," Solomon answered. "My aunt and uncle don't brew. They buy from Abraham. I suppose I've seen the casks and, of course, I know the odor. That's how I find the best tavern in a strange town. But I never thought to ask about the process."

Lucia shook her head at such ignorance. "Well, trust me," she told him. "By next week, this will be beer."

"How does it turn from white to brown?" he asked, not sure he wanted to know.

"Part of the time in the keg is to let it settle," she answered. "If it doesn't, or if it starts to go bad, we add other things."

She went over to another earthenware crock and opened it. Solomon put down the paddle and went over to look. Inside was a grayish coarse powder. Solomon sifted some through his fingers and then wiped them on his tunic.

"What is it?"

"The leaves and stems from the ground cherry," Lucia said. "Sometimes we use eggshells, but this time of year the hens aren't laying, so this does as well. We dry them and pound them as finely as possible. Some property of the plant draws the impurities to itself."

"Fascinating," Solomon said, looking at her.

Lucia smiled up at him. She reflected that she had always been fond of dark men. Her smile dimmed. He wasn't Natan.

"Avois! What do you think you're doing here, mesel?'

They both jumped. Thanks to years of practice, Solomon put himself at once between his interrogator and the door back to the tavern.

"Samson!" Lucia said with annoyance. "You remember Solomon, Master Eliazar's nephew. He came in for some beer but there was no one to take his money since you and Goliath were gone and I had to work back here."

"Where's Mother?" Samson countered.

"Visiting a friend," Lucia answered. "Solomon was just about to help me pour this."

"Well, I'm here now," Samson told her, glaring at him.

"Glad to see you," Solomon lied. "Did you ever find out who took your cart?"

"No. What do you know about it?" Samson took a step forward. Solomon took two back.

"Just what Edgar told me," Solomon said. "It seemed odd that anyone would steal a cart only to leave it at your door."

"Just some *trigoleurs* with no sense," Samson answered. "If I ever find them, they'll learn quick enough not to play their tricks on us."

Solomon had no doubt of that. "So, I should be heading home." He tried to sound casual. "Thank you for the information, Lucia. Good night."

Outside, Solomon leaned against the wall for a moment, until he could breathe properly once more. Where had that man popped from? He could have sworn he hadn't heard the door creak or felt a draft from outside. Of course, there was something about Lucia that focused his senses away from such things. Another good reason not to pursue her. His life depended all too often on being able to keep his wits about him.

The next morning Catherine and Edgar were eating bread soaked in hot water when a pebble bounced against the window. Edgar looked out. John stood below in the street.

"May I come up?" he called.

"Of course." Edgar hurried down to let him in, relieved that they were still on speaking terms. "What brings you here so early?" he asked as they went up.

"I needed to see you before you left," John explained. "I wanted to explain about Giles."

"Oh, that." Edgar rubbed at a sudden kink in his neck. "I'm sorry I lost my temper with him. Do you want me to beg his pardon?"

"It might be worth it just to see you on your knees to anyone." John laughed. "And you may have to do it, but not for my sake. Look, Edgar, from what I understand, Philippe is desperate to recover the Salisbury treasure, especially the arm, but not to bargain for that bishopric. He knows he'll never get Salisbury now. But he does want to be nominated to the next Norman see available and Archbishop Hugh has made the restitution of the treasure the price."

Edgar considered. "The archbishop guarantees the items will be returned to Salisbury?"

"Yes, and he's a man of his word," John assured him. "But if you think we'll ever see another Saxon as bishop there, you've learned nothing from history. Perhaps in a few generations there will be a man with a Saxon name, but I suspect he'll have Norman relations as well."

"Never," Edgar said, but he spoke with more defiance than denial.

John shrugged. "We're all one in the Church, anyway. Remember?"

Edgar sighed. "I suppose so, but it doesn't change how I feel."

"Will you continue your efforts to find the arm?"

"Yes, of course," Edgar said. "I spoke in anger last night. I don't want such a precious relic to be lost forever or sold to the highest bidder even farther from home. But I don't think the man who hired Gaudry knows where the arm is any more than we do."

"But you will go back to the workshop today?" John asked.

"I will," Edgar said.

Satisfied, John took his leave, again apologizing for coming so early.

They finished their Lenten breakfast. Catherine prodded at an undissolved crust with her spoon.

"Everything points to Natan being the last one to have the arm," she said. "What I don't understand is why his accomplices would poison him without knowing for certain where he had hidden it."

"Perhaps they thought they did know," Edgar suggested.

"Perhaps," Catherine said.

"We're not even positive he was poisoned on purpose," Edgar reminded her. "No one knows where or how he came by what killed him. It's even possible that his nephew did it, thinking he would inherit treasure."

"And then beat himself up and kidnap his own son to draw suspicion away?" Catherine asked.

"Catherine, sarcasm is very unattractive," Edgar said. "But Menahem could have killed Natan, found no treasure and then had to deal with the men his uncle had been working with."

"Yes, that would explain a lot," Catherine admitted. "Especially how Natan was willing to eat or drink whatever killed him. But I keep feeling that we're missing something all the same."

"Catherine," Edgar sighed. "I love you. You know I love you. But my temper has been somewhat strained recently and, if you don't stop pushing that lump of bread around, I'm going to take your spoon and twist it into a double knot."

Catherine gave the lump a bash that finally disintegrated it. "I love you, too, Edgar," she said. "But I foresee that we shall someday have a whole set of twisted spoons. It's a very good thing that you're learning how to make new ones."

After that matter had been amicably settled and Edgar had left for the day, Catherine sat and considered what she should be doing. Palm Sunday, the beginning of Holy Week, was tomorrow and there were a number of things she needed to shop for. She had heard nothing from her father and presumed that he was planning to remain with Guillaume until after Easter. She knew even less about Agnes. Was anyone living now at the house on the Grève? While there were many good points about having a room that was all one's own, Catherine admitted it would be nice to be in a place once again where someone else shopped and cooked and cleaned.

You had that in the convent, you know.

That didn't even deserve an answer. Catherine took her basket and went out to fight the crowds in the Halles for bread, cheese and the first greens of spring.

On her return, she found her cousin sitting on the stoop.

"Your guests didn't stay long last night," Solomon began. "Did we offend them that much?"

"Actually, Edgar and the archdeacon had a difference of opinion," Catherine admitted. "It made our entrance almost a model of courtesy by comparison."

Solomon's eyebrows rose. "I miss all the fun," he sighed. "Oh, well. Aunt Johannah sent me to ask if you and Edgar would eat with us Sunday night; it's Erev Pesach, the feast of the firstborn."

"I'll ask Edgar," Catherine said. "But I don't see why not. Is Ullo still staying with you?"

"Yes, but I think he's leaving for Vielleteneuse later today," Solomon said. "Uncle Hubert felt that he should be with his own people for Easter week. He didn't want anyone thinking we were trying to convert a Christian child."

Catherine nodded. "This time of year people are reminded too often of the primary difference in our beliefs."

They were upstairs now. Catherine put the food away and unstoppered the jug. She sniffed.

"It's close to vinegar, I'm afraid," she said. "But we can mix some with water, if you're thirsty."

"No, I'm fine," he said.

He took off his cloak and handed it to her. Catherine sneezed and sneezed again.

"*Marpe*," Solomon said automatically. "To your health."

"Thank you," Catherine answered. "But I'm not ill. There's some sort of powder on your cloak that's tickling my nose."

"Oh, that. Sorry." Solomon took the cloak back and hung it on the hook himself. "I forgot. It's something they put in beer to clarify it. Ground cherry leaves, Lucia said."

"Ground cherry?" Catherine repeated. "Are you sure? I thought that was one of the solanem plants."

"Yes, I'm sure," he said. "Why shouldn't I be? They aren't difficult words to remember."

Catherine ignored that. "Ground cherry is not used in medicine, as far as I know, but Sister Melisande used to warn us not to eat the berries. She said they wouldn't kill us, but we'd get sick. I thought she also said that the poison was strongest in the leaves and stems."

She went over to Solomon's cloak again and sniffed cautiously. "There's something familiar about this," she said. "I wonder what it smells like when it's mixed with beer."

"I thought you said it was poison," Solomon said. "They wouldn't sell very much if the customers died before the first refill."

"I don't think it's that toxic," Catherine answered absently. "You'd need a large dose. And if it were used to settle the dregs, most of it would stay at the bottom of the keg, I'd imagine. Now, where have I smelled this before?"

She closed her eyes and suddenly it came back to her. The odor of smoke in wool, beer and this acrid tang. She had thought it breath from the Hell-mouth as it blew at her that night.

"Natan," she said. "He must have drunk this powder in something the night he died. Beer would make sense. You say Lucia told you about it?"

"Yes."

"She told me Natan loved her," Catherine said. "He would have taken a cup from her hand. But she insists she loved him, as well. Why would she kill him?"

"I can think of a dozen reasons," Solomon said. "Each one ending with '. . . because she loved him.' "

A year ago, Catherine would not have understood. Now it only surprised her that Solomon did.

"Don't say anything to anyone, please," she begged him. "Let me talk to her. For all we know, every brewer in Paris uses this. Or I might be mistaken. We can't accuse her without more proof."

"I agree," Solomon said. "But you shouldn't see her alone. Who knows what she might do if you accused her? And don't forget, she has a weapon, too. She can always expose Uncle Eliazar. She'll be helping Aunt Johannah today. I'll take you there. It will be much safer than if you go to the tavern."

Catherine went with him but vowed to find a way to see Lucia alone. Solomon cared only about proving that Eliazar had nothing to do with Natan's death. He had no concern about finding a treasure or the arm of a saint he didn't believe in.

Perhaps Lucia had told her only the simple truth. But perhaps Natan had promised her a legacy and she had murdered him to keep it.

Then she might be the only one left who knew where Aldhelm was hiding.

Eighteen

Johannah's kitchen, the night of the sarch for unleavened bread,
Saturday, March 22, 1141 / 13, Nisan, 4901

. . . nec tam culpas quam opera punimus, nec in aliquo tam quod
eius animae nocet quam quod aliis nocere possit vindicare
studemus ut magis publica preveniamus dampna quam singularia
corrigamus.

. . . we punish not so much faults as deeds, and we attempt
to correct in someone less what harms his soul than that
which can harm others in order to prevent public injuries,
rather than correct individual ones.
—Peter Abelard
Ethics Book I

*L*ucia was preparing to serve the Holiday meals. She did not appear happy to see either Solomon or Catherine.

"We're busy here," she told them shortly. "I've no time to talk with you."

"I thought you wanted our help," Catherine said.

"I did," Lucia said. "But it seems to me that I've been helping you more. Finding the one who killed Natan clearly has no importance for you."

"Yes, it does, Lucia," Catherine assured her. "I promised I would find out who it was, no matter where the investigation led."

"Even if it came back to your own family?" Lucia asked.

"Yes," Catherine answered. "But my father never did any business with Natan. He's not involved in this at all, even though Menahem still doesn't believe us."

"Catherine, I'm not deaf or blind," Lucia said with scorn. "Nor was I born an idiot. I overheard you talking with the master and mistress. I can see that you and Solomon might be twins, and not just by your looks, either, although I would wager that under his beard, Solomon has your chin, as well. You both move the same way and you talk to each other the way Goliath and Samson and I do. Catherine, you have much more to hide than I, much more to lose. I've known for a long time that you are related to these people, and I don't think you're that careful about hiding it. How can I trust you? I don't even know if you're Christian."

"Oh, yes, I am that," Catherine said wearily. If anything, the past two years had forced her to examine her faith more intensely than she would have ever imagined necessary. "Although none of us can be certain until Judgment Day, I fear."

Lucia took out the Sabbath platter. "And you." She turned on Solomon. "How do I know they didn't tell you to poison Natan? You're the one who seems to get all the dirty jobs around here."

"This is true," Solomon answered. "I've been saying so for years.

It's a shame that you're the only one who has noticed. And I admit that you can't know I didn't kill Natan. I had no reason to, but who can prove that? Personally, I wouldn't poison anyone. It seems so cowardly. There are better ways, especially while traveling."

"Solomon!" Catherine said.

"I am not stupid, either, Catherine," he reminded her. "I've survived journeys as far east as Rus and as far south as Toledo. An unsuspicious man would have his goods stolen and his throat cut the first night out."

Lucia smiled at him. "Maybe you didn't kill Natan," she conceded. "If you wanted to, you would have done it with that knife in your sleeve."

"That's right." He felt for the knife. He had thought it well hidden but must have been careless within the house. Solomon had worn it so long it was as unfelt as his skin. He resolved to take his own advice to heart. "Jews aren't allowed weapons," Lucia reminded him. "You're protected by the king."

Solomon didn't blink. "The king has never been with me when I needed protection."

At that moment, his resemblance to Catherine almost vanished. Beneath his teasing and joking, Catherine realized, he was hard and wary as a hawk. If she had thought about it before, she would have realized that he had to be. In her mind, he was still the little boy who had pushed her out of the tree at the fair at Provins so many years ago and then cried because he thought he had killed her.

It was with difficulty that she remembered why they had come.

"Lucia," she said, "I do have one more question for you. Please. Solomon says you use a powder made from ground cherry in your brewing?"

"No, it goes in after," she answered. "To draw out impurities."

"Then what happens to it?" Catherine asked. "It doesn't float around in the beer like those herbs you put in, does it?

"Wouldn't be much use in that," Lucia answered. "No, it sinks to the bottom of the keg, below the spigot. We scoop it out when the kegs are rinsed."

Catherine was still concerned. "I'd always heard ground cherry was poisonous."

"Poison?" Lucia repeated. "Can't be much, if at all. I've got it on my hands and licked a bit off now and then. It's drying and bitter but it didn't make me sick."

"So you don't think it could kill anyone?" Catherine persisted.

Lucia scrunched her face in thought. "I don't see how," she said at last. "We've been known to tip the keg to get the last of the liquid out. Some probably got into the cup. If anyone has died, it hasn't hurt business. So what are you saying?"

"I'm sure I smelled this powder on Natan's breath as he came at me," Catherine told her. "I thought it would explain how he died."

Lucia stared at her for several seconds. "I see," she said. "You thought I lured him into my bed and then poured him a cup of poison. Do you imagine I saw myself as Judith? We're supposed to die for the Faith, not kill for it."

"By Saint Vitus's guardian eagles!" Catherine said. "You told me to hunt for the truth, but of course you wanted it to fall elsewhere than at your door. You were right before. No one really cares who murdered Natan. All anyone wants is the treasure he left behind. And if it really is the arm of Saint Aldhelm, I'm ready now to let the holy relic take care of itself."

Lucia's expression changed in an instant. "A relic? You think Natan stole a holy relic?"

Solomon answered. "It seems there's one missing and a lot of people believe that it was Natan who had it last."

Lucia sat down. "That's impossible," she said. "He wouldn't have gone near such a thing. It would have disgusted him."

"You're quite sure he never said anything to you about the people he was dealing with or what he was trading in?" Catherine asked once more.

"Nothing more than I've already told you," Lucia said. "I can't help you anymore. And if all you can discover is that Natan may have been given ground cherry powder and it killed him, then you can't help me."

"Do all the brewers in Paris use it?" Catherine asked.

"What?" Lucia was getting up. She left the knife on the table and went for her cloak.

"This powder," Catherine repeated. "Do you grind it yourself, or get it from a peddler? Is it common?"

"I have no idea," Lucia answered, tying the hood. "Goliath gets it

in some village. I suppose it grows there. Other brewers must use it,
too. I have to go. Tell Mistress Johannah I'll be in later to serve the
food for her."

She hurried out, refusing their offer of company.

When she had gone, Solomon and Catherine looked at each
other.

"Which do you think upset her more," Solomon asked, "the
source of the poison or the relic?"

"The relic, I'd say," Catherine said. "She didn't seem to believe
me about the poison."

"Either that," Solomon said, "or she already knew. I wonder
where she's going?"

Catherine took his hand. "Shall we find out?"

Edgar knew there was something wrong before he opened the door.
Usually the warmth came through the cracks in the wood. Today it
was cold. There was no noise, either. No clank of metal or creak of
the bellows. Nothing.

He didn't want to open that door.

He was being foolish, he told himself. Worse, he was acting like a
coward.

He fumbled for the handle to lift the latch. The click sounded like
a thunderclap in the dark silence. The door opened inward. He
pushed it with his foot until it swung all the way to the table, where
it stopped with a thump. At least he knew there was no one hiding
behind it, ready to spring at him. He looked in.

The windows were mere slits high in the wall, just above ground
level. This early in the day, they let in very little light. The old workshop was better in that respect.

He made out Odo first. He was slumped over the oven in a way
that told Edgar the fire must be out. He stepped closer. The back of
the journeyman's head was crushed as if with a huge hammer. Edgar
crossed himself, mumbling from some forgotten corner of his mind,
"*Beati mortui, qui in Domino moriuntur.*"

Blessed are those who die in the lord. Edgar hoped it was true.

Gaudry was sprawled across the table, one hand still clutching a
chisel. He had apparently tried to fight off his attacker, but a chisel
was no use against the knife that had slit his throat through.

"*A porta inferi, Domine, erue animas eorum.*"

Deliver their souls, Lord, from the gates of Hell.

Edgar looked around. He didn't know what else he expected to see. None of the tools had been touched. Nothing broken but the bodies of the men he had worked with. Then he noticed the box where Gaudry had kept the precious metal they used. It was open. He bent to examine it.

The lock had not been broken, but opened with a key. Gaudry had made the lock. He wore the key around his neck. Was it still there, under all the blood? Edgar's courage failed him. The box was empty, as he expected. The reliquary they had labored over for weeks was gone.

Edgar stood up. He thought he was in complete control of his faculties.

"I have to tell someone," he said aloud.

But who? He had no idea where these men lived, who their families were.

At least now there was nothing to hinder finding out exactly where he was.

"No," he said. "First I have to see to the bodies. They need . . . I must find someone to tell."

He backed out of the room. There was a seed of panic sprouting in him. What if he were found down here by the ones who had done this? Did they know they had missed one silversmith? Just as frightening, what if someone else saw him coming from a place where two men had been slaughtered? How would he explain what he was doing there? Who would speak for him?

Despite the darkness, he started to run down the tunnel, heading for the exit by the river. He had to get out into the light, to breathe clear air.

He burst out the door of the shed. A fisherman casting his net above the mill gave him a startled glance, then returned to his work.

Edgar stood bent over, his hands on his knees, gasping. His head started to clear. He checked his hands and feet for bloodstains. None. None on his cloak, either, that he could see. He hadn't touched either body.

I should have at least made the sign of the cross on their foreheads, he thought.

He was suddenly angry with himself for forgetting that simple act of kindness. Catherine's voices would have had a few sharp words for him on the futility of self-recrimination, but they had never bothered to speak to him and he wouldn't have listened if they had. Edgar knew better than to pay attention to such things.

Now he had to decide what to do next. His first thought was to go to his father-in-law, but Hubert wasn't in Paris. Eliazar had nothing to do with this, he fervently hoped. His mind recoiled from telling Catherine, although he knew he would have to eventually. He didn't want her involved in this before it was necessary. Even in his present jumbled thinking it never occurred to him that she wouldn't be, sooner or later. Who else in Paris could he trust?

Only John.

Edgar went in search of him.

"We're wasting our time, Catherine," Solomon said. "She's just going back to her mother's."

"Yes, it looks that way," Catherine admitted. "No, wait, step back. She's turned the other direction, toward Notre Dame."

"Maybe she's going to pray for guidance," Solomon said.

"I hope so."

If Lucia had thought to look back, she would have spotted them instantly. But she didn't even seem to notice what was in front of her, pushing her way through the crowd as if the people were no more than branches in her path.

"That's funny," Catherine said. "She's going into Saint-Étienne."

"I don't know why the bishop doesn't tear that church down," Solomon said. "The place is full of beggars and ripe for a fire."

"Ask him, next time you meet," Catherine said. "Should we follow her in?"

Solomon gritted his teeth. He hated being in those buildings. Even half in ruins, it was still a church. But he couldn't let Catherine go alone.

"We can't stop now," he sighed. "You go in. I'll be just behind you."

At this time of day there was a great deal of activity inside the church. Between fallen roof timbers whole families had settled, with their few belongings. Small children peered at them from behind makeshift barricades along what had once been the ambulatory.

It took a moment for Catherine's eyes to adjust to the dimness of the light. She thought she saw Lucia at the other end of the nave, heading out the door of the left transept. Catherine hurried after, hoping to catch her before she vanished into one of the dozen alleyways radiating from the court.

They came out into the light again. Catherine blinked and spotted the woman they had followed.

It wasn't Lucia.

"What do we do now?" Solomon panted.

"I don't know," Catherine said. "Go home, I suppose. We won't find her in this crowd. I wish we knew where she was going. She hasn't told us everything, I'm sure she hasn't. And I know the news about the relic surprised her."

"Yes," Solomon said slowly. "But was it because she didn't know Natan had the relic or because she didn't know that we knew?"

"You would have to ask something like that," Catherine said. "I hate it when I think I have a problem neatly worked out and you add a new perspective."

"Just trying to be helpful." Solomon smiled. "By the way, isn't that Edgar?"

Catherine turned where he was pointing. Yes, it was. What was Edgar doing out at this hour?

"Edgar!" she called.

She thought he heard her. His stride broke for a second; then he went on, if anything, more rapidly.

"This is definitely something we should find out about," Catherine said, grabbing Solomon's arm and pulling him behind as she ran after her husband.

"Let go. I'm coming!" he said. "But if he goes into the cloister, you'll have to follow on your own."

It had taken Edgar the better part of the morning to find John. That was a clear indication that his mind was not functioning well. Master Gilbert de la Porrée was lecturing today. John wouldn't be anywhere else.

Luckily, Master Gilbert was just finishing when Edgar entered the Bishop's Hall. John was standing with his compatriots, the masters

Adam du Petit Pont and Robert of Melun. They were debating the finer points of the lecture with great enthusiasm.

"I tell you, the man is one step from heresy," Robert was saying with great force.

"I disagree," John said. "You simply aren't following his argument carefully enough."

"And what do you think he's saying?" Robert asked, as if he were prepared to listen but not to be convinced.

John opened his mouth to reply. Then he saw Edgar. "*Benedicite*, Edgar," he said. "You missed a most illuminating talk."

"John, you have to come with me," Edgar said. "Something's happened. Masters Robert, Adam, you, too. Please. I need witnesses to this."

"What is it?"

Edgar lowered his voice, first looking to see who might be listening. Quickly and without much coherence, he told them what had happened.

"The reliquary is missing," he finished. "I think the murderer intends to use it for a counterfeit relic. But with Gaudry and Odo dead, there's no one who can identify him. I beg you to come help me. It's not right to leave them there like that."

They agreed and went with him readily. Across the hall, Catherine and Solomon watched in puzzlement.

"Why would Edgar be in such a rush to meet them?" Solomon said. "Is there some great scholastic debate planned? Another heresy trial?"

"They're all from England," Catherine said. "Perhaps it has to do with Saint Aldhelm. *Avoi*, Solomon! We have to find out where they're going."

They arrived at the shed leaning against the wall by the river in time to see the four men enter.

"We'll never find them if they go into the tunnels," Catherine said.

"Then we need to catch them before they go any farther," Solomon said.

The trapdoor was open when they entered the shed. Leaning over it, they could see a flicker of lamplight ahead.

"You call," Catherine said, suddenly nervous about Edgar's reaction when he found her there.

Solomon went halfway down the ladder and shouted Edgar's name. The light continued moving away from them. Catherine hitched up her skirts and prepared to climb down.

"Just follow the light," she said. "I have to know why he's taking all those men down here."

They were left in the dark once when the path turned abruptly. Catherine did her best to keep her mind on locating Edgar and not on what else might be hiding in the ancient passageways.

The door to the workshop was half-open. Catherine heard a strangled cry of "*Godehelpe!*" She started to enter, but Solomon pushed her back and looked in.

He didn't say anything.

"What is it?" Catherine said. "Let me see."

"No," Solomon answered, his voice more gray than the air around them. "Edgar saw me; he'll be out in a moment."

Catherine stepped back. "Tell me what's in there," she said quietly. "I won't go in. I promise."

"Two men. Dead. A lot of blood." He leaned his head against the low lintel. "*Adonai*, but I'm sick of ugly death."

Catherine was, too. She made no attempt to go in. She felt herself starting to shake and wrapped her arms around her waist in an effort to stop it.

"What by all the burning souls in Hell are you doing here?" Edgar barked in her ear.

"We saw you at the hall and were trying to catch up with you," Catherine said, wrapping her arms around him instead. "It's Gaudry, isn't it?"

"Yes. Now go home, please," he pleaded.

She looked up at him, her eyes huge in the dim passageway. "It could have been you," she whispered. "If John hadn't come by, if we hadn't fought, you would have been here. It would have been you. It would have been you and I'd have never known what happened."

She was still shaking. Her eyes were dry but inside there was an enormous terror, scooping her out to make room for itself. Edgar held her fiercely.

"It wasn't me, Catherine," he said. "I'm all right. Go home. Don't leave the room. I'll be there as soon as I can. Solomon?"

"I'll stay with her."

"Thank you."

Edgar went back inside and closed the door. John was explaining to the other two masters what Edgar had been doing and how this was connected with the theft of Saint Aldhelm's arm.

"We don't even know their parish," Adam said, looking at the remains of the two men. "We'll have to send undertakers for the bodies for now. Have them taken to Saint-Christophe."

"I think that Laudine at The Blue Boar may know Gaudry's family." Edgar remembered meeting him there. "Perhaps they can tell us if Odo has any kin in Paris."

"Do you have any idea who killed them?" Robert asked.

Edgar stared at the bodies. Odo had certainly been hit from behind; anyone might have done it. But Gaudry had to have been pinned down to have his throat cut like that, either by two people or one very powerful one.

"I can't see the canon Gaudry described as having the strength for this," he said at last. "He's supposed to be a small man, a cleric. None of you are particularly frail, but could you have fought a man like this? Look at his arms. He has the muscles of a knight. Yet, who else could have been here? How many people even knew this place existed? We only set up this oven a little over a week ago."

"Edgar, I think it's time we took this matter to the bishop," John said. "He has jurisdiction over crimes involving church property. And, no matter how you feel about him, we must tell Giles du Perche."

"Yes, tell anyone you like," Edgar said. "Tell the king. Tell the chancellor, if you can get him out of bed with Petronilla. Do you really think they'll care? These men were working outside the laws of both man and heaven. They don't even have a guild to bury them."

The other three were silent, admitting the truth of what Edgar said.

"We'll pray for their souls," John said. "And I believe the archdeacon can be persuaded to see to their burial."

Edgar didn't really hear him. He turned his back to the bodies and looked instead at the table against the wall, with the chisels, files, hammers, compass, scorpers and rasps lined up precisely, ready for the day's work. Gaudry was so careful of his tools.

Even Catherine wouldn't have recognized the anger in Edgar at this moment. It was burning cold, drawing all other feeling from him. He had been happy here, accepted for his skill for the first time in his life. These had been good, pious men in their own way. While they had been willing to use their art for ends that might not be approved of by society or the guilds, they weren't the ones who stole from the churches. They had done the work they were given honestly. Edgar was certain that Gaudry would not have mocked God with false relics.

"Edgar."

He turned around. The others were waiting.

"I will find the person who did this," Edgar told them.

"I know," John said. "I'll give you any help you need. Come with us now. We need to arrange for an audience with the bishop and the archdeacon."

The first warm sunlight of spring touched Catherine's face as she and Solomon came out of the shed. The clouds had broken and the river sparkled as if sown with stars. On the opposite bank, men were laughing as they finished unloading a barge. From Goat Island they could hear the bleating of the newborn kids. Lent was almost over, the new year beginning.

"I try to understand," Catherine muttered as they walked along the edge of the Seine to the Grand Pont. "I read; I listen to the priests and the masters. I know that we're on earth only to prepare for heaven. So why do we have to care so much? I shouldn't fear for Edgar's life. I should have . . . accepted it when the baby died instead of grieving my heart out. No one gives me a reason I can believe. Why?"

Solomon didn't answer. He had no answer and, anyway, he didn't think she was talking to him.

When they got up to the room, he helped her pull the cloth off the shutters and open them. As the light poured in, Catherine looked around in surprise.

"I didn't realize how grimy things were," she said. "Smoke from the brazier, grease, mud from the street. Mother would be so ashamed of me."

"I'll go draw a pail of water," Solomon said. "Do you even own a scrubbing brush?"

Catherine admitted that she didn't. Solomon agreed to get one of those as well.

"If we're going to be here all day, we might as well do something," he said. "With all the cleaning Aunt Johannah's been doing this week, I should be an expert, at least in advising."

"You'll do more than that," Catherine said. "If I scrub, so do you."

"Very well," Solomon said. "Wait here. I won't be long."

It really was shameful, the way she had let things go in the dark winter. How long had it been since she'd aired the bedding? She wasn't even sure the last time they'd bothered to put the bed up for the day.

The door opened while she was struggling with the mattress.

"You'll have feathers all over the room, if you're not careful," Lucia said, taking one end of it.

"What are you doing here?" Catherine asked.

Lucia shoved her end of the mattress over the window frame.

"I've been worrying about what you told me this morning," she said.

"This morning?" It was too long ago to remember.

"About a relic." Lucia picked up the felt mattress pad. "I don't think this is worth cleaning," she added. "What sort of relic was it?"

"Natan had a box with him that he wanted Eliazar to store," Catherine said. "We think someone may have hired him to transport it from Rouen to Paris. Only it never reached the people it was meant for, either because Natan hid it or because he was killed."

"I see." Lucia started folding the sheets. "You don't happen to know what it's supposed to look like, do you?"

"Lucia, it looks like an arm," Catherine said in exasperation. "There's only one thing it could be. You can't mistake a reliquary for a salt cellar."

"Yes, I know. I mean—" Lucia stopped. "Did it have any ornamentation, any jewels, for instance?"

"Why? Have you found some?" Catherine asked.

Lucia didn't answer.

"All I know," Catherine continued, "is that the arm was taken from its normal box and put into another, covered in gold leaf. No one told me about any jewels."

Lucia put down the sheets. She lifted her skirts and felt for a pouch she had hung at her waist. She untied it and opened the flap.

The gold had been pounded thin. There were little holes in the corner of each piece that showed where it had been attached. Some of the edges were ragged as if they had been cut with a saw.

"Could these have covered a reliquary?" Lucia asked.

Catherine put out a finger and touched the thin metal. "I'd have to ask Edgar to be sure, but I think so. Did Natan give you this?"

"In a way," Lucia said. "He asked me to keep the pouch for him. He was afraid that the men he was working with wouldn't pay him."

"He must have trusted you a great deal," Catherine said. "Do you know what he did with the box?"

"I'm not sure," Lucia said. "But I have an idea. I wanted to check this morning but there were too many people around."

"Saint-Étienne?" Catherine asked.

Lucia's eyes narrowed. "You followed me. No, never mind. It doesn't matter now. Sometimes Natan and I would meet in a corner of the old crypt. Especially in summer, it was nice and cool."

"You think he hid the arm there?"

"Yes," Lucia said. "He would think it appropriate. No one would expect it of him and I know he wouldn't have desecrated his own home with such a thing. I'm the only one who would know where to look."

"So?" Catherine asked.

"The beggars who are usually in the church will be gone tomorrow evening," Lucia said. "The canons of Notre Dame are giving a special dinner to the poor of the Île. I want you to come with me."

"Me? But why?" Catherine asked.

Lucia wrapped up the pouch and tied it once again around her waist. She licked her lips nervously.

"If it really is a relic of one of the blessed saints, I don't want to treat it disrespectfully," she explained. "I suppose I could ask our priest, but he'd ask too many questions. You're the only other person I know who would know what to say to it. Do you know which saint it is?"

"Saint Aldhelm."

"I never heard of him," Lucia said. "Was he one of the martyrs?"

"No, a Saxon bishop, who wrote poetry and a long treatise on virginity," Catherine said.

"Oh. Then I'm quite sure we would have little to say to each other," Lucia replied. "Will you come with me?"

"Can we bring Edgar?" Catherine asked. "He's quite devoted to Saint Aldhelm."

"No, and I want you to promise not to tell him," Lucia said. "He'll bring his English friends and there will be too many questions about how the relic got there and how I knew where to find it."

Catherine thought about it. "If we find the arm," she said slowly, "we could take it to the archdeacon, Giles, and tell him that Aldhelm led us to his hiding place. He might believe us. Edgar never would. He knows me too well. He doesn't need to come with us, but I can't simply wander off and not tell him where I'm going."

"Come to the tavern tomorrow night," Lucia suggested. "We can slip out the back. We'd only be gone a few moments. No one would miss us. If you don't come with me, I won't go and you'll never find it without me."

Catherine cocked her head, listening. Wasn't it time for the voices of the convent to tell her what a stupid thing she was considering? They were usually very vocal when she attempted any rash act. Of course, she normally ignored them, but it was odd for them to be silent. Perhaps they knew this was what Saint Aldhelm wanted. And it would be wonderful to be able to give Edgar back this part of his lost heritage, even if it would immediately have to be returned to Salisbury.

"All right," Catherine said. "I'll do it. Now, you'd better go unless you want to spend the rest of the day cleaning."

Edgar came home too drained to notice the preternatural cleanliness. He ate his fish cake and bread in silence. Catherine didn't try to break it. It was enough that he was there, alive.

"Gaudry had a wife and five children," he said quietly. "The parish is Saint-Nicholas. He's been taken there. Odo had no one."

Catherine crossed herself and murmured a prayer. "We'll give a candle in his memory," she said.

"The aged and wise archdeacon wants to send to Rouen for further instructions," Edgar added. "We couldn't see the bishop. He's traveling with the court. He won't be back until Sunday." He rubbed his eyes. "I'm tired. And I don't think we'll ever discover who did this or where Saint Aldhelm is being held."

Catherine bit her tongue. "There's nothing more we can do today," she said. "Wash your feet and come to bed."

She filled the tin basin for him, then took pity on his exhaustion and, kneeling on the floor, she took off his shoes and washed his feet herself.

"Catherine." Edgar sounded unsure. "I don't think I can . . . I mean, with all that's happened and finding . . ."

"What?" Catherine looked up and understood. "Oh, Edgar, of course not. This is supposed to be a day of abstinence, anyway. Now we'll have one less penance to do."

"You give such strange comfort, *leoffedest*," he said. "But comfort all the same. Blow out the light."

Nineteen

Paris, the market of the Halles, Palm Sunday, March 23, 1141 / 14, Nisan, 4901, the first night of Passover

Obtenebrescant oculi vestri qui concupiverunt; arescant manus quae rapuerunt; debilitentur omnia membra, quae adjuverunt. . . . Ne cessent a vobis hae maledictiones scelerum vestrorum persecutrices quamdiu permanebitis in peccato pervasionis. Amen, fiat, fiat.

May the eyes of you who are covetous be darkened; let the hands of those who plunder wither away; may all the limbs of those who aid them be crippled. . . . may these maledictions on you endure as long as you persist in the sin of pillage. So be it. Let it be done, let it be done.

—Archbishop Arnulf of Reims
"Warning and Anathema for
Predators upon the Church"

*C*atherine held her shopping basket tightly in both arms to avoid its being crushed by the press of people surrounding her. With her elbows, she forced her way to the dried fruit stall. Even though there was still another week of Lent remaining, the warming weather had brought a sense of awakening. Everyone seemed to feel the need to escape the deprivations of winter even if only by adding something green to the eternal pea or bean and cabbage soup. After the morning procession, all of Paris seemed to congregate at the market.

The jostling was just what Catherine needed to clear her thoughts. There was no doubt that the people around her were alive and had every intention of remaining so. Cheerful vulgarities flew about, full of creative suggestions. If many of them were acted upon, the population would increase remarkably by Christmas.

She managed to fight her way in to the stalls and out again, onto the rue Saint-Denis. People were still carrying the evergreen branches they had carried in the procession, a commemoration of Christ's entry into Jerusalem. It had been five years since Catherine had been in Paris for Palm Sunday. The last time had been just before she left for the Paraclete. Then she had believed she would never step outside the convent as long as she lived.

She heard someone call her name just as she was turning onto the rue Saint Germain l'Auxerrois. She looked and nearly dropped the basket. It was the last person she expected or wanted to see.

Jehan appeared equally delighted. "I have been sent by your father to tell you he has returned to Paris and would like you and your husband to dine with him tonight," he said stiffly.

"Tonight?" Catherine said. "I don't know. I'll ask Edgar."

Jehan turned to go.

"Will Agnes be there?" Catherine hated to have to ask.

He turned back. "No," he said. "She left for Blois last week. I'm surprised you didn't know."

"She doesn't speak to me either, Jehan," Catherine said. "I'm glad Father, at least, has forgiven you."

He looked at the ground and spoke between clenched teeth. "He has only granted me the right to atone. I am to first beg your forgiveness. I shouldn't have abandoned you, no matter what the provocation."

Catherine admitted that the provocation had been great. "As you see," she said, "I arrived home unharmed, with my honor intact."

Jehan snorted his opinion of her honor. "Then I will tell your father you will send word of your decision."

He vanished before she could ask him anything more.

She was halfway down the street before she remembered her promise to Lucia to go with her to Saint Étienne. That was far more important than any daughterly duty. But how could she get away to meet Lucia without explaining where she was going?

There must be a way.

She went upstairs to put on her cleanest clothes and then hurried over to the Grève.

Hubert opened the gate himself.

"Father, I'm so glad you came home!" Catherine hugged him. "We thought you wouldn't be back until after Easter."

"Something Ullo said when he arrived at Vielleteneuse made me think it would be wise to return at once," Hubert said. "Are you well, child? You seem very pale. Is there any news?"

"News about what?" Catherine asked, then blushed. "No, Father, not yet. It's only been two months."

"Yes, I suppose," Hubert conceded. "I do want you to get your strength back before you have another. But there is something wrong, isn't there? Ullo was full of stories about battles and dragons, but there were enough shreds of reality to tell me something had happened. Tell me what's been going on. I haven't seen Eliazar yet. Have they found the person who killed Natan?"

"No, Father, but Uncle has told us why he hired Natan last year." Catherine went on to explain.

Hubert's reaction was much the same as that of Solomon and Johannah.

"Eliazar should have trusted me," he said. "Trying to protect us only made things worse."

"There's more, Father. Someone killed the silversmith Edgar was working for."

"What? Who? When?" Hubert led Catherine up to the great hall. "Catherine. I want you to sit right here and tell me everything that has gone on while I was recovering in blissfully ignorant leisure."

Catherine sat. She started the story after she had arrived back in Paris. Since he had asked her pardon, there was no need to dwell on what happened after Jehan's abandonment of her, or mention that she had entered the city in a beer cart. "Everything" was not that all-encompassing. It was difficult to remember so many events in the correct order. Hubert had to stop her several times and make her clarify herself.

One thing caught his attention even more than the deaths of Gaudry and Odo.

"Solomon said that the man he took the chalice from was Suger's nephew?" he asked.

"He's certain," Catherine said. "You can ask him yourself. We don't know how Gerard is connected with the people here in Paris yet, although I suspect that Argenteuil is one of the places Goliath delivers his beer to."

"It is strange how many trails seem to lead back to this tavern," Hubert admitted. "Suger's nephews. That's all we needed."

"Not 'nephews,' " Catherine said. "There's only the one, Gerard, mayor of Argenteuil."

"No, there's another one, here in Paris." Hubert shook his head. "Simon. He's very ambitious, I've heard, even if at the moment he's only a canon at Notre Dame."

Catherine's stomach felt as if it had just inverted. "Is he a little man, built rather like Abbot Suger?" she asked, her voice cracking.

"Yes, a bit taller, but the same build," Hubert said. "Why? Have you seen him?"

"I think so, in Argenteuil," Catherine answered. "Talking with Gerard. I didn't know he was a canon, much less of Notre Dame. Father, you should know that the canon who commissioned Gaudry to make a replica of the reliquary was also supposed to have been of medium height. It's not much of a connection, but . . ."

She could tell from his expression that his thoughts were following hers. This was becoming dangerous. It was bad enough to accuse a cleric of trading in church property, but not unheard of. To accuse the nephew of the abbot of one of the most powerful houses in France of doing so was madness, especially for someone whose livelihood depended on continued business with that abbey.

"It may not be the same man," Catherine added.

Hubert grimaced. "The Lord would never let my life be that easy," he sighed.

"Edgar has gone to speak with the envoy of the archbishop of Rouen," Catherine said. "The return of the property stolen from Salisbury is all that really matters to him. Perhaps, if the arm can be found, everything else can be handled quietly."

"From what I understand, both Eliazar and Menahem have scoured their homes in search of Natan's missing treasure," Hubert reminded her. "No one has found anything. It's only a matter of time before the whole community falls under suspicion."

Catherine was reminded again of the importance of being able to get away easily that night.

"Father, until you invited us, Edgar and I were going to meet with John and Maurice at Bietrix's to eat and decide what should be done next," she said. "Your information about Canon Simon would be of great interest. Will you come there, instead?"

"I cannot drink that swill they call cider," Hubert said. "I swear they wring it out of their cats."

"It's not that bad," Catherine said. "You could drink water."

Hubert cringed at the suggestion but he agreed to come to the tavern later in the evening, to Catherine's relief.

"Then I think we should discuss your return here," Hubert continued. "There's no need for you to stay in that hovel any longer. Edgar's work has finished and poor Agnes has left. My accounts are far in arrears. I need your help. Will you come home, my child?"

"Oh, yes." Catherine threw her arms about him. "As soon as this matter is finished, we would be happy to."

Hubert patted her back affectionately, although he knew her joy was partly from knowing she would no longer have to cook.

The meeting with Archdeacon Giles was not going well, as far as Edgar was concerned. He had succumbed to John's counsel and agreed to sit silently, unless he was asked a question.

"Whatever he says to antagonize you, ignore it," John had said firmly. "Think of something else. I'll let you know when to speak."

Edgar was doing his best to think of something else but it was difficult when the archdeacon was clearly doing his best to imply that he believed Edgar had murdered Gaudry and Odo in order to steal the arm of Saint Aldhelm for himself.

"Suger, lord abbot of Saint-Denis, requested that Edgar take on the disguise of a common artisan in order to locate the arm," John insisted. "He is well respected by Abbot Suger and it was only out of respect for the abbot and duty to the Church that he was willing to demean himself so."

Edgar listened admiringly. John had a wonderful oratorical style. He was going to make a fine lawyer someday. It wouldn't be surprising if he were one day summoned to debate in the papal curia.

He let his mind wander. By common consent, no one had mentioned Natan, either his involvement or his death. John felt, quite reasonably, that it was only a distraction from the main issue. Natan, like Gaudry, had been no more than a tool, to be disposed of when no longer useful.

Except Natan had died before his usefulness ended. Logically, he should have been stabbed and thrown in the river downstream somewhere. His death would have been laid to the danger of travel. And logically he would only have been killed after he had given his parcel to his employers.

Edgar shook his head. The logic failed; therefore one or more of the suppositions was incorrect. He hadn't been that avid a student, but he had learned that much. He started through it again.

"Edgar?"

He brought himself back. "Yes, John?"

"The archdeacon wants to know if you've had any contact with anyone from Salisbury recently."

Edgar smiled. "Only you, John."

"*Thu fagwyrm!*" John told him pleasantly, then turned back to the archdeacon. "Of course, any number of masters here in Paris will bear witness to my character, if you suspect me of aiding in this theft," he continued. "But I can assure you that Edgar and I both believe strongly that Saint Aldhelm belongs to the land and the people of Salisbury, whoever may rule them now. All we wish is for the poor sainted bishop to be restored to his rightful honor."

Giles looked at Edgar skeptically.

"Aldhelm belongs in England and to England," Edgar said. "There is nothing more I want."

"No reward?" Giles sneered.

John quickly stepped in front of Edgar. "Any temporal reward for such a deed would be an insult," he said.

"Thank you," Edgar whispered in his ear.

"I still don't know how you propose finding the relic," Giles said. "By your own admission, you don't know where it is. No one alive does. Are we to hold a prayer vigil until the good saint reveals himself? It would be most inconvenient considering the season."

Edgar firmly turned his thoughts away from grabbing the archdeacon by the neck and rubbing his face into the stone floor.

John was unfazed. "As you remember, my lord," he said, "the substitute reliquary that Edgar worked on was stolen. It seems likely to us that your arrival may have precipitated the theft."

And the murders, Edgar thought.

"So we think it quite possible that you will soon be approached by someone, perhaps even a cleric," John went on smoothly. "He will have some story about a miraculous discovery of this relic and offer it to you. It will be in a box of yew, plated in gold."

"I see."

Although the archdeacon was very young and the archbishop's nephew, as well, John had heard that Giles was proving himself a competent administrator. He was counting on the truth of the rumors.

"Archbishop Hugh will not be eager to accuse a cleric of Paris of murder," Giles said slowly. "But he would be pleased to inform Bishop Stephen if one of his canons were polluting the honor of the order by participating in this sacrilegious commerce."

"And you would not wish such traffic to continue unchecked and unpunished," John said.

"Naturally not," Giles answered.

"Then we are in agreement?" John asked.

"We are," the archdeacon said. "Only one thing worries me. We are assuming that the relic I will be offered is an impostor. But what if it isn't? How can I be sure?"

"In that case, my lord," John said, "we will have to rely on Saint Aldhelm to make the truth manifest."

* * *

When they were outside again, John congratulated Edgar on his restraint.

"I don't know why you wanted me there at all," Edgar answered. "It was only your intervention that saved his nose from being bent like a crozier."

"I took the risk because I wanted to remind him that you are as wellborn as he," John told him. "Even your rudeness indicates your birth. He had to realize that before he would give any credit to your story."

Edgar stopped dead in the road. "Do you mean that my throwing him out of the house impressed him?"

"Only someone very sure of his place would dare such a thing," John answered. "I couldn't have done it. Especially in that house."

"Yes, you could," Edgar said. "You'd do it for God's honor, that's all. I was thinking only of my family."

John seemed embarrassed. "In any case, I think he's convinced. Now we just have to hope that Giles is offered the false reliquary."

Edgar didn't answer.

"Something else?" John asked.

"If the canon is ordained, he can't be hanged for murder," Edgar said. "At the worst, he'll be shut up in a monastery somewhere or sent on pilgrimage."

"Believe me, Edgar, that can be worse than hanging," John promised. "I've heard about the penances given such men."

"I hope you're right," Edgar said.

That afternoon Catherine told Edgar about her father's offer. "He says he wants me to do his accounts again," she said happily.

"That's good," Edgar said. "You need something to keep you busy."

"Until?" she asked. She could hear the unsaid half of the sentence more loudly than the words he spoke.

"Until we have children," he said. "Until you have a husband who needs a chatelaine to attend to his lands. Of course, you may have to wait some time for that. Perhaps your second husband."

"Edgar!"

"I'm sorry," he said quickly. "Of course we'll go live with your father again. I never imagined we'd do anything else."

"Would you rather stay here?" she asked.

"Of course not," he answered. "This is no place for a man of my exalted rank. I was just reminded of that."

Catherine put a hand on his sleeve. "Edgar, I don't understand everything you're saying and what I do understand frightens me horribly."

She bent to find her *sabots*, hiding her face. When she rose again, she had regained control. "This isn't a good time to discuss the future," she told him. "You're still upset about Gaudry and Odo. So am I. When this business is finished, we'll talk."

"Umph," he said, lacing up his boots.

She assumed that was agreement. There were a thousand things she wanted to say to reassure him. She would say anything to prevent him from slipping into this melancholia. But she was so afraid the words she would choose would be the wrong ones that she couldn't say anything at all.

The walk across the Grand Pont, down the rue de Juiverie and through the alleyways to the tavern was the longest of Catherine's life. She was grateful to see that John and Maurice were already there when they arrived. She wouldn't be expected to say much.

"John told me about your meeting with the archdeacon," Maurice said. "I think your plan is magnificent."

"What there is of it," Edgar said. He took out his cup and started to get up to go fill it.

"I'll do it," Catherine said. "If you'll let me share. I forgot mine. I'll not dip my sleeve in it. I promise."

He handed her the cup. As he did, he squeezed her wrist, quickly. It was enough. She felt instantly better.

She went over to the table and asked Bietrix for some ale.

"Is Lucia in tonight?" she asked.

"She'll be back once it's dark," Bietrix answered. "She offered to work today as they are preparing a feast for tonight."

Catherine had forgotten. The twilight was deepening now. It shouldn't be long.

There was something important she had neglected to tell Edgar. It tickled at the edge of her mind as she walked back to the table.

She sat the cup down and gave Edgar the first gulp. He needed it far more than she. Across the table, Maurice smiled at her. She smiled back. He was looking better fed today. Perhaps the archdeacon had seen that he got a decent meal. Thank goodness Maurice wasn't a canon yet. He didn't need to join them in their fast tonight.

"That's it," Catherine said. "The canon."

"Yes?" John asked.

"I'm sorry," she said. "Nothing."

It had occurred to her that the name of the canon wasn't something to be shouting in a crowded tavern, this one most of all.

Goliath had done business with Natan. Goliath sold beer in Argenteuil. Lucia said her brother liked Natan, but resentment isn't always obvious from the outside and Goliath was the one who bought the powder they put in the beer. Lucia said it couldn't kill anyone, but perhaps if it were concentrated enough, it could. Catherine was sure that the strange scent on Natan's breath was the same as the ground cherry on Solomon's cloak. But, if Goliath were working with Natan, perhaps transporting stolen goods, why kill him? And why use poison? Goliath could take a man out with one hand. Perhaps Goliath had simply provided someone else with the poison. Someone Natan trusted.

Catherine wished her speculations didn't keep pointing back to Lucia. There must have been someone else Natan would have taken a cup from. All the same, perhaps it wouldn't be wise to go with her tonight.

As she was debating this, Hubert arrived and demanded that he be told everything, as a representative of the abbey Saint-Denis, if nothing else. The men were soon huddled over their bowls of beer and a large hunk of cheese that they cut pieces from and ate as they talked.

Lucia's face appeared at the door to the brewery. Catherine got up, murmuring an excuse. If she didn't go, the relic might never be found. None of the men seemed to notice that she took her cloak with her. Bietrix nodded as she walked by.

"I went past Saint-Étienne on my way home," Lucia whispered. "It's almost deserted. Take this lantern. We'll be back before they know you're gone."

In the courtyard Samson was carrying the casks of new beer down to the cellar. He stopped when he saw them.

"Where do you think you're going?" he challenged. "Does Mother know you're out here?"

"I have an errand to do," Lucia answered. "We won't be long."

"Better not," he grunted, lifting the cask again.

It was a short distance to the church. As Lucia had promised, no one was inside. Even the children were in line to receive their share of the alms. The two women went down the ambulatory and stopped at the door of the crypt.

It was hanging by one hinge, stuck halfway open. Catherine knew well that there was no one buried down there now. The bishops and saints had all been moved to Saint-Denis or Notre Dame. But the sense of ruin alone made her skin crawl.

Lucia wasn't bothered by atmosphere. She stepped over the fallen timbers and started down the steps. Catherine followed, holding the lantern close to the stone to avoid tripping on the debris. The wooden ceiling had collapsed in places and what was left was propped up by crumbling pillars of plaster and wood.

"Hurry," Lucia said. "We don't have much time."

They reached the bottom of the steps. To the right were several slabs on which the sarcophagi of great and holy men had once rested. A few were broken, though, the pieces leaning against the pillars. Lucia led Catherine to a far corner, where one burial niche had been built into the wall. She climbed up onto it.

"We usually brought a blanket," she commented. "You can hang the lantern on that hook. I'll need your help."

Catherine did as she was told. As she did, she heard a scraping noise from behind her. She gave a small yip.

"Rats," Lucia said.

Catherine waited. The scrape was not repeated. She got into the niche next to Lucia, who was pulling at a stone set into the wall at one end.

"We found this by accident," she told Catherine. "I needed something to hang on to and there was an iron ring in here and so I pulled, and, you see?"

The stone slid out as if greased. Unexpectedly, it was no more than a handbreadth thick. Their heads were in the way of the light so Catherine couldn't see what was behind, but she had already guessed.

Lucia took the box from the cavity in the wall. It was no longer nailed shut. The rope was wound around it loosely. Lucia set it on her lap.

"I should have known at once that he would hide it here," she said.

"Shouldn't we go now?" Catherine said.

Lucia lifted the box and offered it to Catherine. "I want to see what Natan died for. You open it for me," she said. "You know what to say."

"Lucia, we need a bishop or an abbot at least, for the translation of a relic," Catherine pleaded. "I think we should take this to Notre Dame and let them take care of it."

"No," Lucia said. "This is my legacy. I want to see it now. Then we'll give it to whoever you want."

"Very well." Catherine took the box and laid it in her lap. She tried to think of something suitable to say to Aldhelm, if he were in there. Perhaps it would be better to speak to God directly.

"O Domine," she chanted softly. "Ego serva tua et filia ancillae tuae."

"What did you say?" Lucia asked.

" 'I am your servant, Lord, and the daughter of your hand-maid,' " Catherine said as she opened the box. "You repeat that."

Catherine dropped the lid on the floor. It clattered like the coming of the four horsemen.

"Misericors Dominus et justus et Deus noster miseretur," Catherine said. " 'God is merciful and just; our God is filled with pity.' Say it quickly, Lucia."

She did, staring in awe. "Do you think that's your Aldhelm?"

"Yes."

It was nothing more than a crudely carved box, in the form of an arm. There were scratches on it where the gold had been sawn off. At the wrist there was a hole that had once been covered with glass. Inside they could make out a bone.

Lucia put out her hand, then drew it back. "All the power of the saints should be there, but it looks so helpless now," she said in wonder.

"There is power, but not like human strength." Catherine tried to explain although she wasn't sure she understood completely herself. "This is more of a promise, a symbol of the person this once was. He's in heaven now; he doesn't need this body. We need it, to help us comprehend things that are beyond human experience."

"But can't relics work miracles?" Lucia asked.

"Of course," Catherine said. "Edgar told me that a man was cured of dumbness when the fingers of Saint Aldhelm were put in his mouth, and a woman was cured of a shaking in her limbs when she prayed before his tomb. But it's not the relic that effects the cure, Lucia; it's God who works a miracle because the saint sees our respect and devotion and asks him to."

"Do you think, then, that we could get a miracle for returning Saint Aldhelm?" Lucia said hopefully.

Hope blazed up in Catherine, too, as the one miracle she wanted leaped into her mind. She put away the thought. "I don't know." She shook her head sadly. "But I think we have to return him anyway and try not to look for a reward."

Lucia picked up the lid and wrapped the rope around the box again. They started to climb out of the niche.

"You bitch!"

Catherine slipped and scraped her hand on the stone. Lucia jerked at the sound of the voice, nearly losing her hold on the box containing the reliquary.

"You whore, *jael*, jezebel, *gordine*, slut!" the voice went on in the dark. "Did you think you could hide your disgusting acts? Did you think such filth wouldn't be found out?"

Lucia peered across the crypt. He was out of range of the lantern light but she knew the voice well.

"Samson," she said. "What are you saying? Have you gone mad? Why did you follow us here?"

"I knew that if I watched you long enough, you'd lead me to where he hid it," her brother answered. "How could you disgrace yourself so as to lie with that infidel?"

"What disgrace?" Lucia said. "Our mother keeps a brothel, Samson. At least I give myself for love."

"That's even worse," Samson said. "That just means you're an idiot as well as a heretic."

"Samson." Catherine hated to interrupt a family discussion but she felt the situation warranted it. "How did you know what Natan hid?"

"Because it was mine!" Samson said. "I had made the arrangements. All Natan was supposed to do was bring the goods down from Normandy. But that stiff-necked bastard wouldn't carry anything unless he knew what it was. And then he wanted a bigger share, because of the risk, he said."

"And so you killed him," Catherine said. "You poisoned him because he wanted more money."

"No," Samson said. "I killed him because of her. That oily sneering Jew polluted my sister with his filth. And you let him! You encouraged him, you . . . you . . . heretic!"

Lucia stared at him with loathing. "You couldn't even fight him like a man," she said. "You had to poison his beer and send him out into the night to die alone!"

"I didn't want him to go that easily," Samson told her. "It should have taken weeks. I had a special keg just for him. He thought I'd gotten it from Abraham. That stuff wasn't supposed to kill so quickly. I must have put in too much." He seemed more angry about that than anything else.

"I'll see you hang for this, Samson," Lucia said. "I'll let them leave you on the gibbet by the road until the crows have feasted to bursting on you."

"No, you won't, Lucia." Samson started toward her. "You'll be swimming in the molten lakes of Hell with your lover long before then."

He moved toward Lucia, his hands stretched out to clench around her neck. Catherine tried to move around him but one arm shot out to stop her. She realized that he was strong enough to hold her down with one hand and strangle Lucia with the other.

Lucia screamed and dropped the box as Samson reached for her. "Samson!"

Catherine sighed in relief. It had been so long since she had heard the noise from the corner that she wasn't certain he really had followed them. Samson swung around to face his new attacker, brushing against one of the pillars as he did so. He pulled his knife out of his belt.

"Is this your new lover?" he asked Lucia. "I should have guessed. I saw the way he looked at you. Even better, then. They'll find your bodies here in the morning and he'll be the one who's accused."

"You aren't going to touch them," Solomon said, stepping between Samson and Catherine.

"And how will you stop me?" Samson laughed. "With your fists?"

"No," Solomon said. "With this."

The knife gleamed in the lamplight. Samson stared at it in disbelief.

"Jews aren't allowed to carry weapons," he said.

"Yes, I know," Solomon answered easily. "I'm under the protection of the king. But I decided I would forgo the honor and learn to defend myself. Now, would you like me to show you what I've learned, or shall the four of us go back outside and send for the watch? I'd pick the latter, Samson. You can't kill the three of us at once."

"Oh, can't I?" he said.

He took a step back and shoved with all his might against the pillar behind him. It seemed to Catherine that it took forever to fall and yet she was incapable of moving while it did.

The pillar crashed down, bringing the floor above with it. Lucia screamed. Solomon leaped to one side to avoid being crushed and landed in front of Samson. Behind him the space where Catherine and Lucia had been standing was covered in debris. Dust rose in the light of the lamp Catherine had left hanging on the wall.

Samson stood staring in awe at the damage he had wrought. Solomon never found out what he was thinking at that moment. He didn't give Samson a chance to tell him. With one long sweep of his arm, Solomon drove the knife into Samson's gut, just as he had been taught, below the rib cage and up to the heart.

Samson looked down at the knife, puzzled. Then he toppled over, falling with solid finality. Solomon moved back to avoid being crushed. For a moment all he could do was wonder how in the world he would get the knife back. Then his brain cleared and he turned his attention to the pile of rubble behind him.

"Catherine!" he screamed.

There was no answer.

Twenty

The crypt of the church of Saint-Étienne, a moment later

Absistamus . . . poenarum exhaustim satis est, via facta per hostis.

Let us depart . . . The punishment is complete; a way is
created through the enemy.
—Virgil, *Aeneid* Book IX

Solomon began to pull at the pieces of wood and concrete that had fallen, calling all the while.

A voice came down from above. "Anybody hurt?"

Solomon looked up. A pale face peered over the edge of the hole.

"There are two women trapped under here!" he shouted. "Get help."

"Probably no use." The man did not seem inclined to move. "Kin of yours?"

"My cousin," Solomon said. "Now either you go get help or I'll climb up there and break your neck."

"No need to get in a state," the man said. The face vanished.

Solomon had no idea if the man had gone for help or simply vanished. He had no time to consider. His hands were scraped and full of slivers. Each board he moved shook the ones underneath and he feared that he might send the rubble down to crush Catherine and Lucia, if it hadn't already.

"Catherine!" he called again, his voice hoarse with dust and emotion. "Catherine! Answer me!"

How long had it been? Why was no one coming to help?

"Catherine, listen to me!" he shouted. "I'm sorry I teased you. I'm sorry I laughed when you fell in the mud last week. I'm sorry I pushed you out of the tree when you were five! I promise I'll never make fun of you again! Just let me know you're alive!"

Nothing.

He went on moving the pieces. In the lantern light he didn't notice the foot, grey with dust. He grabbed it and recoiled when his fingers met soft flesh instead of rock.

The foot wiggled.

"Catherine? Lucia?" Solomon worked his way up the leg, removing the debris more carefully. The boards and cement slabs lay at odd angles, leaning against each other instead of on top of the body. As he reached the knee, Solomon noticed the material of a second *bliaut* draped over it. The women had fallen together, huddled to fend off the world crashing down on them.

"Catherine! Lucia!" Solomon called again. "Can you hear me?"

He felt their skin. They were alive, at least, but unconscious. Carefully, he lifted off the tented fragments covering their heads.

Lucia and Catherine were curled face to face under the pillar Samson had pushed over. Between them, standing upright, was the box holding the arm of St. Aldhelm. The box itself had split and the reliquary had cracked. One piece of bone, a fingertip, pressed against the pillar, keeping it from crushing the women beneath.

"That's impossible," Solomon said.

Gently he pulled Lucia and Catherine out of the rubble. He left the arm where it was.

As he lifted her, Catherine stirred and began to cough. "Edgar?"

"He'll be here soon," Solomon told her. "Are you all right? Can you move your limbs?"

"I don't know." Catherine tried to get up. "Dizzy. Let me sit here. Where's Lucia?"

"She's here next to you, still unconscious," Solomon said. "I can't find any injuries, though."

"What happened?" Catherine rubbed her forehead. "Lucia and I, we found the arm. I wanted to take it to Edgar, then something . . . someone . . ." The memory returned. She looked around in panic. "Samson! Where is he?"

"Dead," Solomon said. "Don't worry about him anymore."

Finally, there came the sound of footsteps clattering above, then leaping down the steps.

"Catherine!"

She reached out her arms to him.

"Damn you, Catherine." Edgar sniffed as he gathered her up. "Don't you ever do this to me again." He turned to Solomon. "I thought Catherine was taking a long time in the privy," he said. "And went to see if she'd fallen in. I ran into some idiot in the court who said there were two women trapped in the crypt. Who else could it be?"

He rubbed his cheek against the head lying on his shoulder. Catherine looked up and smiled.

"We found your saint for you," she said. "He saved our lives.

Strange that one never receives the miracle one expects."

Edgar felt her forehead. "Is she delirious?" he asked.

Solomon only pointed to the arm balanced between the floor and the pillar.

Slowly Edgar lowered Catherine to the ground and stayed there on his knees.

"*Halig Aldhelm, giefe thanc for mines wifes lif.*"

Solomon was still trying to wake Lucia. "Is anyone else coming?" he asked Edgar.

"I told the man to go to the tavern and tell everyone to come help," Edgar answered, without taking his eyes from the arm. "They should be here soon. Funny. I thought it would glow or something."

"I don't know why Lucia won't come round," Solomon worried. "She doesn't seem to have been hit on the head. I can't find any injuries at all. Her breathing is regular. It's as if she's asleep."

"Kiss her," Catherine said.

"What?"

"It works in the old tales," she told him. "If there are miracles, why not magic?"

It was clear that she was still dazed by her experience. Nevertheless, Solomon bent over and gave Lucia a kiss.

Her eyelids fluttered open. "Natan?"

So much for magic.

Solomon helped her to sit. She looked around, confused as Catherine had been. She saw the body.

"Samson," she said. "What happened to him? Is he dead?"

"Yes," Solomon answered.

There was a clatter above and the rumble of voices. Edgar pulled himself away from Saint Aldhelm and turned his attention to the body.

"Samson killed Natan?" he asked Solomon.

"Yes, he confessed to it," Solomon answered.

"What about Gaudry and Odo?" Edgar asked. "Did he murder them, too?"

"I don't know. I suspect so, but on orders from someone. We'll probably never know for certain."

Edgar saw the pool of blood seeping out from under Samson's body. "How did he die?" he asked.

"Knife," Solomon answered.

"He was going to kill us," Catherine added. "Solomon stopped him."

"Thank you," Edgar said.

"It was no trouble," Solomon said. "Can you help me turn him? I'm fond of that knife."

They managed to roll the body over and retrieve the knife.

"You're not supposed to have this," Edgar said.

"So Samson told me," Solomon said.

Catherine understood. "So you couldn't have killed him," she told her cousin.

"That's right," Edgar said, taking the knife. "I did it. He attacked my wife and I had to stop him."

Solomon's lips tightened. He understood, too. "Of course," he said. "It doesn't matter what Samson was or what he did. He could be the devil himself, but people would only see a Christian body and a Jew with a knife."

"That's right," Edgar said. "And today is Palm Sunday. Feelings are strong enough at this time of year without adding to them."

"I know," Solomon said bitterly. "I was born here, remember."

"Even though he was my brother, for what he did to Natan, I would have preferred him to hang," Lucia said sadly.

When the others arrived, they were shown the arm, still supporting the pillar. They each fell to their knees and gazed at it with reverential wonder. All but Hubert, whose only emotion was simple gratitude that Catherine had survived unhurt.

"Someone is protecting you, child," he said. "I don't care who, if only they continue to do so."

Lucia directed the men from the tavern to take Samson's body to their mother.

"I'm going with it," she told Catherine. "I'll explain as best I can what happened. She'll have to know what he was doing before she'll keep silent."

"Tell her you what you think best," Catherine said. "I'm sorry it came to this."

"I wanted the truth," Lucia answered. "You didn't create it; you only helped me find it. You needn't reproach yourself." She left.

Catherine reproached herself anyway.

"I shall enjoy telling Archdeacon Giles how Saint Aldhelm revealed himself to us," John said after a few minutes of silent contemplation of the relic.

Edgar was worried. "But what if he sees it as a sign that Aldhelm wants to remain here?" he asked. "I'm not sure that it isn't."

"I suppose the answer will come when we try to remove the arm," John said. "If it won't be budged, then we'll have to leave him here, no matter how we feel about it."

"We should have someone fetch the archdeacon now," Edgar said. "We need him to witness what has happened. If this doesn't prove the authenticity of the relic, nothing will."

Maurice was standing in the middle of the crypt, surveying the damage in the dim light. "I'll go," he offered. "Who else should I bring?"

"No one," John answered quickly. "If word of this gets out, there will be a thousand people in here by morning."

"I doubt even Saint Aldhelm could survive that," Maurice said.

Edgar bristled and thought to tell Maurice all the things the saint had survived in the past. He stopped. There was no doubt in his mind that Aldhelm would be safe. But the more people who knew about his, the harder it would be to see that he was returned home.

Solomon went over to Hubert. "I've had a look at the pillar," he said. "It's fallen on a niche in the wall. The arm isn't supporting it at all. There shouldn't be any trouble removing it from underneath."

"Shssh!" Hubert moved him away from Catherine. "So you don't think this was a miracle?"

"The Almighty One, blessed be he, saw fit to save Catherine and Lucia," Solomon answered. "I believe he used the means to hand, that's all, and within the natural laws he devised."

"So you don't intend to ask for baptism?" Hubert smiled.

"That is not something to joke about," Solomon said. "You should know that better than anyone."

Hubert closed his eyes and the terror of being dragged through the streets and forcibly baptized returned as if it hadn't been more than forty years before. No, it was nothing to joke about.

"Don't tell Catherine and Edgar," Hubert said. "It won't convert them, either."

"I know that," Solomon answered. "They wouldn't believe me, anyway. Even when they see where the pillar is, it won't matter. They need this to be the work of Saint Aldhelm. How could I destroy Edgar's faith?"

Curious faces kept appearing over the edge of the fallen ceiling but no one else came down. Catherine didn't think about it until she heard the altercation.

"Don't you know who this is?" The voice was Maurice's. "He's archdeacon of Rouen. Let him pass!"

A lamp glowed on the steps. Maurice appeared, leading Giles du Perche. Lucia followed them.

"There's a giant at the end of the ambulatory," Maurice said. "He refused to let us come down."

"I told Goliath what had happened," Lucia said. "He's very upset. He loved Samson and trusted him. But even love won't condone what Samson did. Goliath wanted to do something to begin to atone for it."

"That was right," John told her.

"Then Goliath didn't know what Samson was doing," Catherine said. "I'm so glad. I like him."

Lucia came over to her and spoke quickly. "Of course he knew about the trading going on," she said. "He helped with that. He wanted to make enough to build a new brewery. But he had nothing to do with Natan's death, or the others. He swore it and I believe him. That's all that matters to me."

John and Maurice were shining their lanterns on the arm, which was still upright, one finger apparently keeping the pillar from collapse.

"You see?" John said. "Catherine and Lucia were under that. Saint Aldhelm prevented them from being crushed."

"I see," Giles said. "But I don't understand what the arm was doing here or how these women knew where to find it." He looked at Edgar with suspicion. "Perhaps you knew where it was all along," he suggested.

Catherine gasped, afraid of what Edgar might do. But before he could do more than glare, Lucia came forward. She bowed to the archdeacon.

"My lord," she said, "I alone knew where the arm was. I knew my

brother, Samson, was hiding some treasure that he had come by un-
lawfully, although not what it was. I couldn't betray him but it
would have been wrong to allow him to profit from his theft. So I
gave the box to Saint-Étienne to protect. Catherine and I came here
to retrieve it so that it could be returned to your lordship. My
brother followed us and tried to take it back. Saint Aldhelm intervened on our behalf, as you see." She blessed herself. "I swear it, by
Our Lord, the Virgin and all the saints."

"Very well." The archdeacon accepted the statement. He went
over to the arm and studied it. "Are we supposed to assume that
Saint Aldhelm desires his arm to be the foundation of a new church
in Paris?" he asked.

"Perhaps we should see if he will consent to be moved?" John
suggested.

"Yes, I'll agree to that." Giles nodded. "I'll ask him; you two attempt to remove it. Use no unusual force, however. That saint must
come of his own free will."

Giles raised his eyes to heaven. Unfortunately, his view of para-
dise was obscured by the faces of the unwashed, but now well-fed,
poor of Paris staring down at him.

"Go away!" he shouted. "You people have no business here. I'll
have the bishop put you out into the streets!"

The faces vanished. Giles composed himself to pray. He closed
his eyes this time.

John got down on his hands and knees. Beside him, Edgar did the
same. They approached the relic with great respect and not a little
fear. Not sure of the efficacy of the archdeacon's petitioning, Edgar
quietly asked Saint Aldhelm's permission for what they were about
to do.

He put both hands around the reliquary. The wood had bent and
cracked when the pillar landed. He thought it might come to pieces
in his hands, leaving him holding the bones themselves, something
he knew he wasn't worthy to do.

John held the top of the broken reliquary as Edgar slid the bottom
toward himself. It came away easily, leaving the pillar above in place.

Edgar let John take it to Giles.

The archdeacon looked at it. "Oddly enough," he said, "a certain
Canon Simon came to me today with a story of how he had recently

discovered an arm in a gold reliquary of English design. He told me that it had been among the goods of a repentant thief who had come to him for absolution. He wondered if it might not be the one I was looking for." He looked at each of them in turn. "I told him that it might," he said.

Catherine slept that night in a clean feather bed. Hubert had insisted that they return to his home. There Catherine had had the bathing tub in the back garden filled and heated. Then she had scrubbed and scrubbed herself from head to toe and between the toes to get out the grit, the dust and the shock.

Edgar helped.

She woke up far into the day, feeling like a piece of laundry twisted first one way and then the other before it's put into the mangle. She opened her eyes to find Edgar staring into them.

"How do you feel?" he asked.

"Sad," she said. "And grateful."

She snuggled closer to him.

"Saint Aldhelm saved my life," she continued. "But he was the reason it was in danger. I don't understand what he was trying to accomplish, leaving Salisbury and coming here. Three men are dead, four if you include the priest from Evreux, and I can see nothing good that has come of it all."

Edgar picked up one of her frayed braids and wrapped it around his hand. "I know. I don't understand, either," he said. "We can't expect to comprehend the ways of heaven, of course, but it seems to me that some things could be made clearer. For instance, how could Samson have murdered Gaudry and Odo? Who told him where the workshop was?"

"And was it Samson who found out about Uncle Eliazar and Canon Thomas?" Catherine asked. "I can't believe that he's the one who attacked you last year. Even without a knife, he could have killed you easily."

"Yes, I got the impression of a much smaller man," Edgar said.

"You believe it's Suger's nephew, Simon, don't you?"

Edgar unwrapped the braid and twisted it the opposite way around. "I do," he admitted. "He has the connections to have discovered both about Natan's selling Brother Thomas's possessions and to be involved in the transporting of the stolen relic. But I don't think we can prove it. His story about receiving the reliquary that Gaudry and I made as restitution from a thief is plausible enough that anyone who wanted to believe it, could."

"Father won't let him escape so easily," Catherine assured him.

"But if he knows about Thomas's conversion, our silence may be the price for his," Edgar sighed.

"I think that's something we have to let Father and Uncle Eliazar handle."

"As long as Aldhelm eventually is taken home," Edgar said. "I only wish he could travel in the reliquary I carved for him."

"Why can't he?" Catherine said. "Ask Archdeacon Giles. You don't need to say it's your work. The other box is certainly not fit for a saint now."

"Catherine," Edgar said, "about that pillar."

She smiled. "I know. I saw how it was resting. It only shows that Saint Aldhelm is as practical as you. He used the niche to help him protect us."

"I hoped you would see it that way," Edgar said.

That evening they all dressed in their best clothes and went to Eliazar's for dinner.

Catherine was astonished to find Lucia serving at the table.

After the meal she stopped the maid in the hallway.

"What are you doing here?" she asked. "I thought you'd never want to come here again."

"Mistress Johannah needed someone," Lucia said simply. "I told her I would stay through Easter."

"Then what will you do?"

"Mother needs me to help her," Lucia said. "Goliath does his job if you explain it to him carefully, but he can't manage the brewing and keeping track of the payments. Someone has to."

"Lucia, I haven't said anything about the gold," Catherine said. "You could use that to start again somewhere else."

"I don't have it anymore," Lucia said. She seemed embarrassed about it.

"Lucia?"

Lucia looked away, then back at Catherine. She sighed. "I told you what the priest at my parish says. The saints have no need of gold. They don't get hungry or thirsty. They don't have children to care for."

"You gave it to Gaudry's wife, didn't you?" Catherine guessed.

Lucia nodded. "My brother was the cause of her widowhood. It's my duty to see that she's taken care of. Goliath will bring her a cask of our best beer every week and check to see that she and her children are well."

Lucia hurried back to the kitchen. The last look she gave Catherine was a warning.

Catherine returned to the dining hall slowly. She told herself that she wouldn't interfere in Lucia's duty, but that she would see to it that Hubert bought every extra barrel of beer they made, no matter what domestic animal it was wrung from.

A week later, the holy days having been observed, Hubert met at his home with Eliazar, Solomon and Baruch to decide what to tell Abbot Suger about the vipers in his family nest.

"We must tell him something," Baruch insisted. "At least about Gerard. That can be proved. He not only trades in church property, he cheats on the tolls."

"Are you positive we can prove it?" Hubert asked. "What evidence do we have for anything? Gerard had apparently been using Natan to do the actual transactions ever since the mayor caught him selling Brother Thomas's clothes. If Natan wasn't available, he sent goods to Paris with Goliath. But do you think anyone would credit the word of Samson's brother against Suger's nephew?"

"And my word is worth nothing?" Solomon asked.

"Three Jewish witnesses are needed to refute one Christian," Baruch reminded him. "And it still isn't certain we'd be believed. And what if Gerard accuses you of robbing him that night?"

"I see your point," Solomon admitted. "Then what about the tolls? I'm sure there are any number of Christians who would complain."

"The water merchants' association has already decided to send a delegation to the abbot concerning his nephew's extortions," Hubert told them. "I will add my voice. We're a powerful group. The abbot may weigh his love of Cistercian wine against the profit Gerard is making and decide that he prefers the wine."

"And Simon?" Solomon added. "He was the one working with Samson and Natan in Paris. He must have been frantic when the arm was lost. I would wager that it was his idea to kill the smiths when the duplicate reliquary was finished. I'd believe he was the one who kidnapped Silas and hit me over the head." Edgar rubbed at the sore spot.

"I know," Hubert said. "But he insists that he came by the box in the course of his pastoral duties. It will be almost impossible to prove otherwise."

"That archdeacon believes us," Solomon said. "I was surprised to find myself almost liking him."

"His orders were to find the arm and the chalice and return to Rouen with them," Hubert said. "He may leave with a word of caution to the bishop to keep a close eye on Brother Simon."

"Maurice will keep a closer one," Solomon laughed. "I would trust him to settle the score with that Simon long before Bishop Stephen does."

"I would like the criminals punished for their deeds," Eliazar said, "but I know that in this world that doesn't always happen. My heart is more concerned with my brethren, and with my brother. Do you forgive me for putting all of us at such risk last year? When that boy came to me and begged for circumcision, I couldn't deny him."

"We have said it; you could do nothing less," Baruch told him. "It is only your secrecy that we regret."

"Then I ask your forgiveness for that," Eliazar said.

"I, for one, give it gladly," Baruch said.

"Of course," Hubert agreed.

"Solomon?" Eliazar asked.

"Yes, I forgive you, Uncle," Solomon said. "But I still say you should have asked me. Haven't I always been willing to carry out your requests?"

"Ah, well, since you mention it," Eliazar said, "Hubert and I do have another little job for you. Not too long a trip, just to Lombardy and back."

"Alps." Solomon put his head in his hands. "You want me to climb those blasted mountains again. When must I leave?"

*   *   *

The little room was cleared out and most of the furniture put on the woodpile. Catherine stood in the center of the empty space and turned around slowly, remembering.

This had been her healing place. Ugly, cramped and cold, it had taken her grief and made her look beyond it. She knew there were people who would think it a palace. Those beggars who slept between the fallen timbers at Saint-Étienne certainly would.

She still didn't know if their mission had been of any use. Saint Aldhelm was on his way back to England. Edgar had seen the arm laid gently into the box he had crafted so carefully. Catherine had thought he would be proud, but his expression was one she'd never seen before and couldn't decipher.

And now they were going back to her father's home. She would settle in with her books and accounts just as if she had never been away. Only Edgar would be there, too.

Doing what?

He hadn't mentioned it again, but she knew he thought about it constantly. He would have made a bad monk but a good prior. He might even have been happy as a lay brother, working in the smithy at the abbey. But what was left for him here? He wasn't a knight; he certainly couldn't lower himself to be a merchant. Knowing that all her father expected was for him to provide grandsons was not good for his confidence. The work he did best was denied him. Marrying her was a step down socially. They couldn't live the rest of their lives over a weaver's shop while Edgar peddled handmade spoons.

Pity.

She couldn't bear to see him so miserable and she had no idea what to do about it.

She picked up the last of the bundles and went down the stairs to where he was waiting with the donkey.

He was silent as they walked, brooding, she was sure, on the mistake he had made in adding her to his life.

Suddenly his head went up.

"*Deofoles belg!*" he shouted. "Of course! Where else?"

"What is it?" Catherine asked.

"I know where that workshop was!" he said. "I should have realized it at once. So stupid. It just shows that we never see the obvious answer. It was right there under my nose. Hunh! It was right there in my nose."

"Is that what you've been worrying about?"

"Of course," he said. "I hate to leave a problem like that unsolved. It wasn't under the cloister. It was under the brewery. The smell of the malting and the brewing as well as the oven there would cover up anything from the metalworking."

"And that's why Natan also had that odd sulfuric scent on his clothes!" Catherine said. "Yes, it is good to have that settled. I thought you were wondering what you were going to do with yourself now that we've moved in with Father."

"Oh, that." Edgar shrugged. "I'll find something. At least I'm far enough from home that my father doesn't have to know about it. I was talking with Maurice. He thinks that someone should pull down Saint Étienne and rebuild Notre Dame, using the extra space to make it twice as large. The cathedral is in almost as bad repair as Saint Étienne. Stephen de Garlande put a new roof on it a few years ago, but that just kept the rain out. It's too small, especially on feast days."

Catherine laughed. "So you and that scrawny boy who isn't even a canon yet are going to build a new cathedral."

Edgar grinned. "Not tomorrow, of course, but someday. I was simply explaining that there are a lot of possibilities. And, remember, I've proved that, whatever happens, I can take care of us. Even with no land, no name, no wealth, I know that we'll never starve."

He began to whistle. Catherine stared at him in delight.

"Thank you, Saint Aldhelm," she said. "You gave me a miracle after all."

Afterword

The story of the arm of Saint Aldhelm is based on a note in Orderic Vitalis's history mentioning that, while at Salisbury with King Stephen, Philippe d'Harcourt took, among other things, a relic, *"Brachium unum, aureis lammis coopertum, et lapidibus preciosis ornamentum"* (an arm, gold-plated and ornamented with precious stones). This relic was later returned to Salisbury through the offices of Hugh, Archbishop of Rouen. The relic was not named but my preliminary research indicated that it belonged to Saint Aldhelm, monk of Malmesbury, Latin scholar, preacher and the first bishop of Sherborne, the diocese that became Salisbury.

However, when I dug further into this, I began to doubt that the arm was Aldhelm's. For one thing, his reliquary is listed in 1096 and 1214 as being silver, not gold, and yet, in each mention I found of the arm in connection with Philippe, in the 114Cs, it was gold. What bothered me most was that the relic never was named. Orderic doesn't say who it was; neither does Hugh. And William of Malmesbury, who wrote a biography of Aldhelm, never mentions the theft in his *Historia Novella*, although he tells about Stephen's occupation of Salisbury.

Now, in my misspent academic career, I had never before run into Aldhelm. Since I started this book, I can't get away from him. He was very well known in the Middle Ages and beyond and a particular patron of Salisbury. John Crowe Ransom even wrote a sonnet to him in this century, for goodness' sake. It made no sense that there would be so little mention made of the theft of his relic. So now I was partway through a book and not sure I had the correct relic.

Not to bore the reader any longer, I am at this writing convinced that it probably wasn't Aldhelm that Philippe stole. Therefore I worked my story around the facts as I knew them. I don't know whose arm it was, but I'm still looking.

Many of the other characters in the book really lived: Hugh and his nephew, of course; Abbot Suger and Prior Hervé. Suger's nephews, Gerard and Simon, were mayor of Argenteuil and canon of Notre Dame, respectively, and the next abbot of Saint-Denis had some trouble with them, but that is all I know of these men. I have used them for the purpose of the story because they were in the right place for my fiction, not because I have any reason to think that they did something similar. Canon Simon eventually became one of Louis VII's chancellors. I did a lot of reading on Andrew of Saint-Victor and then he didn't appear as much as I expected. He may well return in a future book. Maurice de Sully is a Horatio Alger of the twelfth century, starting as a poor student in Paris and ending up bishop of the city. I hope he lets Edgar help when he starts to rebuild the cathedral of Notre Dame.

John of Salisbury has left so much of his personality and life in his voluminous writings that one can't take too much liberty with him. I don't think Catherine and Edgar could have a better friend.

Writing about Jewish life in France at this time is particularly tricky since so much of the primary documentation has been destroyed. I have tried to extrapolate from what has survived, especially legal documents concerning both Christians and Jews and the responsa of the Tosafist scholars that have been translated. (It is a deep sorrow to me that my Hebrew has never progressed beyond the rudimentary.) Many of these sources indicate both business and personal contact between Jews and Christians. King Louis VII was known to be "soft" on Jews, a failing not shared by his son, Philip Augustus. But Philip won't be king for another forty years. At this time Jews in Paris did not wear badges, were not forced to live in ghettos and did not speak Yiddish. They could own property, do business with and testify in court against Christians. Life was not wonderful, of course. There were repressive taxes and regulations as well as religious and economic animosity from the Christian majority. But there were conversions in both directions and even occasional intermarriage, although both sides found the idea horrifying. While Catherine's acceptance of her family may be unusual, I do not think it impossible.

Despite the above lecture, I want to make it clear that this is a work of fiction. Catherine, Edgar and their families never existed.

The plot and action of the book are my own invention. Because I am also a historian, this book is placed as accurately as possible within my vision of a particular time and place in history. I try very hard to be as accurate as possible. But, as I have said before, I'm not writing a textbook. The main thing is for the reader to enjoy the story. I hope you did.

Sharan